ELIZABETH IS MISSING

ELIZABETH IS MISSING

EMMA HEALEY

ISIS
LARGE PRINT
Oxford

First published in Great Britain 2014
by
Viking
an imprint of Penguin Books

Published in Large Print 2014 by ISIS Publishing Ltd.,
7 Centremead, Osney Mead, Oxford OX2 0ES
by arrangement with
Penguin Books Ltd.,
part of the Penguin Group

CIP data is available for this title from the British Library

ISBN 978–1–4450–9912–5 (hb)
ISBN 978–1–4450–9913–2 (pb)

Printed and bound in Great Britain by
T. J. International Ltd., Padstow, Cornwall

To my grandmothers, Vera Healey and
Nancy Rowand, for inspiring this book

Prologue

"Maud? Was I boring you so much that you'd rather stand outside in the dark?"

A woman calls to me from the warm light of a cluttered dining room. My breath curls towards her, wet and ghostly, but no words follow. The snow, sparse but bright on the ground, reflects the light on to her face, which is drawn tight in an attempt to see. I know, though, that she can't see very well, even in the daylight.

"Come inside," she says. "It's freezing. I promise I won't say another word about frogs and snails and majolica ware."

"I wasn't bored," I say, realizing too late that she's joking. "I'll be there in a minute. I'm just looking for something." In my hand is the thing I've already found, still clotted with mud. A small thing, easily missed. The broken lid of an old compact, its silver tarnished, its navy-blue enamel no longer glassy but scratched and dull. The mildewed mirror is like a window on a faded world, like a porthole looking out under the ocean. It makes me squirm with memories.

"What have you lost?" The woman steps, precarious and trembling, out on to the patio. "Can I help? I might not be able to see it, but I can probably manage to trip over it if it's not too well hidden."

I smile, but I don't move from the grass. Snow has collected on the ridges of a shoeprint and it looks like a tiny dinosaur fossil freshly uncovered. I clutch at the compact lid in my hand, soil tightening my skin as it dries. I've missed this tiny thing for nearly seventy years. And now the earth, made sludgy and chewable with the melting snow, has spat out a relic. Spat it into my hand. But where from? That's what I can't discover. Where did it lie before it became the gristle in the earth's meal?

An ancient noise, like a fox bark, makes an attempt at the edges of my brain. "Elizabeth?" I ask. "Did you ever grow marrows?"

CHAPTER
ONE

"You know there was an old woman mugged around here?" Carla says, letting her long black ponytail snake over one shoulder. "Well, actually, it was Weymouth, but it could have been here. So you see, you can't be too careful. They found her with half her face smashed in."

This last bit is said in a hushed voice, but hearing isn't one of my problems. I wish Carla wouldn't tell me these things; they leave me with an uneasy feeling long after I've forgotten the stories themselves. I shudder and look out of the window. I can't think which direction Weymouth is in. A bird flies by.

"Have I got enough eggs?"

"Plenty, so you don't have to go out today."

She picks up the carers' folder, nodding at me, keeping eye contact until I nod back. I feel like I'm at school. There was something in my head a moment ago, a story, but I've lost the thread of it now. Once upon a time, is that how it started? Once upon a time in a deep, dark forest, there lived an old, old woman named Maud. I can't think what the next bit should be. Something about waiting for her daughter to come and visit, perhaps. It's a shame I don't live in a nice little cottage in a dark forest, I could just fancy that. And my granddaughter might bring me food in a basket.

A bang, somewhere in the house, makes my eyes skitter across the sitting room, there's an animal, an animal for wearing outside, lying over the arm of the settee. It's Carla's. She never hangs it up, worried she'll forget it, I expect. I can't help staring at it, sure it will move, scurry away to a corner, or eat me up and take my place. And Katy will have to remark on its big eyes, its big teeth.

"All these tins of peaches!" Carla shouts from the kitchen. Carla the carer. "Carers" is what they call them. "You must stop buying food," she calls again. I can hear the scrape of tins against my Formica worktop. "You have enough for an army."

Enough food. You can never have enough. Most of it seems to go missing anyway, and can't be found even after I've bought it. I don't know who's eating it all. My daughter's the same. "No more cans, Mum," she says, going through my cupboards at every opportunity. I think she must be feeding someone. Half the stuff disappears home with her, and then she wonders why I need to go shopping again. Anyway, it's not like I have many treats left in life.

"It's not like I have many treats left," I say, pushing myself higher in my seat to make my voice carry to the kitchen. Twists of shiny chocolate wrappers are wedged down the sides of the chair; they squirm against the cushions and I flick them away. My husband, Patrick, used to tell me off for eating sweets. I ate them a lot at home. It was nice to be able to have a sherbet lemon or

4

a caramel cup when I wanted, as we weren't allowed them at the exchange — no one wants to speak to a telephonist who's got her mouth full. But he said they'd ruin my teeth. I always suspected he was more worried about my figure. Polo mints were our compromise, and I still like them, but now there's no one to stop me eating a whole box of toffees if I want them. I can even start first thing in the morning. It's morning now. I know because the sun is on the bird table. It shines on the bird table in the morning and the pine tree in the evening. I have a whole day to get through before the light hits that tree.

Carla comes, half crouching, into the sitting room, picking up wrappers from around my feet. "I didn't know you were here, dear," I say.

"I've done your lunch." She snaps off plastic gloves. "It's in the fridge, and I've put a note on it. It's nine forty now, try not to eat it till twelve, right?"

She talks as if I always gobble everything up as soon as she leaves. "Have I got enough eggs?" I ask, feeling suddenly hungry.

"Plenty," Carla says, dropping the carers' folder on to the table. "I'm going now. Helen'll be here later, all right? Bye."

The front door clicks shut and I hear Carla locking it after her. Locking me in. I watch her through the window as she crunches across my path. She wears a coat with a fur-edged hood over her uniform. A carer in wolf's clothing.

When I was a girl I'd have been glad to have the house to myself, to eat things out of the larder and wear my best clothes, to play the gramophone and lie on the floor. Now I'd rather have the company. The light's been left on and the kitchen seems like an empty stage set when I go in to rearrange my cupboards and check what Carla has left me for lunch. I half expect someone to come in, my mother with her shopping or Dad with arms full of fish and chips, and say something dramatic, like in one of those plays at the Pier Theatre. Dad would say: "Your sister is gone," and there'd be a drum or a trumpet or something, and Ma would say: "Never to return," and we'd all stare at each other for the benefit of the audience. I pull a plate from the fridge, wondering what my line would be. The plate has a note attached: *Lunch for Maud to eat after 12p.m.* I take the cling film off. It's a cheese and tomato sandwich.

When I've finished eating I wander back to the sitting room. It's so quiet in here; even my clock doesn't tick out loud. It shows the time, though, and I watch the hands slowly moving round on top of the gas fire. I have hours of the day to fill and at some point I have to switch on the TV. There's one of those sofa programmes on. Two people on one sofa lean towards another person on the opposite sofa. They smile and shake their heads and, eventually, the one on her own starts to cry. I can't work out what it's all about. Afterwards there's a programme where people run through various houses looking for things to sell. The sort of ugly things that are surprisingly valuable.

A few years ago I would have been appalled at myself — watching TV in the day! But what else is there to do? I occasionally read, but the plots of novels don't make sense any more and I can never remember where I've left off. So I can boil an egg. I can eat an egg. And I can watch TV. After that, I'm just waiting: for Carla, for Helen, for Elizabeth.

Elizabeth is the only friend I have left; the others are in homes or graves. She's a fan of these running-about-selling-things programmes, and has a hope of one day finding a disregarded treasure. She buys all sorts of hideous plates and vases from charity shops, her fingers crossed for a fortune. Sometimes I buy her things too, bits of garish china mostly, it's a sort of game — who can find the ugliest piece of pottery at Oxfam. Rather childish, but I've begun to find that being with Elizabeth, laughing with her, is the only time I feel like myself.

I have an idea there was something I had to remember about Elizabeth. Perhaps she wanted me to get her something. A boiled egg, or some chocolate. That son of hers keeps her on starvation rations. He won't even spend money on new razors for himself. Elizabeth says his skin is raw from shaving and she's worried he'll cut his own throat. Sometimes I wish he would. The miser. If I didn't pop round with the odd extra, she'd waste away. I've got a note here telling me not to go out, but I don't see why. It can't hurt to nip down to the shop.

I write a list before I put on my coat, find my hat and keys, check I have the keys in the right pocket and then check again at the front door. There are white stains along the pavement where snails have been flattened in the night. This street always collects hundreds of

7

casualties after a rainy evening. But what makes those marks, I wonder, what part of the snail makes the stain turn white like that?

"Turn not pale, beloved snail," I say, bending over as far as I dare to get a better look. I can't think where the phrase is from, but it's possible it is about this very thing. I must try and remember to look it up when I get home.

The shop isn't far, but I'm tired by the time I get there, and for some reason I keep taking the wrong turning, which means I've got to walk back around the block again. I feel like I did at the end of the war. I often got lost on my way into town, what with houses bombed to rubble, and sudden open spaces, and roads blocked by bricks and masonry and broken furniture.

It's a small place, Carrow's, crammed with things I don't want. I wish they'd move the rows and rows of beer cans to make space for something useful. It's always been here, though, ever since I was a child. They only changed the sign a few years ago. It's got Coca-Cola written on it now and Carrow's is squashed in underneath like an afterthought. I read it out to myself as I go in and then I read my shopping list aloud, standing by a shelf of boxes. Ricicles and Shreddies, whatever they are.

"Eggs. Milk — question mark — Chocolate." I turn my bit of paper about to catch the light. There's a cosy cardboardy smell in the shop and it's like being in the larder at home. "Eggs, milk, chocolate. Eggs, milk, chocolate." I say the words, but I can't quite think what the things look like. Could they be in any of the boxes

8

in front of me? I carry on muttering the list under my breath as I shuffle about the shop, but the words begin to lose meaning and are like a chant. I've got "marrows" written down here too, but I don't think they sell them here.

"Can I help, Mrs Horsham?"

Reg leans over the counter, and his grey cardigan bags out, sweeping across the penny sweets in their plastic tub and leaving bits of fluff on them. He watches me walk round. Nosy beggar. I don't know what he's guarding. So I walked out with something once. So what? It was only a bag of soft lettuce. Or was it a jar of raspberry jam? I forget. Anyway, he got it back, didn't he? Helen took it back, and that was that. And it's not as if he doesn't make mistakes — I've often been short on change over the years. He's been running this shop for decades, and it's time he retired. But his mother didn't give up working here till she was ninety, so he'll probably hang on a bit longer. I was glad when the old woman finally gave up. She used to tease me whenever I came in because I'd asked her to receive a letter for me when I was a girl. I'd written to a murderer and I hadn't wanted the reply to go to my house, and I'd used a film star's name instead of my own. The reply never arrived, but Reg's mother thought I'd been waiting for a love letter and used to laugh about it long after I was married.

What was it I came for? The loaded shelves frown down at me as I circle them, and the blue and white linoleum stares up, dirty and cracked. My basket is empty, but I think I've been here for a while; Reg is

9

watching me. I reach for something: it's heavier than I was expecting and my arm is pulled down suddenly with the weight. It's a tin of peach slices. That'll do. I put a few more tins in my basket, tucking its handles into the crook of my arm. The thin metal bars grind against my hip on the way to the counter.

"Are you sure this is what you're after?" Reg asks. "Only you bought a lot of peach slices when you came in yesterday."

I look down into the basket. Is that true? Did I really buy the same things yesterday? He coughs and I see a glint of amusement in his eyes.

"Quite sure, thank you," I say, my voice firm. "If I want to buy peach slices, I can buy them."

He raises his eyebrows and begins typing prices into his till. I keep my head high, watching the cans being put into the plastic carrying thing, for carrying, but my cheeks are hot. What *was* it I came for? I feel in my pocket and find a piece of blue paper with my writing on it: *Eggs. Milk? Chocolate*. I pick up a bar of Dairy Milk and slip it into the basket, so at least I will have something from the list. But I can't put the peaches back now, Reg would laugh at me. I pay for my bag of cans and clank back down the road with them. It's slow going, because the bag is heavy, and my shoulder and the back of my knee are hurting. I remember when the houses used to whiz by as I walked — nearly running — to and from home. Ma would ask me afterwards about what I'd seen, whether certain neighbours were out, what I thought about someone's new garden wall. I'd never noticed; it had all gone past in a flash. Now I

10

have plenty of time to look at everything and no one to tell what I've seen.

Sometimes, when I'm having a sort-through or a clear-out, I find photos from my youth, and it's a shock to see everything in black and white. I think my granddaughter believes we were actually grey-skinned, with dull hair, always posing in a shadowed landscape. But I remember the town as being almost too bright to look at when I was a girl. I remember the deep blue of the sky and the dark green of the pines cutting through it, the bright red of the local brick houses and the orange carpet of pine needles under our feet. Nowadays — though I'm sure the sky is still occasionally blue and most of the houses are still there, and the trees still drop their needles — nowadays, the colours seem faded, as if I live in an old photograph.

When I get home there's an alarm clock ringing. I set it sometimes to remind myself of appointments. I drop my bag inside the front door and turn off the alarm. I can't think what it's for this time; I can't see anything to tell me. Perhaps someone is coming.

"Did the estate agent turn up?" Helen calls, her voice broken by the scrape of her key in the front door. "He was supposed to arrive at twelve. Did he?"

"I don't know," I say. "What time is it now?"

She doesn't answer. I can hear her clomping about in the hall.

"Mum!" she says. "Where have these cans come from? How many bloody peach slices do you need?"

I tell her I don't know how many. I tell her Carla must have brought them. I say I've been at home the whole day and then I look at the clock, wondering how I've managed to get through it all. Helen comes into the sitting room, breathing out sweet, cold air, and I'm a child again, in my warm bed, and my sister's icy face presses against my cheek for a moment, and her chill breath whispers over me as she tells me about the Pavilion and the dancing and the soldiers. Sukey was always cold coming home from a dance, even in the summer. Helen is often cold too, from so much time spent digging about in other people's gardens.

She holds up a plastic bag. "Why would Carla leave tins of peach slices in the hall?" She doesn't lower her voice, even though we're in the same room, and she holds the bag high off the ground. "You have to stop going shopping. I've told you I can get anything you need. I come every day."

I'm sure I don't see her that often, but I'm not going to argue. Her arm drops and I watch the bag swing to a stop against her leg.

"So will you promise? Not to shop for food again?"

"I don't see why I should. I told you, Carla must have brought them. And, anyway, if I want to buy peach slices, I can buy them." The sentence has a familiar ring, but I can't think why. "If I were to grow marrows," I say, turning a shopping list to the light, "where would I best plant them?"

Helen sighs her way out of the room and I find I've got up to follow her. In the hall I stop: there's a roaring noise coming from somewhere. I can't think what it is,

12

I can't work out where it's coming from. But I can hardly hear it once I'm in the kitchen. Everything is very clean in here: my dishes are on the rack, though I don't think I put them there, and the knife and fork I like to use have been washed up. As I open a cupboard door two scraps of paper flutter to the ground. One is a recipe for white sauce and the other has Helen's name on it, a number underneath. I get a roll of sticking ribbon, long glue ribbon, out of a drawer to stick them back up again. Perhaps I will make a white sauce today. After I've had a cup of tea.

I switch the kettle on. I know which plug it is, as someone has labelled it KETTLE. I get out cups and milk, and a teabag from a jar marked TEA. There's a note by the sink: *Coffee helps memory*. That one's in my handwriting. I take my cup through to the sitting room, pausing in the doorway. I've got this rumbling in my head. Or perhaps it's coming from upstairs. I start up towards the landing, but I can't do it without holding on to both banisters so I step back and leave my tea on the shelf in the hall. I'll only be a minute.

My room is quite sunny, and it's peaceful here, except for a sort of growl somewhere in the house. I push the door shut and sit at my dressing table by the window. Bits of costume jewellery are strewn across the doilies and china dishes; I don't wear proper jewellery now, except my wedding ring of course. I've never had to have it altered, not in over fifty years. Patrick's matching one seemed to burrow itself into his flesh so that the knuckle bulged above it, he refused to have it cut off and it wouldn't budge, however much

13

butter I greased it with. He used to say the ring being bound to him like that was proof of a strong marriage. I used to say it was proof he didn't take care of himself properly. Patrick told me to be more worried about my own ring, too loose on my slender finger, but really it fitted perfectly and I never lost it.

Helen says I lose my jewellery now, though, and she and Katy have taken most of the good pieces for themselves to "keep them safe". I don't mind. At least they're still in the family, and none of it was very valuable. The most expensive thing I had was a bizarre gold pendant in the shape of Queen Nefertiti's head, which Patrick brought back from Egypt.

I push my hand through a dingy sort of plastic bangle and look in the mirror. My reflection always gives me a shock. I never really believed I would age, and certainly not like this. The skin around my eyes and the bridge of my nose has wrinkled in a very unexpected way. It makes me look quite lizard-like. I can hardly remember my old face, except in flashes. A round-cheeked girl in front of the mirror taking out her curlers for the first time, a pale young woman in the Pleasure Gardens looking down into the green river, a tired mother with untidy hair, half turned from the dark window of a train as she tries to pull apart her fighting children. I'm always frowning in my memory, so no wonder my brow has set that way. My mother had smooth, peaches-and-cream skin right to her death, though she had good reason to be more wrinkled than most. Perhaps it was something to do with not wearing make-up; they say that about nuns, don't they?

14

I don't wear make-up either these days, and I've never worn lipstick, never liked it. The girls at the exchange teased me about it, and every now and then when I was young I'd try some out, borrow a friend's or use one I'd been given for Christmas, but I could never stand to have it on for more than a few minutes. I've got a tube in the drawer from Helen or Katy and I take it out now, twisting the base and applying it very carefully, leaning close to the mirror, making sure not to get it on my teeth. You see these old women with flecked dentures and sooty eyelids and rouge smeared over their faces, their eyebrows drawn on too high. I'd rather die than be one of them. I blot my lips together. Nice and bright now, but slightly cracked, and I am quite thirsty. About time I made myself a cup of tea.

I drop the lipstick back in the drawer and slip a long pearl necklace over my head before getting up. Not real pearls of course. When I open my door I can hear a roaring noise. I can't think what it is. It gets louder the further down the stairs I go. I stop on the bottom step, but I can't see anything. I look in the sitting room. The roaring is even louder. I wonder if it is in my head, if something is coming loose. The noise swells and vibrates. And then it stops.

"There. That's your hoovering done, anyway." Helen stands by the dining-room door, winding up the wire on the vacuum cleaner. Her mouth wavers into a smile. "Are you going out somewhere?" she asks.

"No," I say. "I don't think so."

"What are the pearls for then? You're all dolled up."

"Am I?" I lay a hand against my collarbone. I've got a string of pearls on and a thing on my wrist, and I can taste lipstick. Lipstick, with its foetid waxen smell and its suffocating thickness. I wipe the back of my hand over my mouth, but that only smears it and makes it worse, so I begin to scrub at my face, pulling the sleeve of my cardigan down to act as a flannel, spitting on it and rubbing as if I were both mother and mucky child. It's some minutes before I feel clean again, and I find Helen has been watching me.

"Give me your cardigan," she says. "I'd better put it in the wash." She asks if I want something to drink.

"Oh, yes," I say, shrugging the wool from my skin and dropping on to my chair. "I'm terribly thirsty."

"No wonder," Helen says, turning to leave the room. "There was a line of cold cups of tea on the shelf in the hall."

I say I can't think how they got there, but I don't think she hears me, because she's already disappeared into the kitchen and, anyway, my head is lowered as I'm going through my handbag. I had some malted biscuits in here at some point. Was it yesterday? Did I eat them? I take out a comb and my purse and some scrunched-up tissues. I don't find any biscuits, but there is a note in one of the bag's pockets: *No more peach slices*. I don't tell Helen. Instead I put it under the note with today's date. My carer leaves me one like it every day. That's how I know it's Thursday. I usually visit my friend Elizabeth on a Thursday, but we don't seem to have made any arrangement this week. She hasn't called. I'd have written it down if she had. I'd

16

have made a note of what she'd said, or some of it. I'd have written down what time to go and see her. I write everything down.

There are bits of paper all over the house, lying in piles or stuck up on different surfaces. Scribbled shopping lists and recipes, telephone numbers and appointments, notes about things that have already happened. My paper memory. It's supposed to stop me forgetting things. But my daughter tells me I lose the notes. I have that written down too. Still, if Elizabeth *had* called, I'd have a note. I can't have lost every one. I write things down over and over. They can't all have dropped off the table and the worktop and the mirror. And then I have this piece of paper tucked into my sleeve: *No word from Elizabeth*. It has an old date on one side. I have a horrible feeling something has happened to her. Anything could have. There was something on the news yesterday, I think. About an old woman. Something unpleasant. And now Elizabeth's disappeared. What if she's been mugged and left for dead? Or had a fall and can't get to a phone? I think of her, lying on the floor of her sitting room, unable to get up, still hoping for some treasure to leap from the carpet.

"Perhaps you've spoken to her and don't remember, Mum. Do you think that might be possible?" Helen hands me a cup of tea. I had forgotten she was here.

She bends to kiss me on the top of my head. I feel her lips through the thin hair that puffs from my scalp. She smells of some sort of herb. Rosemary, perhaps. I suppose she was planting some. For remembrance.

"Because, well, you did forget that we'd been out on Saturday, didn't you?"

I balance the cup on the arm of the chair, keeping a hand on it. I don't look up when my daughter moves back. I suppose she must be right. I have no recollection of Saturday, but I have no recollection of not recalling it either. The thought makes me breathe in sharply. These blanks are worrying. More than worrying. How can I not remember last Saturday? I feel the familiar skipping of my heartbeat, the flush of embarrassment, fear. Last Saturday. Can I even remember yesterday?

"So perhaps you have spoken to Elizabeth."

I nod and take a sip of tea, already losing the train of the conversation. "You're probably right." I'm not quite sure what I'm agreeing to, but I like the feeling of falling into blankness, the end of anxiously trying to remember. Helen smiles. Is there a hint of triumph in it?

"All right then. I'd better get going."

Helen is always going. I watch her through the front window as she gets into her car and drives off. I can never remember her arriving. Perhaps I should write it down. But these bits of paper on the table beside my chair, this system for remembering, it's not perfect. So many of the notes are old, no longer relevant, and I get them muddled. And even the new ones don't seem to contain the right information. There's one here with writing still shiny: *Haven't heard from Elizabeth*. I run my fingers over the words, smudging them slightly. Is that true? I must only just have written it. I certainly

18

can't remember having heard from her recently. I reach for the phone. Button number four is Elizabeth. It rings and rings. I make a note.

CHAPTER
TWO

"Elizabeth is missing," I say. "Did I tell you?" I am looking at Helen, but she isn't looking at me.

"You said. What are you going to eat?"

I sit staring over the top of my menu. God knows where we are. I can see it's a restaurant — waiters in black and white, marble-topped tables — but which one? I have an awful feeling I'm supposed to know, and that this is some kind of treat. I don't think it's my birthday, but perhaps an anniversary. Patrick's death? It would be just like Helen to remember and make it a "special occasion". But I can see from the bare trees out on the street that it's the wrong time of year. Patrick died in the spring.

The menu says "The Olive Grill". It's heavy, the cover leathery; I trace the indented letters with a finger, though the name means nothing to me, and the end of the spine slips on the tabletop. I pull it on to my lap and read the contents aloud: "Butternut squash soup. Tomato and mozzarella salad. Garlic mushrooms. Parma ham and melon —"

"Yep, thanks, Mum," Helen says. "I can read it myself."

She doesn't like me reading things out, it causes her to sigh and roll her eyes. Sometimes she makes gestures behind my back. I've seen her in mirrors, pretending to strangle me. "What are you going to have?" she asks now, lowering the menu but keeping her eyes on it.

"Chorizo-stuffed marrow," I read, unable to stop myself. "Are marrows fashionable again then? I haven't seen one on a menu for years."

People used to grow marrows more when I was young and there were competitions for the best ones. That doesn't seem to happen so much now. I got to know Elizabeth because of some marrows. The first time I met her she told me her garden wall had pebbles cemented to the top and I knew exactly where she lived. It was the house with the garden where, more than sixty years ago, some marrows had been dug up during the night. And, I don't know why, but I wanted to have a look in that garden, so I got myself invited round for tea.

"You won't like chorizo," Helen says. "What about the soup?"

"I used to have soup with Elizabeth," I say, feeling a sort of ticklishness at the thought. "After we'd finished at Oxfam. Soup and sandwiches. And the *Echo* crossword. We haven't done that in a long time." And I still haven't heard from her. Not a word. I can't understand it. She never goes away; something must have happened.

"Mum? You've got to order."

A waiter is standing by our table, notepad out ready. I wonder how long he's been there. He bends right over to ask us what we want, his face unnecessarily close to mine. I lean away from him. "Helen, you haven't heard anything about Elizabeth, have you?" I say. "You would tell me if you had?"

"Yes, Mum. What are you going to eat?"

"I mean, it's not like she can go off on holiday." I close the menu and look for somewhere to rest it, but I can't find a space; there are things in the way. Shiny things, like Elizabeth has. I can't think what they are. They stand on her table, alongside Branston Pickle and salad cream and bags of Maltesers. The bags are usually open and the chocolates roll out on to the floor like some sort of cartoonish trap. I often worry about her slipping on one. "If she'd had a fall I wouldn't know," I say. "I doubt her son would bother to tell me."

The waiter straightens up and takes the menu from my hands. Helen smiles at him and orders for us both; I don't know what. He nods and wanders off, still writing, past walls streaked with black paint. The side plates are black too; I suppose that must be fashionable. The restaurant is like a sheet of smudged newsprint, one that's been scrunched round an apple for the winter, unreadable except for the adverts.

"There's no way of finding anything out for yourself. That's the problem," I say, feeling a sudden lift as I unexpectedly catch hold of my subject. "*Families* are informed, but not friends. Not at our age, anyway."

"This used to be the Chophouse, d'you remember, Mum?" Helen breaks in.

What was I saying? I can't remember. Something. Something something something . . .

"Do you remember?"

I'm blank.

"You used to meet Dad here, didn't you?"

I look around the room. There are two old women at a table by a paint-streaked wall; they peer at something lying flat on the table between them. "Elizabeth is missing," I say.

"When it was the Chophouse. For lunch."

"Her phone rings and rings."

"The Chophouse. Remember? Oh, never mind."

Helen sighs again. She's doing a lot of that lately. She won't listen, won't take me seriously, imagines that I want to live in the past. I know what she's thinking, that I've lost my marbles, that Elizabeth is perfectly well at home and I just don't remember having seen her recently. But it's not true. I forget things — I know that — but I'm not mad. Not yet. And I'm sick of being treated as if I am. I'm tried of the sympathetic smiles and the little pats people give you when you get things confused, and I'm bloody fed up with everyone deferring to Helen rather than listening to what I have to say. My heartbeat quickens and I clench my teeth. I have a terrible urge to kick Helen under the table. I kick the table leg instead. The shiny salt and pepper shakers rattle against each other and a wine glass starts to topple. Helen catches it.

"Mum," she says. "Be careful. You'll break something."

I don't answer; my teeth are still tight together. I feel I might start screaming, but breaking something, that's a good idea. That's exactly what I want to do. I pick up my butter knife and stab it into the black side plate. The china breaks. Helen says something, swearing I think, and somebody rushes towards me. I keep looking at the plate. The middle has crumbled slightly and it looks like a broken record, a broken gramophone record.

I found some once in our back garden. They were in the vegetable patch, smashed to bits and jumbled together. Ma had sent me out to help Dad when I'd got back from school and he'd handed me his shovel for digging a runner-bean trench, before disappearing into the shed. The records were almost the same colour as the soil and I wouldn't have found them, only I felt something snap as I dug and a few moments later the shards caught between the prongs of my garden fork.

When I realized what they were I scraped them out of the earth and dropped them into a sunny patch of grass to dry. I couldn't think where they'd come from. Only Douglas, our lodger, had a gramophone and I thought he'd have said if any of his records had broken. Anyway, he was a nice boy and wasn't the sort to dump things in the garden.

"What on earth are they?" Ma said as she came out to collect some washing and found me kneeling over the pieces.

I'd brushed the dirt off and begun to fit them back together. Not because I thought the records would ever play again, but because I wanted to see which ones they were. Ma rubbed at the dirty marks on my face where I'd tried to brush my hair away with soil-covered fingers and said she thought it must be the neighbours who'd chucked the records over the fence.

"There's a new tenant every week next door. Heaven knows who they are at the moment," she said. "It's not the first time I've found rubbish out here." She looked down at the black parodies of discs. "Fancy breaking all these. Good for nothing now. Hey, Maud, toss them in the bottom of the runner-bean trench. For drainage."

"All right," I said. "I just want to put them together first."

"Why? You making stepping stones for the lawn?"

"Could I?"

"Don't be daft."

She laughed and stepped daintily from one broken bit to another, the washing basket on her hip, till she was at the kitchen door. I watched her go in, the red of her hair dull against the bright red brick of our house.

It didn't take me long to connect the pieces, and it was nice work in the winter sun, listening to the music of the pigeons as they cooed to one another. It was like doing a jigsaw puzzle, except that even when I'd finished there were still some bits missing. I could read the labels now, though: "Virginia", "We Three" and "I'm Nobody's Baby".

I sat back on my heels. These were my sister's favourites, the ones she always asked Douglas to play. And now here they were, smashed up and buried amongst the remains of rhubarb and onions. I couldn't think who would do it or why. I shuffled the bits together again, scattering them into the bean trench, and when I walked back to the house I saw Douglas

25

standing at his window. I thought for a moment he was staring down at me, but then a flurry of birds dived from the dark of the hedge and I turned just in time to catch the shape of a woman scurrying away.

"I have to pick Katy up in less than half an hour," Helen says, getting her coat on, despite the fact that I'm still finishing my ice cream.

It's nice and cold against my tongue, but I can't work out what flavour it's meant to be. Strawberry, I suppose, from the colour. I'll need the loo, too, before we go. I wonder where the Ladies is. I wonder if I've been to this restaurant before. It reminds me of the lovely old Chophouse that Patrick and I used to meet in when we were courting. It wasn't expensive, didn't have exotic food or white tablecloths, but everything was nicely cooked and well laid out. I used to walk down from the exchange at lunchtime and wait at a table by the window. Patrick would get a tram from the pier where his firm were working on plans for rebuilding, and he'd come loping along, hair swept about and cheeks red, and he'd grin as soon as he saw me. No one grins at me like that now.

"Do you need the loo, Mum?" Helen's holding my coat out for me.

"No, no, I don't think so."

"Okay then. Let's go."

She's not very pleased with me. I've obviously done something. Was it embarrassing? Did I say something to the waiter? I don't like to ask. I told a woman once that her teeth made her look like a horse. I remember Helen telling me I'd said it, but I don't remember saying it.

"Are we going home?" I ask instead.

"Yes, Mum."

The sun went down while we were eating and the sky is an inky colour, but I can still see the road signs through the car's windscreen, and am reading them aloud before I know it: "'Give Way'. 'Level Crossing'. 'Reduce your speed.' " Helen's hands go white on the steering wheel. She doesn't speak to me. I shift in my seat, suddenly aware of my full bladder.

"Are we going home?"

Helen sighs. This means I've asked before. As we turn on to my street I realize how urgent my need to go is. I can't wait any longer. "Drop me here," I say to Helen, scrabbling at the door handle.

"Don't be silly, we're nearly there now."

I open the door anyway and Helen stops the car with a jerk.

"What the hell d'you think you're doing?" she says.

I scramble out of the car and make off down the road.

"Mum?" Helen calls, but I don't turn round.

I hurry towards my door, body bent forward. Every few seconds an extra-hard squeeze of the muscles is required. The pressure in my bladder seems greater the closer I come to home, and I unbutton my coat as I walk, groping desperately for my key. At the door I shift from foot to foot, frantically twisting the key in the lock. Something is stopping it from turning properly.

"Oh no, oh no," I moan aloud.

Finally I feel it catch and turn. I fall through the door and slam it behind me, handbag thudding to the floor. Clawing at the banister, I rush up the stairs, coat sailing away as I shrug it off. But I get to the bathroom too late. Hand on my waistband, I start to wee. I tear down my trousers, but have no time for the rest, and so sit on the loo urinating through my cotton knickers. For a few moments I let myself slump forward, head on hands, elbows on knees, the sodden trousers clinging round my ankles. Then, slowly and awkwardly, I kick off my shoes and pull the thick wet fabric over my feet, dropping it into the bath.

There are no lights on in the house — I couldn't stop to switch any on — and so I sit in the dark. And begin to cry.

The thing is to be systematic, try to write everything down. Elizabeth is missing and I must do something to find out what's happened. But I'm so muddled. I can't be sure about when I last saw her or what I've discovered. I've phoned and there's no answer. I haven't seen her. I think. She hasn't been here and I haven't been there. What next? I suppose I should go to the house. Search for clues. And whatever I find I will write it down. I must put pens into my handbag now. The thing is to be systematic. I've written that down too.

I check that I have my key three times before I move off the doorstep. The pale sunlight slants on to the lawn beside me as I shuffle along the path, and the smell of the pine trees makes me feel optimistic. I don't think

I've been out for a few days. Something happened and Helen has been fussing. But it's all a blank, which makes me feel dizzy.

I've wrapped up warm in a suede duffle coat, over a knitted jumper, over a wool dress, but I'm still chilly. I go past Carrow's and catch sight of myself in the window. Back hunched, I look like Mrs Tiggy-Winkle without the spikes. As I walk I check the pens in my bag and the paper in my pockets. Another quick check every few steps. The most important thing is to write everything down. For a moment, I'm hazy about just what it is I have to write, but the route I'm following reminds me. Past the last of the prefabs, which has been painted a sickly green-and-yellow by its owner. (Elizabeth laughs at its ugliness and says if she could find a ceramic replica it would be worth a fortune.) Then the back of a hotel, where the road is slick with a murky liquid (Elizabeth says it's the tea dregs that are thrown out after breakfast), and under the beautiful acacia tree, stretching from a snail-covered front garden (Elizabeth's taken cuttings every year, but they always fail).

Elizabeth's house is white-painted, with double-glazed windows. The net curtains give it away as being the home of a pensioner, though of course I can hardly criticize, having them myself. It was built just after the war, part of a street of new homes, and the garden wall has never been changed. The first owner cemented coloured pebbles to the top and no one has ever removed them. Elizabeth wouldn't dream of having them chipped off now. I was always curious about these new houses as a girl, and I remembered this one especially, because of the pebbled wall.

I ring the bell. "It echoed through the empty house." The phrase bubbles up from somewhere, but bells always echo through houses, surely? Empty or not. I wait, and work a hand deep into one of the earth-filled barrels by the front step. These are usually crammed with flowers, but not even a green shoot breaks the surface now. Elizabeth must have forgotten to plant any bulbs this year. I pull my hand out quickly. I can't think what it was doing in the soil. Was I just feeling for bulbs, or am I supposed to be looking for something else?

I face the door, wondering how long I've waited here. Five minutes? Ten? I check my watch, but it doesn't give me any clues. Time is so elastic now. I ring the bell again, carefully making a note of the time, and then watch the second hand as it moves round. After five minutes I write: *No sign of Elizabeth*, and begin to walk away. Perhaps she *is* on holiday, as someone suggested. Or is staying with her son? But I would have written that down, I'm sure of it. I have old notes like that. These little snippets of news are things to talk about, as well as information for myself. "Do you know, Elizabeth's gone off to the South of France?" I might say to Helen, or "Elizabeth's staying with that son of hers," I could tell Carla. News of that kind is valuable. Helen has been known to stay an extra thirty seconds for it in the past.

So I know I'm not forgetting this time. Elizabeth must be missing. But all I've established so far — all I've proved — is that she is not at home this minute.

At the gate I have a thought, and I turn back to look in through the front window. Pressing my nose against the cool glass and cupping my hands round the top of my head, I can just see through the net curtains. They give the dark room a misty quality, but I can make out the empty chairs and plumped cushions. Her books have been pushed neatly into their shelves and her collection of majolica pots and vases and tureens stand in a line on the mantelpiece. "You never know," Elizabeth always says, after she's done laughing at my reaction to the veiny ugliness of a moulded leaf or the sick-makingly intricate scales of a fish, "one of them might be worth a fortune." She can't see the things properly of course, only a vague brightness of the colours, but she likes the feel. The animals and insects in relief. She can trace the contours where they rise from the surface of the pottery, the glaze almost as smooth as a frog's skin, almost as slippery as an eel's. She lives in hope of discovering one that's really rare. And the promise of money is the only reason her son allows her to keep them. Otherwise they'd be in the wheelie bin without a word.

I take out a thick pen and a bright yellow square of paper ready to articulate my meagre findings: *Very tidy. No Elizabeth, no lights on*. Backing away, I stumble into a flowerbed and my foot sinks into the soil, leaving a perfect print of my shoe. Good thing I'm not planning anything criminal. I walk carefully around the edge of the bed, to the side of the house, and look in through the kitchen window. There are no net curtains here and I can clearly see the bare wooden worktops and gleaming sink. *No food out in kitchen*, I write. *No bread, no apples. No washing-up.* It's not much, but it's something.

I walk back home through the park. It's not raining, so I may as well get some fresh air. The grass is slightly frosty and I enjoy hearing it crunch under my feet. Somewhere on the other side of the bandstand is a dip, like a meteor crater, filled with flowers and benches. Helen did that. It was one of her first big commissions, and though I don't recall all the details I do remember they had to move tons of soil. It's a deliberate suntrap, and even tropical flowers thrive there. She was always good at making things grow. And she would know the best place to plant marrows: I must remember to ask her when I see her next.

I've been walking past this bandstand for seventy-odd years. My sister and I used to come this way when we went to the pictures. They often had music on here during the war. To cheer everyone up. The deckchairs would be out and filled with men in khaki uniforms, hardly camouflaged against the bright grass. Sukey would slow down to hear the band and smile at the soldiers; she always knew one or two from dances at the Pavilion. I'd run back and forth between her and the gates, wanting to get into town, impatient to see whichever film it was we were heading for. I wish I could run like that now, but I wouldn't have the puff.

At the steps out of the park I pause to look back; the sky has darkened and a figure kneels on the grass. The sound of a boy calling to someone from the bandstand makes me hurry, shivering, towards the street. On the third step down there's a shiny bit of stone. My foot slips. I try to grab at the handrail, but miss it. My nails scrape along the brick wall and my handbag swings wide, pulling me with it. I land, heavily, on my side, clenching my jaw muscles at the pain in my arm. Blood rushes about my body as if it doesn't know where it should be, and I find I am staring and staring, eyelids stretched wide, eyes drying.

Slowly the shock of it recedes and I can blink again, but I'm too tired to get up at once, so I roll over and rest where I am for a minute. I can see the rusty underside of the railing and beneath that some gritty-looking paint which has been stencilled into the shape of a fox. There's soil in the creases of my palm, though I can't think where it's from, and the sharp juts of the steps dig into my back. At least I have finally fallen. These steps have always been a worry. And I haven't hit my head, though I've bashed my side and my elbow and will have bruises tomorrow. I can feel them spreading under my skin, staining me like blackberry juice. I remember the pleasure of studying my bruises as a child, the black and navy of them, the cloud-like shapes they made. I was always finding blotches on my hips from knocking into furniture, or purplish fingernails from getting my fingers caught in the mangle. Once, my friend Audrey slipped while she was mucking about hanging over the edge of the East

33

Cliff, and I got a dark line across my chest from smashing into the railings when I grabbed at her. And then there were the marks left by the mad woman after she'd chased me home.

I'd been sent out for groceries, and I found her at the counter. She was mumbling something to the grocer as I asked for a tin of peaches and Ma's ration of cooking fat, and I stood away from her while the things were being weighed and wrapped, looking into a high corner of the shop. There was a strange aniseed smell, and somehow I felt it was coming from the mad woman, though perhaps it was just the jars of liquorice which stood along the windowsill. I paid and left and was holding the groceries against my chest, waiting for a tram to pass, when suddenly there was a great bang! on my shoulder. My heart jumped and my breath whistled in my throat.

It was her. She had followed me out and hit me with her umbrella. She always carried an umbrella, a shabby inky thing, half unfurled in a way that made it look like an injured bird. She used to stop the buses by standing in front of them and waving the umbrella, and then she would lift her dress and show her knickers. They said it was because her daughter had been knocked down and killed by a bus, before the war. People talked about it in whispers, or they made sly jokes, but if you asked a question you'd be told to be quiet, not to pry, just to keep away from her, as if she had something catching.

The end of the tram was trundling away at last, when bang! she hit me again. I leapt across the road. She followed. I ran up my street, dropping the tin of peaches in panic, and she chased me, shouting something I couldn't catch. I got through the kitchen door, calling for my mother, and she rushed out to see the woman off and retrieve the peach slices.

"I've always told you, don't look at her, don't talk to her, keep your distance," Ma said when she came back in.

I told her I'd done all that and she'd still chased me.

"Well, I've never seen her in the grocer's before. We should probably fetch a policeman, but I can't help feeling sorry for her. I suppose she doesn't like seeing young girls about the place," Ma said, peering out of the window, in case the woman was still about. "Because of her daughter being killed by that bus."

My fault for being a young girl, I thought. But I wondered later if she'd just been hungry and had wanted my rations. There was a bruise on my shoulder for weeks after that, dark against my pale skin. It was the same colour as the mad woman's umbrella, as if it had left a piece of itself on me, a feather from a broken wing.

CHAPTER
THREE

I've rung the doctor. Carla told me not to but I've got a very sore arm. I think it might be a symptom of something more worrying. She says it's just the way old people are in the morning. She doesn't use the words "old people", but I know that's what she means. When she realizes I have rung the doctor anyway she calls my daughter to come and tell me off.

"For God's sake, Mum, you've been asked to leave the poor man alone," Helen says, sitting on the window seat, looking out for him.

"But Helen, I'm ill," I say. "I think I'm ill."

"That's what you said last time, but there's nothing wrong with you. You're just not young any more; the doctor can't do anything about that. Oh, here he is now." She leaps up from the seat and goes to open the front door.

They talk in the hall, but I can't catch what they say.

"Well, Mrs Horsham," he says, coming into the room, winding up the earphones to a Walkman, or whatever they are now. "I'm rather hard pressed this morning. What did you want to see me about?"

He's young, my doctor. Very young and very handsome, with dark hair falling over his forehead. I smile at him, but he doesn't smile back. "I'm all right," I say. "What's the fuss?"

He breathes out through his nose, an impatient sound, like a foraging animal.

"You called the surgery, Mrs Horsham. You said you were in urgent need of a house call." He looks at Helen, then sits down, holds my wrist in his hand and presses it, looking at his watch. "Can you remember what it was about?" he says. "You've been ringing fairly frequently of late. And people don't usually ask for house calls when they are *all right*."

Helen shakes her head at me behind him.

"I haven't been calling frequently," I say, still looking at Helen.

"That's not quite true, is it?" he says, scribbling something on a notepad. "In fact you've phoned us twelve times in the last fortnight."

Twelve times? He must have me confused with somebody else: the wires must have been crossed, or perhaps the telephonist put the wrong person through.

"Now, I'm not suggesting you're making things up, really I'm not, but I wonder whether there isn't something else going on here." He takes out a little torch. "Perhaps it's not something strictly medical."

"I'm sorry," I say, turning from the light, which is like a fly buzzing in my face. "But I really don't think it can have been me who phoned all those times. I usually have very good health."

"I know you do," he says, putting a hand on my forehead so I can't move away and pointing the torch at one of my eyes. "Which is why it's a little frustrating to

37

be called out by you when I have genuinely ill people to see."

I don't know what to think, I can't concentrate with this light flicking, flicking over my skin, but he tells me I must open my eyes. "I don't understand it," I say. "I'm not like my friend Elizabeth. She can barely leave the house. Her sight's poor and she's unsteady on her feet. Whereas I —"

"Whereas you are in great shape for your age. I know."

He puts the torch away and I frown at him. For a minute I can't think what he's here for. "But I meant to tell you, Doctor," I say. "My friend Elizabeth. She's missing."

"Oh, Mum. Don't start that again," Helen jumps in. "Sorry, it's a bit of an obsession of hers at the moment. I've told her I'll find out what's happened."

"It's not an obsession. I don't know how long she's been gone —"

"I'm sure your friend will be in touch. You must relax and let her family take care of her. Okay? Relaxing is the key. Right. I must get to my other patients." He picks up his bag and turns to Helen. "I see she's had a blood test this week too." There is a brief look at me. "You might want to arrange for a faculties assessment. At some point."

He is already inserting the little plugs, the wire shells, back into his ears, while he talks on to Helen, and I wonder briefly what it is he listens to. I cup my hands over my own ears, straining to hear the sea-like music of my circulation, the singing of my blood. But hands don't work as well as shells; they don't create the right echo, or whatever it is. Helen comes back after letting the doctor out and sits on the arm of my chair.

"You didn't have to cover your ears, Mum," she says. "He wasn't shouting. But now will you promise not to phone the surgery again? And to stop all this nonsense about Elizabeth?"

I don't answer.

"Mum?" She grabs my arm and I cry out. "What's the matter?" she says, pulling back my sleeve. There are bruises, staining my skin, spreading round the elbow, fanning out like wings. "My God. Why didn't you tell the doctor about this? I'll call him and ask him to come back."

"No, don't," I say. "I can't stand that fly in my face. I don't want him here again."

"I'm sorry." Helen slides down into a crouching position in front of me. She holds my hand. "I'm sorry I didn't believe you. I'm sorry I didn't tell the doctor to look at you properly. How did you get these bruises, Mum?"

"It was an umbrella," I say, but really I can't remember.

She sits, stroking my hand for a few minutes, and I close my fingers over hers, feeling the skin around her nails where it's pink and raw from scrubbing soil away. This is the closest we've been in a long time.

"I sat and held my mother's hand when she was dying," I say, though I had meant to keep the thought to myself.

"You're not dying."

"I know. But it reminded me, that's all. She died never knowing. I don't want to die like that."

Helen sits up a little. "Never knowing what, Mum?"

"About Sukey." I clutch at her fingertips. "So that's why I want to find Elizabeth."

Helen sighs and drops my hand. "I'd better go soon. Can I get you anything?"

I tell her there's nothing I need and then change my mind. "I'd like a new jumper."

One of the last times Elizabeth went shopping, before her sight got too bad, before she stopped going out of the house, she bought me a silk glasses case. I notice it whenever I open my handbag. The pale silk catches the light and the coolness of the material reminds me of its presence whenever I get out my money or feel for my bus pass. I keep my spare pair of glasses in it. I only really need glasses for reading, but they make you wear them all the time once you reach a certain age. It's part of the uniform. How would they know you were an old duffer otherwise? They want you to have the right props so they can tell you apart from people who have the decency to be under seventy. False teeth, hearing aid, glasses. I've been given them all.

Helen always makes sure I have them before we leave the house. She stops short of checking I have my teeth in, but she makes a special point about the glasses. I think she thinks I'll start bumping into things if I forget them. So I always have one pair on a chain around my neck — ready for any reading eventuality. They're not helping much at the moment. I'm looking for a jumper.

40

A nice sensible colour and thin wool. Just like we used to wear. If I can keep that picture in my mind, I don't think I'll forget what I'm looking for. But I haven't come across it yet, and I'm ready to drop.

I dig into a square bin full of socks, sagging against the side, my arms lost in the fabric. An image of my mother battering a mass of clothes against the sides of a suitcase blinks into my head and is gone. "I can't understand why it's so difficult to find a *normal* jumper."

Helen and Katy sigh, and I wonder how long we've been walking around, how long we've been searching. I'm starting to regret this trip. It's a pity, because I used to love shopping. But the shops are so different now, everything jumbled together, jumbled about. So many odd colours. Who is it wears these bright orange things? They must look like road diggers. Young people will wear almost anything, it appears.

Just look at Katy. Seems funny I should have a granddaughter with "piercings", though I suppose she is considered quite unremarkable by other teenagers. Perhaps I would have "piercings", too, if I were young now. She leans on a rail of floral skirts, mimicking my own pose; only Helen stays completely upright, standing in the middle of the lino path, forcing other shoppers to dodge past her.

"Mother, we've shown you a hundred jumpers," she says. "You've rejected them all. There are no more left to show you."

"Can't have been a hundred." I do get annoyed at Helen's exaggerations. "What about over there? We haven't looked in that bit yet." I point to the other side of WOMEN'S WEAR.

"Grandma, we've just come from there."

Of course we have. Have we?

Katy pushes herself away from the skirts, hooking a cream jumper off a rail next to her. "Look, this one is nice. It's the right sort of colour."

"It's ribbed. No good." I shake my head. "I can't understand it. All I want is a jumper with a round neck. Not a polo, not a V. Warm, but not too thick."

Katy grins at her mother before turning to me. "Yes, and it can't be too long, but mustn't be too short —"

"Exactly. Half the jumpers don't even cover your belly button. And I know you're making fun, Katy," I say, though I only know after I've started to answer. "But it's not much to ask, is it? A normal jumper."

"And a *normal* colour. Black or navy or beige or —"

"Thank you, Katy. You may laugh, but you can't really expect me to wear one of these odd colours. Puce or magenta or teal or whatever they are." I can't help smiling; it's nice, being teased. Elizabeth often teases me too. It makes me feel human. At least someone assumes I'm intelligent enough to get a joke.

My granddaughter laughs, but Helen puts her hands up to her head, surveying the rails and rails of clothes. "Mum, can't you see that to find a jumper that is the length, thickness, colour, neck-type and goodness knows what else that suits you personally is an impossible task?"

"I don't see why. When I was young I could always find the right sort of jumper. They had more choice in those days."

"What — during rationing? I doubt that."

"They did. Or at least, you could always find someone to make you what you wanted. And Sukey used to bring me beautiful clothes."

My sister always dressed very stylishly, especially after she married. She cut things up and made them new, of course, but still Ma used to wonder where she got the money, never mind the coupons, and Dad would shake his head, talking about the black market. I got a lovely velvet bolero from her once. I wore it far too often, for very ordinary occasions, and wished later that I'd saved it for best. I was wearing it the last time I saw her.

She had come through the kitchen door while I was cutting the bread. I'd changed out of school uniform into a dress and my bolero, but couldn't match my sister in her duck-egg-blue suit and Lana Turner pincurls. She was seven years older than me, and ten times more sophisticated.

"Hello, Maud," she said, kissing me on the top of my head. "Where's Ma?"

"Putting on another cardigan. Dad's getting the fish and chips."

Sukey nodded and sat down at the table. I pushed the teapot into a beam of light, thinking that would keep it warm for a little longer. Our kitchen was usually dark until just before sundown, when the rays would make it through gaps in the dense bramble hedge in the

43

back garden. We used to time our evening meal to catch those last few moments of sunshine.

"Is Douglas in?" Sukey leant forward a little to look down the hall, towards the stairs, as she spoke. "Is he sleeping here tonight?"

"Of course. Why wouldn't he be?" I laughed. "He's our lodger. Sleeping here is what he pays for." I looked up from my task of laying the cups out. Sukey wasn't laughing; her face was pale and she couldn't seem to keep still. She twisted the ring on her finger and spent an age arranging her jacket on the back of a chair.

"I'd thought I might stay," she said finally, and must have realized I was staring, because she suddenly smiled. "Is that so odd? So wrong?" She seemed to be genuinely asking.

"No," I said. "You could stay in my room. Your old bed's still there."

Ma came down the steps into the kitchen, greeting Sukey and kissing her. "Your dad'll be back with the fish in a minute," she said. "Have a cup of tea. Pour it, would you, Maud?"

"Thank you, Polly," Sukey said, the way she always did if I made tea.

"Shall I make your bed up now?"

"Never mind, Mopps," she said, her voice low. "I'll have to think about it first."

I poured the tea, feeling like I'd missed something. Dad arrived and we laid the hot fish and chips out on plates, the stinging smell of vinegar rising on the steam. Sukey seemed calmer now, but she dropped her teaspoon when Ma asked how Frank was.

44

"Well enough," she said. "He's going away this evening, taking a load up to London. They're packing the van up now, which is why he couldn't come. All these people moving back home."

Sukey's husband had inherited his parents' furniture-removal business and spent the war helping people move out of bombed buildings into new lodgings. Now he was helping them to go back where they'd come from.

"Perhaps you can come over for your dinner while he's away?" Dad said. "Be nice to see you more often."

"Yeah, I could. Just while Frank's gone. It's such a big house, and it seems silly to eat on your own, doesn't it?"

"*Sure* does," Douglas called as he came into the kitchen. He collected American phrases from the films and used them as often as possible. It was irritating, but both Ma and Sukey had told me I mustn't mind because of him losing his mother in a night raid. "How you *doing*, Sukey?" he said as he took his place at the table and began on his dinner.

"Fine, thanks, Doug."

We ate quickly, not wanting our chips to get cold. Dad told us about a change in his rounds since another worker had come home from the army, comparing his postal routes with Douglas's milk deliveries, and Ma complained about the queue at the butcher's. I only half listened, distracted by Sukey and then by Douglas. I couldn't help trying to anticipate where he would put in the next bit of American slang. It tended to come out strangely twisted by his Hampshire accent.

"I was thinking of going down to Tub Street, to the *movies*," he said, when he'd finished eating. He was looking at Sukey, and the last of the light showed the places on his face where his stubble didn't yet join. There was a C-shaped patch of smooth pink skin on his cheek, and another under his chin.

"Bye, then," Sukey said, opening her compact and pressing the puff to her nose.

She swiped it expertly across her forehead, reminding me of her promise to teach me how to use make-up, and Douglas watched her for a moment before going off to get his coat from the hall. If only there were a kind of make-up for Douglas, I thought, a compact with powder to fill in his beard.

When Ma got up to clear the dishes and Dad went to put the greasy newspaper in the outside bin I leant towards Sukey. "Are you going to stay tonight?" I asked her. I'd been thinking during dinner and had come up with several possible explanations. "Has something happened between you and Frank?"

She shook her head. "I told you, Mopps, I need to think. In fact, I'd better be getting back now. Bye, Ma, Dad. See you." She was nearly at the door before I remembered.

"I got you a gift, Sukey."

She smiled; properly, genuinely, for the first time.

"It's for your hair," I said, spoiling the surprise slightly. I'd bought two matching combs on Saturday at Woolworth's, one for her, one for me. They were fake tortoiseshell and covered with crudely moulded birds,

46

but when I'd held them up to the light the wings had almost seemed to flutter.

"It's beautiful. Thank you, darling," she said, opening the tissue paper and sliding the comb into a wave of hair above her ear.

She kissed me before she slipped out the door, and I still had her lipstick on my forehead when Douglas came back from the pictures. He laughed as he smudged it off with his thumb. I remember thinking it was funny, because when he teased me about it he mentioned the exact shade: Victory Red.

"Can I help?"

The girl at the make-up counter is dull against the lit-up glass, dressed in white, her face various shades of beige. All around her are gold and see-through powder compacts, open like clams. What I need is the bottom half of a blue and silver one, but I won't find it here. "I want some lipstick," I tell the girl.

She nods and waves limply at a plastic display.

"Victory Red," I say.

"I'm sorry?"

"I wanted Victory Red." The sweet wet smell in these places is overwhelming. I feel like I'm breathing through treacle. Helen and Katy are trying on various perfumes a few feet away, making faces and coughing. They are looking for a gift for Carla, because she did something, or didn't do something, or because I did something.

The girl looks at the stand, pulling out several little tubes and replacing them roughly. They clack against the plastic. "I don't think we do that one," she says. "How about this?" She holds up a shiny, squarish cylinder. The sticker on it says "Seductive Scarlet". Sounds promising. I take it from her and draw a streak over my hand, the colour seeping into the wrinkles.

"Yes, that's nice," I say, handing it back. "But I'd prefer Victory Red. Do you have that?"

"Sorry, we don't do that one." She smiles and slouches against the counter. There's a sour smell under the perfume that makes me think the shop uniforms are all nylon.

"Really? What a nuisance. Why's that?"

"It's just a bit old-fashioned. Why not have this one instead?"

I want to ask Katy's opinion, but I can't see her. Or Helen. I walk past the other shining counters. No sign of them. The light drops as I move into another department, full of glistening leather bags and cheap jewellery. The racks are over twice my height and crowded with goods which reflect the spot lighting into my eyes. Music is blaring out, the words seem to tumble from the singer's mouth chaotically, and I feel as if my balance is going.

Somehow, I get tangled with a display of long bead necklaces. One strand round my coat button, another attached to my glasses' chain. My hands aren't steady enough to undo the clasps, and the more I pull the worse it gets. I start to think I'll be trapped here for ever. Sweat collects along my spine. A girl comes towards me, not Katy, and a sudden sense of panic makes me rip the button from my coat. I leave my

48

glasses, still attached to the beads, dangling sadly against the rack, and I back away on to the escalator, teetering at the edge of a step and gripping the handrail for support. There's a stripe of lipstick on my hand, suffocating my skin, and I rub my other hand over it, suppressing the ghost of a shudder. I've always hated how the stuff smudges.

The department I arrive in is COOKWARE AND GLASS. The music, bouncing off the hard surfaces, is so loud I can hardly think. My specs are gone and I search in my bag for the pale silk case. These second-best glasses feel funny on my face, and I have to keep adjusting them as I wander amongst the shelves of crockery. I can't think what I'm here for, and no inspiration comes. The cut-glass vases and stoneware lasagne dishes give me no clues. I stand and read out the cleaning instructions on a metal wok: "Remove stubborn residues with a sponge scourer or nylon cleaning pad only. Do not use metal scourers or any abrasive cleaners."

A woman with orange fluffed-up hair gives me an odd look as she walks past. How long have I been here? I can't see the time. I might have been standing next to this shelf for hours. If I could just find a member of staff . . . I hear a shop assistant ask someone if they need help, but I can't see over the stands and I can't tell which side the voice is coming from.

"That is the last one, but my manager might give you a discount, as it was on display."

I rush one way, but there is no one there, so I hurry in the opposite direction. As I turn a corner my bag catches something on the edge of a shelf. There is a smash. I freeze. "Waterford Crystal," I read from the display. There's a couple of seconds' silence. No one comes. I start to move away.

"Oh!" A woman in the dark-blue shop uniform hurries to my side. "You've broken this vase. Look, it's smashed to bits. You might have to pay for that," she says. "It's a hundred and twenty pounds."

I begin to shake. A hundred and twenty pounds. That's a fortune. I feel tears come into my eyes.

"I'll have to find my manager. Will you wait here?"

I nod and take out my purse. I have two five-pound notes and one twenty, as well as a bit of change. I can't work out what it all comes to, but I can see that it's not nearly enough.

"What should I do? Take her address?" the woman says, coming back. She looks over the shelves at someone I can't see and then asks for my address.

I can't remember it. She thinks I'm lying, but I'm not lying. I can't remember my address. I can't remember my address. "It's *something* Street," I say. "Or *something* Road."

The woman looks at me with disbelief. "Did you come here with someone?" she asks. "Who was it? We can page them."

I open my mouth, but I can't remember that either.

"Okay. Come with me," she says.

She puts her hand on the back of my arm and guides me across the shop. I can't think where we're going. We walk through a department full of those beds for sitting on, comfy, bouncy sitting beds, and I long to collapse into one. Finally we come to a high desk.

"Can you remember who you came with now?" she shouts, as though I'm deaf.

I tell her I can't, and my stomach closes in on itself.

"You need to give me a name so I can page someone."

She is still shouting. I can't think with her shouting. A man in an overall, wheeling a trolley of strange mutilated-looking dolls, stops. "Bloody hell, Grace," he says. "What are you doing?"

"We've got a vase smashed in Glass, and this lady's lost and I don't know who to page to come and get her," she says, not lowering her voice much.

We're standing near a bank of TVs. The flickering screens, like a thousand birds flapping their wings, make me feel dizzy. They make me think of Sukey sliding the comb into her hair, and of the hedge next to our house, and of the woman in the foliage turning to run from Douglas's gaze.

"Just page her name and say she's here," the man says. He turns to me. "What's your name, love?"

For an instant I think I have forgotten that too. But then it comes to me, and the next moment I hear the woman's voice pronounce it over the tannoy. We wait. I don't know how long. The woman goes off to talk to someone and I can see those sitting beds in the distance. Surely no one would mind if I went for a rest.

The first one I come to is a "Prima Sudeley Sofa, large, in mushroom chenille". It's lovely and cosy. I sink

51

into it. It's such a relief to be sitting that I'm in danger of nodding off.

A sudden loud announcement wakes me. Something about discounts on bath mats. I lever myself up from the sofa and stand for a minute.

"Oh, Mum. Where on earth have you been?" Helen says, coming out of a lift. "We've been looking for you everywhere."

She takes my arm, and we go back down in the lift; she will hold my arm but won't catch my eye in any of the mirrored walls. The brown-tinted glass deepens her frown. She is cross with me. I worried her, wandering off like that, she says. Funny how things are reversed. Helen was always running away when she was a child. I'd find her school satchel half packed with spare jumpers, bruised apples and favourite shells, or, if I missed that sign, I'd be forced to go looking for her across the heath. When Patrick was back from the Middle East I left him to deal with it, not bothering to unpack the bag or chase off after her. She knew it, too, knew I'd ignored her one repeated act of rebellion. And I paid for that when she was a teenager. Strange now to think that she's the child who stayed here and my son, Tom, who hated to spend a night away from home, has made his life in another country.

We find Katy when the lift doors open, a security guard watching her paint each of her nails with a different-coloured polish from the set of testers on a counter. He looks at me as I walk past and seems about to speak. I feel a sudden jolt of memory, though I can't quite place it.

52

"I think I may have broken something," I say, as we walk through the doors, into the street.

"No, Mum, your arm's just bruised, remember?"

CHAPTER
FOUR

"I went to Elizabeth's house. See?" I say, holding my notes up for Carla. She doesn't look. I slap the bits of paper on to a little table and just miss knocking over my morning tea.

"So? She wasn't in."

"No, but there was no sign of her either."

Carla turns a page of the carers' folder; she's got some sort of flowery perfume on today and it clouds up around her with each movement. "Was anyone else there?" she asks, when she's finished writing. Her eyes widen for a moment and I can tell there's some awful story coming. "I've heard of cases where young crack addicts move in with old people," she says. "They locked an old man in Boscombe in his room and asked all their crack-addict friends to smash the house up and . . ." she pauses, waving one hand in the air ". . . have orgies."

I look at my notes. "But the house was very tidy," I say.

Carla puts down the folder. "Well, there was an old woman who was bound in a basement, and the robbers took everything and then tortured her and locked her in, and nobody knew she was there. For days and days."

54

I watch Carla's face as she talks. Her eyebrows move up and down and the end of her nose turns pink. I wonder why she is so preoccupied with old people being locked in rooms. Neither of these scenarios seems very likely, but I write them down anyway.

"Perhaps I should go back to the house?" I say.

"No," she says, her tone changing. "You mustn't go out. Write that down."

I sit for a while after Carla's gone, staring into space, and then shuffle through my notes, making changes, putting Katy's name above the list of subjects she's studying at school. There's a letter from my son, and a photo of him with his wife and children. The photo is neatly labelled on the back: "Tom, Britta, Anna and Fred in the Mecklenburg Lake District". It's not Tom's writing. Anna and Frederick look just like their mother: evenly tanned skin, treacle-dark hair. Their smiles take up all their faces. Tom looks messy and blotchy in comparison, his smile cheekier, more knowing. The place looks very pretty, but I don't suppose I'll ever see it for myself. Tom stopped asking me to go and stay with them in Berlin years ago. The letter says that Anna has started at the gymnasium. "Secondary school" is in brackets next to this word, and I write it down on the paper with Katy's school subjects, reading it back to myself before finding another note: *Elizabeth locked in room — crack addicts in house. Bound and tortured in basement.* I frown at my own writing. I must be going barmy. Crack addicts? The police would have been called. But, I think, why not go to the house anyway, check on Elizabeth?

I wrap up warm, walk past the acacia tree and knock at Elizabeth's door, just in case. When there's no answer I get out my pen: *Still no Elizabeth at house*. I step back, and my head seems to empty itself, my stomach sinks, the muscles in my neck seize up. I can't think what I'm doing here and I scrunch the bits of paper in my hand. Several fall to the ground: *Crack addict*, I read. *Crack addict. Elizabeth locked in her room. Bound in basement*. Could I really have written that? It seems ridiculous. Elizabeth doesn't even have a basement. I peer through the letterbox, but I don't know what I'm looking for. I'm not entirely sure what crack is; how would I know if I saw it? The smell of cooking drifts into the air around me. A salty, meaty smell like frying bacon. It seems for a moment to be coming from inside the house, and I wonder if someone could be in there, cooking.

"What are you up to?" A woman, in one of those shiny coats you wear for rain, comes out of the house next door. She puts a hand on the fence between us, her coat whispering loudly like an unruly child. Her other hand holds the lead of a bouncing dog. He claws at the wood of the fence and sniffs. It must be the bacon smell that's got him excited.

"I'm looking for Elizabeth," I say.

"Yes, you're a friend of hers, aren't you? Don't worry, you never remember me." She chuckles to herself and I feel my face go hot with embarrassment. "Visiting, are you? Think you'll get a surprise."

"Why? What's happened? Is Elizabeth all right?"

"I haven't seen her, to be honest with you, but she's been having a clear-out, by the looks of things. Her son's taken masses of boxes of stuff to his car." She pulls the dog back from the fence and grins.

I stare at her. "Peter's been removing things?"

"And about time, don't you think? The state of that place. Full of rubbish." She waves a hand and then runs it through her short blonde hair; her coat whispers something, but I can't catch the words. "I've had to tell him about it often enough. Was getting to be a health hazard."

I stop myself from rolling my eyes. What an exaggeration. Elizabeth's a bit untidy, that's all. It's the collecting, the china, the hoping for a fortune. But tidy people like to tell untidy people off. Peggy at Oxfam is like that, muttering to herself if you leave the price tags in a tangle.

"So he's finally got round to doing something, and I'm glad. Cleared quite a lot of things out, far as I could tell."

"What's he taken?" I say. "Elizabeth needs her things."

"I can't know that, really, can I?" She lets the dog lead her towards the road.

I follow on my side of the fence. Elizabeth's side. "But you didn't see Elizabeth?" I say, my voice rising. "When Peter was getting rid of things. You didn't see her?"

The dog strains at the lead and points his nose at the house opposite. I turn, too, and, yes, that's where the bacon smell is coming from. Not Elizabeth's.

The woman opens her car door and shoos the dog in. "No. I didn't see Elizabeth. But then I never do, except when Peter takes her out. I must admit I wasn't sure about him before, but now he really seems to be looking after her properly. A good boy, isn't he?"

I look away. I don't think Peter is good at all. "But she isn't in and I haven't heard from her . . ."

"Must be with Peter then."

I bite my lip. That doesn't sound right.

"I've got his number if you want it?" the woman says, struggling to make the dog sit. "If you're worried, I'm sure he wouldn't mind you calling him."

"Please."

She slams the car door, making the dog whine, and goes back into her house. The dog and I stare at each other through the car window; the shaggy hair above his eyes gives him a puzzled frown, as if he's thinking: What am I doing in here when you're out there? I have an urge to let him out and take him home. Could I do it before the woman comes back? No, she's already returning, with a slip of paper.

"Tell Peter I send my best," she says as she hands it to me over the fence. "If you remember."

I feel myself flush again and stand outside the house for a while after she's driven off, trying to think of something else to look for, something to prove that I'm not a silly old woman. The slip of paper flutters about in my hand. I find I'm missing the dog. If only I could get my hands on a bloodhound. Then we could follow Elizabeth's scent trail. In the meantime perhaps I should put a note through Elizabeth's door. Just to say

I've been. Just to say I was looking for her, in case she comes back. Dad did that for Sukey.

None of us had seen her since the night of the fish and chips, and before a fortnight was up we knew there was something wrong.

Sukey always came to us for at least one meal a week, and sometimes Frank would come, too, bringing extra food, or things he knew Ma would find it hard to get hold of, like soap or matches. He did lots of people favours and seemed to be able to get extra things, including servicemen's rations — tiny tins of butter, cheese or jam. Ma would use those things first so that Dad didn't see the tins. She didn't want to break the law, but she couldn't turn down extra food. Not when it was so scarce. "And your dad can keep his conscience," Ma would say, "because it's not him has to queue for two hours and then make three meals a day out of a slice of ham and half a tomato." So I never said anything. And neither did Douglas, though he would narrow his eyes at Ma exclaiming over the things and packing them away.

There was no one in when Dad stopped at Sukey's house on the way home from work, and no one in the week after. Ma went round a few mornings, too, and looked for Sukey at the shops in town, but she never saw her. It didn't make any sense to us. One minute everything was fine, and the next she'd vanished. And Frank, too. He was never at the house either, and Ma said he must have stopped in London. Dad tried the hospitals, thinking perhaps there'd been an accident, but neither Frank nor Sukey had been brought in. I kept looking at the comb I'd bought, thinking of the matching one I'd given Sukey. I felt there must be a way to find her, and the next time Dad went round to her house I asked to go with him.

I was surprised when he said I could — he always did his little jobs alone — and I started to regret my request as we walked the ten streets to Sukey's in silence. It was a blue-skied, windy day, and the smell of bonfires wafted over us, following the undulating roads. Once, a man appeared at the crest of the hill, chasing his hat down towards us, but when I stopped it for him and handed it over, he looked at me strangely before throwing it up in the air and running after it again. Dad said he must be a bit touched and told me not to stare. It was the only time he spoke.

We passed Douglas's old house on the way. Half of it had been blown off by a bomb two years before, but the inside wall was almost unscathed, and you could see a first-floor room above the heap of rubble. A clock still sat on the mantelpiece next to a statue of a bronze horse, and, as if to prove this hadn't been caused by bad luck, the mirror was unbroken. A lot of the wallpaper had come away, but some hung on, and the green and white flowers on their pink background seemed unfairly exposed to the daylight and the rain and the passers-by. I had been to see the house several times since Douglas moved in with us, and had stared up at it, trying to imagine our lodger living there with his mother.

60

At Sukey's we stood on the doorstep and Dad peered in through the windows of the front rooms. But there was no one about, and the sound of a dog, barking madly somewhere in the distance, made the place seem truly deserted. The dining room was as full as ever of other people's furniture, with bookcases and lamps and empty plant pots piled against the inside of the glass, looking as though they were desperate to escape some terrible fate within. Most of Frank's house was used for storage. There was money in it, apparently, and his mother had made adjustments to each of the rooms when she'd run the business, moving walls and blocking up doors to create more space for the stuff of other people's lives. Frank once told me he'd had to sleep on a walled-off part of the landing until his parents' deaths, as his mother wouldn't give up the space for him to have a bedroom.

The windows to the cellar had been bricked up, with just grilles in the front for air. I tried to get a look through, but of course it was too dark to make anything out, so I went round to the yard behind, where Frank kept his vans. The dog's bark was louder here, and the sound moved with the direction of the wind, so it seemed as if the animal was circling the house. Only one van stood on the frost-polished cobbles, and it didn't look like it had moved for a while. GERRARD'S REMOVALS had become RRARD'S REMO under the dust. I licked my finger and was uncovering the G from its cloak of grime when I heard a noise, a faint squealing somewhere above me, and looked up at the windows of the old stables.

61

For a moment I thought I saw fingers, the tips pressed against the glass, the skin flattened and white as they squeaked down towards the bottom of the pane. Coming closer, though, I saw the fat peach fringe of a standard lamp, resting flutteringly on the inside window ledge, and knowing that the stables, too, were full of furniture, I guessed the squeaking had been mice nesting in amongst it. Even so, I started up the outside staircase, determined to get a better look. The door at the top was locked, or had something heavy resting against it, so I peered through its small window, squinting at the dark, dusty interior.

And then I saw it. A face looking back at me from deep in the room. I slapped a hand to the glass, shouting, before I realized what it was. My own reflection in a dressing-table mirror, which had been left on its side against a four-poster bed. Dad had come running at my shout, but drifted away again when he saw I was all right. And I was glad he didn't come up. Something else I could see, through the grimy glass panes, was a box of rations stamped BRITISH ARMY.

I made my way back down the stairs, and in the quiet following my own voice I listened again to the hoarse bark of the dog and looked over the fences of the nearby gardens to see if I could locate it. Dad had his hands in his pockets and was staring at the ground when I came round the house, and he didn't bother to comment on the absence of Frank or Sukey. Of course, he had come and knocked before, had stood and waited before, had searched and peered and then come home alone before. After a few moments he got out a pencil and wrote a note on the back of an envelope; he always carried a little bundle in a rubber band. I didn't read it before he pushed it through the letterbox.

"Hello?" It's a man's voice, thick and slurred. I'm on the settee in my sitting room. The phone's just stopped ringing and it's pressed against my ear.

"Hello. Who is it?" I say.

"Peter Markham. Who's *this*?" The words are clearer now; there's a whine to the voice.

Peter Markham: I know that name. "Is that Elizabeth's son?" I ask.

"My mother's name is Elizabeth. What do you want?"

"Oh, did *I* call *you*?" I say.

"'Course you phoned me." He says something under his breath. "Bloody" something. "What is it you want?"

"Perhaps Elizabeth asked me to call you," I say.

"Asked you? Why?" he says. "Where are you calling from?"

"I don't know why," I say. "It must be important."

I hold the receiver away from my ear and pause to think, gripping the phone until the plastic creaks. When did I see Elizabeth? And what did she ask me to call about? I can't remember. I rest the receiver on the arm of my chair and flick through the bits of paper on my lap, shuffling past the number for Peter Markham, a shopping list and a recipe for gooseberry crumble. The drone of a car somewhere in the distance is like a fly buzzing under glass, like a memory flinging itself at the surface of my brain. I pick up the phone and hold the next note under the lamp: *Where is Elizabeth?* My stomach drops. "She's missing," I say aloud.

There's a crackling noise as Peter breathes hard into the mouthpiece. "Who is this?" he says, his voice sharp.

"My name's Maud. I'm a friend . . . of Elizabeth's," I say. "I had your number and I was a bit worried about your mother."

"It's the middle of the night, for fuck's sake."

I look at the clock above the gas fire; it says three o'clock. It's not daytime. "I'm sorry," I say. "I'm not so good with time now. Oh dear, I am sorry. I'll leave you in peace. As long as Elizabeth is all right."

The voice begins to sound muffled again, groggy. "I already spoke to your daughter. Yes, Mum's all right. I'm going to put down the phone now, okay?"

There is a click at the end of the line, and a long beeping noise. He has hung up. I quickly retrieve my pen. *Elizabeth all right says son,* I write. *Said fuck on phone,* I add, though I'm not sure why it's significant.

I replace the receiver carefully and find I'm thinking about Mrs Winners. I haven't thought of her for years. She was the first person on our street to get a telephone. It was solid and beautiful, with a polished wooden base. She was very proud of it and always stood by the window when "phoning" so everyone could see, waving as you went by and pointing to the receiver. The shallowest pretext moved her to invite people in to use the phone and I was amazed at the things she could find out through it. Not only news about her family — there were always stories about her cousin in Torquay and her sister in Doncaster — but things about the town, about the war. It seemed you could find anything out by telephone, and I wondered who it was she spoke to and how she remembered all the information. She rang lots of people for us when Sukey disappeared, always telling my mother to keep her spirits up, and sometimes I'd come home from school to find her in the kitchen with Ma, drinking tea and passing on crumbs of hope, and I would sit and listen, too, refilling the teapot when Ma asked.

I put my notes aside and make a pot of tea now. I don't do this very often, as tea is quite tricky. But this time I remember to warm the pot and put in just three spoons of tea. As it's only for me. I carry it through to the sitting room and put it on the coffee table, curving my sleeve-covered hands around it for warmth. Steam rises from the spout and clings to the underside of my chin. The feeling is so particular, so familiar, and yet I can't think what it signifies. I try not to move, hoping the meaning will curl into my mind, but all I can think of is Dad putting something in the outside bin.

I've brought the tea cosy which Elizabeth gave me into the sitting room, but I never usually use it. I'm afraid it's rather ugly, and bits of wool come off and get into the tea. It begins to feel like drinking a cloth pulp. Elizabeth's own tea cosy is similar, but she has somehow managed to stop the wool from shedding. "I've drunk the excess wool away," she told me. "It's probably expanding inside my internal organs." I make her a pot of tea whenever I'm at her house and she reminds me how to do it if I get lost halfway. She says it's a luxury for her, as she's too weak to lift the teapot herself now. Her carers sometimes make a pot, but they never stay long enough for her to drink more than one cup, and she can't refill it after they've gone. And of course Peter never gets her anything. He just comes in, dumps her shopping and leaves.

Elizabeth tells me he barely says a word to her and spends most of the time in another room. The kitchen or greenhouse. It's cruel, when she's stuck in the house all day and what she wants most is company. And then she said something recently. Something about him lying to her. There were things going missing, and then he lied. I wish I could remember the details. I pick up my notes again: *Elizabeth all right says son.* Somehow I don't feel reassured. I fetch the tea cosy and put it on, fitting it neatly over the pot, no wrinkles. I don't care about the shedding. It's nearly four o'clock in the morning and I'm not drinking the tea anyway.

There was a lot of not eating and not drinking in the weeks after Sukey disappeared. And a lot of not talking too. Ma and Dad barely spoke in front of me, but I overheard bits of their conversation when they thought I was out of earshot. The word "police" came up a lot.

One Sunday we were sitting at the kitchen table not eating lunch and not looking at each other, the light beginning to dim outside, when Dad got up.

"Come on," he said. "We'll go and ask the neighbours."

He swung his jacket on to his back and held the kitchen door open for me. I remember looking at Ma still sitting at the table; she didn't turn to watch us go.

She had already spoken to Sukey's next-door neighbour, a woman who used the same greengrocer's as us, but all she'd had to say was that there were some funny types around nowadays.

"You never know, someone might know something," Dad said as we jogged along towards Sukey's road.

The laundry had its doors open and there was something almost heady and luxurious about the scent of the soap. But it was a false smell, and somehow it made Sukey seem further away. We began at the house next to Frank's yard. Dad knocked on the door, and it opened quickly, as if the man had been standing behind it. A head poked out: "Yer?"

The head was shaggy and a bad smell came from the dark corridor, souring the scent of the laundry.

Dad cleared his throat. "I was hoping you might . . . I wanted to ask . . ." He paused, took a breath. Moss was growing along the brick by the door frame and I curled my fingernails into its soft dampness.

"I'm looking for Susan Palmer. I mean" — Dad shook his head — "Susan Gerrard. She lives at number twenty-three. Have you seen her?"

"Never seen her." The head shook its unwashed hair. "What — gone missing, has she?"

Dad nodded.

"What's it to you?"

"She's my daughter," Dad said.

"Oh, right. Well, Frank's at twenty-three, and she's all right if she's with him, I should think."

"He's not there either."

"There you are then. Taken her off somewhere." A smile appeared under the hair; there were gaps in the teeth and a tongue was rubbed into each space.

Dad cleared his throat again. "She would have told us. I mean, they're married," he said. "She would have said if she were going off with him."

"Oh, they're married?" He sounded disappointed. "Then I couldn't speculate, I'm afraid."

We tried the next house along. While Dad knocked, I leant over the string that had replaced the railings and looked at the rubbish that had collected below street level. The old man at that address hadn't seen Sukey either, but he knew Frank.

"Lots of women going off now," he said. "Seen it in the papers. Don't seem to like it when their husbands come home, and so they're off to London or some other ungodly place. Frank's a good 'un, she should be happy with him. He moved my sister down from Coventry, didn't ask a penny. Said he had another job and could put her things in with it. My sister wouldn't have been one to leave her husband, if she'd ever had one, that much I *can* tell you."

Dad carried on down the street. I stood and watched him make his way to the end of the road. The sky was grey and the red of the bricks dulled, but it wasn't cold.

"No one's seen anything," Dad said, coming back to me. "Or they're not saying if they have. Careless Talk and all that. You'd think the war was still on. Shall we go home?"

I thought about the dress pattern that Sukey had started for me. I could picture it spread out on my bedroom floor. I couldn't help thinking that she would walk in any minute and pick up the scissors. I hadn't touched it since she'd cut out the sleeves, and I couldn't bear the idea of going back to look at it.

"Let *me* knock at one," I said, and stepped up to a thickly painted door. The paint had run and then set in drips as if it were rain, and I traced the bumps as I waited for an answer. "I'm looking for my sister, Sukey," I blurted out when the door opened. "She lived just down there. I don't know what's happened to her. She didn't say she was moving away, and I can't find her now. There's no one at her house. Have you seen her? She's got a comb like this."

I was close to crying, felt embarrassed and childish, and wished I hadn't knocked on the door at all. The woman, wearing a hair-net and standing just inside the door frame, looked quickly along the street.

"How many doors've you knocked on then?" she asked.

"I don't know, maybe ten. No one's seen her." I breathed against the tears.

The woman shot another look towards Sukey's house. "What number was your sister at?"

"Twenty-three."

She nodded. "No, they wouldn't have said, prob'ly. Look, I don't know where they went — I wasn't sure they'd gone, to be honest — but they had some trouble, I know that much. All sorts in and out of that house. And one night she runs out screaming." She paused to let me gasp. "But it was quiet the next day and I sees her in the street, right as rain. So . . ."

"When was that?" Dad said, coming to stand behind me.

The woman looked over my shoulder at him. "Few weeks ago? Not sure. Seen *him* carrying a case since. Thought I saw her, too, but like I say, can't be sure. And before you ask, no I don't know where they were going."

Dad was quiet for a bit after the door had closed, and then he turned to me. "Right," he said. "You can do the talking from now on, seeing as how you got that woman to tell you something."

He pushed me forwards to the house at the corner.

"Yes?" A man opened the door and stood with his shirt open. Its creases were sharp and it gave off the warm smell of freshly ironed cotton.

"I'm looking for my sister," I said. "She lives at that house." I pointed a finger, my arm shaking. "But she's not there now. I thought she might have left a . . . forwarding address, or something?"

The man stepped over the threshold and leant over to look at Frank and Sukey's front door, as if he needed reminding that there was a house there at all.

"Sister? Oh. Dark hair? No, no, I can't say that I know where she's gone. Had a bit of a row, though, I think. I remember something of the kind, anyway. Missing her, are you? I'm sure she'll be back. Though now I think about it, it's been weeks since I saw Frank."

"You know Frank?"

"We've had a bit of a drink of an evening. Done me a couple of good turns, has Frank."

70

That made two people Frank had helped. I tried the house opposite Sukey's next. The front door had frosted glass with a net curtain behind it. A woman in a very stiff-looking housecoat came to the door. I asked her if she'd seen Sukey.

"Can't say I remember," she said, fiddling with the lace collar under her chin. Her voice was rich and had a dry rasp to it which caught at my nerves. "I'm not one of these busybodies who watches everyone."

"But someone told me she'd run into the street, screaming," I said.

"Did they? Did they, really?" The woman looked accusingly at every house along the road, as if she were trying to find out who had given the game away. Then she shook her head very firmly. "I never heard anything. Not a hint. People don't go about screaming in this street."

"That's funny. You see we've had . . . accounts that she came out . . ." I looked into the woman's face, the implacable lines of it, and sighed.

"Accounts, eh? I'm sure. And I bet they don't know the half of it either. Like I say, I never heard anything, but I know your sister was up to something. I know it. Sorry if it pains you. She had men round."

"Men?"

"Yes. One at least. Young one. Here all the time, he was. Told me some nonsense about him being her parents' lodger, but I knew . . ."

"Douglas, you mean?"

"A name like that, yes."

"Oh, but that's true. He *is* our lodger."

"Is he now? Is he? Well, that's as may be." I thought she was going to say more, but she just nodded at me until I stepped down on to the pavement.

I moved on one; the next door was answered by a couple. They knew Sukey a bit. Had invited her and Frank in a few times, but never had an invitation back. They didn't seem to mind, though.

"Frank gave my Don a bit of work when he came out of the army," the wife said. "So kind of him, really kept us going, that did."

"Someone else said they'd seen Frank leaving with a suitcase," I said.

"Yes, well, since Don got a job at Muckley's we don't have very much to do with them, as I said. Not that we aren't grateful for the work he did put Don's way."

I thanked them and started to walk back towards Dad. Thinking that made three favours.

"Hey, love?" A young woman came out of the stiff-house-coated lady's door, wrapping a long mackintosh around her thin frame. I stopped and waited for her.

"I heard the screaming," the woman said. "Sorry about my aunt, she's got a dread of the unrespectable. But, look, it's not what you think. It can't have been Frank that your sister was afraid of."

"Then who?"

"I don't know, but I saw Frank come home after that, so you see, it couldn't have been him."

I looked up at her and shivered. Had someone else been in the house that night?

"I saw them with suitcases, too."

72

"Both of them?"

"Well, Frank anyway. A few weeks ago, that was. I know Sukey didn't like what was going on and —"

"How d'you mean?" I asked.

"Child, your family's obviously the law-abiding sort." She looked over at Dad as she said this. He had picked up someone's lost glove and was arranging it over a railing at the end of the road. "But Frank . . . he isn't. Sukey didn't like his 'business dealings'." She emphasized the words with a raise of her eyebrows. "You never know. Perhaps they've gone away to make a fresh start."

"But she hasn't contacted us for weeks. She wouldn't do that, she'd tell us where she was if she could. My dad thinks she's been kidnapped or killed or something. He won't say it, but that's what he thinks."

"It is odd. She's a real family girl, isn't she? Talks about you a lot anyway." She smiled sadly at me. "Don't know what else to say. Have you checked the hospitals?"

"When you heard her screaming, was that the same night they left?"

The woman frowned and twisted the material of her mackintosh in her hands. "Don't think so. Can't be certain. Time gets a bit mixed up sometimes, doesn't it? I mean, the way I remember it, Frank went off with a case and came back the same night. But that doesn't seem to fit, does it?"

"And you're sure you haven't seen them since?"

"Definite. There were a couple of men hanging around outside last week, but neither one was Frank. Probably police, knowing him."

I nodded, looking over at the house. I felt something should be making sense by now. The woman squeezed my shoulder and slipped away, and I stood wondering when Sukey had spoken to her about me.

"Well?" Dad said when I got near him.

I shrugged. "She did come out screaming. That woman said to check the hospitals."

He nodded, though I knew he'd done that already, and we started walking.

"You think she's been kidnapped or something, don't you?"

"It's the 'or something' I'm worried about, poppet. She should never have married that man. I knew he was the wrong sort."

I didn't know what to say, so we walked in silence for a few minutes. I tried to remember anything else that might be helpful. "That woman I spoke to last said Frank had 'business dealings'." I tried to replicate the emphasis the woman had given the words, and Dad's face creased. I thought he was going to cry and was amazed at the power of the words, but as we got to the end of the street I saw he was laughing.

"Oh, Maud, what's that supposed to mean?" he asked, waggling his eyebrows in the way I had.

"I don't know," I answered, allowing myself to smile. "I thought you would know."

74

"You said something about Elizabeth's son," Helen says. We are in her dining room, and she is crouching down, getting out place mats for the table. There are people coming for lunch, but I can't remember who or why. Katy rests against the door post, a silly smile on her face. She taps at one of these tiny phones.

"Did I?"

"Yes. Peter's his name." Helen's voice is muffled by the cupboard she has her head in.

"I think I spoke to him," I say, searching through my notes.

"Yes, I did, too, and it turns out Elizabeth's not missing, is she?"

I flick through the paper.

"That's what you said, Mum." Helen pulls her head out of the cupboard to look at me.

"I said, *he* said she was all right."

"That's good news then, isn't it?" She gets up and puts a pile of mats on the table.

I'm still frowning over my writing. "I don't know," I say. "He swore at me."

Helen bangs the cupboard door shut and the plates on the dresser rattle. The noise makes me swell with irritation for a moment. She puts a hand on a plate to silence it and then turns to lay the tablecloth out. She's a bit haphazard about it and can't seem to get it even. "You could help, you know," she says to Katy.

My granddaughter nods and shifts a foot from the door, but she doesn't make it any further and she doesn't take her eyes from the phone.

"He was quite angry," I say. "Helen, if a friend of mine called you and said they were worried about me, what would you say?"

"I'd say, 'You *should* be worried because she's quite dotty.' "

"Helen."

"Okay, okay." She drops the edge of the tablecloth. "I'd say, 'Thank you for your concern, but there's nothing to worry about. The men in white coats are coming for her soon.' "

I sigh.

"Fine. I wouldn't say the last bit." She picks up the tablecloth again. Pulls it towards her.

"But you wouldn't get angry."

"No." She walks round to pull the other side, sighing in Katy's direction.

"You see, Helen? I don't trust him."

"Oh, Mum."

"Surely only someone with a guilty conscience —"

"You called him in the middle of the night. He was bad-tempered, and no wonder. That doesn't mean he lied or that he's done his mother in."

"I know. But I think he's hiding something."

"Right, Katy, go and hang about somewhere else." She opens a drawer and rakes through it. "Mum, put these out, would you?"

She hands me a bundle of knives and forks. I put them down in the centre of the table and follow her to the kitchen. There's a smell of rosemary and mint and I hope we're having lamb, but knowing my daughter, it's as likely to be some sort of tafoo or torfo business.

76

"Mum!" she says, turning round and bumping into me. "Stay in there and set the table, will you?"

"Sorry." I go back to the dining room and stand still for a minute. I can't think what I'm supposed to be doing, but I can hear someone in another room.

"Katy, I've told her a hundred times," a voice says. "And I can't take her there. Peter was adamant. I just wish she'd forget about it."

There's a murmuring answer and then: "Oh, very bloody funny."

I follow the noise. Helen is in the kitchen.

"Back again?" she says. "I asked you to help me. Have you got a bit of paper?"

She puts out a hand and I give her a blue square. She fishes in a drawer for a pen, writes "Set the table" and hands the square back to me.

"Give me the rest of the notes," she says. "I'll put them somewhere safe."

Back in the dining room, I begin to arrange things on the table, mats spaced evenly, spoons above. I pick up a knife and fork and stand thinking for a minute. I can't remember which side they go. Fork right? Or fork left? I lay them down where I think they should be, but for the next place along I change my mind. I take another knife and fork. Looking at my hands, I try mimicking the action of cutting up food. Do they look right where they are, or should I swap them over? I try swapping. They look the same.

When Helen comes in I am still examining my hands, looking at the wrinkles on the knuckles, the papery skin, the brown spots.

"Have you finished, Mum?" Helen asks. "What are you doing?"

I don't look up. It's such a little thing — knowing where to put cutlery — but I feel like I've failed an important test. A little piece of me is gone.

"It looks very nice," she says, her voice too bright. She walks round the table and I watch her out of the corner of my eye. I see her look at me. I see her hesitate and then quickly swap the knife and fork. She says nothing. Doesn't point out my mistake.

"I don't want to set the table again," I say.

CHAPTER
FIVE

It's dark out here, but there's a glimmer of grey light somewhere low in the sky; it will be day soon and I must finish this. A mist of rain clings to my hair, to my arms and thighs. It makes me shiver but thankfully doesn't disturb the soil. That stays in its perimeter pile. I have to lean right in to dig now. A long breath, pulled deep into my lungs, leaves me with the raw wet taste of the bruised earth. My knees shift, nestled in the sodden ground, and the fabric of my trousers slowly draws moisture up my legs. Soil is caked on my hands and driven into my fingernails to the point of pain. Somewhere, somewhere, the other half of the compact hides. In front of me is a hole, a hole that I've been digging, in the middle of the green garden carpet. And suddenly I can't think what I'm doing here, what it is I'm looking for. For a moment I'm too frightened to move, not knowing what I might do next. It could be anything: I might tear the flowers from their beds or chop down the trees, fill my mouth with leaves or bury myself, for Helen to dig up again.

Panic starts to seep from my stomach, and my shoulder blades shudder together. The cold has got into my joints and I ache with it. Slowly I brush what dirt I can from my hands and, wiping them on the green carpet, the garden carpet, not moss, the other thing, I push myself steadily upright. And still I have the urge to go on digging, to search for something in the ground. But what can be here in my own garden? Unless it's something I've planted. Have I put something here? And forgotten?

I sway on my feet, the grey, shadowless garden shimmering around me, but then a spark of pale gold drops over the trees in the distance. Dawn plummeting into the day. I press a foot against a mound of soil and work it into the hole, trampling the newly flat earth. It's dawn and I'm out in the garden. And how lovely, really. How nice. To get some fresh air and watch the sun coming up. I'm shaking still as I walk back to the house, but there's no need. I just came out to see the dawn and have a bit of air and some exercise. Nothing to worry about. And now I'll go and do something I haven't done for ages.

I'll have a bath.

Inside, I run the taps, adding some sort of gloopy, flowery liquid, something Helen must have bought for me. I peel my trousers from my knees, the skin greyish after its dawn encounter with the wet earth, and take off the silky nightdress I have on top. I never sleep in this; I must have put it on especially. I wish I knew why: such a stupid thing to wear. I squeeze the fabric in my fist, listening to the muffled fizz of bubbles forming in the bath.

No, I think, perhaps it was a treat. A lovely silk nightie for a lovely golden morning. And why not? I drop it on to the floor and clamber carefully into the bath. I like being in the water. Old people aren't supposed to have baths, we're meant to shower while sitting on a little stool. But you can't think when you're having to balance on a bit of plastic with water gushing over your head. And I need to think.

My hands tremble as I reach for the cake, the slippery washing cake, but really I don't know why, I'm having a lovely time, and anyway, I won't mind so much once this dirt has come away. My mouth has that stale, grimy taste that makes me think of the time I spent ill in bed as a child, and I rub the edge of the washing cake against my lips. It's wonderful getting clean again after you've been working hard. I wish I could remember what I was supposed to have been working hard at.

When I'm clean and dry I rummage in the wardrobe for one of Patrick's old shirts. Helen wanted to take them all to wear when she's gardening, but I kept a few. Some of them are very good, he had them specially made for him in Kuwait, and the material is soft and thick. It's nice to be able to put one on, a reminder, a comfort. I can almost convince myself they still smell of him, though of course they've been washed many times between his death and now. This shirt is white with dove-grey stripes, the cotton cold at first. Too big for me, but that's what's nice. I tuck it into my trousers and button my cardigan over it before going downstairs. Carla has arrived and is making a pot of tea.

"Thank you, Polly," I say, but she doesn't seem to hear.

"The bath is filthy," she says as I come into the kitchen. "And there's a big lot of dirt on the lawn. What have you been doing?"

I wince at the question. Why is it I can remember the garden and the soil and the dew, but none of the reasons for being there? I work the sleeve of my cardigan down over my fingers, picturing the pale-gold sky, the sparkling grey of the leaves, colourless until the light hit them. I can see it all perfectly, I just can't think when it was. One of those nights spent waiting for Sukey to come home? Some point in the past, anyway. I never wake up in time for the dawn now.

"Although it's just as likely to be a son," Carla says.

I've missed some earlier part of her speech, and I don't know what she's talking about.

"You're lucky you have a daughter. They say sons steal from their old mothers. It was in a report I saw on the news."

"But I do have a son," I say.

"Millions of pounds, stolen every year."

"I don't have millions of pounds," I say.

"And all kinds of antiques, Georgian, Victorian."

"I don't have any antiques either." Oh, this is no good. What sort of a conversation consists of people saying whether they have something or not? I stop listening, stop answering, but an image shimmers in the air, of bookcases and lamps and empty plant pots piled up at a window. Of deep-grained, solid furniture and dainty silver ornaments, of dark-glazed vases and plates made to look as if worms were wriggling across them. The sort of things Elizabeth is always looking for. They didn't use to be so sought after, not when I was a girl, and people sold them off for next to nothing. There were none of these dim, expensive shops or excitable TV programmes. The only place I ever saw real antiques was at Frank's.

He had hundreds jumbled into his house, and they were always being moved so that just as you got used to swerving to avoid a chest of drawers it would disappear, to be replaced by a set of nesting tables put down exactly where you were likely to trip over them. Altogether, the house felt like some sort of nasty trick. A trap. Sukey didn't like it either, and some of the things made her afraid, though she only admitted to that once.

I'd tripped over a revolving bookcase and bashed my knee on a grumpy-looking grandfather clock on my way to the sitting room. Sukey was curled on a high-backed settee, drawing a needle slowly through some delicate blueish material, strands of her hair catching on the settee back, looking like creepers growing up a wall. Ma had sent me round with rags and darning wool, convinced that my sister wouldn't be coping with all the housework, but Sukey never seemed to need much help, so I sat down by the fire and warmed one side of my face until it was burning hot.

Frank's removal men were unloading a van in the yard, and they came through the sitting room on their way to the cellar, carrying boxes, spindly little tables and heavy dining chairs. Sukey nodded at them as they emerged empty-handed, trying to rid their lungs of the dank cellar air.

"Old woman from the Avenue's died," she said. "So Frank's bought more junk, much good it'll do us. Though it might come in handy for firewood, I s'pose."

She said the last bit loudly, and a soft-faced, sweating removal man stopped on his way to the cellar with one of the sharp-legged tables. "If that's what you're going to use it for, I'll break it up now, save me a trip to yonder hell pit," he said, putting the table down and leaning on it. Sukey smiled at her sewing, lifting one shoulder very carefully so as not to disturb the perfect line of stitches, and the man picked his table up again, chuckling to himself. She looked at me when he was gone.

"Oh, Mopps," she said. "But just look on the mantelpiece. See what Frank's keeping for himself from the house clearance. Ghoulish, I call it."

Sukey often complained about the "junk" that Frank brought home. Paintings of boats all done in brownish paint and ugly plates teeming with insects. This time it was a glass dome the size of a coal bucket full of stuffed birds. I got up, pressing a hand to the fiery side of my face, and peered in. The birds were brightly coloured, green and yellow and blue. Some had their wings spread out; some had beaks poking into flowers; others, as I moved round, pointed straight at me. Their glassy eyes seemed not to fit quite in their sockets, and their feathers had a dullness to them which made me think they'd been dyed. I couldn't look away.

"Horrid, aren't they? For some reason, Frank's taken a liking to them and so we're to have them here from now on. And Mopps, no matter how many times I say to myself, 'They're stuffed and dead, Sukey, get a hold of yourself,' I still can't shake the idea that they're going to fly out at me." She pulled her row of stitches straight. "Silly, isn't it?"

I looked at her and nodded, and that made her laugh.

"But I can just hear it, Mopps. The glass breaking and the blighters fluttering out, flapping their wings, coming to peck my eyes out."

"Blimey, your missus has a mind on her," one of the men said, coming into the room with Frank. They carried an old settee between them. "You want to watch she doesn't come up with too many ideas about you."

"That's just where I'm lucky, Alf," Frank said. "She's managed to get the idea into her head that I'm a catch. And I'm not complaining."

They took the settee into the cellar and Sukey watched them disappear down the steps before turning to me. "Get my shawl to cover those birds, will you?" she said. "I can joke all I like, but I really can't bear to see them any longer."

She looked quite desperate, and I went off to find the shawl which she thought she'd left on a chair in the kitchen, or on the coat stand in the hall, or possibly in the bedroom wardrobe, and if not there, then definitely on the towel rack in the bathroom. I walked through the kitchen, trying my hardest not to trip over or scrape my skin or knock my elbows, and had to hold the door open for two men carrying a large piece of furniture in from the yard. It was covered by a cloth, but I guessed it was a dressing table from the shape, with a mirror fixed to the top. The edges of the cloth rippled with the movement and made it seem as if the dressing table were floating between the men's hands. One of them, a man with a face full of vertical lines, asked me to open the next door for them. I ran over to do it but, forgetting it opened outwards, pulled instead of pushed, banging the door in its frame and making the plates on the nearest dresser clink together alarmingly. The men laughed.

"You 'aven't quite got your sister's delicate touch, 'ave you?" the line-faced one said.

They floated the furniture into the sitting room and I started up the stairs, stopping halfway and breathing quietly, listening to the house. There were creaks, deep and almost human, as if the house was straining under the weight of other people's possessions. These were covered by the dissonant chiming of two clocks somewhere downstairs, and once I heard the cursing of a removal man as he walked into or fell over some piece of furniture. I hoped it was the line-faced one, and looked out of the window.

There was no one in the yard now, and yet I could hear a faint rustling from outside, the sort of sound a blackbird makes when it's foraging for worms under a hedge. A short, angry fizz of foliage followed by another. I couldn't see anything, but the thicket near the lane bristled, and for some reason the sight of it made me shiver. There was no wind that day and everything else was still, but I'd seen birds shake the hedgerows before, rearranging their wings inside them. Why should it frighten me now?

I carried on to the landing, nearly falling over an elephant-foot umbrella stand and squeezing through an army of old gramophones, their horns like marrow flowers. None of these would play, but Frank kept them because if you stripped out the insides you could keep all sorts of things in them. Sukey told us that over dinner one evening, and Dad made muttered suggestions that the things wouldn't be legal, guessing the contents based on the gifts Frank had given us: ham, nylons, marmalade, dried fruit, butter, eggs. The list had made Ma very cheerful indeed, though she'd been careful not to let Dad see.

Sukey's shawl was on the towel rack and, as I pulled it free, I caught sight of myself in the bathroom mirror. I was surprised to meet myself here, and surprised by the way I looked. My face wasn't the barrier I thought it was, it seemed so unguarded, so easy to read, so open to misinterpretation. My eyes were ringed with darkish circles before I ever lost an hour of sleep and my lips were red as if I'd been biting them in agitation. My nose was shiny too. Sukey had promised to teach me to use powder several months before, and I reminded her as I went back into the sitting room.

"I don't know, Mopps," she said. "Perhaps you're too young. Perhaps I shouldn't have promised. Dad'll probably have a fit."

I was about to protest when I hit the peak of my ankle on a low tea table and I squealed instead, lifting my foot. The line-faced man came in and laughed.

"Clumsy one, you, eh?"

Flustered and irritated, I tossed the shawl at Sukey, thinking she would catch it, but she wouldn't take her hands from her sewing and it sailed on to her head, draping her, shroud-like. She cried out as she stabbed herself with her needle.

"It's to cover the birds," she said, drawing the material off and pushing her hair back from her face. "Not me."

"Sorry," I said, stepping quickly over an empty iron plant-pot holder, wanting just to get out of the house.

"Mopps?" Sukey called after me. "Mopps!"

I carried on to the yard, the clear path and the cooler air already making me feel better. I got to the side of the house and stopped, stretching my limbs in the uncluttered space, and heard that rustling in the hedge, that blackbirdish noise, and again felt the inexplicable shiver of dread. Sukey had drawn up a window, and I turned away as she leant out.

"Oh, get away. Get away. Why are you always here? I can't bear it!"

I thought for a moment she meant me, and had told her to go and boil her head before I saw she was facing the hedge. As I looked, I was able to make out a woman, standing, her lower body pressed to the other side of the fence, one arm deep in the foliage. The other was bent at the elbow so that she could press something against her mouth. Or into her mouth, I thought, as I saw her jaw work. The thicket was made of small hawthorn trees and the woman seemed to have a fistful of leaves, which she was chewing. She stared at Sukey as she chewed, not in the least bothered by her discovery, and Sukey stared back, horrified. Of course, I knew who it was. Everyone knew the mad woman.

"We need Doug," Sukey said.

"Doug? You mean Frank," I said, and called for him.

When he came out, shouting and threatening and raising his fist, I went back inside to Sukey. She laughed off her fright, saying the woman must be some sort of gourmet. "I mean, I don't blame her," she said. "Hawthorn's delicious, isn't it, Mopps? Remember we used to call it bread and cheese?"

I nodded, but I didn't like the brittle tone to her voice.

"We used to prefer it to Ma's sandwiches, remember? Better than meat paste. Better than carrot simmered in Bovril." She paused, like a moment in a film, one hand on her hip. And then she suddenly sagged against the mantelpiece. "But, Mopps, there must be hawthorns enough in the park. So why here? Why does she have to come here?"

She looked at herself in the mirror above the fireplace, her eyes studiously avoiding the newly veiled glass dome of birds, and then she raised her hand up until it covered her mouth, reminding me for one awful moment of the position of the mad woman.

Carla has suggested I try church. She's a Catholic and thinks it might be a comfort in some way. I've surrendered and let her give me a lift to a service this morning, on her way to another old crone. I insisted on an Anglican church, though I don't really believe in any particular god and I'm not sure what to expect. Ma stopped going to Holy Communion after Sukey went missing and I never restarted the habit. Patrick didn't believe in anything either, and Helen's quite a determined atheist. But lots of old people go to church. Elizabeth goes.

The church she goes to is an ancient stony building with comically serene-faced martyrs in the stained glass. Everyone in the congregation is a bit dressed up. Or they've made some effort, anyway, winding silk scarves around their necks or sliding sparkly things into their hair. I feel rather drab and shy for a few minutes. But then I remember that I am old and nobody is looking at me.

I take my hymn book and sit down. "Hymns Ancient and Modern," I read. A couple of people turn to look at me. There can't be more than a dozen people here. The smell of wood and polish reminds me of school. It's quite comforting, as is all the shined brass and flower arrangements. I start to understand why the elderly go to church.

There are flowers on the end of each pew and I reach a hand out to brush the petals in the nearest arrangement. One of the flower heads comes away and I close it in my fist. The action is familiar and I repeat it, opening my hand before crushing the flower again. But I can't think what it means and, anyway, it's the wrong sort of flower. It should be a yellow marrow flower, and these ones are white, as if left over from a wedding. Perhaps someone got married yesterday. Young people still do that in church, I'm told. I squeeze my fist while the vicar clears his throat and people on other benches bow their heads in prayer. The petals of the flower are soft and crushable. I like it like this, mangled and real rather than stiffly sitting in its arrangement. These bunches on the pews are too much like those you find preserved under Victorian glass domes, crisp and dry and slightly unnerving.

We stand and sing and sit and pray. I'd forgotten how tiring these services can be. I can't keep up and I lose track of where we are, so I just mime along with everything. The vicar looks puzzled when he sees me moving my mouth during his talk, his speech, from the pulpit. Finally it's time for tea. There's a huge metal urn on a trolley at the back of the church and lots of greenish cups. Far too many for the number of people.

A woman in a padded body-warmer the same colour as the cups comes towards me with a tin of biscuits. "We haven't seen you before," she says.

"No," I say. And then I go blank. I can't think where I am. Or why. I wobble slightly on the flagstones and my breath catches. I take two biscuits from the tin, balancing them on my saucer.

"Are you local? Or visiting?" she asks.

"I don't know," I say, feeling foolish and panicky. "I mean, where are we exactly?"

She smiles. It's a kind smile, but it's full of embarrassment. "This is St Andrew's."

The name means nothing. I don't like to ask any more.

"Perhaps you usually go to the chapel?" she suggests. "There's one just a couple of streets away."

I shake my head. I haven't forgotten my religion, I know I'm not a Wesleyan or Baptist or anything. I'm not even really a Christian.

"Sorry," I say. "I'm a bit forgetful."

The woman looks as though she thinks this description doesn't quite cover it, but she nods and takes a sip of tea before introducing me to the vicar. Luckily, I have been practising my name in my head.

"How do you do?" the vicar says, shaking my hand. His hands are incredibly soft, as if they have been worn smooth by the amount of handshaking he has had to do. "I hope you enjoyed the service."

I wasn't aware that it was the sort of thing you were supposed to enjoy, so the question rather takes me by surprise. "Oh," I say.

He and the woman in the body-warmer start to move away, frightened off by my inarticulacy, and I look down at my tea and biscuits, uncertain what to do with them. I watch as a man takes two sugar lumps from his saucer, drops them into his tea and stirs. And, with a sigh of relief, I do the same with my biscuits, stirring the pulpy mixture round and round. When I look up, everyone in the little group of people is staring at me, except the woman in the body-warmer, whose eyes are fixed on the ceiling.

She nudges the man next to her and he coughs. "No, she wasn't well at all," he says. "It was Rod who found out about it. He used to pick her up. Didn't you, Rod?"

A small man with a comb-over nods. "Yes, that's right," he says. "So, naturally, her son rang me. I told him we'd pray for her . . ."

"Of course, of course."

"Actually, I'd been to the house several times needlessly before I got a call. Rather annoying. Stood outside waiting, and no answer."

"Elizabeth," I say suddenly. I hadn't meant to.

The woman in the body-warmer looks at me, finally.

"Elizabeth," I say again. "She's missing."

"Yes. That's right, dear. She *is* missing from our congregation. Never mind." She turns to the others.

I bite my lip in humiliation, but I must catch at the chance before I forget. "No," I say. "I've been looking for her. She isn't at home."

"Not at your home?" the woman asks, careful with each syllable. She really is very irritating. I suppress the urge to scream.

"No, no, she's a friend of mine. She's gone missing."

The comb-over man frowns and smooths a hand over his head. The long, thin hairs seem to be embedded in his scalp. "She's not missing —"

"Where is she then?" I ask. "I've been to her house."

"Well, dear," the woman says, looking at the group. "Perhaps it was the wrong house."

Her voice is quiet, as if she doesn't want anyone to hear her suggestion, but her words are very clear and they are listening closely. The vicar coughs and shifts his feet and the other man smooths his head again. Her tone is final and I can already feel the conversation moving on. In a moment someone will mention the weather. I get a flash of heat. How dare they dismiss me, these people who are supposed to care about Elizabeth? How dare they?

"I didn't go to the wrong house," I say quietly, steadily, the assertion making me feel like a small child. "I'm not stupid. Elizabeth is missing." I take a shuddering breath in the silence. "Why don't you care? Why won't anyone do anything?" I think I'm beginning to shout, but I can't help it. "Anything could have happened to her. Anything. Why will no one do a thing to help find her?"

Frustration constricts my breathing. I squeeze the cup in my hand and then throw it at the ground. It smashes easily on the stone floor of the church and the sound rings through the building as the syrupy, crumb-filled tea soaks into the mortar between the flagstones. The woman in the body-warmer puts down her cup and picks up the broken remains of mine.

"Perhaps I'd better take you home," she says.

She leads me gently away from the vicar and puts me in her car. And she is very patient when I give her the wrong directions to my house and we have to go round the one-way system a second time. As she drives along I write a note to myself: *Elizabeth not at church*. The woman sees me writing it and reaches over to pat my hand.

94

"I shouldn't worry if I were you, dear," she says as she helps me out of the car. "God looks after his flock. You must look after yourself."

She offers to collect me for church next Sunday, but I tell her I'm not really up to it. She nods in understanding and there is a touch of relief in her smile.

CHAPTER
SIX

The police station is still in its original building. The stone front, with "1887" carved above the door, and the big glass hallway lantern, are somehow reassuring, but the floor inside looks as though it's wet and I'm not sure about stepping on it. I stand for a moment at the threshold, wondering how "drunk and disorderlies" manage on the slippery surface, and I put a hand against the wall when I go in, keeping to it as I walk round.

After a few steps I find I am leaning on a noticeboard. I stop and read out the words of a poster pinned in the middle: "Cash-machine criminals operate twenty-four hours a day." I wonder what a Cash-machine criminal is and how they manage to stay awake for so long. The thought makes me feel tired. There's a wooden thing for sitting, a long wooden seat, next to me, but I can't sit down, I must keep on. I must do the thing I came to do. For a moment I can't think what it is. My mind is blank. My arm starts to shake and my heart beats in my stomach. I take a deep breath and put a hand into the pocket of my cardigan, looking for a note. I must have written it down, whatever it was. There must be a reminder somewhere.

I pull out lots of coloured squares of paper, the edges curling against the skin between my thumb and forefinger. I don't like having to take my other hand away from the wall to shuffle through them. I don't feel I can trust my balance. I find a pink square with today's date — if it is today's date, I'm not sure. And a yellow square with my daughter's telephone number on it, in case of emergencies. There's a recipe for vegetable soup, though most of it seems to be missing, and the ingredients list stops at *onions*. But I can't see anything to tell me why I'm here.

"Hello, Mrs Horsham," a voice says.

I look up. There's a desk on the other side of the room with a sign saying POLICE RECEPTION. I read it aloud. A man is behind the desk, but I can only just see him through the shine on the glass divide. I push the notes back into my pocket and walk past a bench, worn and wooden. Is that where they put the newly arrested people, I wonder? Is this place full of drunks and prostitutes and street thieves at night? Doesn't seem possible. Now, in the middle of the day, it's all-quiet and I can hear the echo of my footsteps as I walk towards the desk.

When I get closer I can make out the dark epaulettes, like tiny wings, on the man's white shirt. He smiles up from his computer screen and I find myself smiling back, the way I used to with Frank, the muscles around my lips automatically obeying his. I can't think how he knows my name.

"Same as usual?" he says, his voice sounding metallic through the speakers.

"Usual?" I say.

"Elizabeth, is it?" He nods, as if encouraging me to say a line in a play.

"Elizabeth, yes," I say, amazed. Of course, that's what I've come for. I've come for her. "Do you know about Elizabeth?" I ask, feeling a rush of relief. Perhaps someone is investigating after all. Someone is looking for her. Someone knows about her disappearance. A weight lifts from my shoulders. How long have I been struggling to make anyone listen?

"Oh, yes, I know all about Elizabeth," he says.

Tears of relief come into my eyes and I smile through them.

"Missing, right?"

I nod.

"Probably that no-good son of hers, don't you think?"

I move my shoulders in helpless agreement.

"And no one else seems to think she's missing. That it?"

"That's it exactly, Officer," I say, clinging on to the counter.

"Thought it might be." He grins at me for a couple of seconds. I have a sinking feeling. "This'll be the . . . let me see . . ." he clicks at the computer a few times ". . . fourth time you've been in."

Fourth time? "So," I say. "Is someone looking for Elizabeth already, then?" I know as soon as the words are out of my mouth that it's hopeless.

He laughs. "Oh yeah. I've got every man on the force out. Sniffer dogs, forensics, flying squad. They're all out there" — he pauses to skim a hand through the air — "looking for your friend Elizabeth."

I go hot at his words. My armpits prickle. I can see what he thinks of me now, and I feel sick. The tears spill over, finally, and I turn away so he won't see them.

"Forget the drug dealers and the rapists and the murderers, I told the team," the policeman says. "What about that no-good son of old Lizzie . . ."

I don't hear any more because I'm hurrying out of the building and into the street. The cooler air catches at the wet patches on my cheeks. I stand by the bus stop and cover my mouth with the sleeve of my cardigan. This was a last hope. If the police won't take me seriously, what chance is there of ever seeing Elizabeth again?

I don't remember going to the police station about my sister; Dad went on his own to report her missing, and again after we'd spoken to her neighbours. He and Ma went often after that, to find out what was being done, what might have been discovered, but they never took me with them. I do remember a policeman coming to the house, though, to ask us about Sukey. He was there when I got home from school.

"I did say I'd pop in," he said, sitting at our kitchen table, the plate in front of him loaded with slices of cake. He had shiny brown hair and dark shadows under his eyes. And he wasn't in uniform. "But this screaming business seems to be totally unrelated, happened weeks and weeks ago according to neighbours — I had a constable check. And it's like they told you at the station: people are being reported missing left, right and centre nowadays. The men can't get used to being back on Civvy Street, or the women can't get used to having their husbands home again, and so they're off. And we get the poor abandoned folk crying to us."

"But Frank always was home," Ma said, putting the teapot down and sliding on to the chair next to me.

"Eh? Didn't fight?" The policeman looked up from his cake, a crumb falling from the corner of his mouth.

"Runs a removal firm — Gerrard's," Dad said, looking at the crumb where it lay on the table. "Reserved occupation. And, anyway, Frank's gone missing too."

The policeman nodded slowly. "Oh, yes, yes, that's right. Gerrard's. I know it. He helped my aunt move a few things after she was bombed, matter of fact. It was that bomb over at the school, d'you remember that one? Yes, he did us a real favour there. Still" — he cleared his throat and pressed a few stray currants together with his fingers — "I knew he'd gone because he's wanted for questioning."

"Is he?" Dad asked.

The policeman gestured with fingers still pinched around the currants. "Coupon fraud," he said, putting the dried fruit into his mouth. "A serious business. It's helping people to more than their fair share. And that in turn encourages others to buy things on the black market."

Ma cut more slices off the cake and refilled his cup of tea.

100

"Black market, eh? Something else I imagine Frank knows all about. So you haven't found him?" Dad said.

"No. And that does put another spin on things. Him being wanted." He took a slurp of tea. "I suppose they might have decided to do a runner together? You said something about him having a suitcase."

Dad leant away from the table and put his hands into his pockets, gazing at the floor. "I really can't believe that Sukey would have gone along with anything criminal," he said.

I kept my eyes lowered and fiddled with the handle of my cup, remembering Sukey's fur collars and new snakeskin bag, the boxes of British Army rations in the old stables and all the extra food we had for dinner whenever she and Frank came round.

"Well, no, it would hardly be worth running anyway," the policeman said, reaching for another bit of cake. "There's not much of a case, if I'm honest. But if it's not that, then . . ."

"Then Frank's done something to her and made a break for it," Dad said.

"Frank never would!" Ma said, jumping up and throwing her teaspoon into the sink.

Dad lifted his head to look at her and must have caught sight of Douglas in the hallway, because he called his name. "This is Sergeant Needham, Douglas, come about Sukey. Sergeant, this is our lodger."

Douglas stepped down into the kitchen, leaning awkwardly against the shelves by the door. He nodded at the sergeant and then shook his head when Ma offered him some tea.

"Did I hear you talking about Frank?" he said, turning his head sideways and tugging at the hem of his pullover.

"Yes," said the sergeant. "Mrs Palmer here doesn't think he can have anything to do with her daughter's disappearance."

"Doesn't she?" Douglas asked, looking at Ma where she stood, still facing the sink. "Well, I do. He's a jealous man is Frank. Got a temper on him too."

"Jealous, is he?" said the sergeant. "Why's that, then? Anything to do with you, is it?"

"No," Douglas said, pronouncing the short word slowly and carefully. "But Sukey's told me he can be jealous." Douglas kept his eyes fixed on the sergeant. His face seemed stiff, like a mask, and I had the mad idea that when he spoke he did it without moving his lips. "Jumps to the wrong conclusions, she's said."

Dad took his hands out of his pockets and rubbed them over his face, and Ma turned and leant back against the sink, gripping the edge behind her. I wondered why Sukey would tell Douglas anything and why she hadn't told me. I wondered if it was true. "When did Sukey say that?" I asked, not meaning to. Immediately, Dad told me I should go upstairs.

"This is no discussion for you," he said.

I left the table, but lingered at the top of the steps up to the hallway. The kitchen looked cosy and bright, the light from the range competing with the overhead lamp. I could almost believe it was a normal family tea, with the cups out and the teapot steaming. Except, of course, there was a policeman in Ma's usual place, finishing off the cake and writing things down in a little book.

"Yes, when *did* she tell you that?" he asked Douglas, turning a page of the notebook.

"Lots of times. She told me lots of times, Sergeant," he said. "Over the summer . . ." I could only see a section of him, from chest down, but his arm moved and I guessed he'd shrugged.

"What, when she came for dinner?" Ma asked, her legs still visible against the cupboard under the sink. "I never heard her."

Douglas's pink jaw jutted out below the top of the door frame as he bent forward and I thought he was going to say something, but the sergeant swallowed the last dregs of his tea and scraped back his chair.

"Time I was off," he said. He pushed his cup away, wrote something in his notebook and stood up. "Thanks for the tea, Mrs Palmer. I will let you know if anything presents itself. But don't worry. People are moving around all the time at the moment. Can't keep still. More than likely they've gone off to try another town for a bit and will be back when they realize everywhere's the same. Anyway, the law'll catch up with Frank before long."

He stood on the spot for a few more seconds, facing Douglas, before following Dad to the front door. I moved quickly into the sitting room and heard Ma say something to Douglas about not having any cake left.

"That was the last of the dried fruit Frank got for me," she said, and I imagined the face Douglas would make at the mention of him. "How was your film?" she asked, changing the subject before he could start on Sukey's marriage. There was a murmured answer too low to catch.

"What?" Ma said. "I thought that one was supposed to be funny. Weren't you paying attention?"

Meanwhile, Dad was thanking Sergeant Needham for coming.

"Not a problem. I'll let you know if Gerrard turns up, or that suitcase he was carrying."

They stopped at the door to look back down the hall and allow the sergeant time to brush the crumbs from his trousers. "That boy reminds me of someone," I heard him say as he left. "Just can't think who."

I have chucked all the notes on Elizabeth into the wastepaper basket. It looks like a tub of confetti. I feel terrible, abandoning her like this, but what can I do? There's nothing to "go on", as they say, and no one who can help. I have been to the police station four times. I know because I have it written down. Four times, and they will do nothing. They think I'm a dotty old woman. I think they might be right. I look out a big sheet of paper and a red pen and I make a notice to put on my sitting-room wall: *Elizabeth is not missing.* Even if I don't believe it now I might in a few hours. Sooner, perhaps. I don't want to be drawn back into looking for her. It's useless. No one will believe me and I'll only drive myself mad if I carry on. Anyway, there's so much I can't remember, perhaps I have got it completely wrong, perhaps Elizabeth is at home and I've been fussing over nothing.

Carla sees the notice when she arrives and nods approvingly. "Quite right," she says. "You concentrate on keeping safe and well. Better safe than sorry, eh?" She bustles about as usual, telling me of muggings and armed robberies. I try to keep up, but I feel it doesn't really relate to me any more. "The elderly are just very bad with safety," she is saying. "They don't see their locks are turned properly or their windows are shut tight. It's because you grew up in a different time. I bet you knew everyone then, huh?"

"Don't be daft," I say. "The town was full of all sorts when I was a girl." Men just demobbed getting drunk in the pubs, American and Canadian soldiers waiting to go home, evacuees from London or Birmingham with no home to go back to, and convalescents hoping for a cure from the sea air. Carla disappears upstairs to do my bedroom before I can finish the thought, and I wander into the kitchen. My sandwich hasn't been made yet so I put some bread in the bread-heater, the bread-browner, and get out the butter.

"How much toast d'you think you eat?" Carla says, suddenly reappearing. "You must get through a loaf a day."

"Well, there's no cake left because of the sergeant," I say.

"If there's no cake it's because you've had it," she says, running the tap and whisking Fairy Liquid into a mountain of foam.

I don't much like her tone. I move out of her way and check the front door before going to sit down.

105

Carla comes into the sitting room to give me my pills; I don't know what they're for.

"And then, of course, there's the key safes," she says as she stands by the coffee table, writing in the carers' folder. "You have to have them so us care workers can get in and that, but it would only take one bad lot, wouldn't it? Someone tells someone the code, and the criminal doesn't even have to break in." She puts her hands to her head and then lifts them into the air.

"They can't be that dangerous," I say. "Or they wouldn't make everyone have them. Even Elizabeth has one." My mind rushes to tell me something. Elizabeth has a key safe. Key safes make it easy to get into a house. I write it down and put Elizabeth's name next to it. "Elizabeth has a key safe," I say again. "If someone had got in . . ."

"Not that again," Carla says. "I thought you'd given it up?" She points to the sign on the wall.

"Oh, yes," I say, laying down my pen. I feel disappointed, as if I've lost something valuable.

"Okay. Bye." She goes to the door. There is the sound of her trying to open it. It bangs as if it's stuck. "Hey!" she calls. "You've locked it. Where's the key?"

I get up and show her the little pot on the radiator shelf where I keep it. "You said to check the locks," I say, showing Carla the note I wrote on the subject.

She stares at me. "But you don't check them while I'm still here."

When she's locked me in again I go and look for my sandwich; there's a piece of toast on the sideboard and I put down my handful of notes to get the butter, but I can't find any in the fridge. There's a big sign above the stove telling me not to cook anything, but I really fancy an egg with my toast. Surely boiling an egg is allowed. That's hardly cooking at all.

I turn on the gas and fill a saucepan with water. While I'm waiting for it to boil I pick up my notes to read: *Key safes make it easy to get into a house.* Elizabeth's name is next to it. I read it several times. There's something significant about it, I just don't know what. I've also written: *would only take one bad lot.* But that's true of everything. And anyway you can't go around being afraid of everyone. You have to let some people into your home.

Sukey was the one who suggested Douglas as a lodger. She was working in the NAAFI canteen, which had been set up in a hotel on the clifftop, and Douglas was doing milk deliveries until he was old enough to join the army. The canteen was on his route, and Sukey liked him. They used to chat before she opened in the morning, mostly about films, she said.

I met him one day when Sukey took me to work. It was the week after our school had been hit in a night raid. They hadn't got the facilities for us to join the boys' school yet and Ma didn't want me hanging around at home all day. We had to get up really early and I was still half asleep when we arrived. Sukey sat me down in the kitchen while she weighed tea and coffee into white cloth bags and ran backwards and forwards to check the hot-water urn. I thought she looked funny in her blue overalls and little cap, but she didn't seem to mind. There was a lovely smell of cooking and she gave me beans on toast and a sausage to eat.

"Shouldn't really," she said as she passed me the plate. "Only meant to be for the Yanks."

It was mainly American soldiers they served there then, and I kept listening out for an accent as I ate. I was just finishing when I heard one.

"Sure thing," it said, and, "That'll be just fine."

I looked round and saw Sukey come in with a boy. He carried a crate of milk bottles and set them on the counter in front of me. I was surprised at seeing an American milkman and stared at him.

"This is Doug, Mopps," Sukey said, a hand on his shoulder. "Say hello."

"Hello, Doug," I said, looking past him as Sukey picked up a couple of milk bottles and went back out of the kitchen.

"Hello . . . Mopps," he said, frowning a little at the name. His eyes followed Sukey as she walked away.

I laughed. "That's not my real name, silly," I said.

He looked annoyed at that and turned to me. "What does she call you that for then?" he said. His accent was no longer American and I wondered if Sukey knew he'd been pretending.

I put the last bit of sausage into my mouth. "It's a nickname," I said, chewing.

"Bit stupid, isn't it?" he said, still frowning.

I shrugged and rested my fork against the side of my plate. "Bet Doug isn't your real name."

108

"'Course it is," he said, his eyes sliding back over to Sukey as she came in and dropped another bag of tea on to the scales.

"Isn't it short for Douglas?"

His mouth flattened and he looked down at the milk bottles, pulling them from their crate jerkily.

"Isn't it?"

"Yes."

"So Doug is a nickname, then?"

He stopped what he was doing and looked at me. "You've beaten me there," he said, and he blushed and flicked another look at Sukey. I'd embarrassed him, and I felt sorry.

"Doug's a good name," I said, trying to make it up. "I like it."

That made him smile, and I felt even more sorry. He was nice-looking, Douglas, with a soft oval face and brown hair and very straight eyebrows. He was tall, but he stooped and ducked his head when he spoke, and he looked at you sideways, so people didn't always notice his height.

"I hope you're being nice to Doug," Sukey said, coming over to put the empty bottles down on the table.

I nodded, trying to think of something to say. "Hey, we saw the mad woman outside," I said, because we had, though only briefly.

"Hush, Maud," Sukey said. "Don't call her that. You don't know who she might be. Imagine if Ma did something funny and someone called her mad. And you weren't listening to me. Doug's going to be our new lodger." She ruffled his hair in the way she usually ruffled mine, and he blushed again. "D'you want something to eat?" she asked him.

"No, I'd better be getting on," he said, and he quickly filled the crate with empties, carrying them out and waving awkwardly when Sukey called cheerio.

"Has Ma ever done anything funny?" I said to Sukey as soon as he'd gone.

"'Course not, silly," she said, gathering up the bottles of milk. "You should just be a bit less quick to judge, that's all. Do you like Doug? Ma's been looking for someone to take the room since old Miss Lacey went to her niece. I meant it, though. Be nice. His mum's just died. Bomb dropped on their house."

I felt even worse about the nicknames thing then, and I promised I'd be kind to him. I meant it too. But I thought of the way Sukey had ruffled his hair and offered him food, looking after him the way she looked after me, and I wondered whether I ever stared at her the way Douglas did.

There's a funny smell coming from somewhere. I look round the sitting room, pick up a cushion and sit down on the window seat. I can't see anything. I can't work out where the smell's coming from. I've been digging a whole lot of my notes out of the waste-paper basket, wondering how they got there. I've rescued a scratched blue and silver compact lid from the bin, too, so that makes twice it's been dug up. I'm just getting the energy to go and see what's causing that awful smell when Helen walks in.

110

"Mum! You've left the gas on!" she shouts. "I've told you not to use the hob. You could have blown the whole bloody house up! Ugh, you can smell it in here too."

She stands in front of me and leans past to open the window, wafting the air with the curtain. I look at the underside of her chin. It's very soft-looking. Vulnerable. "I'm sorry about the nicknames," I say.

Her chin folds into itself as she looks down at me. "What?"

"No, I don't know," I say. I wonder if she will get me a cup of tea in a minute. But we might not have any milk, because I upset the milkman. Oh, everything is so muddled. There is a breeze from the window; it gets me right in the lower back and makes me shiver.

"Couldn't you smell it?" Helen says.

"I thought I could smell something, yes," I say, pulling a bit of material over my knees for warmth. "Sausage and beans and — what did you say it was?"

"Gas."

"Oh. Has there been some kind of leak, then?" The material in my lap won't lie flat. I try to smooth it down, tuck it round me, but it keeps moving. When I look up Helen is still waving the curtain about. The movement makes me blink.

"No, Mum," she says. "You left the hob on. This is why you mustn't cook."

"I don't cook, usually, Helen," I say. "There's a sign in the kitchen —"

"I know there's a sign. I wrote it." She drops the curtain and pushes her fingers into her hair.

"But I can do a boiled egg," I say.

111

"No! No, you can't. Mum, this is what I'm saying." She makes her hands into fists, pulling at the roots of her hair. I can't work out why she's so upset. "Do you understand? You really mustn't try to cook anything. *Anything.*"

"All right. I won't," I say, watching her walk about the room. "I'll have a bit of cheese or something instead."

"D'you promise?" she asks. "Will you write it down?"

I nod and take a pen from my handbag. There's a jumble of coloured paper on the table next to me and I make a note under a list which starts: *Compact, vegetable marrows.*

"And write on the sign too," Helen says. "I'll come with you and help."

She puts out a hand and I hold it to stand up. Somehow I've managed to get the curtain caught in my trousers, and Helen has to untuck it. She walks very close on the way to the kitchen, her fingers covering mine once on the handrail. When we get there I realize I've left the pen in the sitting room. Helen runs to fetch it.

"Even eggs," she says, coming back. "Write 'even eggs' on the sign."

I do as she says and then put the pen down. "What does that mean?" I ask. "'Even eggs'? What does that mean?"

CHAPTER
SEVEN

That old Eric Coates tune is in my head. "Calling All Workers". It spins round and round, getting more manic by the second. Bouncier, louder, more militaristic. I imagine a crazed smile on my face, my arms moving as if they're pulled by strings. I used to feel restless like this when I was a girl. Everyone telling you to get on and help, to work, for the war effort, but not giving you anything specific to do. I switch on the TV, but can't focus on it, so I potter about the house, tidying up, doing a bit of cleaning, arranging, dusting. I plump the cushions on the settee and put the books neatly away. I spray polish on to the coffee table and fetch a cloth to rub it with. Carla comes in just as I'm buffing the first smear of spray into a shine.

"There's a busy bee," she says, taking off her coat. "You doing some cleaning? I should write it in your folder." She nods at me, flipping through the pages with her pen poised, but then she turns and makes a little noise. "Oh, but what's going on?" she says. "Are you going to burn them? Why have you piled all the books into the fireplace?"

"What are you talking about?" I say, dropping the cloth. The books are neatly in position. They fit perfectly in the little alcove next to the TV. It looks very nice.

"And, er," she says, "what are you using to clean the table?"

"A cloth," I say, frowning at her. She seems to be full of silly questions today.

"No, I don't think it is a cloth."

She has the lump of material in her hands, ready to straighten it out. When she holds it up I can see what it is. A skirt. One of Sukey's. A skirt of dark-brown jersey, covered now in matted polish and crumbs. I must have pulled it from the wardrobe in my old room. There are lots of Sukey's things in there. Things I cut up and adjusted and wore, and things I kept just because I couldn't bear to throw them away. And now I've gone and ruined something.

Carla grins. "Novel way to use a skirt," she says. And then she catches my eye and tilts her head to one side. "I'll put it in the washing machine. Not to worry. It'll be good as new."

When Carla's gone I find I don't have the patience to sit down. I have a nagging feeling that there's somewhere I'm supposed to be. I put on my coat and walk out. I can't think where I'm going, but that doesn't matter, I'm sure I'm supposed to be somewhere and I must come to it eventually.

A bus goes past as I reach the top of the road. I hope I didn't mean to get on it. If I did, it's too late now anyway. I keep myself steady with a hand on someone's garden wall while I turn to look back down the street. There is moss, wet under my fingers, and I find I'm scratching it off, enjoying the feel of the roots breaking from their hold. A few brightly coloured scraps of paper are dotted along the pavement. They must be mine, my notes, my paper memory. My pockets are stuffed full of lists and memos. For a moment I can't be bothered to go back and pick these lost ones up, but I bend for the nearest, feeling a creaking in my joints, knowing something critical might be lost if I don't retrieve it. This nearest is a blue square of paper: *Oxfam 2p.m. today*. I still help out there.

Two p.m. today. Does that really mean *today*? I have a feeling it doesn't, but I wouldn't like to let them down. Those awful images of skinny children with swollen bellies and flies around their mouths would haunt me if I did. And if it's a Tuesday, Elizabeth will be there. I walk to the bus stop, reaching for the nearest scraps of paper as I go. I'm sure these terrible famines didn't happen so much when I was young. I find half a bar of chocolate in the pocket of my coat while I'm waiting and eat it on the bus.

The Oxfam shop is in the arcade. It used to be a posh jeweller's, and it's where my sister got her engagement ring. My old hairdresser's is here, too, though it's been closed a long while. The windows are dusty, and the old-fashioned hairdryers, which have been left behind, stand, slowly disintegrating, like a row of overgrown harebells in a sandy field. The shop next door sells all sorts of bathroom gifts. Salts and oils and bubbles, and glass trays for soap and shells dyed different colours. We get quite a lot of their things given into Oxfam. I would have loved the shells when I was young. I had a collection once, and still have some of them stored away at home, in a chest made of glued-together matchboxes. I used to pick them up from the edge of the beach, my parents shouting at me not to get too close to the barbed wire. I liked to hold them to my ears and listen to the rush of the waves.

I had a lot of pink ones and some speckled grey. I never got further than that in identification, though. Uncle Trevor gave me a book on shells when he found I was collecting, but I wasn't interested in knowing the names and, as I looked through the pages, the drawings of the horrid slug-like things that had lived in my beautiful collection began to make me feel sick. I didn't like to think of those ugly slimy things in connection with the pearly, perfect shells. The word "mollusc" angered me and eventually I threw the book away.

I am hit by the musty smell as I go into our shop. We can never seem to get rid of it, despite steam-cleaning all the donated clothes. The air is stale and sourish; it's the only thing I really dislike about working here. That and Peggy. She looks up from behind the counter as I walk in, her pale, starch-stiff hair catching the light. She is only sixty-eight and so is better than me by a good dozen years.

"Maud?" she says. "What are you —?"

"Am I late?" I say, pushing at a rack of clothes so I can get past.

"No, Maud. We don't need you . . . I mean" — she leans her hands on the counter and puts on a high-pitched, wheedling voice. It's the one my daughter uses when she is trying to persuade me that throwing half my possessions away or giving up cooking is "for the best" — "we decided you weren't to worry about coming back here, didn't we? Do you remember?"

I lower my head and pretend to look through the basket of things on the front desk. I feel a sudden welling up of hatred for Peggy as I poke at the soiled leather bookmarks and plastic napkin rings. I do remember. She and Mavis decided I wasn't up to working here. Well, I was always at a disadvantage. The others had jobs in shops when they were young. Peggy was at Beales, Mavis managed Carlton Shoes, and Elizabeth's father owned a baker's shop, which she had to serve in as a child. But my dad got me a job at the exchange straight out of school, so I was never anything other than a telephonist. I found the till at Oxfam difficult enough as it was, and then I began to get the different coins confused, giving people too much change. When I was flustered by a customer it was even worse. One day I stood staring at a pound coin, unable to recognize it. The man at the counter kept sighing. "You can't be that bad at maths," he said.

I don't know what I gave him in the end, but Peggy was very angry.

She taps her varnish-encrusted nails on the counter now, waiting for me to answer. I carry on rummaging through the basket and my finger catches on the back of a little picture frame. "That's funny," I say, pulling it out. "Elizabeth has a frame like this. It holds a picture of us just after we met. It's unusual, isn't it?" I smooth my thumb over the corner. The frame is made of creamy porcelain with flowers delicately sprouting

117

along both sides. A tiny cherub's head pokes out at the top, looking down at where the photo should be. "I wouldn't have thought there would be two alike," I say. "She bought it from here a few months after she'd started."

"God, yes, she was always buying bits of china. I see you have a good memory for some things, Maud."

"I really think it is her frame. But she would never have given it away." I look up at Peggy. "Was the photo in it?"

"Possibly, but we would hardly have tried to sell it with a photo still inside. Anyway, I doubt very much that it's Elizabeth's frame."

The door opens and Peggy smiles briefly at someone entering the shop. "You can always give us the two pounds for it, if you want it. Buying things is the best way for you to help us now."

I know what this means. But I'm not ready to leave yet. "Shall I make you a cup of tea?" I say, laying the frame down carefully in the basket. "I can remember where the kettle is, and you're stuck out here . . ." I begin to move towards the back room. Peggy's frown fades.

"Well," she says. "Well, that would be nice. I'd like an instant coffee."

I fill the kettle and switch it on. One thing I do remember about Peggy is that she can't bear to throw photos away. I've always thought that fact made her seem more human. Under the work table piled high with donated clothes there's a drawer she keeps the old photos in. The wood squeaks as I pull it out, and I flick

118

a look towards the door, glad the kettle makes such a noise, before sitting down to sift through the pictures.

Lots of them are of pets, a couple of family groups, and a few on stiff card from long ago — a man in uniform about to go off to fight in the Great War, and a woman with leg-of-mutton sleeves standing by an aspidistra. I set them aside, searching through several layers of snapshots before I find a highly coloured photo of two ordinary-looking women in soft floral blouses. Elizabeth and me. We are standing just outside the arcade, the painted iron gates curling prettily behind us. Elizabeth's grey-streaked hair is pinned tightly to her head and mine floats away into the air. We smile at the camera, showing off the wrinkles that prove we are past middle age, and Elizabeth holds something up. It's a frog-shaped jug she bought on her first day at Oxfam. "Just a replica," she said, and hideous if you ask me, but Elizabeth's hands are holding it as though it were very precious. That was the day we met, the day I found out that her garden was the one with the pebbled wall, the day I decided we'd be friends. I can still remember the way my face ached from laughing. She would never have thrown this picture away. My eyes fill with tears. I'm starting to think she must be dead. The mounds of discarded clothes on the table suddenly take on an ugly significance. All the hours Elizabeth and I spent going through the donations, and I never thought that one day one of us might be going through the things of the other.

I put the photo in my pocket and the kettle pings. I take Peggy's mug to the counter.

"Oh, *Maud*," she calls out as I leave the shop. "I asked for coffee and you've given me tea!"

I walk back through the park. There's a plank for sitting on, a long sitting plank, by the bandstand that looks towards Elizabeth's road, and I have a rest, watching a man top up a compost heap. It's cold and it looks like rain, but I don't feel like going home yet, I want to sit and think about this new find and let the fresh air free me of the shop's musty smell. What is it about old clothes that makes them smell like that? Even clean clothes seem to give off that sour smell after a time.

It's the smell from the suitcase I remember most. Dad was the one who brought it home, nearly three months after Sukey disappeared and about a week before my fifteenth birthday. I didn't recognize the case at first: Dad was crying when he handed it to me and I could only look at him, feeling a falling in my chest like guilt or fear. The skin on his face was creased and he made a dry sound in his throat. I'd never seen him cry before and was too shocked to comfort him. He sat down on a chair by the stove and turned his face away. Ma didn't comfort him either, she just laid the suitcase on the kitchen table.

Sukey had got it for her honeymoon, a bulky thing, made of brown leather, with a brown leather handle and brass clasps. A point of pinkish light shone through the window, picking out the places on the clasps where the brass was scratched. I ran a finger over one, dulling the metal, and Ma brushed my hands away

120

to open the case. That sour-clothes smell filled the room, lying over the usual kitchen smells — fried onions and dried herbs and soap flakes — like a thick layer of dust.

We stood and looked at Sukey's things. The clothes were screwed together and twisted against the striped canvas lining. Blouses and pullovers and false fronts, a fur collar and a pair of fawn trousers with tiny pleats on the waistband. Underneath was a dress, once beige, which Sukey had only recently dyed a deep-navy colour to make it new. And then there were the underclothes, knickers and camisoles, patched in silk and trimmed with lace. They weren't dirty, but the shine on the material was gone, as if they'd been handled by lots of people.

"Oh dear. I can't think how you wash this," Ma said, taking out the dyed dress. "With cold water, perhaps. How much soap d'you suppose, Maud?"

I kept my eyes on the suitcase, wondering how long it was since Sukey had touched the things inside. This was all we had left of her. I wanted to curl up in the case and shut the lid, not take everything out and wash her away. A blue glass bottle nestled against the sleeve of a blouse as if held in the crook of an arm. Sukey's perfume, Evening in Paris. I pulled it free, automatically splashing my wrists and neck before I thought what I was doing. Ma stared at me through the haze of cheap, sweet scent, too light to linger long in the air, and then began to grab at the mass of cotton and jersey and wool as if she were kneading dough, battering the clothes against the sides of the case. Smaller things fell away, slipping on to the floor, and I was bundling up several pairs of silk drawers when Douglas came in. He paused, stared, turned sideways and dropped his eyes.

"Sukey's?" he asked. "Where from?"

"Station Hotel. Police found it," Dad said.

He was staring into the wood burner in the range, his face red from the heat. I was grateful he wasn't crying any more. Ma had stopped her kneading when Douglas came in, and stood rigid, a silk scarf and the belt of a dress reaching like creepers up to her elbow. I slowly unwound them and pushed the knickers I'd gathered from the floor back into the case.

"They've been through it already," Dad said.

So that was why everything had been in such a mess. I imagined big policemen's hands rooting through the underwear. It was a horrible thought. Perhaps Douglas was thinking that, too, because he looked sick for a moment.

"Find anything?" he asked.

Dad shook his head. "Nothing really. Except her ration book."

"She left it in her suitcase." Douglas made it sound like the answer to a riddle. "And the people at the hotel? What did they say?"

"They've no recollection of seeing her. Her name's in the register — receptionist's handwriting, not hers — but they didn't recognize her photo."

"So did she stay there or not?" I asked. My chest felt full of air and I thought my lungs might burst. Nobody answered. Ma didn't move, didn't say anything, but I saw tears fall on to silk, and watched as they made dark

122

circles on the material. It was me who washed everything in the end.

I'm halfway along Elizabeth's road before I know where I'm going. It's full of children in dull, untidy uniforms, on their way to, or possibly from, school. I stumble through a knot of them; they smell of unwashed gym kits and cheap aftershave and I find I'm staring at their rucksacks and record bags expecting to see a brown leather suitcase with a brown leather handle. Even at Elizabeth's door I'm still glancing back to check. I ring the bell, look through the front window and peer in at the kitchen, but I can't see anything. The house seems dark and unlived in.

"Look, it's some geriatric burglar!" someone shouts.

A gang of children, teenagers I suppose you'd call them — Katy's age — swagger about the pavement, slapping at their fellows and dragging their bags along the ground. The boy who shouted is grinning at me.

"How you gonna get in?" he calls. "Stannah stairlift?"

The others laugh, and I turn to see where he's pointing: the landing window is open. How useful it would be if I really did have a stairlift to take me up there; I might just fit through that window. I wonder if it has been open before? I nearly missed it this time. I wonder if anything else is open. I try the side gate, but that's wishful thinking. If only I could pull the outer wall away to see if Elizabeth is in there, take the front off like a doll's house. Or like Douglas's house after the bombs were dropped. Of course, I wouldn't really want anything like that to happen and I feel slightly ashamed of wishing for a bomb. But I do want to ask about the open window, so I step round to the next-door neighbour's. There's no bell, and when I knock a dog starts barking. It gets louder and more aggressive-sounding as I wait, until it seems as if it's right behind the door. I begin to back away but, just as I reach the pavement, the door opens and the dog bounds out. It runs around me, whining and sniffing.

"Don't worry," the owner says. "He won't bite or anything, he's just curious. Did you knock?"

I stare at the owner. He's young, just a boy, and has messy brown hair. Very messy. The dog licks my hand, and I pat it on the head.

"You must give off good vibes," the boy says. "He only usually does that to people he knows."

I smile, glad to have been singled out. Glad to have found a friend. I always wanted a dog when I was young. My parents said we couldn't afford it, and they were probably right, but I was haunted by a story about a dog that was found dead in someone's yard. It had been tied up and left without food and water after the owner had gone away. Mrs Winners told us about it to prove we shouldn't give up hope, that people were moving "at the drop of a hat" nowadays, doing moonlight flits, that Sukey might have done the same. "No time to even consider their pets," she said. "It's the way of the world now." But it was the other details that struck me at the time. The yard was one near Frank's, and the dog was found only a few days after Dad and I had been to his house. "It must have barked and

124

barked," Mrs Winners said. "Hoping someone would come and rescue it." How I wished — for years, I wished — that I had been that someone, had followed the barking when I'd heard it, and saved the dog.

This dog in front of me whines as if it knows the turn of my thoughts. I pat him again, longing to be young and supple so I could crouch down and rub his coat properly.

"Shut up, Vincent," the boy says. "He's just going for the sympathy vote. Hoping you've got a biscuit on you."

I begin to look through my bag.

"Oh, no," he says. "Don't. We've got plenty, he's just greedy. You're not a friend of Mum's, are you? Did you want something?"

"No," I say. "No. Thank you."

"Wasn't it you who knocked?"

"I don't think so," I say, walking away. The dog follows me to the end of the path and then runs off when its owner calls. I keep looking back towards Elizabeth's house as I walk home. If only there were some way of getting in.

It starts to drizzle in the park, and that quickly becomes a downpour. I stand for a moment under some trees. I stood here once, long ago, with my mother. I remember it being dark like this, the sky glowering and the earth too sodden to give off that fresh smell of the outdoors. I'd followed her here, more or less, after a row with my father.

She'd been at the garden gate when I got home from Audrey's, and I could see Dad silhouetted in the light of the kitchen door. "How could you, Lillian?" I heard him shout.

My first instinct was to run into the larder and cover my head, but instead I waited on the pavement, half hidden by Mrs Winners' hedge.

"What was I supposed to do?" Ma yelled back, pulling her mackintosh close against the rain. "There are still four mouths to feed in this house. And it's not like I can ask Frank for help any more."

"Frank! Again! You never stop talking about that man. Never mind he was the death of our daughter —"

"He never was! He just isn't a sour-faced Methodist like all the people you admire. And don't think I don't know who's put that idea in your head."

I couldn't hear what Dad said to that, but I heard Ma shout.

"Yes, I mean Douglas! He could never leave Sukey alone — of course he'd like to accuse Frank."

I looked at the windows above, hoping Douglas wasn't in, and then watched as Ma marched off down the road, raindrops making the brim of her hat sag sadly. When I finally moved I found Dad still standing by the kitchen door. He threw his hands up as he spotted me.

"You're determined to get wet through, too, I see," he said.

After a moment I followed him inside. Douglas was sitting at the table, concentrating on his food, and I wondered how much he'd heard. There was a towel hanging on the back of a chair by the fire — it smelled of gravy but I rubbed my face and hair with it while

126

Dad told me I deserved to get pneumonia. I took my wet skirt off and hung it on the chair where the towel had been, and Douglas stared at me for a moment in my petticoat.

"What's going on?" I asked, as no one had bothered to tell me.

"Frank's back," Douglas said. His eyes were narrowed, and he was holding a spoon as though he might try to stab someone with it. "They arrested him off the train from London."

"Arrested him? Why? Have they found — I mean, is there any news of Sukey?"

"Nothing yet. Just the coupon fraud so far." He shook chutney off his spoon fiercely; it spattered on to his pullover and he muttered something under his breath. Dad sat down to his own half-finished meal, frowning at the shredded cabbage.

"But you think there will be something?"

"No doubt. When they find out what sort of a man he is. A drunk, a criminal. The sort of man that should never have been allowed to marry Sukey. The sort of man no parent should ever allow near his daughters."

Dad's fork clattered against his plate. "Thank you for that, Douglas," he said. "I'm sure you mean well, but you can keep your opinions to yourself in the future."

I leant against the sink, watching Douglas's face as it screwed tight before relaxing enough to chew. For a few minutes he looked like his old self, ducking his head and bending right over his food to eat. I almost expected him to sit back with a "This chutney sure is swell." But he was staring at his left-over mutton gristle when he spoke again.

"Mr Palmer," he said, "you do think it was Frank, don't you?"

Dad stared at him across the table.

"You do think it must have been him? You do want him to be locked away?"

"We don't know if she's dead," I said.

"None of that will bring her back," Dad said at the same time, then, turning to me, "Maud, the police told us. The likelihood now is that she isn't still living. You must understand that."

I looked away at the rain-soaked garden, wondering where Ma was.

"Maud?" Dad said again. He reached a hand towards me.

"Yes, yes," I said, pushing away from the sink and taking Dad's old greatcoat from its hook. I was trying to be as mechanical as possible, trying not to let myself think.

"You're going after your mother?" Dad got up as I made for the kitchen door. "Don't, Maud. You should know: she's been using Sukey's ration book."

"That's what you've been arguing about?" I said, moving stiff and puppet-like.

Dad nodded, and Douglas behind him. I looked at them sitting together, a united front. No wonder Ma preferred the dismal night to the two of them, here like this, stony-faced and against her — still eating, I noted, the food they were so morally opposed to having. I felt

128

something rush up through me and my breath rasped into my throat.

"If Sukey's dead," I shouted, "what does it matter?"

I banged out of the house and took the route I'd seen Ma take, down the street and into the park. It was still raining heavily. The grass was waterlogged and the air was cold. I wished I had better shoes on and realized I didn't know where I was going, or how far Ma might have walked. But I was too angry to stop and go back home. Angry with Dad's petty worries in the face of Sukey's disappearance, angry at his weak acceptance of Douglas's interpretation, and angry at having been made to take sides. I kept going, past the bandstand and on to the North Gate, before turning back towards the wilder bit of the park.

It was there I found Ma. She had stopped under the trees, where it was still wet, but not so exposed. The park seemed like a flat sea and Ma, standing, looking out, was a ship's captain, surveying the water, the tall dark trees behind her a huge wave about to engulf the ship. I thought she might have been crying on the walk there, but it could just have been the rain. She saw me and held her head up so I could see her eyes under her hat.

"If you're going to weigh in about that book, then you can cook your own meals, same as they can from now on," she said, but then she opened her arms and I went straight to her.

"She wasn't with him," she said into my hair, which the rain had plastered to my scalp. "Frank's come back, but she wasn't with him."

I pressed my face into her shoulder and she stroked my wet head.

"I thought. I'd hoped. You know what I'd hoped. But she wasn't with him. And do you believe it, Maud?" she asked, holding me away from her for a moment. "Do you believe Frank could have done it? Douglas said he was a nasty drunk. Was he?"

A copy of the *Echo* blew past and I watched it flapping like a fish as it came to rest against the nearest tree. "I did see Frank drunk once," I said, feeling I had to say something. "But he wasn't nasty to Sukey. Not exactly. Sort of the opposite. Sort of."

Ma nodded, smiled a bit. "Thought so," she said.

"And he probably didn't like Doug very much because of the amount of time he spent there."

"What?" Ma said, turning my face up to hers and smoothing my hair back.

I felt a drop of rain splash on to my face. "Doug," I said. "One of Sukey's neighbours said he was there all the time, and I s'pose Frank didn't much like that."

"Douglas was there all the time? Why?"

I shrugged. "The woman thought he was Sukey's fancy man. But that's stupid, isn't it, Ma? Isn't it?"

She let go of me and began to walk back across the park. I followed, avoiding the puddles which her feet found and trying to draw a dry breath in through the rain. As we got to the darkly covered bandstand a shadow slipped beyond the trees.

"Come on, just come out of the rain," someone said from the blackness of the bandstand, and Ma and I stopped as one, straining to see into the gloom.

130

"It's pelting it down. You'll catch your death." It was Douglas's voice, and then his face, shining down at us like an owl's. He started at the sight of us and his skin seemed unnaturally white.

"Who were you talking to?" Ma said, looking round.

"You," he said, though he looked over our heads, at the expanse of inky turf. "I thought you should come out of the rain. Who else would I be talking to?"

Ma stared at him for several seconds and then turned very deliberately towards the trees. There was nothing there. "Well, I don't want to huddle under a bandstand for the rest of the night," she said. "Let's get home."

Our footsteps on the path held a liquid ring and I was glad to be heading for our kitchen and a hot fire, but before we reached the steps down to the street I looked back. It only took a moment to recognize the figure of the mad woman. She was crouched on the open grass, pinned by the rain, her umbrella propped against her side, unopened. And I suddenly knew that it was she Douglas had been speaking to, she he had been pleading with to come out of the rain.

CHAPTER
EIGHT

"'Snake and kidney pie', that was one of Dad's. And 'Nosmo King sits here,' d'you remember, Helen? He'd put the NO SMOKING sign on your place mat. Used to drive waitresses mad with his nonsense."

My son is over from Germany with his wife and children. They're talking and laughing, their voices echoing over each other the way they do underwater. I can hear what they say — making jokes of some kind — but somehow I can't make the sentences fit together. I lose track. Still, I laugh along with the others; it doesn't matter what the joke is, it's nice to laugh. My face aches from smiling. And I am so warm. My daughter's on one side, my son on the other.

I've got a bit of a rhyme running through my brain, but it runs too fast to catch it all. There was an old woman who lived in a shell. That's not quite right, but I can't think what it was she did live in. Anyway, I feel as if I'm inside a shell, and I'm an old woman, so perhaps I'm allowed to change the rhyme a bit. There was an old woman. I used to read that to these children of mine. Tom and Helen. I used to read it to them.

Of course, we're really in a sort of café, not a shell. It has a glass-domed ceiling and pearly walls and lots of those things for drinking, for putting drink in, on the table. Katy is laughing with her cousins opposite me and I've finished whatever it is I've been eating. Broth, perhaps, without any bread. That's what the old woman gives the children.

"Shall we think about getting you home, Mum?" Helen stretches herself as she stands, showing off her long legs. She might be fifty, but she's as lithe as anything. Being a gardener must keep you fit.

My left side feels suddenly chilly where she was sitting against it. A current of cold water in a warm sea. "No, I'd rather stay a little longer," I say, not getting up. "I'm having a nice time."

Helen bites her top lip with her bottom teeth; they are tiny pearl squares against the flesh. "It will take an hour to get you home and settled," she says. "I know you're enjoying yourself but —"

"Oh, let her stay a bit longer." Tom puts an arm round my shoulder. "Not often you get out, is it, Mum?"

"I take her out every week actually. I'm *here* for her, unlike some people." Helen's tone makes me wince, but Tom smiles.

"I know, dearest sister. You are a saint. No, really, I'm not being sarcastic." He stands too. "You know I appreciate everything you do for Mum, but I don't see her that often, so it would be nice . . . Look, we'll drop her home if you like. And you can get off."

Helen tilts her face towards the sky; a cloud shaped like a shoe is visible through the glass in the domed ceiling. "You wouldn't know what to do with her when

133

you got her home," she tells Tom. "She needs everything set out for her, otherwise she gets confused."

"Britta can deal with that, just tell her what to do."

There's a silence. I wonder whether to shout that I'm not an imbecile.

"No, I'll stay," Helen says finally. "After all, Katy's having a good time too."

"Just you who's here on sufferance." Tom sneaks in the last sentence, and gets a whack on the shoulder from his sister.

Katy *does* seem to be enjoying herself. I suppose she doesn't get to see her cousins very often. They always take a while to warm to each other. A shame, because by the time they're getting on it's usually time to go. I watch them laughing and chatting. They look very different. Katy's got her mother's blondish curls, always a bit messy. She never listens when I tell her to run a brush through them. Not even when she was a little girl. "I'm not going to meet the Queen," she used to say. Made me laugh to hear her. Anna and Frederick would never need to be told; they both have dark, glossy hair which lies very straight. Both children smile at me and call me Grandma, but I feel like they are strangers.

"I like your socks, Anna," I say, though I hadn't meant to break into her conversation. "They're very smart."

She looks at me, startled, and pulls the socks up higher, over her knees.

"There you are," Britta says. "I told you Grandma would like them. They're your favourites, aren't they,

Anna?" She smiles at me the way parents do when their children aren't being quite as polite as they'd like them to be.

Anna nods, but she seems to have forgotten what she was talking about before. My fault. I try to think of something to say, to help her out.

"I used to have socks like that. Good job too. Girls wore skirts to the knee when I was young, and we had no tights. I remember walking along the front with my parents. And, oooh, it was freezing."

We'd started at the top of the cliffs, making a zigzag down towards the beach. Dad didn't want us going too far on to the sand, what with all the barbed wire still piled up and the who-knew-what which had been buried to keep the Nazis away. So I didn't paddle, but I did get close enough to feel the spray of the sea and to find shells, like tiny pleated skirts, washed up and blown on to the path. We walked a long way that day, past the pier, watching the waves crash against the beach, and Dad held my arm as if I might vanish, same as Sukey. I hated being so closely held, especially with him and Ma arguing all the way. She'd said something about Frank when we were only yards from the house and Dad hadn't let the subject drop since.

"If only Sukey had left him," he said. "Every other couple in this country seems to be getting a divorce. Why couldn't they have done that? Then she'd have been back living with us, safe."

"You said last week you didn't hold with divorce," Ma said.

"Well, it depends on the character of the husband, doesn't it?" He looked for a moment at Ma. "Or the behaviour of the wife."

I held a shell to my ear, letting the hollow gush drown their voices, and then pulled away from Dad as we reached the dancing shack. It was a sort of wooden hut on the path, by a turning up towards town, where they'd sold drinks and things before the war. It was shut now, with boards nailed over the windows and the old awning just a tatty fringe. It smelled of the sea, salty and rotten, and of wood and damp. Grass had sewn itself on to the roof so that it seemed to have hair which waved in the wind. Sukey had called it the dancing shack because the grass made the hut look as if it was swaying to some unheard music. Salt had caused the grain of the wood to open and pucker and there were holes where knots had fallen out. We used to run our fingers over the walls and feed tiny stones and shells and even handfuls of sand through the holes. I had liked to think of it filling up a bit more every time we came to the beach. And one day the hut would be whipped away, leaving a densely moulded copy in its place. Like a giant sandcastle.

Letting my parents walk on, I ran a hand over a weathered board, knocking my knuckles against it, and heard a sort of flapping shuffle somewhere close by. I looked up at the grass on the roof, but couldn't see anything, so I walked round behind, wondering if there was a nest somewhere. My friend Audrey had had pigeons breeding in her family's beach hut the spring before and she'd been terribly upset about her father

136

smashing the eggs. I reached the far corner, still not able to see anything, and was about to poke a finger through a hole, when I saw the gleam of an eye.

I jumped back, nearly falling over the slope of a dune. This wasn't a pigeon. It was a human eye. Someone was inside, looking out. I could hear a voice from within, whispering. Whispering about glass smashing and birds flying. Whispering about a van and soil and marrows. Whispering until the whisper broke and whoever it was inside the dancing shack was suddenly shouting.

"I'm watching. I'm watching you."

I didn't doubt it. The eye stared straight at me through the hole in the wood, and, desperate to get out of its line of vision, I ran after Dad, my heart thumping. When I looked back there was a figure coming away from the hut, an umbrella in her hand. It was the mad woman. She shouted after me, repeating in a yell the words she'd whispered, and then, just before I was out of earshot, I thought she said Sukey's name. I stopped and nearly went back, but she was always shouting and I was frightened. So instead I caught up with Dad and let him hold my arm the rest of the way home.

I'm quite tipsy by the time Tom helps me into the car. Helen buckles me in and gives him a list of instructions for taking me home. She wants to make sure he doesn't forget to lock me in the house. Tom drops the paper on to the dashboard and hugs her before she hurries away.

"Has she gone to tell the woman off and get our peach slices back?" I ask him.

137

"What?"

"Nothing," I say. "It was nonsense." I'm quite emotional, partly because I don't know when he and the family will be over from Germany next, and partly because of the wine. I have a little sob in the car and the children shift about behind me.

We go home a funny way — Tom no longer remembers the roads — and we pass Elizabeth's house. The side gate is open. I sit up and look back out of the window.

"Could you drop me here?" I say to Tom. "I'd rather walk the last bit."

He looks unsure, but slows the car. Side gate, I say to myself. Side gate side gate side gate.

"Helen said to make sure she was in the house, Tom," Britta says from the back seat. "I don't think we should just let your mother out here."

"I'm not an imbecile," I say over my shoulder. "And I haven't forgotten where I live, yet. I often walk back through the park, and I'd like to do that today." I put cold hands to my hot face: lying makes me flush.

"Okay, Mum," Tom says, pulling over. "If that's what you want. But don't tell Helen, or it'll be curtains for me."

I smile at the twinkle in his eye. He always was the more charming of my two children. I get out, untangling myself from the seatbelt, and blow kisses at the grandchildren. Britta gets out, too, and gives me a hug.

"I only want to make sure you are safe," she says.

I tell her I know, I tell her I'm grateful. And I wave them off, watching until the car disappears around a corner. All the time I'm trying to cling to two words as they slip, easily, through the gaps in my brain. I am outside Elizabeth's house, the sun is slanting on to the drive and the side gate is open. I can see a sliver of garden through it, golden green. A figure comes down the path from the front door. Curly hair, check coat. She smiles at me. Elizabeth. It's her. She's been here all along. "Elizabeth," I say. "How —"

It's not her. It's someone else. As she comes close I can see she's much younger than Elizabeth. She smiles as she passes me and gets into one of those mobile-library vans. I nod and stroke the top of the pebbled wall as if I'm admiring it, and then walk on, along the park fence and past the acacia tree. *The slender acacia would not shake/ One long milk-bloom on the tree.* The poem comes into my head unbidden. I was made to learn it at school. The teachers thought I ought to know it and I felt I ought to like it, what with it being called Maud. I did like it in a way, all the dewy flowers and things, but the meaning was completely obscure and it seemed to get very morbid at the end. Audrey was made to learn "The King's Breakfast", because her father owned the dairy, and that seemed much more fun: *I do like a little bit of butter to my bread.*

I wait by one of those striped crossings, lima crossing, llama crossing, trying to remember more words. I wonder about milk-bloom, what exactly milk-bloom might be. Just a moment ago I had

139

something to do. I watch a few cars go by, a lorry, a library van. Perhaps I was going to see Elizabeth, except that I can't have been, because she isn't there. I wander towards the house anyway, wishing I could see inside. That would be something. As I get close I find the side gate is open. There's no one about so I walk up the path and slip through, into the garden.

The smell of honeysuckle is thick in the air and I run a hand up the side of the wall, where moss and ivy-leaved toadflax have gathered. There are several patches of raw earth in the lawn and I wonder if moles have moved in. I walk over to a little hill, finding the soil damp. The smell of it is fresh and sharp, and it makes me think of a song, but I can't think of the name and I can't find the record. I can't find it, but I'm sure it was buried here. I put a hand against the apple tree and dip my fingers into the soil, pushing it aside to dig deeper into the ground. I want something smooth and round, silver and blue, but a stone catches the side of my nail and makes me pull away sharply. What on earth am I doing? I look at my hands, covered in dirt, and sigh. How often I seem to catch myself doing something stupid.

I wipe the soil on to my trousers and peer into the dining room through the French windows in case Elizabeth's inside. But her chair by the window is empty. This is where she always sits, looking out and watching the birds. The chair I usually sit in has been pushed back against the wall. No one is expecting me. I let out a breath and leave a cloud on the window.

The greenhouse surrounds the kitchen door and I remember when it was full of tomato plants, seedlings or wintering geraniums. It still smells of damp soil and wood stain, but almost everything has been replaced by cobwebs and boxes and old-people paraphernalia: a rusty wheelchair, two walking sticks and an old bath seat. There are a few empty plant pots, chalky to the touch, lined up against the wall. I drag them across the concrete floor, but there is no key under any of them. The desiccated remains of roots cling to the bottoms and these break away nicely under my fingers, like tiny strips of old wallpaper, leaving white lines on the terracotta. I sit down in the wheelchair, putting my feet up on the footrests. My head is muzzy, as if I've been drinking.

There's a key safe on the wall and I stare at it for a moment. I have one myself, for the carers. A tiny square box which requires four numbers to unlock it. If I was able to guess those numbers I could get into the house. I think through all the possible significant dates. But I can't remember Elizabeth's birthday, or her son's. If I ever knew them. I take bits of paper out of my pockets. A lot of them are appointments. The dentist. The optician. A fête Helen said she would take me to. I can't remember if we ever went.

Elizabeth's anniversary. Go round for cheer up. It's on a bright yellow square. I read it several times, but I can't remember what date that was. I shuffle through again. More old reminders: *sun hat in Helen's car — leave it there.* Then, on a pink square, I see it. *5th July. Go round and cheer Elizabeth up. (Would have been*

141

diamond wedding anniversary.) Diamond, that's sixty years. Silver for twenty-five, gold for fifty. Patrick and I just made our golden anniversary. We had a big party in the garden, invited the family, and friends and neighbours. It was a lovely September day and after everyone had gone home he and I sat on the swing hammock until well after dark, watching a bat flit round and round the house. He died before our fifty-first.

I stare out at the garden again, feeling very lonely. I don't know what I would have done without Elizabeth after Patrick went. Those silly games we played at Oxfam — buying up the ugly china and hiding the pricing gun so that Peggy couldn't find it — and all the tea-drinking and crosswords and ploughman's lunches: they kept me going. I struggle up from the wheelchair and stand in front of the key safe. Sixty years. That would make it 1952? I type it in. No luck. I press my forehead against the cool glass of the kitchen door and scrunch the note into a ball.

A dog barks in someone else's garden; the bark has a rusty quality and I find I can't bear the whine of it. I rattle the kitchen door handle, desperate to get away, and my stomach gives a lurch as the door opens into stillness. It was unlocked. I pause on the threshold, trying to think what it means, trying to separate the feeling of something being wrong from the memory of our own kitchen door when I was a child. Never locked until night-time; always unguarded, just like this one.

Dull light filters through a floral blind, making the surfaces blotchy, and the kitchen smells of disinfectant.

142

It gets me in the back of the throat. I open the top cupboards and the bottom cupboards and find they're empty. The fridge is on, humming away, but it's only got an old tub of margarine in it. I'm hardly sure the lack of food is significant, though. I often have to bring supplies to Elizabeth. Her son keeps her on starvation rations: cheap, tasteless food which she hates.

The dining room doesn't look the way I expect and I see for the first time how shabby and downtrodden the carpet is. There's something missing. I stare at the polished wooden table and try to remember what should be here, but I can't think of anything in particular. I stand behind Elizabeth's chair and look out of the window; watching the birds is something we often do together. Elizabeth can identify them just by their shape, she doesn't need to see the colour or anything. Even now she can tell a sparrow from a robin in the twilight.

The blackbird spots me from across the garden and half hops, half flies towards me. He lands on the bit of concrete outside the glass and looks in, turning his head one way, then the other. He wants some raisins; Elizabeth keeps a box by her chair and feeds him from the window. He skitters away, before coming back to stare up at me again. I can't see raisins anywhere. I'll have to check in the kitchen while I make Elizabeth a pot of tea. I wonder if I've remembered to bring any chocolate. I rummage in my handbag, taking out some tissues and an old prescription. I can't find any Elizabeth will be disappointed. I wish I had remembered. Perhaps I can make something, scrambled eggs or tomatoes on toast. I could lay the table now. Funny. There's no tablecloth. No place mats or coasters either. Elizabeth's particular about those things. I'll eat over my knees, in front of the telly, but Elizabeth likes to have everything nice. The salt and pepper are missing too. And the mango chutney, salad cream, Branston Pickle. Elizabeth needs a lot of condiments to go with all the bland food her son gets her. Turning towards the door, I see the writhing shelf of majolica ware is gone, the vases of worms have wriggled away, the plates of beetles and millipedes scuttled off. I hear my breath quicken in the silent room. There's something wrong here; I'm not just visiting. I take out my notes. Elizabeth's name is written over and over: *Missing, missing, missing.*

An engine grunts into silence somewhere close by, and I shuffle into the hall, blinking at the light which pours through the bubbled glass in the front door. I can see the Hoover marks on the carpet, and on the mat there is a letter addressed to Elizabeth. I bend to pick it up, my hand shaking as I push it into my pocket. A car door slams.

"I'll just get the rest of the boxes. You sit tight."

It's Elizabeth's son. I know his voice, and I wonder who it is he is calling to. I hear the scrunch of his feet on the crumbling concrete drive, see the blur of a man through the bubbled glass. Should I run and hide? Or will he see me if I move? I stand hunched forward, waiting. The footsteps move away, round the house; there is the clunk of the side gate's latch. I pull back a tiny bit of net curtain from the hall window. It must be

144

Peter's wife in the car, looking anxiously through the windscreen, but there's no Elizabeth with her.

"Left the bloody door open. I'll just have a quick check inside." Peter again; he lays a bath seat in the boot of the car and comes back towards the house.

I look around in panic. I mustn't be found here, I mustn't be discovered. I hear the scrunch again of footsteps, the metallic screech of the greenhouse door. My heart pounds. Could I make it up the stairs in time? I am about to stand and brazen it out when I catch sight of the larder door. The wood creaks and judders against the frame as I pull it open, but the man is busy stumbling over something and shouting about pots left in the way. I throw myself inside and shut the door.

The larder smells of polish and stale chocolate and I'm squashed in against some things, some long thin things. One has a sponge on the end, one has a brush. I can't think what they're called. There is a Hoover here, too, with a name written on it. "Hoover Hurricane Cyclone System. Two thousand watt power edge cleaning." I whisper the words to myself. It makes me feel better. Footsteps go past, padding on the carpet, sticking on the kitchen lino. I shut my eyes, hearing how jagged my breathing is, hoping it isn't too loud. A fridge door opens and closes. The footsteps go past again and up the stairs. I keep my eyes shut and half crouch against the wall. It's a familiar position. I used to hide in our larder when I was a child.

Ours was in a corner of the kitchen, and I especially liked it if there were other people in the room who didn't know I was there. I remember the smell of it. Soil-covered vegetables and pickling spice. Children were always having secret breakfasts in the books I read, and I longed for the things they ate. Sausage rolls and fruit tarts and meat pies. I particularly liked pastry. But we never had so much of that sort of food that it would be left over in the larder. Occasionally I would open a jar of jam or a bowl of stewed apple and eat it with a spoon, or take a slice off the boiled ham. But it wasn't the same. And I'd be in trouble if I was caught. Still, I liked being in there, where it was dark and cool and safe, and when Sukey went missing I started to linger there again. Breathing in the familiar smell, enjoying the fact that no one knew where I was.

I was standing inside one day, delaying going back to the sitting room, when I heard someone on the steps down from the hall. I knew it was Douglas straight away. He had a sort of loping walk, long strides, but strangely quiet. The scrape of a chair and the crack of a knee made me stare hard at a plate of carrot biscuits, trying to imagine what he was doing. It must only have been a few days after Sukey's suitcase turned up, because it was still lying on the floor of the kitchen, waiting for its contents to be sorted and washed, and I distinctly heard the brass clasps snap as Douglas unfastened them.

I pushed lightly at the door then, not thinking that I'd give myself away, just desperate to know what he was doing. It opened half an inch, the catch nearly noiseless, and I could just see him, side on, pushing his hand into the tangle of clothes. His mouth was open and I could hear his breathing, uneven, like waves washing on to a beach. It made me worry that he might hear mine and I moved back from the door a little way, knocking into a shelf. The jars clinked and I gritted my teeth at the noise, but the wireless was on in the sitting room: *Lorna Doone*. I could hear music and West Country accents loud enough to cover my twitchings. Douglas kept flicking glances at the steps up to the hall and didn't look in my direction.

After a while he pulled the case away from the dresser and opened it flat. He started to take out the clothes, draping them over a chair. A peach camisole, a shell-coloured slip, a pair of stockings. Everything seemed to be underwear. I couldn't think what he was doing. Except that there had been something in the paper about a man stealing women's knickers off washing lines, and for a second I wondered if Douglas had been that man. But then he started to feel around the sides of the case and I shook my head at my own thought. He was searching for something.

I lift my head from the wall. About time I got out of here. Ma will be wondering where I am.

"That's the lot," a voice says.

There are feet on the stairs above me. The noise gives me a jolt and I stop. My hand rests lightly on the door, not pushing.

"Everything else can wait for the clearance men," the voice says.

I look round the larder. No jars of jam, no sacks of potatoes. Instead there's a Hoover, a broom, a mop.

147

Still, I can't think where I am. A door slams and a car starts up somewhere outside and drives away. I breathe in slowly and step out. This is Elizabeth's hall, Elizabeth's house, but Elizabeth is not here. The stairlift is at the bottom of the stairs, so she can't be up there. Or if she is, she's trapped, because she can't make it down without that machine. The top banister looms over me as I walk up, looking like prison bars, but when I reach the landing I find all the doors are standing open, and that makes me feel better, though I don't know why. Elizabeth's room smells of her rose talcum powder, and for a minute my brain is unreasonable. How can her scent be here, and she not? How can one sense tell me she is near and another say I'm wrong? But there's no wastepaper bin full of tissues, no Rennies next to the bed, and the dressing table's uncluttered surface makes me swallow against tears.

Elizabeth was burgled a few years ago. The police called it a distraction robbery. A woman kept her talking in the garden, saying she'd lost her cat, while someone else ran in and grabbed the jewellery off the dressing table. I remember exactly what they took: a gold chain, a cameo brooch and an opal ring. Elizabeth hadn't seemed to mind much about the things, although I think the ring was expensive. She said she thought that it brought bad luck anyway, being an opal. "Well, I hope it brings the thief plenty of bad luck," I said, feeling quite fierce about it. She smiled at that, but she was nervous about being in the house on her own. I thought her son might take her to stay with him that night, but he was busy and thought she was fussing

148

about nothing, as no one had actually broken in. I couldn't take her home with me, it was too far for her to walk, so I stayed the night, sleeping on the other single bed, which had been her husband's. We talked into the dark and sang old songs until we fell asleep.

I lower myself on to the bed now, digging a pen and a bit of paper from my bag: *Elizabeth's house searched — DEFINITELY not there.* That's something to show Helen. I tuck the note away, and find I am listening to something. I imagine my ears, pricked like a dog's, pointing up and alert. A whirring has started somewhere close. I know the sound, so familiar, so associated with Elizabeth. A mechanical noise, one note gradually getting louder and nearer. It's the stairlift. The stairlift coming up towards me. My mouth goes dry in panic. There is no one in the house. No one. So who is coming up the stairs? My heart beats harder and harder in my chest until I think it might give out, and my legs feel weak, but I make myself stand.

The lift stops. I don't want to move, to betray the fact that I'm here. I stand for a long time, hardly daring to breathe. When nothing happens I drop a balled tissue on to the carpet, marking my place, and walk out on to the landing. The lift is empty. It has stopped two thirds of the way up and there is no one on it at all. I stare at it, my tongue sticky with fear. Shaking, I back away into Elizabeth's room and shut myself in. I collapse back on to the bed and my hand touches something hard. The stairlift remote control. I was sitting on it. My breath rings out as I sink backwards and lie still, looking up at the ceiling, watching the shadows change. Every now and then a car goes by and I can hear the whoosh of it as it turns the corner in front of the house. I imagine the sea is just outside and the cars are waves. Or that I am holding a shell to my ear, listening to the rush of my own blood.

Eventually I get up, bring the stairlift to the landing with the remote control, settle into it, and ride down.

CHAPTER
NINE

Helen should be here soon. Any minute her car will drive up in front. If I kneel on the window seat, lean on one hand and put the side of my head against the glass, I can see almost to the end of the street. I want Helen to come. I want to see her car drive up, hear the reassuring sound of tyres scrunching on the tarmac outside the house. There's nothing I need. I just need her, my daughter. I lean over again to look up the road. The wind catches the shrubs in the front garden, beating them against the gate post, and the noise of it — the rustling, the sharp shuffling — makes me shudder. I find I'm staring very hard at the gaps in the branches. A car comes by, the headlights swinging on to the house and the gate and the hedge, and for a second I think I see someone crouching amongst the leaves, a hand crushing the fragile stems, and a mouth open — to eat or shout.

I scramble backwards, the cushion slips from under me and I lose my balance, dropping on to the floor. There's a sudden sharp pain in my thumb and a crunching sound. I whip my hand up in shock, letting out a wail and holding my thumb in the other hand. I hold it tight, and the pain subsides. I can't think what

I've done. "Hush, hush," I say, cradling the hand. Helen used to hold my thumb when she was a baby. Sometimes she holds my hand now, but not very often.

There's the sound of a car behind me and I turn in hope. But it only glides past, not stopping. It wasn't Helen at the wheel, anyway. The street light shone on a fair-haired man. So the street lights are on, but I didn't notice it get dark. I stare out of the window and feel a hollowing of my insides. Helen doesn't come this late. She isn't coming tonight. Or perhaps — it's unlikely, but perhaps — she has already been. And I've forgotten. I stare out at the empty street. Tears make the lights sparkle and I lift a hand to wipe them away, feeling a sharp pain in my thumb. I gasp in shock, but I can't think what I've done to it. I look across to the telephone, but it seems miles away, far too far away for me ever to get to it. I seem to have this feeling more and more. I suppose it's my age; it's how I always thought getting old would be. But I remember this sort of tiredness when I was ill the summer after Sukey disappeared.

I hadn't been sleeping and my brain seemed to be too hot and tired to work properly. I forced myself through the kitchen door one morning, on my way to school, and found that I couldn't make it to the end of the road. I was walking for what felt like miles, but had barely got past Mrs Winners' gate. I looked back towards home, but it seemed to have moved further off, as if it was going out for the day, same as I was. I didn't

152

know what to do and so I just stood still for a moment, hoping to get my breath.

And of course it was Mrs Winners herself who found me, collapsed on the pavement, not unconscious, but not quite right in the head either. I remember the feel of the pavement, chalky under my hands, and the smell of perfume as Mrs Winners came out of her house. I remember thinking it was really lovely, the way a warm jumper is when you're cold. I kept breathing in the scent as she helped me up and back to my house.

I was in bed for weeks and weeks after that, staring at the light patterns on the walls and straining to hear the radio in the sitting room. Ma had it brought up to my bedroom for a while, but it made me sleep fitfully and what I needed most of all was rest. Both my parents were very worried, I found out after. Dad hardly ever came in to see me because he was sure I would die and he couldn't face it, what with Sukey gone.

Ma was more anxious about my mind. She said I talked a lot in my sleep and some of it frightened her. I'm not surprised I talked. I must have been really delirious at one stage because there were several times when I thought Sukey was lying on her old bed staring at me. And once when I saw Douglas doing the same.

I had lots of strange visions. I saw Sukey with her hair tangled, telling me she didn't have a comb, and I kept saying, "I gave you one, Sukey, don't you remember?" And I saw hundreds of snails all over the ceiling. And, once, I saw the mad woman leaning over me, her teeth bared and her umbrella raised. And I heard songs over and over, silly Vera Lynn songs that

153

I didn't even like. And I thought I heard mice scratching in the skirting and bombs dropping over the town, and my friend Audrey calling me. And there was the constant roll of waves close to my ear, though I had no shells to listen to. And one time I was sure someone had come in the back door, but when I called down I got no answer.

"It's nice to be home," I say to Helen. "Nice to be back in my own home after all this time." We've come from the hospital. I had to go because of some problem. What was it now? Anyway, it's nice to be home.

"You were only at the hospital for a few hours, Mum. Don't overdo it." She drops her car keys on to the coffee table.

"No, Helen," I say. "It was longer than that. Several weeks. Perhaps months. A long, long time."

"A few hours," she says again.

"Why must you argue? I'm just saying that it's nice to be back." I hit my hand on the chair arm and it makes a muffled thud. It's all bandaged up.

"Okay, Mum, you're right," I hear Helen say. "It is always nice to be home again, isn't it? And I thought you'd feel better after a visit. I know it wasn't very nice, I know it was a bit sad, but at least you can stop worrying now."

I don't know what she's wittering on about. Can't she see my hand's a giant white cocoon? I can't move it like this. "I don't think I need to have these bandages on any more," I say. "I think it's about time I removed

154

them, don't you?" I start to unwind the white strips of material.

"No, no, no! Mum, please." She rushes towards me and cradles my hand in hers. "You have to keep them on until the sprain has healed. It will be a little while yet."

"Nonsense, Helen," I say. "I haven't sprained it. It doesn't hurt." I pull away from her and wave my hand in the air to prove it.

"Even so. Leave it on, for me? Please?"

I shrug and tuck the hand between my thigh and the side of the chair so I don't have to look at it.

"Thank you," Helen says. "Shall I make you some tea?"

"And a little bit of toast?" I say. "With some cheese?"

"Maybe later, Mum," she says, leaving the room. "The nurse said you should cut down a bit."

Oh, yes. I forgot. The nurse says I'm getting fat. She says it's because I forget when I've eaten.

"You're not getting fat," Helen calls from the hall. "You just need a better diet. More varied. Less bread-based."

I have a note that the nurse made for me: *Are you hungry? If not, don't make any toast.* I'm surprised they let me decide for myself if I'm hungry. No wonder you hear about old people starving to death in hospitals, what with nurses telling them to stop eating all the time. Beneath the note is a list of care homes and I feel a sudden weight on my chest. Am I to go into one? I listen to Helen in the kitchen, to the innocent sound of cups being taken down from the cupboard.

Would she? I look at the list more carefully. My hands are shaking. There are a few names with cross-throughs, and lots more with question marks. One or two of the cross-throughs have NOE next to them. What does that mean? NOE. It looks like my handwriting, but Helen's is very like mine. *Mill Lane NOE*. Or perhaps more like NoE. North of England, perhaps. Is that where the home is? My God, that's it. But how would I ever see Helen or Katy if I moved there? This one is crossed through, though, and maybe that's why: too far away. I relax a little. Still, I don't want to go into a home. Not yet. I'm not old enough. I must tell Helen. I must call her now and tell her. As I get up to find the phone the bits of paper fall from my lap on to the floor.

"Damn and blast," I say, getting on to my knees to shuffle them together. My left hand won't move. It's covered in white bandages, though I can't see why; it feels fine. Perhaps Katy was playing nurse again. Well, I can't keep it like this. I pull at the end of the material and unwind it. A piece of plastic falls away as I do. The hand looks crumpled and pale. Katy did it too tight. I hope she doesn't grow up to be a real nurse. I start to scoop up the bits of paper and a sharp pain shoots through my thumb. I cry out.

Helen rushes into the room. "What happened?" she says, breathless.

"My hand, my hand," I say. Waving it at her. It doesn't hurt so much now I'm not trying to use it, but the memory makes me rock about and wail.

156

"I told you not to take the bandage off," Helen says. "Christ sakes, Mum." She holds my wrist tightly and starts to wrap the material round again. "What are your notes doing on the floor?"

I look at the bits of paper; one has a list on it. "I don't want to go into a home, Helen," I say.

She stops winding. "You're not going into one, Mum."

I nod, but I can still see the list lying on the carpet. Helen looks too.

"Oh, God. I thought you'd chucked that list away. That's your old list," she says. "For . . ." She stops and narrows her eyes. "Don't you remember? What you were looking for?"

I have to tilt my head to frown at her, but my neck muscles are still tight from shock. What could I have been looking for? "Elizabeth," I say, and I feel as if my limbs are suddenly lighter; my back straightens. "So it's no E. No Elizabeth."

"Right." She finishes safety-pinning my bandage and pulls the notes into a pile. "Only you don't need these numbers any more, do you? And we were going to put the list in the recycling so you don't call the care homes again."

"Were we?" I say, snatching at the paper. "I think I'll hang on to it for a bit, anyway."

Helen tries to tug the list from my grasp, but I won't let go and she soon gives up. "Well, that was a waste of time," she says. "I'll finish getting the tea."

"And a little bit of toast?"

★   ★   ★

157

Toast was practically all Ma would allow me to eat that summer I was ill. Thin soup with dry toast; creamed rice for a treat. I knew I was nearly better the evening she brought me a little mutton chop.

"Though I don't know how you deserve this," she said, resting the tray on my lap. "What with all the bread and jam you had at breakfast."

"I had porridge for breakfast, didn't I?" I said, hardly paying attention, my mouth watering at the smell of the meat. "You gave it to me."

"Yes, and then soon as I was out to the grocer's you sneaked down for bread and jam. Half the loaf's missing."

"Ma, I didn't —"

"Maud, love. You can have whatever you want, I'm glad you have an appetite again, but I have to plan what I'm going to do with our rations and —"

"Ma, really," I said, chewing my first mouthful quickly and swallowing so I could defend myself properly. "I didn't have the bread. It wasn't me."

"That's funny. Can't have been your father." She moved my glass of milk a fraction and unfolded a tea towel for me to use as a napkin. "D'you think Douglas would take food? Doesn't seem like him."

It really didn't seem like him, but there wasn't another explanation. "I suppose he could have come back and made a sandwich to take on his late-morning rounds," I said.

"I gave him a good breakfast, though," Ma said, looking offended. "I never send him or your father off without that."

158

I wiped my mouth and shrugged. "Perhaps h[...]
for someone else."

"What, you mean he's feeding someone? If he is, I'll
be wanting their coupons."

"There was someone in the house," I say, hanging on to
the banisters. Why won't anyone believe me?

"I do believe you, Mum," Helen says. "But it was just
a carer. A new carer, that's all. She wasn't a burglar.
There was no need to call the police. Mind out the way,
will you?"

She pushes by, and I watch her running a cloth along
the skirting board. She leans and swishes her hands
along, like some sort of athletics. Like those exercises
we were supposed to do when we were young. Bending
from the waist to keep trim. They always showed fields
full of women doing them at the same time. Smiling. It
never made me smile to do them.

Helen follows the skirting into the sitting room, and I
follow her. "One two three four, one two three four.
Keep smiling, girls."

"What are you on about? God, it was embarrassing.
Heaven knows what she thought. You accusing her like
that. Telling everyone you were being robbed. By the
carer," she adds, when I look at her blankly.

"What would you do if you came down to breakfast
and found a stranger in your kitchen?"

"Not a stranger, a carer."

"Yes, you, so she says. But how do I know she's
telling the truth? She could be anyone."

159

Helen lets her hands drop to her sides and leaves the room. This is supposed to mean something. I push my toes into the carpet as I go after her, careful not to slip, careful. "I'm not safe in my own bed," I say, though I'm losing track of what it is I'm in danger of. Surely it wouldn't be possible to slip over when I'm in bed. "Helen, where exactly is it best to grow marrows?" She doesn't answer and when I get to the hall it's empty. "Oh, where have you gone?" I say. "Why d'you keep hiding?"

"I'm not hiding," Helen says, coming out of the dining room. "I'm trying to get the soil off the walls. You've scuffed it over everything. Again. I don't know how you manage it."

She scrubs at a low bit of wall, moving up the stairs. I watch her heels on the steps, bouncing, and follow slowly, trying to place my feet in exactly the same position, trying for the same bounce. It's better walking after another person. You can see how the steps work, and you can trust where they are when someone else has tested them first. I watch closely, but I don't notice when she stops, and my shoulder bumps her on the hip.

"Oh, Mum, will you stop following me?" she says. "Stay in the kitchen, I'll be back in a minute."

I tramp back down and look out of the window. There's a cat on the lawn and I try to open the kitchen door, but there's something wrong with the handle. "You've left me open to attack here," I say to Helen when she reappears. "With these flimsy locks. And this door is made of Bakelite or something, what's the use of that?"

"The wooden one was rotted through. What was the use of that?"

"And I want that thing removed from outside the door. It spits the key out to anyone."

"Not unless you have the code."

"Well, someone's been writing it down. Leaving it for burglars. I've got one of the notes here, look." I find my bag and unzip the pockets; it's awkward because my left hand's bundled up in a sort of mitten, but soon I can push my right-hand fingers into the creases of fabric. Each one seems to be full of tissues, twisted like the limbs of trees and fraying into dust at the edges.

"How are the carers supposed to get in if we take the key safe away? And that's your old bag, Mum. What are you looking for? There won't be anything in there."

She's right: the only bit of paper in here is an envelope. Addressed to Elizabeth. Did I say I would post it to her? I must have forgotten. I hope it wasn't anything important. I turn it over, trying to remember. There is a note taped to it: *From Elizabeth's house.* And underneath: *Where is Elizabeth?* Where *is* Elizabeth? I look at the envelope sadly. I suppose I should send it on. But where to?

I'm craving apples as I push my finger into the corner of the envelope. The crisp paper tears at the crease, and soon it is past repair so I may as well open the letter properly. I rip the envelope flap into scruffy shapes. There's just a slip inside, from the library. An overdue notice for a book. The library van has tried to collect it for the past few weeks. It is overdue by months and the fine is more than ten pounds. I feel funny about having opened it now. Post is property, and opening it is like breaking and entering. My postman father was always very definite about that, and he'd be furious if he could see me now. He nearly caught me opening a letter of Douglas's once.

The address on that envelope, to "Mr D. Weston", was in Sukey's handwriting. That's what made me snatch it up from the kitchen table. Ma always left our post in a heap there; Douglas's along with ours. I never got anything, except occasionally a postcard from Uncle Trevor or a note from Audrey, but I liked to look through the pile anyway, trying to work out who the letters were from. Ma's sister, Rose, had pretty but messy handwriting and Uncle Trevor's was very black, with deep marks in the paper. Audrey always left blotches between her words, and I could picture the sides of her hands stained with ink. I knew Sukey's writing of course, though she didn't send us letters. It would have been a bit funny, seeing as she was only about ten streets away. I think we got one when she was on her honeymoon, but that was the only time.

The letter to Douglas came about a week after we'd last seen Sukey, about a week before my parents started to worry. I was surprised no one had noticed the writing, and when Douglas didn't pick it up on his way out to the pictures, a terrible curiosity overcame me.

I was stewing apples for the morning and I had to lay down the spoon to feel the envelope. It was just paper inside, folded once, I thought; perhaps twice. I held it to the light with one hand, stirring the apples with the other, but I couldn't see anything; the paper of the envelope was too patched with labels over labels, to make it last longer. "Paper is a Weapon of War — save every scrap." It was difficult to forget the warning, though there was no war any more to need weapons for. I'd meant to drop it back on the table, but for some reason I turned to the pan and, without really deciding to, angled the letter into a wave of steam. The apples simmered away, giving out their fruity, spicy smell, and I kept still, watching the paper buckle slightly with the moisture. My face was damp from standing over the saucepan and soon the hand holding the letter was too. The edge of the envelope flap started to come loose and I helped it along with my little finger, and in a few minutes it was halfway undone. That was when Dad walked in.

I hadn't heard his footsteps on the stairs and in a panic I dropped the envelope into the saucepan and stirred. He opened the kitchen door to put something in the outside bin, and the cold air found my damp skin, making me shiver. Dad took Ma's shawl from a chair on his way back in and put it round my shoulders.

"Must be nearly done now," he said, tapping the handle of the pan.

I nodded stiffly, praying he wouldn't look in it. When he walked back up to the sitting room I sagged against the stove in relief and then lifted the letter out with a spoon. It was a soggy mess, and there was no way I'd be able to draw it apart without tearing the paper. I pressed it between two sheets of newspaper and laid it on a shelf in one of the top warming ovens to dry, hoping that the ink hadn't blurred too much, hoping no one would notice the faint blue tinge to the stewed apples when we had them at breakfast the next day.

Douglas got home as I was washing up the pan. Ma had come down to the kitchen to say goodnight and she asked him how his evening had been. He was as vague as ever about the film he'd seen.

"Er, it was one where . . . it was one of those ones with fancy costumes. It wasn't very good."

"*The Wicked Lady*, was it?" I said, turning with soapy hands to watch his face.

"Yes, that was it."

"That's not showing any more."

He swung stiffly towards me, but his eyes didn't lift from his shoes. "That can't have been it then. I must have got it wrong."

The hurt in his pose reminded me so much of the first time I'd met him, the blushing and embarrassment at his being caught out with the nicknames, that I felt a flood of guilt. Water dripped from my hands on to my slippers. Why was I always so cruel to him? I didn't think I meant to be. I almost told him about the letter then, but thought that admitting I'd been trying to read his post might not make him feel any better.

CHAPTER
TEN

I hate this place and hardly ever come here. I hate the smell of the books, musty and unclean, and I never borrow books myself. So often you open one and find it stinks of cigarette smoke or has the remains of someone's dinner smeared over the pages. Of course, I don't read now, so it hardly matters.

"Mum, please keep your voice down," Helen says. "You're the one who asked to come."

She edges away slightly and I walk over to the desk, feeling in my pockets. I can't think why I'd have wanted to be taken here; I've got a slip from the library, but it's addressed to Elizabeth, not me. The man behind the desk sweeps his fringe from his eyes, and I feel panicked for a moment, by his expectation, by the thousands of books on their shelves. Even if I knew what I wanted, how could I ever find it? "I'm looking for something," I say to the man. "I just can't recall, you know."

"A book?"

I say I suppose it must be, and he asks what sort of book it is, but I don't know. He asks if it's fiction.

"Oh, no," I say. "It's a true story, only no one will believe me."

His brow wrinkles and he smooths his fringe over the lines. "What's the story about?" he says. "Perhaps I will know it."

"It's about Elizabeth," I say.

"Elizabeth. Could that be the title?"

I watch as he taps at letters on his computer with strangely flexible fingers.

"There's something with that name in the crime section," he says, and points me, flexibly, in the right direction.

Helen is rummaging through some papers, so I go over to the shelves alone. There aren't so many books here as there used to be. A lot of space has been given over to computers. They look very bright and enticing, but I've tried a few times and I just don't think I'll learn now. This set of shelves has the word CRIME pasted over them and there are lots of books with bones on the covers, or dripping blood. Mostly they are black books with neon writing. Something about them feels oppressive, frightening, and I don't think I'd like to enter any of the worlds inside them, but I take one anyway and read the blurb. It's about a woman on the run from a serial killer. I put it back. There are four books with cream covers next to it, mysteries set in Russia. I don't think I'm quite up to that. I have enough mystery in my life as it is.

Helen comes quietly over to look with me. "I can't be bothered with these," I say. She shushes me and looks round, but there's practically no one here. "We used to press flowers in books," I say. "Sukey and I, when I was young."

We always meant to make a picture, but never got round to it. And years later I found the dried and flattened celandines and forget-me-nots, violets and buttercups, stuck between the pages of my father's old set of Mrs Radcliffe. We pressed grasses, too, and clover leaves.

"And Helen, that last time she came to dinner, I remember, I gave her a comb and she put it inside a hardback book and pressed the covers together until the comb inside crunched and all the delicate little amber teeth fell out. And she said, 'It's beautiful, thank you, darling,' and kissed me before she slipped out the door. And I had her lipstick on my forehead." I think that's how it was. But Helen doesn't think so, and she doesn't want to argue about it here, and do I want a book, otherwise we'll go.

There's nothing I want so we start to walk out, past the desk. The man there has strange bendable fingers and he sweeps his fringe to the side as he looks at me. His fingers, I think, are like a fringe themselves, like the peach fringe of a standard lamp. For a moment I expect to see bookcases and clocks and empty plant pots jumbled against the desk, but there is only a trolley of books. *The Mysteries of Udolpho* is waiting to go back on to a shelf. I pick it up, weigh it in my hands and then, holding it by its hard covers, I shake it to see if anything falls out. The spine makes a creaking noise.

"Hey! Hey!" the man at the desk says. "What are you doing? You can't treat the books like that."

"Sorry," I say, dropping it on to the trolley. "I was just checking." I leave it where it lies and walk out to the street. Helen walks with me. "Are we going home?" I ask. She doesn't answer, and I suppose this means we are and she can't be bothered to tell me again. I squint at her, but I can't tell if she makes any gesture. The sun's in my eyes and it's difficult to see. The shape of her is distorted by the light, circles of her silhouette removed as if by a pastry cutter. She walks in front, getting further ahead, and I struggle to keep up, struggle to make out which way she's going. I shut one eye and keep the shadow of Helen ahead of me; I just need to concentrate on that, and not worry about directions or people or cars or the sun. Just focus on the shadow. I mustn't let it get away. It might lead me to Sukey.

"Mum! Wait."

I turn to look behind and the light shines straight on to my daughter's face. How did she get here? And was she always so wrinkled? I can see where freckles melt into the lines around her mouth. She's outdoors too much and that's bad for the skin; it ages you. I can't think how old she is, though; I ought to know.

"Who were you following?" she says.

I think for a moment, trying to make sense of the words. "Douglas," I say. "I was following Douglas."

It was his loping shadow falling across the bramble hedge that told me he had come home early. And a moment later I heard the creak of the larder door and the scrape of a spoon on glass. I was up and dressing before his shadow fell again across the hedge, not wanting to miss the opportunity to follow him as he left

168

the house. For weeks I'd lain ill in bed, going over everything in my mind, knowing he was up to something, what with searching Sukey's suitcase and calling to the mad woman in the park. Now food was going missing and I was determined to find out why. I ran quietly, in his wake, slinking along the wall like ribbon on a spool.

Being out of bed was a shock and my legs protested at the sudden exercise. The outside air was full of the sharp scent of freshly cut pines and the low sun shone in my eyes, forcing me to walk against it as if it were a strong wind. I was used to the dimness of my curtained room, and the light felt like a blast of sand. Douglas was a dark blur some way ahead and I focused on that rather than try to see where I was. He paused once to look at the wreck of his old house, but it was only when we turned on to Sukey's street and blue shade washed over me that I could look about properly, only then that I knew where we were going. I followed him up the lane by Frank's house, keeping close to the wall so as not to be too near the hawthorn hedge, always suspecting that the mad woman might be there, leaning into it.

At the turning to the yard I stopped, sagging, hot and tired, against the wall, and pressed the toe of my shoe into the flesh of a leaf which lay on the ground. The mark, so definitely my doing, gave me courage, and I moved one eye slowly to the very edge of the building, my cheek brushing the brickwork. The sun was again blinding at this angle, and so I crept out, mole-like and praying that I wouldn't be seen. But the yard was empty, except for the same old van that was always there, and I went to rest against it, shifting my shoulder blades against its hot metal wall. I hadn't expected the answering shifting inside. It was like a foot dragged along a floor, and fear had propelled me halfway across the yard before the doors opened and Douglas stepped out.

"What? In there?" I said, hardly coherent with the exhaustion of being out of bed after so many weeks of illness.

"Maud," Douglas said, trying to block my view into the van. "How did you . . .?"

My steps slid back across the cobbles and I looked past him to see a mess of broken furniture, tea chests and dust sheets jumbled against the wooden supports. There was a smell like old hedge cuttings and there were crumbs on the floor.

"Someone lives in there," I said.

Douglas ducked his head.

"Who? Douglas, who is it? Is it Sukey?" I felt a rush of something through me; my heart seemed to beat up through my shoulders, my neck, as if it were trying to escape through my head.

Douglas put a hand out, steadying me as I staggered. "No. No, Maud, it's not Sukey."

For a moment I wasn't sure I believed him, I didn't want to believe him. "Tell me the truth," I said, jerking away from his hold. "I know Sukey was in a van. The mad woman told me. She told me before I got ill."

"Did she? It was nonsense," he said. "Ravings. It's she who's in the van. This is where she's been living."

170

I shivered at the thought, seeing now the scattering of stripped hawthorn stalks and the bundle of packing blankets that she must have been using as bedding. I thought for a moment that I could smell liquorice. There was a piece of cracked mirror wedged behind one of the upright slats. Did she look into that, I wondered? And if so, what did she see? I crawled into the van, wanting to look in the same bit of glass, and saw Douglas's hand, framed by the mirror, a crinkled package of newspaper visible between his fingers.

"What's that?" I said, whirling round, reminded of the reason I'd been following him. "You've been feeding her. You've been feeding the mad woman."

He looked for a moment like he might deny it.

"Ma's noticed the food going missing," I said, and he grimaced. "Why? Why are you giving her our rations?"

"She's been living here a while. Perhaps before Frank went to London, before Sukey disappeared. I think it's possible she saw something."

"Saw what?"

"What happened to Sukey, or where she went. Sometimes I think she's trying to tell me."

The smell of the mangled leaves and stalks was sickening in the heat and I began to shift towards the doors. "You mean you talk to her? You have conversations?" I thought he must be nearly as mad as the mad woman.

"Don't look like that. She's not an animal, she can speak."

"I know," I said, though it seemed so strange to be talking about her, to be allowed to actually talk about her. It was like discussing an animal, but a mythical one perhaps, a griffin or a unicorn. "I know, only she usually shouts. About watching people and smashed glass and vans and marrows and flying birds."

"And about Sukey?"

I stopped in my outward scramble. "Once, perhaps. I thought she said Sukey's name once. What does that matter?"

He didn't answer. Instead, he climbed into the van beside me and pointed towards the wall. The sharp broken teeth of a comb grinned out under the mirror. It was deformed now, but I knew that comb, and I reached for it.

"How did she get this?" I said. "Where did she get it? What's happened to my sister?"

"Give that to me!" I shout. "Get off the phone."

Helen turns to look at me, curling a hand against her chest.

"It's not yours. Give it back."

She shakes her head and waves me away. I shout her name and she frowns, half stands. I rush over, yank the wire out of the wall and push the coffee table over, sending everything flying on to the carpet.

"What's got into you?" Helen cries. She has dropped the phone and stands back against the window seat.

I stamp on a glass and kick my alarm clock across the room. I can feel the pulse in my neck beating, and there's a pressure building in my head. I close my eyes and shriek.

"Mum? Stop it. What's happened?"

172

Helen skirts round and puts her hands on my shoulders, but I throw her off and hit out, catching her in the stomach. "Get out!" I shout. "Get out of my house!" I pace across the room and she backs away quickly, clutching her middle, her mouth trembling.

"I can't leave you like this," she says. "Mum?"

I scream again and push over a chair. And then she's gone. And my alarm clock is broken. The wires exposed, the tiny cogs biting into the carpet. I must have dropped it. I'll have to tell Helen to get me a new one. There's a glass broken too. Little shards of it scattered over the rug. I find a piece of newspaper in the waste-paper bin and gather the bits up, pricking myself several times. The paper begins to darken, drawing the blood into pretty patterns around the margins. I try to piece the shards together, and I feel for a minute the sun on my back and the grass under my knees, and I listen for the pigeons' breathy coo. I expect Ma to come out in a minute and tell me to throw the pieces in the runner-bean trench. But of course she never will, and I twist the paper closed, carrying the broken contents out of the room and up the stairs. Into my room. I shut the door and sit down at my dressing table and suddenly I can't think what I'm doing here. I was going to the kitchen, wasn't I? I let out a little laugh at myself. How silly to end up in the wrong room. I must be going mad.

I walk back down and put the newspaper in the bin. I push it right down as far as I can. I had to be careful to put anything dangerous well out of reach when Tom and Helen were small because, once, Helen got into a neighbour's bin and found a cake that had been laced with rat poison. She ate it and she got Tom to eat it, too, though he was the elder and should have known better. I thought they'd both die and was out of my mind with worry, and I had to make them both be sick, pushing a spoon down along their tongues till they gagged and brought it all up. I remember their little hands hitting at me and then the terrible sound of their retching. But, thankfully, they were all right afterwards. I got them to a doctor and he said there was no damage done; I'd acted quickly enough.

Of course I was upset with Tom, but I was angry with Helen. She was always up to mischief, her fingers grubby from mucking about in the garden, digging up worms and making snail farms. Tom was more inclined to lie on the settee reading car magazines. Irritating when I wanted to hoover the cushions, but not half so difficult to keep an eye on. I stayed angry at Helen for a long time after the cake incident, and laughed when Patrick made jokes, even years later, about not being able to trust anything she'd baked. "You're not trying to poison us, are you?" he'd say, just when she would be proudly presenting her pineapple upside-down cake or her banana bread. "Because you've got form." Young girls don't appreciate that kind of teasing, and there were often tears. But even that was a relief. To think they'd both been in danger like that and yet here they were still with us, fussing over teenage romances and getting into trouble at school and making a mess of my sitting room.

174

Someone's still making a mess of my sitting room. There are things all over the floor and my coffee table lies on its side. I pick it up and put everything straight, the pens back in their pots and the notes in neat piles. Someone's unplugged the phone and I have to stoop awkwardly to get the wire into the wall. I'm shaking as I bend down and I feel as if something has happened. The skin in my throat is tight, the way it is after you've been crying, or shouting. Elizabeth says her son has a habit of shouting, has a terrible temper on him. It makes me sorry for her. Helen gets cross sometimes, but not like that, and Patrick could be brusque, but he wouldn't yell and scream like some husbands. My parents never shouted either, even when I'd done something really naughty like jump in the river at the Pleasure Gardens. Frank shouted at me once, though.

It was at his house. Sukey and I were making a blind for the kitchen. "To keep the mad woman from peering in?" I'd asked, but Sukey didn't seem so worried about her at that time, and she told me off again for calling her mad. Said she was a "poor thing", said we were lucky not to be the same way. She'd not been really angry, though, and had put my hair up like the NAAFI girls', rolled round an old stocking-top, and had even let me wear some of her perfume. I was teaching her to sing "I'll Be Your Sweetheart" while we knelt on the floor, carefully cutting the precious material. We'd sewn the little pockets for the dowelling rods and were sliding a length of wood into each when the front door crashed open.

Frank's face, red beneath the tan, seemed to appear feature by feature as he swayed along the hall towards us. He staggered across the kitchen to the sideboard, knocking over a chair, and I watched in horror as he picked up a knife. But he was only threatening a piece of cheese, lying half wrapped in paper, which Sukey had refused to let me finish off at lunch.

"No, Frank," Sukey said, getting up and standing in front of me. "I'm saving that."

"What? This again?" he said, his voice thick and slurred beyond her skirt. "Can't I have a bit of cheese in my own home? Who are you saving it for?"

"Not *for* anyone. But what would you know about keeping house, eh? I'm the one who works out the meals, so leave it to me. I am your wife."

"My little wife," he said, letting the knife clatter on to the plate, his voice sharpening for a moment. "My lovely little little little little little wifey." His arm curled round Sukey's waist, and she tried to push him away.

"Frank, you're standing on the blind fabric," she said. "Get off it."

He looked down at his feet for a few seconds, his fair hair flopping over one eye, and he saw me.

"Got Maudie here, too, have we?"

I nodded, shuffling back against the cupboard out of his way.

"Making a blind?" he said, looking at his feet again.

I held up the length of dowelling rod in evidence, and he let go of Sukey.

"How d'you make a Venetian blind, eh, Maud?" he said, leaning a hand on the counter behind me and bending very close, his breath like the waft from a pub door.

I couldn't guess. I felt too scared to breathe. The arm that had been around Sukey's waist flexed above my head.

"Poke him in the eyes."

The answer seemed horrible to me, and I shuffled further away, but Frank grinned, his teeth bright and keen in his tanned face.

"Eh, Sukey?" he said, pushing himself upright. "Venetian. Blind?"

"It's not a Venetian blind, though, is it?" she said, righting the chair. "It's a Roman blind."

"Still works. Here, Maud. How d'you make a Roman blind?"

"Shut up, Frank," Sukey said. "You're drunk." She pushed him sideways and finally succeeded in getting him off the fabric.

"Drunk? Not a chance." He shook his head and had to reach a hand towards the counter again.

I stared up at him, trying to find the familiar Frank in this vague and fevered version. He noticed my stare and made a face, putting out his tongue and flaring his nostrils. Somehow he looked more like himself, and I laughed despite my fear.

"Yes, you are. Go to bed," Sukey said.

"Only if you come with me."

"Ugh, Frank, Maud's still here. She doesn't need to hear your filthy talk. Go to bed. Sleep it off. Go on."

"Send your bloody little princess home then, if she's too good to be in the same room as me." He made

177

another face, but this time I didn't laugh and he turned away.

"Don't start shouting, Frank," Sukey said. "And don't start that stuff again. Of course you're good enough."

"That baby-faced lodger of yours doesn't think so. Always hanging about."

"What do you care what Doug thinks of you?"

"I just don't get what you've got to talk to him about all the time," Frank said. "And I know he goes back and bad-mouths me to your parents. Your dad doesn't like me as it is."

Sukey sighed and turned to me. "P'raps you should go home, Mopps," she said. "We'll finish the blind another day."

"Yeah. There'll be many more days for finishing off blinds and chatting about what might have been."

I couldn't understand what he was talking about, but I stood up and slipped past him as quick as I could, and was almost at the front door when I remembered my coat. I tiptoed back down the hall, but Frank saw me.

"What the hell are you still doing here?" he shouted, his face truly contorted now. "Go on, bugger off!"

I gave up my coat and ran out of the house, crying until I reached the Avenue, where I stopped and wiped the tears away. Then I walked round and round Ashling Crescent until I was calm enough to go home.

CHAPTER
ELEVEN

Something's happened. I have to get up, get out, get to Sukey. I pull on a man's striped shirt and worn, unfamiliar trousers and push things into the pockets: tissues, a roll of Polo mints, a plastic pearl necklace. I wonder if this is a dream. I don't think it is. My bedclothes are all of a tangle, but I can't waste time straightening them, and I start to write a note, but I can't think what to say. The stairs creak as I creep down and the front-door latch clanks noisily in my hand. I pause on the threshold, the muscles of my face taut, but everything is quiet as I set off towards Frank's house.

The air outside is cold and fresh and almost sweet; I'm enjoying the feel of it on my tongue and several minutes of walking go by before I realize I've lost my way, that this is not the road I thought. The next street is just as strange and my heart gives a thud in my chest. I'm running out of time. I've got to get somewhere, or to someone. It's urgent. My footsteps echo slightly in the dark and a fox runs out in front of me. He stops and looks at something on the other side of the road. I stop too.

"Hello, fox," I say, but he carries on staring at the opposite pavement. "Fox?" I say again, and wave my arms. For a moment it seems really important to get his attention, to have my presence acknowledged. I rummage in my pocket, working a mint out of its packet, and throw it on to the middle of the tarmac. It lands with a ticking bounce at the fox's feet, and he turns, a point of light gleaming from each of his eyes. "Hello, fox."

He runs off and I walk on. It's these acres of new houses that have me confused, I see now, though how I got here I don't know. I'll never find my way with the roads in a jumble like this. And I'm exhausted. I can't have walked very far, but my legs are heavy and my back's sore. I feel like an old woman. I work another Polo from its wrapper and throw this one on to the pavement behind me. It shines white, bright on the dark stones. At least I'll know if I'm going round in circles. A car stops at the end of the road and a man gets out. He wanders towards me, his hands hooked in his belt, his shadow reaching out from the car lights. I begin to back away.

"Where are you going, love?" he says. He's looking right at me. I can tell even though his face is just a silhouette.

"Home," I call as I turn away, trying to force my legs to go faster. "My mother's waiting up."

The man makes a noise, a sort of snort. "Is she?" he says. "And where's home?"

I don't know. For a second I don't know. But it doesn't matter, I say to myself, I wouldn't tell him anyway. I wouldn't tell him anyway and I'll remember in a minute. When I get on the right path, I'll remember. Soon the man is a good way behind me, still standing by his car. I turn down a street, then another, walking without seeing. On a pavement I find a Polo mint, white and shining in the night. I bend to pick it up and see a big turreted house in the distance. Perhaps I'll recognize something when I reach it. I look into the front garden as I get near, but it's just a dark space.

"Thought home was the other way?"

A man leans against a car. The lights glint off his fair hair, and that makes me think of Frank. He's waiting for me. But he should be waiting for Sukey. "What are you doing here?" I say.

"Taking you to the station. Car's waiting."

"Station?" I ask as I get in. There's a mint in my hand and I pop it into my mouth. "Are we getting a train?"

The man doesn't answer me but asks if I want the window up or down.

"Down," I say, putting my hand on the inside of the door. I want to leave something behind me, something to tell people I was here. The mint slides against my tongue and I spit it out as far as I can into the night. The man laughs and I laugh with him. "Frank," I say. "Frank."

I walked right into him one day after school. He was standing by Mrs Winners' hedge, looking towards our house, and he turned round as we collided, putting out his hands.

"Maud," he said. "I was just thinking about paying you lot a visit." There was a deep dent in the hedge

181

where he had been leaning into it and I thought he must have been waiting there for a long time.

"How are your parents?" he asked, and I opened my mouth but found I was unable to make any sort of expression, and I wondered if I was imagining him.

"They haven't heard from Sukey, then?"

I shook my head and studied his face. I suppose I wanted to see if he looked guilty. But he only looked shabby. There was stubble on his chin and his hair was a bit longer, his clothes were crumpled and grubby. I was shocked at the change. Where were the perfect creases down the front of his trousers, the starched collars, the shined shoes?

"Can't understand it," he said, leaning over me, his hands on my shoulders. "I mean, if she was going off somewhere you'd think she'd tell her husband, wouldn't you?"

The words gave me a little flutter of hope. I thought of Sukey hiding from Frank. Hiding away somewhere safe. Of course she wouldn't contact anyone if she was hiding.

"But I s'pose she might tell her sister, mightn't she?" Frank looked down at me with his usual smile, eyebrows raised, a kind of forced gleam in his eye. It looked wrong on this new, scruffy face. His hands pressed down heavily on my shoulders and I realized he was studying me too. "Did she tell you things, Maudie? Things about going away? About me? About anyone else?"

"Nothing, Frank," I said. He dropped his hands, and my spine lengthened, my bones rose up. I felt light, too light, as if I might float into the sky and disappear. I wished he'd weigh me down again, but I couldn't think how to ask.

"I miss her," he said. "Miss having her about the place, her bits of things. I don't know what they are. Hair things and bits of material. Bottles of scent."

"Evening in Paris."

"Yeah, that's it." He stared down at me. "You remember better than me. Come and have a drink."

I didn't say no, but I must have looked doubtful.

"Oh, come on, Maud," he said. "I thought you weren't a kid any more. Come and have a drink. Does me good to talk about her, you know?"

I knew. Ma and Dad hardly ever talked about her and I felt as if saying her name at home was forbidden. And here was someone who wanted to remember her properly, with words. I let him lead me to the end of the street and down the hill.

"What else does she have, Maud? What else? You remember."

"A blue suit?" I began. "And lipstick. Victory Red. And an old compact that matches her perfume. Silver and navy-blue stripe."

"Yeah, that's right. What else?"

"Shoes with buckles down the front, a green, scalloped tea dress, those earrings that look like sweets . . ." Thinking about what Sukey wore made me look down at myself. At my brown T-bar shoes and open-knit socks. I didn't notice Frank stopping, and so I walked into him for the second time.

"Hide your school tie, for God's sake. We're here," he said, and went in.

It was a pub. The Fiveways. It had what Dad called "a reputation" and I felt a shiver of apprehension. I'd never been in a pub before and I thought perhaps I shouldn't go in then, and so I dithered, playing with a button that had come off my cardigan. I didn't want to leave the familiarity of the pavement, but I desperately wanted to talk about Sukey, and so I dropped the button against the hinge of the cellar door. Somehow the idea of it waiting out here, for me to come back, made me feel better and I pushed the slim half-door open and went in after Frank.

It was smoky inside and the air was hot, and I couldn't see Frank at first. I wandered in the direction of the bar and felt a hand on my back. "Go and sit over there before the landlady sees you," he said, pushing me towards a table by the door. "I'll get you a drink."

I felt a stab of nervousness at that, but I went and sat down on a wooden stool. The bar was a few feet away, with dark-clad men's backs lined up in front of it so I could hardly see the woman serving.

"Back so soon, Frank?" I heard her say. "Must've only been gone a couple of hours."

I leant an elbow on the table. It was slick with spilt beer, and wetness seeped through my cardigan. I was taking it off when the door opened and a thin, sweating man walked in.

"Hello, girlie," he said, hanging over the table.

A drop of his sweat hit my chest, bleeding into my school shirt, and I thought of Ma's tears on the silk of

Sukey's nightdress. I watched the circle of moisture spread flatly, turning the fabric transparent, and tried not to breathe so that it wouldn't stick to the skin underneath. The man said something, but I couldn't take it in, only aware of his breath against the top of my head. I was starting to sweat myself, with fear, and I couldn't bear the idea of mine mingling with this man's.

"Is that a yes, then?" he said, and I turned my face away.

Frank had started to come towards me, and he winked as he walked. I felt odd, as if I had somehow taken Sukey's place. Here I was in a pub with her husband, being bought a drink. And where was she? Had we switched places? Was Sukey at home with my parents, playing Patience and listening to the wireless?

Frank put the drinks down on the table. He looked at the sweating man, moving very slowly. "Can I do anything for yer?" he asked.

The man raised two moist palms as he backed away and I gratefully picked up the nearest glass. I could see Frank was having beer and I hoped he hadn't bought the same for me.

"Ginger ale," he said. "That all right?"

I nodded and breathed a sigh of relief. The noise in the pub grew as more people piled through the door.

"'Ello, Frank," someone said as he brushed past. "You both back down south again?"

"That's right," Frank said, keeping his eyes on me.

I stared down at my bare knees, rubbing my nails over the reddish patches.

"You look just like her, you know?" Frank said, putting a hand to my chin.

I smiled. I wasn't convinced, but I smiled all the same and Frank leant towards me for a moment, closing his eyes at me like a cat.

"How are things at your place, then? Just the same, are they?"

He rested a hand round his glass and a bead of moisture dripped slowly on to his thumbnail. It seemed to linger a moment on the cuticle before dropping like a tear, and I was distracted as I answered. "Not really. Ma and Dad are very worried —"

"Wotcha, Frank?" a fast-looking woman shouted across the pub. "When you going to give me them nylons you promised me?"

Frank turned slightly to nod at her before letting his eyes drift back to me. "And Douglas?" he asked. "He still there, is he?"

"Where else would he be?"

"Well, I don't know, he might have gone and grown up. Might have stopped hanging round your mum, waiting for handouts."

"He's our lodger. He doesn't get handouts."

"Your lodger, yeah. That's what you think." He took a long drink of his beer and someone pushed past just as he was lowering his elbow, jolting him so that beer ran down over his sleeve. "Fucking watch it!" he said.

I waited for him to say sorry for the swearing, but he didn't. Instead he gulped down the rest of his drink and stood up. "I'll get another round," he said, and when he came back he had a glass of whisky or brandy or

186

something too. I bit my lip as he put it on the table. "You do look just like her," he said. "You've got that same disapproving expression." He raised his glass in a mock-toast and I pushed my own away. "I've been in nick for two weeks."

"I know. Douglas said." I wondered if I could ask about the coupon fraud or if it would make him angry.

"Douglas would. He would know all about it."

"This the missus, Frank?" said a man in his shirtsleeves, rolling his cap in his hands. "Bit young for you, isn't she?"

Frank swore at him.

"Come on, Frank. Get a sense of humour."

"Tell you what, Ron. I'll get one when you start being funny."

Ron let his cap unfurl with a flourish. "Fine. Fine," he said. "Only being friendly."

"Go and be friendly somewhere else."

"You got a right one here, love," Ron said, raising his eyebrows. "Hope you can handle him."

I frowned after him as he walked away. "People seem to think I'm Sukey," I said.

"No, they don't."

"They do. You said I look like her. Everyone else seems to think so too."

"You don't look that much like her, Maudie. You're still a kid. You look like a kid."

I was hurt. "Why d'you bring me to a pub then?"

"I wanted a drink, that's why. And because I wanted to say something to you."

I finished my ginger ale and twisted sideways on the stool.

"Eh, eh," he said, reaching over to pull me round again. "We're having a conversation here. Look at me."

"What is it you want to say, Frank?" I said, annoyed and wanting to go home. "Ma and Dad will be expecting me."

"My God, you bloody sound like her as well. You'll be telling me I've had too much to drink next."

"You probably have had too much."

"Yeah, well, so would you . . ." He looked down at the floor and sat like that for so long that I thought he'd forgotten me. I pulled my beer-damp cardigan on. "And so your parents don't want anything to do with me," he said suddenly. "They think I killed her, or something."

I didn't know what to say, and I stared at him, thinking that his hair and even his stubble looked angelically blond in the light from the bar.

"Your dad wrote me a letter," he said to his beer glass. "Want to see what it says?"

I didn't answer, but he fished a crumpled envelope from his jacket pocket and threw it into my lap. It was the note I'd seen Dad push through the door when we'd been to Frank's all those months ago: "I know this is your doing. You won't get away with it." I was shocked. I had thought Dad was leaving a message for Sukey.

"Well, he never liked me. Wasn't much I could do about that. 'Specially with that little rat-faced idiot whispering in his ear all the time." He looked up at me

188

with narrowed eyes and a curled lip. "He told me to keep away."

"Who did?"

"Your fucking lodger."

I left after that, telling him it was the third time he'd used bad language and wincing at how much I sounded like Dad. I found the button from my cardigan on the way out, still nestled in the cellar door's groove, and I pressed it hard into my palm as I walked home.

"Fucking let go of me, you fuck," a woman shouts, twisting her body round. A policeman holds on to her arm and signs a book on the counter. "Fucking pigs," she shouts again.

I try to block her slurred voice from my ears and slowly drop the last two Polo mints on to the floor. When they're gone I start on the plastic pearls, breaking them from their string and sending them tiptoeing across the room. I wonder if this hallway's been used for a film. It's very familiar. There is a big glass lantern hanging from the ceiling and a shiny black and white floor. I concentrate on these things, rather than look at the people. I don't want to think about the people. The shouting woman is led away through a door, but I can still hear her, and a man on the bench next to me starts to sing.

"*Que sera, sera.* Whatever will be, will be. We're going to Wem-ber-ley. *Que sera, sera.*"

His frayed football shirt is wet and smells of beer, he swings his feet and one catches a bead, sending it skittling back towards me. I pick it up and curl it into my hand before sliding along the bench away from him.

"That's all we need," the policeman behind the counter says. "The next bloody Pavarotti."

He goes to open the outside door and another policeman brings someone in, dripping blood. His nose is a mess and his eyes are rolling around in his head. "We're going to need a doctor," the policeman holding him says. He has blond hair which catches the light and makes me think of Frank.

"Her perfume was Evening in Paris," I say. "And she had earrings that looked like sweets." No one seems to hear.

"*Que sera, sera,*" the singing man sings, swaying over towards me. His beer smell is mixed with vomit, and he's sweating.

"I goin' to file a complain'," the bleeding man says through the blood. He swings his fist, but doesn't manage to hit anything.

I shrink further into the corner. I don't know what I'm doing here. The lights are very bright and I'm squinting against them. Eventually I shut my eyes altogether. Perhaps this is some kind of nightmare and I'll wake up in a minute. The noise gets louder and a policeman shouts over the top.

"No more cells, Dave! Give 'em a caution and chuck 'em out."

There's scuffling, swearing. Someone comes close and breathes over me. Then the noise recedes a little. I keep my head down and my eyes screwed tight. I sit like that as long as my muscles will stand it. And then,

190

"Mum!" I hear through the noise. "Mum, it's me, open your eyes."

Helen is leaning over me. She strokes my arm and manages to block out everything else in the room. I put a hand to her face, but I can't speak. I feel I might cry in relief.

"Let's get you home," she says, pulling me up from the bench.

There's a Polo mint on the floor and I reach for it as she guides me through the crowd of football supporters, stepping in a patch of blood on the way out. She keeps an arm round me as we walk, and I keep an eye on the ground. When we stop to cross the road I pick an earring up from where it lies on the pavement. A striped earring, like Sukey had.

"Mum, put that down," Helen says. Her voice sounds funny. "Where did you get it? Don't collect old rubbish. Come on."

She walks ahead and I drop the earring. It bounces off my body as it falls and lands in a puddle.

"I thought it was mine . . ." I say, forgetting why.

"At least now I know where the piles of junk have been coming from," Helen says. The light glitters off her cheek as if she's been sweating. "What were you thinking?" she asks. "Coming out at this time? I'm worried about you. Perhaps we should see Dr Harris again."

I can't answer her, even if I knew the answer, even if I could remember the question, but until we drive off I can still look at the earring in the puddle. There was a time when it could have meant something, when I would have taken it home with me.

I took masses of things home with me when I still had hope of finding Sukey. Bits of paper, nail files, hair clips, an earring. A striped earring, like a humbug, which made me want to put it in my mouth and taste it when I found it lying on the bandstand steps. I couldn't bear to walk past something that might be Sukey's and not pick it up. I'd fill my pockets and later pack the things into my matchbox chest, or arrange them on my window-sill. Sometimes I'd examine the finds, writing down what they were and whether Sukey'd ever had anything like it. Once or twice Douglas came in asking what I'd found. He looked at the bits, touching them lightly; and he never said anything, but I felt he was searching for some significance, creating scenarios, coming up with stories for each object, ways they might point to finding Sukey or finding out what had happened to her. I started to believe I would really discover something important and so I looked even more carefully. For evidence.

Mostly I looked after school. I didn't want to go home anyway, to sit by the range and carefully not talk about my sister for fear of upsetting Ma or starting a row with Dad. I didn't want to go home and change into the clothes Sukey had made. So I wandered about the streets in my uniform, scouring gutters and hedges. I often walked down Sukey's road and traced the journey she would have made from her house to ours. Or walked the way she would have gone to the shops or the station. It was the Station Hotel where they'd found the suitcase, and if she'd left town I thought it would probably have been on the train. Sometimes I leant on the platform railings watching the trains coming in, imagining Sukey stepping from a carriage in new London clothes. "I just went to do a bit of shopping," she would say. "What's all this fuss?"

I spent hours staring at our matching combs, holding them up to the light to see how the wings seemed to flutter, and I wondered at myself. She had been frightened by those birds in the glass dome, so why had I given her such a precise reminder? I wished more than anything to speak to her about that. To tell her I hadn't meant any harm. I thought if there was a single chance of finding her it was worth trawling the streets. I usually arrived home pinched with cold and too tired to eat. It was soon after that I got ill. I'd stopped sleeping long ago, it seemed, and instead just lay in bed trying to think where Sukey might be. It's not that I deliberately stayed awake, but my mind wouldn't shut off and I went over and over that last meal, trying to remember everything she'd said. Things about Frank; things about Douglas. I was tired all the time and I couldn't concentrate at school. I had a job pouring the tea straight in the evenings.

"For goodness' sake!" Ma shouted one Monday morning, throwing a skirt down at her feet. "More bits of rubbish." She had been turning out my pockets to do the laundry. "Maud, you have to stop bringing this stuff home with you." She waved an old Coty lipstick lid around in her hand. "You're going to send me mad.

D'you hear? What's it all for? What are you planning to do with it?"

I felt limp and exhausted next to her show of energy. "I thought they might have been Sukey's," I said.

CHAPTER
TWELVE

Have you moved?

"No," I say. "I've been here ages."

I'm sitting in a sitting thing, for sitting on, facing a computer screen with red writing running along it: "Please make sure your GP has your new address." Every now and then there is a high-pitched beep and a name flashes across the screen. "Mrs May Davison". "Mr Gregory Foot". "Miss Laura Haywood". Helen squeezes my wrist when I start to read them out loud. She is sucking on one of those strong mentholly lozenges you get for sore throats, so I suppose we must be here for her.

There's a child bashing a plastic brick against a table of toys in the corner. He looks like a Ken doll whose head's been squeezed. Helen tells me to keep my voice down and holds out a cardboard box of sweets. I take one and pop it in my mouth, wincing at the way the sweetness of it makes my jaw swell, and watching as the boy's mother reaches to take his brick away. She isn't quick enough and he's off, scampering past other patients, who pull in their legs to make room but can't avoid being bumped by the little body. He runs, staggering like a slapstick comedian, into the far wall, and then throws the brick back towards his mother with sudden violence. A man tuts, rolling his eyes and smiling at me. I smile back, and then, getting the sweet between my teeth, spit it out in the direction of the brick. Helen makes a squawking noise and starts to apologize, but I don't hear what she says as the screaming laughter of the boy drowns out her words. He twists about in a sort of joyous dance, making his way almost gracefully now between the rows of people. And he comes to a rest against my knees, landing lightly like a bird, no longer laughing but opening his hands to show me what he's been carrying about with him.

Another plastic brick, a little metal car missing a wheel, a chubby doll's arm, and several other things. I can't think what they are. He balances them all on my lap, and I pick them up one by one, turning them in my hands and describing them to him. "You see here, they've made semicircles in the plastic for fingernails," I say.

He stares at me solemnly, not giving any sign of having understood, and so I put down the doll's arm and balance a squat, splayed thing on my palm. I can't work out what it is, I can't think past its peculiar shape. I say nothing for several seconds.

"Fog," the boy says finally.

"Fog," I repeat, supposing that must be the word.

He presses a little tab at the back and the fog jumps, not very sharply, as my hand is too soft a surface, but enough to bring the toy to life for a second. The boy makes a gurgling sound and presses the tab again. This time the fog flips over, leaping with its own show of joy, and lands on the seat next to me. Serious again, the boy cradles it for a moment and then pushes the fog through an opening in my handbag.

There's a beep and I look up to see my name in lights. I stand and the toys fall from my lap. The boy shrieks with laughter, throwing the car and the brick into the air. I hear them clatter to the floor a second time, but I don't take my eyes off the computer screen.

"Sorry again," Helen says to someone, picking up her coat and leading the way. "Come on, Mum."

In a small room the doctor is staring at his own computer screen. "Hello, Mrs Horsham. How's your thumb? Won't be a moment. Sit down."

Helen puts me in the chair next to his desk. I can't remember why we're here. "You sit next to the doctor," I say to Helen, getting up.

"No, Mum. We're here for you."

I sit down again and ask for one of her sweets. "You're eating one," I say when she says no. "Why can't I?"

The doctor swivels round to face us. He says he's going to ask me some questions and then he asks me what day it is today. I look at Helen. She looks back but doesn't help. He asks me the date, the season, the year. He asks if I know which country this is, which town, which street. Some questions I know the answers to, some I make a guess at. He seems amazed when I get it right, but it's not very difficult, this quiz. It reminds me of the one they had at the day centre. Elizabeth and I went there once, to see what it was like. They asked things like: "Can you think of a colour beginning with B?" Elizabeth was outraged. "What sort of a quiz is that for adults?" she said.

"A lot of bloody stupid questions," I say.

"There's no need to get agitated, Mrs Horsham," the doctor says, adjusting his neckcloth thing, not a scarf, not a cravat. "I have to assess you, you know."

"No, I didn't know."

"Yes, as I explained, that's what I'm doing now. So. What's this building?"

I look around at the walls. There are lots of notices about washing hands and sterilizing things. "Washing hands can prevent: Diarrhoea, M-R-S-A, Noro-virus," I read. The doctor turns and looks at the poster. He makes a closed-lip smile at Helen.

"Do you know what floor we're on?"

I think for a moment. Did we come up stairs? A lift? I look at the window, but the blind is drawn down. What makes a Roman blind? "Poke him in the eyes," I say. No one laughs. Well, I never liked that joke either. There is some throat-clearing from the doctor and from Helen. She pats my leg and the doctor pats his desk as if it were my leg.

"I'm going to name three items," he says. "And I want you to repeat them back to me, okay? Train, pineapple, hammer."

"Hammer," I say. "Hammer." What were the other ones? "Hammer . . ." My notes are in my handbag and I have to reach under the chair. I start to shuffle through them, but I can't find the answer. I find a little plastic frog instead.

"It's best if you don't use memory aids," the doctor says.

That's all right, it's no good anyway. I can't find anything helpful. There is a note here about Elizabeth, though. It says she's missing. It says: *Where is she?* That's the real question. Why isn't the doctor asking that?

"Now I'd like you to count backwards from one hundred by sevens. D'you understand?"

I stare at him.

"Mrs Horsham? So it would be one hundred, ninety-three, eighty-six, and so on. D'you see?"

"I see, Doctor, but I don't think I could have done that even at your age."

"Please try."

He's already looking down at his papers and making notes. There's something else I have to remember; all this nonsense is interfering. "One hundred," I say. "Ninety-three . . . ninety-two, ninety-one?" I know I've gone wrong, but I can't think where.

"Thank you. Can you repeat back to me the three items I mentioned a moment ago?"

"Three items," I repeat, not quite sure what the words mean because I'm scrabbling in my brain for the other thing, the important thing.

"Never mind. What do we call this?" He points at the telephone.

"A phone," I say. "That's it. Elizabeth hasn't phoned. It's been a long time. I don't know how long."

"I'm sorry about that," the doctor says. "What about this?" He holds something up; he doesn't even say Elizabeth's name.

The thing is thin, made of wood. He waggles it between his fingers, the way we used to in school, a trick to make it look as though it's floppy. I can't think what it's called, though. Not a pen. "A tray," I say. That's not right but I can't find the word. "A tray, a tray."

"Okay, not to worry." He puts the thing down and picks up a piece of paper. "Take this in your right hand," he says. "Fold it in half and put it on the floor."

I reach out to take the paper. I look at it, and look at the doctor. I check both sides of the paper. There's nothing on it. No writing. I let it lie on my lap. He leans over and takes it off me, putting it back on a pile. Then he holds up a card with the words CLOSE YOUR EYES written on it. I'm beginning to think he's bonkers and I'm glad Helen is here. The doctor puts the card down and hands me some more paper and a thing. A thin thing made of wood.

"Now, I wonder if you could write a sentence for me, please. It can say anything at all, but it has to be a full sentence."

My friend Elizabeth is missing, I write. Helen sighs next to me. "Pencil," I say when I give it back to him.

"Yes. Great. Actually, you need to keep that, because I'd like you to draw something. I'd like you to draw a clock face. Can you do that?"

He hands me a board to rest on. I start to draw, but my hand shakes slightly and I don't make a very good

200

job of it. Somehow the lines go the wrong way, like when you try to draw something while looking in a mirror. I forget what the drawing is supposed to be, but the shaky circles remind me of a frog, and so I turn it into that, adding big round eyes and a jaunty smile, and, when the pencil slips, wild hair and a beard. I put the drawing on his desk. The doctor can make of that what he likes.

He writes something on his notepad. He writes and writes. He doesn't look up and he doesn't speak. I wonder if he is trying to get something down before he forgets it. There are little bean-like things lying on the desk, round and soft, their shoots curling off under a box of tissues. I can't think what you call them, but I know what they're for. I pick one up and hold it to my ear, but I can't hear anything.

"Not even as good as a shell," I say.

"I haven't got the player on at the moment," the doctor says, still scribbling. "Would you like to hear some music? Do you think that would help you?"

"I don't know."

"Perhaps your daughter could find something you like. What did you use to listen to as a girl?"

"Ha-ha-ha-ha-ha-ha-ha-ha-ha-ha," I say.

The doctor looks up from his writing. Helen goes very still.

"Ha-ha-ha-ha-ha."

"Mum? Mum? What's happening?" She reaches out and grips my arm, her face white beneath her weather-beaten skin.

And now I'm really laughing. "It's the 'Champagne Aria'," I say. "Ha-ha-ha-ha-ha."

It was Douglas's record, the "Champagne Aria", sung by Ezio Pinza. I liked his name and I liked the song, but I liked the laughing at the end best. It was one of the first records Douglas played to us, long before Sukey was married. The very first was John McCormack singing "Come into the Garden, Maud", and it amused me because it had my name in it, but I'd already been forced to memorize the words to the poem at school and I was keener on discovering less familiar songs.

We had seen Douglas's gramophone amongst his belongings when he was moving in and, after a lot of pestering from me, Sukey finally asked if we could come into his room and hear it. It seemed a completely different room with Douglas living there. We'd always had a lodger, but they'd been old ladies for the most part, kind enough, but somehow hardly leaving an impression on the place. Douglas had few possessions, but they were more solid than the old ladies' things had been. A set of books, a set of tools and at least two dozen records. The gramophone was just a little portable machine, like a deep attaché case, but I thought it was quite fantastic. I particularly liked the little tins of needles and the round sort of brush for the records and the way the handle fitted into a clip in the lid. We sat in his room to listen, the sunlight lining the floorboards and soaking the rug. Once I'd heard it I made him play the "Champagne Aria" several times in a row, and I lay on the rug laughing along with the end, hands on my stomach, feeling my diaphragm jerk. I remember the smell of the warm dust and the vinegar which Ma had used to wash the floorboards.

I still have the record somewhere, Douglas left it for me, but I haven't heard it in a long time. We don't have a gramophone, so there's nothing to play it on.

After that first private concert I used to sneak into Douglas's room occasionally to listen to records. I knew his rounds as well as I knew Dad's and I had the route by heart — from the dairy on Sutton Road, down past the station to the clifftop hotels. I knew when he was furthest away and when he wouldn't be able to pop back unexpectedly. I used to push bundled pairs of woollen socks into the horn to muffle the volume, play the aria again and feel my diaphragm jump under my hands. I did that often while I was still recovering from my illness, after Sukey disappeared, and I used to search through his other belongings, too, opening drawers and rifling through his things. Having seen him search Sukey's case, I thought it was only fair. But his clothes were neatly folded, the books carefully ordered with nothing slipped between the pages, and I couldn't find anything peculiar.

Once, though, on the way out of the room, after I'd brushed my fingers over the gramophone and poked in the little needle tin and gone through the set of Dickens, I saw an umbrella propped up in the corner of the room. A shabby black umbrella. It was so much like the one the mad woman had, and the memory of her chasing me was still so vivid, that I screamed. I felt

203

very stupid immediately afterwards and left the room, glad that no one was at home to catch me.

Katy's brought a flat silver computer with her. Its mass of wires stick out like an uncared-for shrub hastily planted in the middle of the kitchen table. She fusses about with speakers and other things, trying to get them to work, and I try to focus on the booklet in my hand. It's got pictures of brains and simple thick-lined drawings of old people leaning on each other and smiling. I know I'm supposed to read it, make sense of it, but I can't concentrate. There's a new loaf in the bread bin.

"Mum thought you'd like to hear some old music," Katy says, pushing the teeth of a plug into the wall. She clicks a button and Vera Lynn blasts out, making meeting again sound like some kind of threat.

"Good God," I say, covering my ears.

"Sorry." Katy quickly jabs at a button, lowering the volume. "There. How about that? Does it jog any memories?"

"Not really," I say, flicking through the pages of this little book. It's not much of a story and it's a bit unconventional for children. There are pictures that show someone's brain cut through. I don't think it's suitable for Katy really, and I wonder if Helen knows what it's about.

"But it's nice to hear the song again?" Katy asks.

I nod, and let my eyes drift back to the bread bin. Perhaps she wants me to tell her about the war. That would be a first. She's always stared into space when

204

I've mentioned anything in the past. But there is something I wanted to ask her, or possibly Helen. I was waiting for Helen to arrive. I've underlined her name on my note, but I can't remember what it was about now. The song comes to an end and I'm just about to suggest a piece of toast when the next one starts. The bread, soft with a crusty top, is ready sliced, but now I see there's a notice above it: *No More Toast.*

Katy is grinning at me, moving her head to the music. I sit still. I don't sigh. I don't roll my eyes. I look carefully at every page of the little book. But I don't think about it. I don't want to. I hate the sight of the squiggly lines spidering over the brains. And the word "plaque" makes me angry. I put the booklet under a sheet of newspaper.

"I think I've heard this song in a film," Katy says. "Or on an advert maybe."

"Where's your mother?" I say. "I've something to tell her."

"Erm. She's showing someone the house, but you're not supposed to know that."

"Showing them? What for?" I picture Helen unhinging the front of the house for huge people who peer in as if we were the Borrowers. That's just what it was like with Douglas's house. When you walked past you could look up and see the furniture and knick-knacks set out neatly. You could see him, too, sitting there in the half-room, drinking tea and listening to his gramophone, and Sukey would be there, checking the time on the mantel clock. "But how would

205

they have got there?" I ask Katy. "When the stairs had been blasted away?"

She turns the music up and looks intently at the screen of her computer. "This is fun, isn't it? Mum said the doctor said she should play you music."

So that's what this is about. "Did he?" I say. I nod, and it seems like the right response, but I never did like Vera Lynn. I remember reading once that she'd never had a singing lesson in her life. Doesn't surprise me. Lot of rubbish, her songs. Who ever heard of a bluebird at Dover? Anne Shelton was the one we liked best. You never hear her any more.

The music stops.

"Grandma!" Katy says. "Lot of rubbish? You can't say that about Vera Lynn." She looks shocked and I can't tell if she's serious. "I can't believe you don't like it."

"Well, Katy, it's just —"

"You're a traitor to your generation," she says. "Imagine if I didn't like . . . er . . . Girls Aloud or someone." She gasps. "I don't like Girls Aloud. Am I a traitor to my generation, too?"

Now I know she's joking and I start to smile.

"I bet you don't even like watching *Dad's Army*," she says. "I bet you just pretend to laugh at the jokes. Don't deny it. I'm on to you now, Grandma."

Two strangers appear at the top of the kitchen steps. They gaze down at us, nodding, as if we were part of the fittings. "Who are you?" I say.

206

Helen pops up behind them, waving her hands, making some sort of sign. I can't tell what it's supposed to mean.

"Anyway," Katy suddenly says in a loud voice, "is there something you'd rather listen to? I can find anything." She stretches her fingers over the computer's keyboard and makes a false sort of laugh. Something is going on.

"Ezio Pinza," I say.

She looks at me blankly, so I tell her about the "Champagne Aria". I tell her about lying on the floor and the dust and sunlight. The song is found easily, in seconds, and Pinza's voice expands into the kitchen. Katy presses something that makes the song start again every time it ends so that the laughing almost seems to come at the beginning of the song, and she lies on the floor at my feet.

"Ha-ha-ha. Yes, I see what you mean," she says. "It is fun. I'm not sure about *you* lying on the floor, though. We might never get you up again."

Strands of her hair mingle with a mess of crumbs, but she doesn't seem to care. And she does look a bit absurd holding her hands over her stomach like that. I start to feel embarrassed for the child I once was. She closes her eyes and I reach over the top of her head for a slice of bread. Katy doesn't seem to notice. And she doesn't notice when I get the butter out of the fridge. The sign says no toast, so I'll just have bread and butter. I can't think where the plates are for a moment, and there's no time to search, so I lay the bread on a sheet of the *Echo*.

"Ha-ha-ha," Katy says, hands on her stomach, as I get out a knife. "Ha-ha-ha," as I'm digging a thick wedge out of the butter. "Ha-ha-ha," as I run the side of my tongue along the soft, salty, buttery bread.

"Ha-ha-ha," I say, when I've finished, and I begin to squeeze the newspaper up into a ball, but it won't scrunch properly. There's some sort of booklet between the pages. The feel of the stiffer paper refusing to crumple makes me think of clearing out the range, of the sweet but unpleasant smell of prunes heating in gravy, of getting home after seeing Frank at the pub.

I had heard the clock in the sitting room chiming five as I opened the kitchen door and I thought I'd get a row when I walked in, but there was no one about. The range was alight and Ma had left a note on the table saying she and Dad would be home at six o'clock and asking me to add a few potatoes to the hotpot. It was an amalgam of two different stews, one with prunes, and I wasn't particularly looking forward to it. The smell as it started to warm up in the stove was sweet and starchy, and I was glad Ma was out so I could help myself to something first. I cut a finger-thin slice off the loaf and, as Ma didn't like me to waste precious butter, I used the last of the margarine instead, putting a tiny knob of it on to a dish and sliding it into one of the warming ovens for a moment, to soften it and make it go further. When I pulled it out again several old sheets of newspaper came with it.

There was practically a whole *Echo*, I thought, as I spread the marg on my bread and took a bite, Ma or I having left a sheet there every time we'd laid something inside for keeping warm or softening. I began to wrap the spare sheets around the potato peelings on the table, but found that there was a springy square inside which wouldn't crumple. It was the apple-stewed letter, the still-gummed envelope, brown at the edges. The address, to D. Weston at our house, was blurred but distinguishable and I traced Sukey's handwriting with my finger for a few moments without thinking. It was only as I was following the zigzag of the W again that I got a jolt. The words were readable.

I'd checked the envelope several times in the days after I'd half drowned it in the apples, peering between the sheets of paper while Ma's back was turned, but the address had been totally indecipherable, the ink just watery blotches. Whatever had been inside was lost, and the dismay had made me put it from my mind. Then, what with collecting "clues" from the local streets, and being ill, and following Douglas, I'd forgotten it altogether. And somehow those months of heat, the drying and browning and crisping of the paper, had made the words rise up again, blue like a flame. I felt a balloon of hope inflate inside me. What if the letter had news of Sukey? What if it told us where she'd gone? It seemed possible in that moment that she might just have gone away, run off to be a pilot in Australia, or a mannequin in Paris, or anything.

I crammed the rest of the bread and marg into my mouth and picked up the butter knife, slitting open the envelope as I chewed. The paper inside smelled strongly of apples where it had been soaked in the stewing fruit, but the words were readable.

> *Doug —*
> *So sorry. So silly and wrong of me. So glad you wrote.*
> *Please let us be friends again. But I really must tell Frank.*
> *He will understand, I promise.*
> *Sukey*

I was still reading the words when Ma and Dad walked in. I pushed the paper into the pocket of my skirt, realizing at the same moment that Douglas was in the house. His gramophone was on upstairs and the "Champagne Aria" was in my head. I wondered how long the music had been playing, how I hadn't noticed it before. The knowledge that Douglas had been nearby when I'd thought I was alone gave me a sudden chill, and I only half heard my parents tell me they'd been to see Frank. He was out of gaol, they said. Which of course I knew, though I kept quiet about meeting him, knowing Dad would have had a row with me for going into a pub.

"'Course he wasn't at home when we got there," Dad said. "But we met him in the street on the way home. Tight. Which is hardly remarkable."

I felt a little nervous glow of secrecy at Dad's words. So, I thought, Frank hadn't stayed too long after I'd left, just long enough to get really drunk. I wondered if he'd gone home to have dinner, or to get the nylons he'd promised that woman. "And what did he say?" I asked.

Dad half huffed, half laughed in response. "Says he thought Sukey was staying with us." He tapped at the edge of the sink. "With her own house half a mile down the road. Can you credit it?"

Ma had her head turned away. Dad must have been going on and on all the way there and back. She'd probably had enough. Six o'clock struck; the music on the floor above was silenced and Douglas started down the stairs for dinner. I felt for Sukey's letter inside my pocket. "So glad you wrote," she had written, as if she couldn't speak to Douglas directly any time she liked. As if there was something between them that had to be kept secret. I listened to his footsteps descending, light and uneven. Could he have been her lover? Was that possible? Even thinking the word "lover" seemed ridiculous. But, I thought, didn't that explain everything? Sukey's strange behaviour at that last dinner, Frank's jealousy, the neighbour telling me that Douglas was at her house all the time. Perhaps even the broken records in the garden. She or Douglas might have smashed them in a fit of pique after they'd had a row. "Let us be friends again."

Ma looked in the oven to check the stew and, finding it was there and cooking, patted my arm. Dad sat down at the table without taking his overcoat off and talked to the range more than us.

"Three months, and he doesn't think to check on his wife? I don't believe a word of it. And if he had to drive

211

a load up to London, why did he come back on the train? That's what I don't understand. Where's the van he drove up in?"

Douglas's steps had stopped in the hallway, and I could see him looking at himself in the mirror as I slid over to the dresser to get forks and spoons and clear away the knife I'd used for the margarine. He was a nice-looking boy, Douglas, but he was just a boy. Even I could see that. It was too fantastic to think Sukey might have loved him. Too fantastic. And yet, as I laid the table, I couldn't help feeling that the crinkling of the letter in my pocket was a kind of answer.

Ma took the hotpot from the oven and sat down holding it in front of her as if she wasn't sure what to do with it now. I went and guided her hands to the table, taking the dishcloth and ladle in order to serve.

"Unshaven, Frank was, and no collar," she said to me, letting her hands go limp. "I don't see how he can have become so dishevelled in so short a time. But I suppose that's gaol for you. It must be hard, and the food's bad, I'm told. 'Course it's not much better on the outside, with flour being put back on rationing. And now they say bread will be too! And there's no cooking fat in the tin, despite the tiny amounts I've been using. We're only halfway through the month. But we've got nothing left."

She stared at the stew as I served it out, and I moved carefully, feeling the letter against my thigh as if it were as hot as the dish I was holding. Douglas still stood in front of the mirror and I had a sudden idea that we were all of us standing behind some sort of glass wall,

212

unable to reach each other any more. Dad didn't move when I asked for his plate.

"Question is," he said, "did he take her to London with him or did something happen here?"

CHAPTER
THIRTEEN

"I wish you'd tell me what it is you want."

Helen stands behind her car, one gardening glove on, calling from a distance as if I were a dangerous animal. Apparently I was very angry when she came near me earlier, and she has a pinch mark on her arm which I am trying not to notice.

"I want the thing," I say, the tang of cut grass in my throat, the threads of leaves and green skin under my fingernails. "The other half of the thing that will lead me to . . ." It's gone. I fold a stalk over itself until it snaps. "Tell me. Tell me who it is. Who's missing, Helen? Who am I looking for?"

She says Elizabeth's name, and hearing it is like falling into a soft bed. Bits, bits fall from the stem of a hydrangea as I run my hand down it. I put some of the leaves into my pocket before weaving my arms amongst the flower heads, holding my breath against the sour-milk smell of the sap.

"Elizabeth," I say to the globe of petals. "Elizabeth."

I throw empty stalks over the gouged lawn and then follow roots through the soil with my hands, pulling ragged wool-like strands out, one after another. The rich feel of the earth is glorious and the movement is

214

soothing, until I get to a long, pale strand that won't budge. I tug it as far as I can, shaking it violently in frustration, and then I push my fingers into the dirt to try to loosen its grip.

Helen cries out as if it's some part of her I'm trying to loosen. "Please, Mum. Not the choisya, Dad and I planted that, and you always say it smells lovely."

I leave the shrub alone. Here by the gate is a box of glass things, those things for drinking and jams. They are all open and for the taking and, although I can't think why you'd want one I reach in, the glass ringing and squeaking. One has BRANSTON PICKLE on the label and I get a sudden vision of Elizabeth's dining room. Of salad cream and white pepper and majolica plates hung on the walls. Of ceramic lizards and turtles and stag beetles scrabbling from ferns and grasses towards the ceiling. Of Elizabeth laughing at my disgust when she brings out a teapot with its spout shaped like a snake. I cradle the jar in my arms. It still has its lid, though many of its brothers don't, and I have to unscrew it to drop in the thing for hair that I've got in my pocket, a ring thing to tie up your hair. It's wet, as if it's been on the ground, and there's a broken Polo mint stuck to it, and I've got a little plastic frog here too. They all go in together.

On the edge of the pavement is a snail, slowly suckering along, and I prise it from the ground as a woman with a long black ponytail comes out of my house. Her hair thing is just like the one in my jar.

"I've put the medication on a plate," she says. "But I really have to get to my next lady now."

215

"I know," Helen says. "Thank you. Thank you for calling me."

The woman stops by a small, roundish car. "Will you be all right?" She isn't talking to me.

I drop the snail into the jar and watch as it bubbles its juices against the glass. I can make my own majolica ware.

"Yes," Helen says. "I'll just stay with her."

"You'll have to call someone else if —"

"I know. Thanks."

The woman looks back at the lawn. "At least you know about plants. So you can put it right later, maybe."

Helen laughs, not very happily, and the woman gets into the car and drives off. I walk in the same direction, going into other front gardens, gathering things. Masses of things. A bottle top, a plastic cameo brooch, a beetle lying with its legs in the air, a handful of sand and some cigarette ends. I put them in the pickle jar and shake, catching sight of the name BRANSTON over and over. And I think of Elizabeth over and over, and it's like a pain pulsing through my skin with every heartbeat. I can see Helen two houses back, watching as I sink my hand into a mound of sand piled up by a fence. Someone is cementing over their garden. Elizabeth's son is always threatening to do that. How horrid that would be, what a terrible thing. "No birds will come," I told her. "It will be like a desert." And how would we ever get at the ground beneath? It would be lost for ever.

216

I walk past the ugly house and the tea dregs and the acacia, the way I've always walked, and then further on, until I can hear the sound of trains. I stare hollowly across the street. On the opposite side is the Station Hotel. It's an old people's home now and I read the name aloud: "Cotlands Care Home". It's a tall Victorian building, still stately even with its change of purpose. The care-home sign is loose on its screws. They seem to have been pushed out by the brick, as if the old building were rejecting its new title. I remember when I was young how it seemed to bristle at the smears of coal dust over its stone front. I always stared at it in those days. It's where Sukey's suitcase was found.

I'd been there once before, just after the case arrived on our kitchen table. I'd gone to stand against the railings of the station, staring at the dozens of windows, and wondering what Sukey had been doing in a hotel in her own town, wondering if she was somehow still living there, hoping she might look out and see me and come running. Of course, she didn't, and I went home to another silent dinner.

But finding the letter again, reading it, and having the word "lover" jostling next to Douglas's name inside my head made me think more sharply: a hotel — wasn't that the very place people went to have affairs? Hadn't I seen that a dozen times at the pictures? And so I made my way back there one lunchtime, instead of going home, stooping to pick up a discarded ticket stub as I went through the doors.

Inside, the hotel seemed to be just one long staircase, winding round and round — as if the people who stayed there didn't do enough travelling. From the bottom it looked like a well, like the rabbit hole in *Alice in Wonderland*. I thought Sukey could easily have fallen down it and never found her way back. And I walked up slowly, looking down at the station from the windows, at railway passengers and porters with laden carts. The scent of onion soup drifted up from the hotel kitchens, mixing with the smell of the acrid banister polish. The combination made me feel strangely hungry and I felt in my pocket for a carrot biscuit, knowing I had none, and finding only the ticket stub and Sukey's slow-roasted letter again. Every now and then a non-stopping train would hurtle through the station and cause a whirl of steam to fly up above the building, and I lingered at the top landing, to watch as the paperboy struggled to hold on to his wares and his hat.

Along the corridor the numbered doors were shut and I couldn't bring myself to try the handles, so I squinted in the dim light at the worn carpet and peeling wallpaper. Had Sukey and Douglas met here? Had they whispered to each other? Exchanged kisses? It seemed so unlikely. And yet I couldn't help a stabbing jealousy at the possibility that I'd been left out of it all, not trusted with the truth. I picked at a piece of wallpaper, curled over itself by a light switch, tearing it carefully away from the plaster and putting it into my pocket. On the way back to the stairs a man passed me; he opened a door and I caught a glimpse of someone inside. She had soft, dark hair and a blue suit, neatly fitted to her figure. Something coiled fast and tight inside me and I stared, hardly hearing the man as he spoke.

"Get back from the door, will you?" he said, his eyes too big for their lids.

I didn't move, couldn't even swallow, but I took him in now, thin and dusty-looking, his slight frame hardly able to block my view into the room. And then the woman turned. But her nose was heavier than I expected, her lips fleshier, her cheeks flatter, and the coil became a lump in my stomach. I fell back against the wall.

"What on earth's the matter?" the woman said, coming out and taking my wrist, her fingers plumply pressing at my pulse. "Looks like she's seen a ghost."

At the woman's voice the man seemed to shake off his dust and his eyes fitted better into their sockets. "Lord help us, girl," he said. "You gave us a fright looking in like that. What is it? Don't like my face?"

I withdrew my wrist from the woman's hand and slinked away to sit at the top of the stairs, listening to the station guardsmen make announcements on the wind. I couldn't find the energy to get up, so I lay back, my legs extending the length of the short flight, and let the rumble of trains vibrate through me. I made a study of the sand that had been trodden into the carpet, imagining I could taste sea salt on the air, until the woman from the room discovered me.

"You again?" she said, doing a little two-step of surprise as she reached the landing above. "What are you lying there for? Are you hurt?"

"Not really," I told her, getting up.

"Are you a guest?"

"No. I just came in. Sorry."

"Just came in to lie on the stairs?" She began to walk down past me and I followed.

"No, it's just — I thought you were someone else."

"Who did you think I was?"

I didn't answer, and she asked me if I thought I was in shock.

"I know *I* am," she said. I told her I supposed I might be and she suggested I have a small glass of brandy. "I'm having one, at any rate."

She left me in the hallway while she went into the bar. This wasn't the Fiveways, and they'd never tolerate a girl in there. "Poor thing came in to have a shock," I heard her say, catching glimpses of the blue suit through the swing doors as people went in and out. Even after seeing her face I couldn't help but imagine she was Sukey. She pointed towards the foyer, and several men turned to look at me. One of them was Frank.

He saw me of course, and a moment later was pushing the bar door open. I'd hardly thought of him until that moment, and had only imagined what Sukey and Douglas might have been to each other. I felt a sharp pain on Frank's behalf, the pain he might have felt if he'd known about them. And then I wondered if he did know. If Sukey had told him, like she'd said she was going to in the letter. I remembered the way he'd spoken about Douglas, calling him a "rat-faced idiot", and that made me think he did know. And what did that mean? What might he have done if he'd found out?

220

I couldn't face him, and turned to run back into the stairwell.

"Maud?" he called after me.

"Oh, Frank," I heard the woman say. "Is she with you?"

I rushed up the stairs, higgledy-piggledy, turning and turning until my thighs burned and I was back at the top landing, looking for the runs of sand in the steps' creases. Frank had started on the first flight and then given up. I saw his face appear between two landings directly below me as he leant backwards over the handrail.

"Come down here, will you?" he said, his voice spiralling up after me. "I can't be doing with these bloody stairs."

"What are you doing here?" I asked, sending the words down through the floors.

"Having a drink. Not a crime, is it?"

"But why here? Where her suitcase was found?"

"You're talking about Sukey, aren't you?"

"Of course I'm talking about Sukey. Who else would I be talking about?"

"All right. What was the other bit?"

I realized he was what Dad would call "tight" and so I repeated my words slowly. "Sukey's. Suitcase. Was found. Here."

He opened his mouth, but looked away as the woman came to the bottom of the stairs, a glass in her hand. "Want to come down and have this then?" she said, her voice echoing.

I did want it: the liquid was honey-coloured and I imagined it would be sweet and warming and that I might somehow learn something from drinking it, but I'd never had spirits before. "I'm not sure I ought to," I said.

"Suit yourself." She knocked the whole thing back before disappearing again into the bar. I was disappointed, and it was only years later that I finally tasted brandy for the first time, and the burning unpleasantness made me glad I hadn't bothered that day.

"How does that woman know your name?" I asked Frank.

"Who? Nancy? She works here. Her husband's an ex-POW. Poor bastard, touched, he is. Can't bear to live at home, so they live here. I gave them some bits of furniture a while back, to make it more homely."

I laughed. It was Dad's "I might've known" laugh. "Seems there's hardly a person in the town you haven't done some sort of favour for."

"That's a bit of a push," Frank said. "Who else have I done favours for that you know of?"

"People on your street."

"Who wouldn't do their neighbours a good turn if they could?"

"It's *why* you did the favours that I wonder about."

"What's got into you?" he asked. His head disappeared a moment and his hand slid up the banister. I wanted him to stop, to stay where he was and not come any closer. I needed to think, to unmuddle my head, to remember the questions I most

222

wanted to ask. I thought about running to the POW's room.

"Does she work at the desk?" I said. "Nancy? Is she the one that wrote Sukey's name in the register?"

"What are you talking about, Maudie?" Frank asked, just a hand on polished wood slowly following the curve of the staircase. His voice curled towards me, sinister and momentous without a body, and I felt the banister like a conductor, sending a current of electricity from his hand to mine. "What are you doing here? Did you come to find me?"

"No."

"But you're angry with me." The hand disappeared and he took the few remaining flights at a run. They weren't too much for him, after all. "What is it? What's happened? You've discovered something?"

I stepped back, disturbed at having to look up at him instead of down, and crumpled the letter in my pocket in answer.

"What have you got there?" he asked with a half-smile, as if I were a child playing a game.

"A letter."

"From who?"

"Sukey. She sent it before she disappeared."

I had expected a conversation, I thought he'd ask what the letter said, that I'd have time to question him, but I didn't even see his expression change before he lunged at me. With a single movement I found I was bent back over the banister, and he was trapping me there with one hand on my collarbone. The sudden strength of him was a shock. I squeezed my fist around the letter and pushed deep into my pocket, the fabric grazing my skin. He gripped my wrist and tried to jerk it upwards, dragging my skirt up with it.

"The letter says she was going to tell you something," I said, clamping my arm to my side, determined to ask my questions anyway. "*Did* she tell you something?"

"Give me the letter, Maud."

His hand slid above my elbow, forcing it to bend, and my arm rose helplessly. "Tell me," I said, trying to hang on to my thoughts, to remember what I was supposed to be asking. It seemed odd to be talking still when I was so like a ragdoll in his hands.

"How can I when I haven't read it?" He had clenched his teeth and was twisting my arm back, his skin hot through the material of my school blouse. That moment, I scrunched the letter into a ball and dropped it over the banister the way you'd drop a penny down a well.

Frank swore as it fell, and tried to snatch it from the air. The action forced me further over the banisters, and my feet left the floor. I tried to catch at the handrail, but missed. Sickness rushed up as I felt the ground far below do the same, and then Frank's hands were on me again. He pulled me roughly on to the landing, and it took a moment before I realized I was safe, not falling.

When I looked, his face was white. "Thought I'd lost you," he said, and it was unnerving to see how thoroughly the blood had drained from his skin. "I thought I'd lost you." He made light grabs at my limbs, like an incompetent doctor checking for broken bones;

224

he seemed to have to prove to himself I was really there.

"Don't worry, I'm not a ghost," I said, though my heart was still beating so hard it was difficult to draw breath, and I wondered what my face had looked like when he touched me. He hung over the banister and his shirt clung to him, showing the muscles in his shoulders and back. I took a step towards him.

He breathed out heavily and started down the stairs. "No, stay where you are," he said. "I can't be trusted."

I stood for a moment, listening to his footsteps as they descended. The blood that had been rushing around my head slowed, leaving the beginnings of a headache, and I let myself imagine, once, what it would have been like if Frank hadn't stopped me falling. I felt the way my head might have caved in and how my neck would have crumpled. I pictured blood on the tiled floor, and people screaming. I thought of my parents, already suffering from Sukey's absence, and I guessed at what might have happened to Frank. He'd have been accused of pushing me, surely? Halfway down the stairs he stopped and his face appeared again between the floors.

"Tell me something about Sukey, Maud," he said. "Not about this place — tell me something else."

"What, for instance?"

"I don't know. Something you did together. That you remember."

I scuffed my shoe over the sand-sodden carpet. "We went to the beach," I said, beginning to walk down after him. "The day they removed the barbed wire. That was

225

before you were married. Before the war was even over."

"I know. Go on."

"And I buried her in the sand." My voice echoed off the walls strangely as I followed him down, but I could still hear the way she'd laughed that day and see the sand slipping over itself, streaming into the crevices. "And I pushed shells into the sand to make her a dress. And afterwards, when she'd dug her way out, she shook her hair, and Ma was cross because she got sand on the sandwiches and when we ate them later they were full of grit. But the shell dress was really brilliant," I said, reaching the bottom of the stairs. "Sukey made me collect white ones for the skirt so it would look like it had a petticoat. I wish we'd had a camera."

"I wish you had too," he said, pulling the collar of my blouse closed around my neck. "Get home now, Maudie," he said. "I'm going for another drink."

He bent to pick up the browned and crumpled letter, slipping it into his pocket as he walked away.

"Come and stand under here, Mum."

I'm wobbling on my feet; it has started to rain and someone's cigarette smoke lingers in the air. Helen is cowering under a bus shelter. She stands right back against the seat as I get near and seems not to be breathing. I put a hand up to her face and she screws her eyes shut for a second, raising an arm. There is a livid mark on her wrist that looks like it will bruise.

"How did you get this?" I say, taking her wrist as gently as I can, feeling her pulse, strong and quick.

226

"It doesn't matter," she says.

"It matters to me. You're my daughter. If you're hurt, it matters to me. I love you very much."

She stares at me for a moment and I worry I haven't used the right words, and then I feel a sudden exhaustion. My limbs won't hold me up. I'm like one of those toys that flop over when you press the bottom in; the wire in my joints has uncoiled. But Helen's hands are under my arms and I find the seat beneath me. I try to settle the glass pickle jar on my lap, but I can't get it to stay put. The seat is at an angle and either I or the jar keeps sliding off. The contents jumble and something moves, oozily covering the frog's eye. It's irritating. I turn to say something to the woman who is sitting next to me, but tears are running down her cheeks.

"There there, dear," I say. She sobs and presses the back of her hand to her mouth. I don't know what to do to help her. I can't work out who she is. "Tell me what the matter is," I say. "I'm sure it can't be as bad as all that." I pat her shoulder, wondering how I got here. I don't remember getting the bus. Perhaps I'm on the way back from some appointment, but I can't think what it would be.

"Is it man trouble?" I say. She looks at me again and smiles, though she's definitely still crying. "He been unfaithful?" I ask. "He'll be back. Pretty girl like you." Though in actual fact you couldn't call her a girl.

"It's not a man," she says.

I look at her in surprise. "Woman, is it?"

She frowns at me and gets up to look at the bus timetable. Perhaps she thought I was prying. Two

227

pigeons nod at each other on the branch of a tree; they seem like me and this woman, chatting to each other, as if they are our bird selves. I try to wave at them, but I have to be quick to catch the jar from sliding off my lap. When the woman turns back I look at her face properly. The tears have been wiped away. It's Helen. The seat seems to tilt under me. It's my daughter, Helen. I've been sitting in a bus shelter with her, not knowing who she was.

"Helen," I say, touching her wrist, noticing a dark mark on it. "Helen." I didn't know my own daughter.

"You're exhausted," she says. "You can't walk back. I'm going to go and get the car. Okay, Mum?"

My stomach seems to have dissolved inside me. I didn't know my own daughter, and it feels like a reproach to hear her call me Mum. I scrabble about in the jar, for something to do. There's a bit of mint stuck to a hair band and I nibble the edge, but it doesn't taste right and there's some sort of grit on it. An old woman comes towards the bus stop.

"Hello, dear," she says, sitting and rummaging in her bag.

"Hello," I say. I notice she has tatty carpet slippers on. She must be even dottier than me.

Helen says hello too. "I have to run and get my car," she says. "Would you mind keeping an eye on my mum? It'll only take me a few minutes." She looks over at the timetable with a frown. "You won't let her get on a bus?"

The woman agrees, uncurling a bit of plastic inside the bag. Helen pauses on the kerb, biting her top lip, and then begins to leap between the cars, waving back at me.

"Taking you out for the day, is she?" the woman says, unscrewing the lid from a bottle and taking a long drink. "Wish someone would take me out." She jerks a hand behind her. There's a stone building with a sign hanging from its facade.

"Cotlands Care Home," I read.

"That's it." The woman's hair is in tight, white curls, very neat. They don't match the tatty slippers. "My son asked me to come here. Said it was for the best. I'd be closer to him. He'd be less worried. He could come and visit more, take me for drives in the country. But does he?" She shakes her curls. "And so I'm stuck here with these Filipino midgets. Oh, they're not bad people. Very kind. Smile all the time. But so tiny! I feel I've dropped into Lilliput, you know? And I'm only five foot two."

She takes another swig from her bottle, and the sound of her swallowing is comforting. She drinks with a focus that makes me think of Frank and the sweaty heat of a pub and I expect to look down and see my bare knees, but I've got trousers on and a jar of jumbled things in my lap.

"And after a while in there you lose yourself. I can't remember what I like or dislike any more. They say 'Mrs Mapp doesn't like peas,' or 'Mrs Mapp loves Starburst,' and then they ask, 'That's right, isn't it, dear?' and I nod, but I can't for the life of me remember what peas taste like and I've no idea what a Starburst is. Same with TV. They put something on and they say, 'Like this, do you?' and I nod. But I couldn't tell you what the bloody hell it's about."

I look back towards the care home. There's something in that jumble of words, something important, but I can't grasp on to it. A tiny brown lady is coming out of the gates.

"And worse than that is my name. It's Margaret, by the way Margaret."

"Nice to meet you, Margaret."

She shakes her curls again. "Yes, yes, you too. But you see, in there, they insist on calling me Peggy. Peggy! I hate that name."

"Me too," I say, thinking of the Oxfam shop.

"Peggy, you no get bus now," the small brown lady calls, smiling.

"I know that," Peggy says. "I'm only having a chat. Here, quick," she says to me, throwing the bottle into my lap, where it clinks against the pickle jar. "Can't get caught with this. Would get a right old lecture. Pity, because gin's the only thing I *know* I like."

"Inside please, Peggy," the little woman says.

"See what I mean? Peggy this, Peggy that. Bloody nightmare. They even put it on my records. So now I'm Peggy Mapp, not Margaret Mapp."

"They put it on your records?" I say, and feel a little jolt.

"Yes. If you called and asked for Margaret, they'd probably say I didn't live here. Half of them don't know my real name." She pauses to sigh. "You see, there was another Margaret when I first got here and they wanted

230

to make sure they didn't get us confused. She's dropped dead since, of course. But I'm still Peggy."

I watch her go in with the tiny carer, and the bus arrives. I'm about to get on when there is a shout from across the road. The driver calls out of his window to someone. There's a great to-do over something, and the doors fold shut. Helen is here too, talking, talking, but I can't concentrate on what she's saying. I'm thinking of all the different names there are for Elizabeth. Eliza, Lizzie, Liz, Lisa, Betty, Betsy, Bet, Beth, Bess, Bessie . . .

CHAPTER
FOURTEEN

"What about this, Mum? Do you want this? Keep packing, just look quickly."

The white glare from the window softens as Helen holds something up in her hands. I can't see what. It's a shadow, a vague shape. I turn my head, trying another angle, but it stays vague.

"I don't know what that is," I say, dropping the sleeved thing, the buttoned and sleeved thing I've been trying to fold, and putting a hand back to press a knuckle against my spine. I'm uncomfortable sitting like this, twisted round on my bed, but I can't see anywhere else to sit. There's a suitcase at my feet, and we're surrounded by the musty smell of clothes left too long in a wardrobe. "It's like the Oxfam shop in here," I say. "Are we going on holiday?"

Helen drops her hands, and the white light from the window makes me blink.

"No, Mum."

"Because I don't think I can go on holiday. I think it would be too much for me. I think I'd rather just stay at home."

"You're moving house, remember? You're moving in with me."

"Oh, yes," I say. "Of course. Of course, that's what all the boxes are for." I fold the jumble of sleeves and buttons, whatever they add up to, that are lying on the bed, laying them in a suitcase and throwing a pair of knickers on top. "Are we going on —" I remember in time and stop myself, but Helen still sighs. She toes something across the floor.

"Do you need that?" she asks.

It's a pickle jar. There are things squeezed inside: a glove, breathing dampness on to the inside of the glass, two bottle tops, a KitKat wrapper, some cigarette ends spilling the last of their tobacco. "That's important," I say.

"How can it be important? It's disgusting." She picks it up with the tips of her fingers and peers at the things, before tossing it with a heavy, dangerous clink, on to one of the piles of clothes.

The jar rolls down the slope of fabric, sending the sand inside whirling about like one of those snow shakers they sell at Christmas. I pull it on to a sheet of newspaper to wrap, but the metal lid pierces through the first layer and I have to wrap another round it. Helen rolls her eyes.

"Oh, Helen," I say, pressing pleats of paper over the word "pickle". "If I move, how will Elizabeth know where I am?"

"I'll tell Peter," Helen says. "I'll tell him to pass the message on. I'll do it tomorrow."

I explore the jar's contours with my fingers, watching her pulling things out of a cupboard. "You'll tell Peter?"

She nods, not looking at me.

"How will that help, Helen?" I say. "He won't tell Elizabeth. He won't tell her anything. He's done something to her. I don't know what. Hidden her away, or worse. She's gone, and I don't know where."

"Okay, Mum. Okay," she says. "What about this?"

It's a ceramic spoon shaped like the head of a cow. The handle of the spoon has been made to look like the cow's tongue. It's very ugly.

"Yes. Yes, I need that," I say, reaching for it. "It's for Elizabeth." I find a piece of newspaper and scrunch it round the cow's head. The printed words are cut in half by the creases in the paper. I try to read them, but they don't make sense. I don't think they make sense.

"Elizabeth! Again. You chucked most of Dad's stuff in the blink of an eye, but you're desperate to keep all this crap, even though half of it doesn't mean anything to you."

I feel something filling my chest and grip the cow spoon tightly in my hands. The newspaper splits. "I can keep what I want, can't I? I don't see what it's got to do with you."

"You're moving into my house."

"So it's your rules, is it? And I have to do as you say? I don't think I want to live with you if it's going to be like this."

"Well, there's no choice now. The house is sold."

For a moment I can't make sense of the words. It seems an impossible sentence. "You've sold my house?" I say, feeling sick. The floor I'm sitting on seems not to be quite stable, as if it's gone already. "How can you sell my house? It's mine. I live here. I've always lived here."

"Oh Mum, you agreed months ago. It's not safe for you to live on your own any more. Can you keep packing, please? I'll get you a cup of tea in a minute."

"Who agreed? You've no right."

"You and me and Tom agreed."

"Tom?" I say the name, I know it's someone particular, but I can't think who.

"Yes, Tom, does that make it all right now, if he agreed too?"

"Tom?" I say, looking about at the piles of clothes. "Is that the man we're giving all these things to?"

"He flies in from Germany once a year and flies out again and you think he's wonderful. But he's not here day after day arranging your appointments and talking to your carers, checking your cupboards and taking you out shopping, buying you new underwear every time you lose yours and picking you up from police stations at two o'clock in the morning."

She keeps talking. She doesn't stop when I ask her to. She stares at the things in her hands and recites something; it sounds like a list of some kind. I wonder if I should be writing it down and I reach for some paper. I write *Tom*, but it comes out funny. The paper isn't flat and the pen slips over the ridges of whatever is underneath. I can't think what the word means anyway. I take a hand mirror from a table and put it on another bit of newspaper. When I look at it closely I can see an eye staring back at me.

"Oh," I say. "Is it something to do with the mad woman?"

Helen turns to me. "What?"

I point at the mirror, whispering, "Is she hiding in here?"

Helen stares, but doesn't answer. And I can't think what I was asking her anyway, the questions have lost their definiteness, tangled amongst the cobwebs in my head. I yawn and put a newspaper package on the floor next to another, similar one; they are strange muffled shapes and I push them away. There is something frightening about their facelessness. That must be what my thoughts look like, masked and unrecognizable. I search for something else to wrap. "Helen, who are we giving these things to?"

She closes a suitcase and snaps the clasps shut. The noise, the sharp secret-breaking noise, makes me think of another case, and of my mother standing at the kitchen table, and of my father turning his face to the fire.

"We got her case back," I say to Helen, though she's already on the stairs. "But there was nothing in it. It was just full of newspaper." Something tells me this is wrong, that I'm mixing it up, but I can see the bits of paper floating, rustling, out of Sukey's case, covering the kitchen floor. "I remember it so clearly," I say. "Getting the case back from the police and opening the lid, and there it was, full of newspaper. I'm sure that's how it was."

I follow Helen to the front door and stand, pushing a hand into the choisya bush, while she goes to the car

236

and lifts in the suitcase. It's a heavy thing, one of those hard ones for taking on planes. I only used it a few times, when I was still able to visit Tom in Germany. "Are we going on holiday?" I say.

Helen slams the boot shut and walks back to the house. When I get upstairs she is manoeuvring my matchbox chest out of the wardrobe. I made this when I was a child. A hundred tiny boxes, all joined together with glue, which has yellowed and crackles now between the cardboard. I used to store my collection of shells in the drawers, and bits of broken pottery, and insects and feathers. And useful things, too, like thread and pins. Sukey was always opening the wrong box wanting a button or a needle, and she'd scream on seeing the furry body of a bumble bee or a tiger moth lying in its bed of newspaper. She complained, but I had a feeling she enjoyed the fright of it.

"I thought I'd thrown these away," I say. "Are we going to go through them all?"

"I'd rather just chuck them," she says, though her hands hover over the boxes as if she's trying to decide which one to open first.

"But Helen, what if there's something I want in there? You know, I used to collect matchboxes when I was a child."

"I know, Mum. And we used to find dead insects in them when *we* were children. Your secrets, we called them. Boxes full of disintegrating bees and wasps and beetles."

"Yes, I collected those too. Was that you?" I say. "Was it you who screamed?"

"It was probably Tom."

She starts to pull out all the little drawers, leaning away as if something might spring at her. "D'you want these old feathers? This button?"

She tugs at a drawer near the bottom and I have a sudden tightening in my stomach.

"Piece of old wallpaper," she says, shaking the little drawer. "And a bit of a fingernail. Ugh. What d'you have that for?"

She passes me the drawer, but it seems only half there. I can see the bottom of a tea chest more clearly, fluffy balls of dust gathered in the corners where the newspaper lining has wrinkled away. And the fingernail is nestled amongst the dust and odd bits of different-coloured thread, pearly and splintered like a broken shell. And when I look up, Frank is there.

I didn't really expect to see him again after the time in the hotel. I'd tried to talk to Ma about him, but Dad said he didn't want the name mentioned in his house. And that was that. Until nearly a week later, when I found him making another dent in the hedge at the end of our road.

"Been waiting near on an hour," he said, as if I were late. "What time d'you finish school?" He looked smarter; his hair was slicked neatly into place under his hat like it used to be and he'd had a shave.

"I got held back," I said. "Not concentrating in class."

He walked to the edge of the pavement. "Which class was it?"

238

"Don't know," I said, making him laugh. I pulled the branches of the hedge through my fingers, careful not to knock any leaves off, and then took a step towards my house. "I'd ask you in," I said.

"Yeah, I know. But I'm not welcome." He followed me home anyway, glancing at the sitting-room windows before throwing his cigarette into the front garden. "Actually, I was going to ask you to come and see me. There's something I want you to have."

"Now?" I asked, not sure I wanted to go anywhere with him after last time.

He shrugged, nodded, and I looked at him for a moment. His gaze was very steady and, when he smiled at me, narrowing his eyes and adjusting his hat, I found I was smiling back without thinking.

"I'll have to tell them something," I said.

I ran down the path to the back door and waited in the kitchen for a few minutes, checking that Ma hadn't left anything in the range for dinner. She and Dad had gone to London to find out if Sukey had been seen. Dad thought it was likely that Frank had taken her there and lied about it; Ma thought Sukey might have gone to find Frank and missed him somehow. Douglas had said he was going to the pictures, but he'd said that several times recently and then hadn't been able to recall what it was he'd watched, so who knew where he really was. Either way, I didn't want Frank to know that there was no one at home to miss me.

He was at the end of the street when I came out, looking into the park. It was only then that I realized how gloomy the evening was. The red of the bricks was fading, and the pine trees were black above our heads. It was dinner time and we walked through empty streets to Sukey's house, past the laundry, its hot, clean scent like a fierce cuddle. Frank stuck a cigarette in his mouth, taking a box of matches from his pocket and rattling it.

"Last one," he said, sliding the tray out. He struck the match and flicked it into the street. "Want the box?" he asked. "Collect them, don't you?"

"I did," I said. "When I was younger." I took the box and slipped it into the pocket of my skirt, feeling shy and irritated. I didn't like being reminded of how recently I'd been a child. I felt he was mocking me.

"What d'you collect them for?" he asked.

"I don't know. To put things in, I suppose. Like I say, it was just something I did when I was a kid."

"To put things in, eh? Secret things, would they be?"

"No. Just bits and pieces, spare buttons. Nothing important."

He looked down at me, and smiled, as if he knew better, and I blushed and felt guilty, asking myself if I was hiding something without knowing it.

"I wonder what sort of secrets a girl like you would have."

"I don't have any secrets," I said.

"Don't want to tell me, eh, Maudie? But p'raps you will, one day."

He kept grinning, not noticing that I wasn't smiling back. I didn't know what to say. I was annoyed at not being believed, but also strangely pleased. I think I liked the idea of having secrets.

When we got to the house he waited so that I had to go up the front steps ahead of him, and he unlocked the door by reaching past me. I stared at the key in the lock as his breath lifted strands of my hair. The hallway, usually so full of furniture and other things to trip over, was nearly pitch black. It smelled of sawdust and stale cigarette smoke, and I walked forward slowly with my hands out, hearing the front-door bolt being thrust into place. I'd got about ten steps along, surprised that I'd managed to avoid hitting anything, when I felt Frank's arm around my waist. I nearly screamed.

"Gone too far," he said. "Here's the front room." He pushed me in and then went off down the hall himself.

I could see better in here, with the street light coming in through the window. Bars of yellow light lay over the bare floor and I went to step on them, letting them shine over my shoes. A bare floor. My gaze shot over the rest of the room. There were no rugs and most of the furniture was gone. No curtains, no settee, no glass dome full of birds. There was nothing familiar to tell me where I was and there wasn't a trace of Sukey. It was strange and disorientating and reminded me of the way the town had felt on mornings after bombs had been dropped. All that was left were a few tea chests next to the fireplace and two armchairs with dust sheets over them. They'd been pushed opposite each other and one was taken up with a worn rug and some army blankets.

"This where you're sleeping?" I asked when Frank came back.

"Don't look so shocked. It's *my* house. And the rest of the furniture's been sold, 'cept for a few bits in the attic I can't get rid of. My old mum would have had an apoplexy if she'd seen how little I sold it for, but I had some debts that couldn't wait. And I'm not going to be here long."

He lit a candle and put it on the floor between us. The light made his face look almost ghoulish and I shrank back.

"Wooooo!" he said, raising his eyebrows and laughing. "Like one of them Karloff films, in't it? Oh, don't worry, I'm not going to slit your throat." He dragged one of the tea chests over towards him. "This is what I wanted to show you."

I had a sudden panic that it would be something improper. I wasn't really sure what that might be, but I had an idea that I wouldn't be able to talk to my parents about it. I shifted my feet, remembering the heavy clunk of the front-door bolt as it had been drawn into its fitting.

"I can't keep these things here much longer," he said. "You can take anything you like."

I was ready with my refusal before he'd got the lid of the chest off, but then he pulled out a fur stole, holding it in front of the candle. Its magnified shadow scurried over the blank space above the mantelpiece.

"She only had that one suitcase with her in the hotel," he said. "All the rest of her clothes are still here. Thought you might know what to do with them. She liked giving you things to wear and that. And you've got the figure for them."

242

His eyes slid over me, starting somewhere towards my middle, and I couldn't help covering the place with my hands, convinced I could feel an ache there.

"Frank," I said then. "Is Sukey dead?"

I saw him wince, his hand tightening on the fur. He stared at the candle flame. "I shouldn't have gone to London after that bloody lunatic had got into the house."

"What?"

"That mad woman. She got in somehow when I was out one night, months ago. Scared the living daylights out of Sukey."

"Did she run out? Screaming? Sukey, I mean. Did she run out on to the street?"

"Yeah. Neighbour complained. Fussing woman across the road. Was it her that told you? Anyway, the night I had to go to London, Sukey found the mad woman inside again. Gave her a fright. She seemed all right when she went off to yours for dinner, but when she came back she said she couldn't stay in the house. Her idea was to stay at your mum and dad's and, well, we had a bit of a row on account of Douglas being there and I don't like him. In the end I got her to take a room at the Station Hotel instead. They owe me a few favours. We decided she'd stay there until the weekend, until I'd sorted out my bit of business, and then get the train up to London and meet me on Saturday afternoon. I was worried after she didn't turn up, but when I couldn't get hold of her at the hotel I assumed she'd run home to your lot and didn't want to tell me."

But she hadn't run home. She'd left the hotel, left her case full of clothes, and vanished. I dropped on to my knees and gazed into the chest. Here were the things she'd decided not to pack. The green and white day dress, with scalloped shoulders, and the red sailor suit with its pleated skirt. And here was the cocktail jumper, with the pearl button at the back, which she had knitted herself from a Hollywood pattern. All her beautiful clothes. All the things she'd collected and worked on.

Frank went to get something to drink and I laid the things over the arm of his chair as I dug through them. Soon I'd emptied the whole chest and there was just dust at the bottom. Dust and something else, something shell-like. I picked it up and held it to the candle.

I nearly dropped it when I realized what it was — part of a broken fingernail, painted pink. I could see the white marks on the inside where it must have folded before it snapped, and I curled my fingers into my fists against the ghost feeling of breaking a nail. I didn't know if it was Sukey's, but there was something odd about it, something sinister. I slipped it into the matchbox in my pocket as Frank came through the door.

"What you got there?" he asked, frowning, with a quick movement like an animal catching a scent.

"Nothing," I said, pushing the box deeper into my pocket and pulling a blue princess-line dress from the chair. "D'you recognize this?"

244

He said he didn't, and when I told him it was Sukey's favourite for dancing, that she'd been wearing it the night she met him, he looked bewildered.

"I didn't remember that," he said, reaching to squeeze the fabric in his hand. "Tell me about something else. Tell me about when she wore all these other things."

I pull a shirt with grey stripes from a twist of clothes, stroking the front of it over my knees and smoothing out the wrinkles. I don't remember Sukey wearing this. It's soft and nicely cut, but it's far too big. I look back into the case. A hard case like you take on planes. There's an elastic band over the clothes and a pair of trousers is tangled in it. Fawn-coloured trousers. But these aren't Sukey's either. I'm sure I'm dreaming. This room is the wrong shape and my furniture is in the wrong place: wardrobe, chest of drawers, dressing table. They loom darkly in their mistaken corners. And lots of things are wrapped in newspaper, so I can't see what they are. I put on the shirt, wondering when I'll wake up, and a woman comes in. My mother, it must be, though she doesn't look quite like herself.

"Good morning," I say. But the words are difficult to produce. My mouth is too soft for the consonants.

"Er, well, it's night-time. What are you doing banging about? Have you got another bottle of gin in here or something? I thought you'd gone to bed."

"I am awfully tired," I say.

"It's been a long day." She smooths my hair from my forehead and helps me to get under the bedcovers, where it's warm as if someone has been sleeping there.

She definitely isn't my mother. Perhaps she's one of these missing women from the newspaper. Perhaps we both are. "You don't still shop at the same fishmonger's, do you?" The words are not quite definite: it's annoying, but the sound somehow matches the dough-like quality of my thoughts.

"No," she says.

I don't think she's understood. I put a hand out towards her and my elbow knocks a glass. The woman catches it before it falls, but liquid slops over the rim. Inside is some sort of preserved corpse. Like we had in school. Rabbits in formaldehyde, showing their guts to the class. I can smell the dull chemicals, the undertone of rotting. "That's disgusting. What's it doing here?" I say.

"Your teeth?" she asks.

A girl I don't recognize pushes her head through the door. "What's going on? Is it a midnight feast? Shall I make hot chocolate?"

"Are you missing too?" I say.

Her eyes slip to the woman's; she looks embarrassed, caught.

"Yes, make us some hot chocolate then, Katy," the woman says, and she speaks to me in a low voice. She tells me she's my daughter, that this is her house, that I live here with her. She tells me it's late and time to be sleeping, that I am perfectly safe, that no one is missing.

"That's not true," I say. "That's not true." I pat at my sides, but I can't get to my pockets beneath the duvet. I squeeze at it, feel under the pillows, and then reach for some discarded clothes. My feet are too hot and are beginning to sweat. "It's not true," I say, tangling my hands in the clothes. The woman draws back the covers, and now I can get to the notes in my pyjama pockets. I hadn't quite known what I was looking for, but I shuffle through the pages and here, here is Elizabeth's name. She's the one that's missing. It's a relief to find out.

The girl comes back with mugs and I take a sip of my drink. It's sweet and cloying, like melted lipstick. "What was that about Elizabeth?" she asks, grinning.

"For pity's sake, Katy. Don't get her started," the woman says. "I've been through it umpteen times already today. You are aggravating sometimes."

The girl continues to grin. She has a little fox-like face and it makes me nervous.

"You'd better go to the loo before going back to sleep," the woman says. She takes my mug and folds the duvet away from me. The air feels cold on my feet where they are slightly damp.

"Where is the loo?" I say.

She points and I follow the direction of her finger, passing a mirror in the hallway. I'm wearing Patrick's shirt. I'll have to change it, but I can't think where my room is; everything looks strange. I get a fluttering in my chest and I take a step towards a door. There's a sign on it, LOO THIS WAY, as if someone knew I'd be looking! I don't know whether to be grateful or afraid.

Through the door there's another sign taped to the wall. This one has an arrow pointing right. The last door just has LOO written on it. And here I am. I draw down my pyjama bottoms and little bits of paper flutter out of my pockets on to the floor. I reach for them, but I can't get them back into my pyjamas while the material is bunched below my knees. I put them on the radiator next to me instead. Elizabeth's name is on them.

"Elizabeth," I say as I pull the flush. "Elizabeth is missing." It's somehow comforting to say it, but I feel the worry of it begin to pull at me too. I have to come up with a way of finding her. I have to make a plan: I must write it down and tick off the points as I go.

The only paper I can find is a newspaper on the hall table, an *Echo*, and I'm not sure if it will do. The front page comes away as I try to read the headlines, but I take it along to a sitting room anyway and settle into a comfy chair, spreading the sheets over my knees. There's something narrow and hard lying on the cushion next to me. It's smooth and shiny with lots of little numbered buttons. I wrap it up in the paper and look for apples, but I can't see any, so I wrap a pen instead and then I wrap a set of keys.

"Oh, Mum," Helen says, standing over me. "No wonder I can never find the remote." She peels newspaper from something, letting the page fall to the floor.

I pick it up and wrap it round my hand. "Where are the apples, Helen?" I say. "We'd better get started, we'd better put them away, or they won't last till the spring."

★ ★ ★

248

I used to like wrapping apples. It was one of those jobs people gave you to do as a child, and I can still recall the sharp smell of the newspaper ink mixed with the sharp smell of the fruit. One year Ma and Douglas and I packed them together. We stood in the kitchen, newspaper in the middle of the table, apples in a tub at one end and boxes ready at the other. There was a breeze rustling through the dark hedge outside our warm and cosy kitchen, and the fire in the range was slowly dying down from dinner. The kitchen light was on the blink and kept flickering above the table as if a moth were inside the bulb.

Ma was the fastest wrapper; Douglas the slowest. He had a bad habit of reading the old newspapers. He couldn't seem to help it, even though he'd more than likely read every article already. There'd been a horrible murder of a woman staying at the Grosvenor Hotel the month before and the reports were hard to miss, though Douglas didn't say anything about it. The eleven-year-old king of Iraq had arrived in Britain and Clement Atlee was coming to give a speech in our town. Douglas laughed when I asked if he thought the two were related.

"They've finished those new houses across the way, look," he said, lifting a newspaper and letting the light skitter over it.

"They did that months ago," Ma said. "That's from February, that paper is. There'll be people living there by now, I expect."

"Yeah, there are. Frank moved a family in from Christchurch," I said. "And that was March."

249

"Did he, love?" Ma said, her voice faraway, calm, but her eyes wide. She pointed to the ceiling and then put a finger to her lips, reminding me not to mention Frank in front of Dad.

I rolled my eyes. "Frank said they got him to move stuff in even before it was finished. He got to look over the whole lot, gardens and everything. Really nice they are, he says."

Douglas looked at me and then away. "How long before?" he asked, finally scrunching his page round an apple. "Before anyone moved in or before the whole street was finished?"

"I don't know. He helped them fix up their gardens though. As a favour."

"Fix them up how?"

"Well, he brought them extra soil and dug the ground over and helped them plant things. Vegetables."

"Didn't know Frank was green-fingered. Which vegetables did he help plant?"

The boards creaked as Dad started down the stairs. He made the steps creak in a very particular way, not like Ma or Douglas, not like me. They seemed to groan under him. He came into the kitchen and grabbed a box of apples for the loft.

"What are you all talking about?" he said.

"Those new houses," Ma said. "Meant to be nice."

Dad grunted, starting back up the stairs.

"They've big gardens, haven't they?" Ma said. "Be nice for a family. Maybe you'll live there one day, Maud. When you get married."

250

For a second it seemed like an obscene suggestion. My face and hands went hot and the smell of the apples seemed to thicken unbearably in the air. Ink came off my fingers, smearing on to the skin of the apple I was holding. I wiped it on my jumper, feeling I'd sullied the fruit in some way and that it wouldn't be good to eat next year.

Douglas was studying a page of adverts. I watched him till I'd filled a box, and then I pulled at the paper. "Why are you looking at the ads?" I asked.

He tugged it back out of my hand. "I've read everything else."

Ma told me to leave him alone and keep up. "I've filled twice as many boxes as you," she said.

Douglas smiled and left the rest of his paper on the table, saying he'd take a box up to Dad. I separated a sheet of newspaper from the pile and wrapped it round an apple, pressing the creases flat against the skin and reading the words that were still visible: "According to the Postmaster General the Post Office is experiencing difficulties in the aftermath of six years of unremitting warfare. Applications for telephone installations have now reached 300,000." I thought of Mrs Winners and how annoyed she'd be to lose her position as the only person on the street with a phone and I was about to say something to Ma when I noticed a headline bunched around the apple's stalk: WOMEN: CONTACT YOUR HUSBANDS.

It was another story about the Grosvenor Hotel murder. The reporter said that the town was in a panic since the discovery of a second body further along the coast, and now local people were worrying that more of their womenfolk had become victims of the vile murderer. In the opinion of the writer, police who were investigating the crimes were being kept busy by dozens of men whose wives, it turned out, had just run off. Hasty war marriages had led to even hastier departures. The article urged these women to let their anxious husbands know they were alive and well, because in light of the recent murders, it was important that they weren't registered as missing.

I read the story again. Could Sukey be reading the same thing? I remembered the little flutter of hope I'd felt at the idea that she was just hiding from Frank, and I went through the pile of papers on the table with a new sense of purpose. There were several other articles about both men and women going off without saying a word to their families, and a letter to the editor from a man who'd found his wife was living just the other side of town under an assumed name. He'd only discovered her because she still went to the same fishmonger's.

So that could be it, I thought. She might have run away from us, from Frank. But the panic that the first reporter had written about had begun to infect me too. What if the alternative was Sukey lying murdered somewhere amongst gorse bushes? What if the murderer had attacked three women, not two?

CHAPTER
FIFTEEN

If I turn left and left again I'm in the kitchen. I have that written down. And there's a soapy smell in here that reminds me of the walk to Sukey's house and a woman bundling a mass of sheets and towels into a washing basket.

"That letter's for you," she says, straightening up and nodding to the envelope on the counter. "From Tom, and he's sent us a photo of their cat, for some reason. I'm sure he expects us to be thrilled. What d'you want for breakfast?"

"I'm not allowed to eat," I say, picking up the photo. "That woman told me."

"What woman?"

"The woman," I say. God, I'm sick of explaining myself all the time. "That woman who works here." Is that right? "She works here."

"What are you talking about?"

"You know the one . . . Yes, you do. She works here. Always busy. Always cross. Always in a rush."

"I think you mean me, Mum."

"No," I say. "No." But maybe I do mean her. "What's your name?"

She makes a face at her pile of washing. "I'm Helen," she says.

"Oh, Helen," I say. "I've been meaning to tell you. That girl you've hired, she doesn't do any work. None. I've watched her."

"Who are you talking about now? What girl?"

"The girl," I say. "She leaves plates by the sink and there are clothes all over the floor of her room."

Helen grins and bites her lip. "Pretty good description. Mum, that's Katy."

"I'm not bothered about her name," I say. "I'm just letting you know what she's like. You should ask her to leave, I think. Get someone else, if you must. I always did the housework myself at your age, but then the younger generations expect everything to be easy."

"Mum, that's Katy," Helen says again. "Your granddaughter."

"No. Can't be," I say. "Can't be."

"Yes, Mum. My daughter and your granddaughter."

She puts the washing basket on the table and shakes out a large piece of material. Some socks fall into the basket. I feel I've had a shock, but somehow I can't quite think what it was. I stare into the half-closed eyes of the cat in this photo. It's black and white and lolls in a mass of bright nasturtiums, crushing them beneath it, and I wish I could lie down in a bed of flowers, but Helen would tell me off. She's very precious about the things she grows.

I move about the kitchen, opening and shutting drawers. There are a lot of orange balls stuffed into one of them, like the eggs of some exotic bird, except

254

they're not smooth, but crinkled like screwed-up newspaper. I begin to flatten an egg out, and find it's made of thin plastic and there are handles at one end. I can't think what sort of bird it is, though. I ask Helen and she grimaces.

"Oh, God. I really ought to do something with those. I don't know how I manage to forget my bag-for-life *every single time*." She looks at me for a moment, and then smiles. "Must be catching."

The front door opens and Helen takes the flattened egg and shoves it back in the drawer. She says something I can't catch. Something about clothes on the floor. I look at the socks in the basket.

"Hi, Grandma," Katy says, coming to stand in front of me with outstretched arms. "This is me."

"Hello, you," I say.

"So do you know who I am?"

"Of course I know who you are, Katy, don't be ridiculous."

Katy laughs and turns to her mother. "She's cured!"

"What is she talking about?" I say, looking over at Helen. "Your daughter's mad."

"Oh, Grandma," Katy says, putting an arm around my shoulders. "One of us is."

She takes her arm back and moves away and I follow her into the corridor, but in an instant I find I'm lost: everything is unfamiliar. I feel as though I've gone through the mirror in that story — what's it called? I look at my notes and find one with directions to THE KITCHEN. I follow them. Perhaps there'll be a little

255

bottle or a cake with an EAT ME label. I find Helen instead.

"Helen, where am I?" I ask. "This isn't my house. Is it?" Somehow, I can't be sure. It's someone's house. I have been here before. Perhaps it is mine — I can't think of another house just now, I can't think of any other rooms to compare this one to.

"This is my house," Helen says, putting down a tray and holding a chair out for me to sit in. "Let's have a cup of tea, shall we? I've made you some toast."

I pick up my cup and she watches me drink.

"I might get some cake when I'm out," she says. She has a crafty look. She's trying to hide it behind a smile, but I can see it. "What kind of cake would you like?"

I ask for coffee cake. I don't like coffee cake so I can't be tricked into eating it. She takes the tray away. She's taken it somewhere, or to someone. To the Yanks in the NAAFI, is it? To serve them breakfasts of sausages and beans. I wonder if she'll bring me any.

Her shield, her winged rain shield, is lying on the table. So I'm not the only one who forgets things. I put my hand through the loop of material on the handle and hold my arm up, watching the raining-rain shield dangle as I drink my tea. There is a newspaper here, too, and I fold it into a tiny rectangle, making the creases as sharp as I can.

A girl walks past the door, collecting things from the shelves in the hall. She's stealing them to give to the mad woman. I can see her from where I'm sitting, putting a coat on, stuffing her pockets. I stand and grab my bag. The front door slams, but I open it only

256

moments later and follow her down the path. At the turn in the road she stops. I stop, too, and pretend to be looking at the heads of some dying sunflowers. They hang over a garden wall, the seeds falling on to the pavement. I gather some up and put them in my pocket. When the girl starts walking again I copy her. And then, as I get to the main road, I see her break into a run. A bus is waiting at the stop, she jumps on it and it pulls away. I've lost her. She's gone. And she won't come back, never never never. I turn towards home. There are bits of rubbish all down the middle of the street. A trail of banana skins and newspapers. There's something I was going to do with newspapers: use them, read them, something. I bend to peel a bit from the tarmac, trying to read the words. But there are sludgy smears across the page and it doesn't smell right. I drop it by my feet.

A miniature bottle lies against the kerb. What's that story about a little bottle? "Drink me," it said. I can't remember the rest. Anyway this bottle says MACALLAN WHISKY and I don't think it was whisky in the story. That's something Frank used to drink. He had a bottle with him once when I met him. It wasn't miniature either.

He drank it sitting in the car at the end of our road while I told him everything I could remember about Sukey. He said he wanted to think of her the way I did, wanted to try and get her straight in his head so he'd never lose her. We sat close in the half-dark, a street lamp breaking through the shadows, lighting up swirls of cigarette smoke. It was stuffy, but I didn't mind: cars were wonderful. In a car you could just sit, you didn't have to be getting on with anything, you didn't have to prepare vegetables, or dig the garden or run sheets through the mangle.

In Frank's car all I had to do was talk, to remember the details he'd forgotten: the name of Sukey's perfume, the flowers she liked, the columns she always read in magazines, and, once again, what she'd said the night she met him. He liked that memory best. How Sukey had come home happy and dancing, how she'd taken off her blue dress and sung to herself as she put cold cream on. And how she'd lain in the dark, in the next bed, and told me she'd met this man, this handsome man, who'd winked at her and grinned. And how she'd known — right then she'd known — she'd met the man she was going to marry.

I told the story, studying the shape of the space between us, the gap between his thigh and mine, and he stared out at the street. And then he cried, not really with tears, but hunched over with his eyes shut. I touched his hair, at the back, where there wasn't any Brylcreem, and he curled his fingers round my wrist and brought it to his mouth. I found I was trying not to breathe.

"This evening, Maud," he said, "when I saw you coming towards the car, I thought for a minute it was her. You don't know what that did to me."

He held my wrist for a long time. When he let go it was to take a drink from the bottle of whisky which rested on the floor against his ankles. A crease had formed in the sleeve of my jacket — Sukey's blue suit

258

jacket — and I smoothed a hand along it, trying to make the material lie flat. And suddenly he leant over, pressing his face into my neck. I kept very still. I didn't dislike it exactly, but I was in terror of what might happen next.

"Frank," I whispered.

He sat up then and I clambered, blindly, clumsily, from the car, hurrying when I realized he was getting out too. But he only leant against the lamp post, watching as I walked home unaccompanied. It made me think of the time when he and Sukey were courting and I would see them huddled together there, under the dimmed street light, wrapped in his big tweed coat, kissing. That was another memory I saved up for Frank.

"Strange company you keep," Douglas said as I came through the back door, the overhead light shining harshly on his face, making him look ill.

"What are you talking about?" I asked, struggling out of my jacket.

"I saw you. In the car," he said. "With Frank."

There was a newspaper, folded very small, lying by his clasped hands, and I looked at it carefully while I thought how to answer. The Grosvenor Hotel murderer had been caught and there seemed to be no doubt he'd be hanged, despite the fact that the trial wasn't due to start for months. "Of course. Always waiting around outside, aren't you, Doug?" I said. "I'd say you were the strange one."

He looked down at the newspaper, too, and I caught a flash of the hurt my words had caused, the hard blink, the creep of a blush. I felt a sudden exasperation with him and batted the newspaper on to the floor. He didn't react, but stared at the table where the paper had been before picking it up again and squeezing it.

"It's not the first time you've been with him," he said. "And wearing her clothes too. What are you doing, Maud?"

I shrugged, the jacket still in my hands. I hadn't even looked at the velvet bolero Sukey'd given me since Frank had let me have all her other things. It was wonderful to dress up, and to go out after dinner in new outfits, even if it did mean lying to my parents about where I was. I didn't know what I was doing, but I wouldn't feel guilty. I wouldn't let him make me feel guilty. "She was *my* sister," I said, but he wasn't listening. His eyes weren't on mine. They were running over me, narrowing over my body.

"They're *her* clothes," he said, standing. He took a step towards me. "Take them off. Give that here."

He yanked at Sukey's jacket, looking at me so fiercely that I backed away, letting go of the collar before it tore. "Doug," I said. "It's nothing to do with you."

I got to the sink and he put his hands on it, trapping me.

"Playing at being her. That's what you're doing. Wearing her clothes. Going out with her husband. What does he do? Take you back to their house? To their bed?"

"Don't be disgusting," I said, cheeks burning. "We just talk, about Sukey, that's all." I looked away, trying to put some space between us, and he grabbed my chin

260

with his fist, squeezing it the way he had squeezed the newspaper, shifting closer.

"You're even wearing her lipstick," he said, his face an inch from mine. "Get it off."

The side of his hand rubbed over my mouth roughly, pulling at my skin and crushing my lips against my teeth. I could feel the make-up smear across my cheek and tried to turn my head away again, but he held my chin tightly.

"Stop it," he said, his breath hot on my face. "Stop trying to replace her. You can't ever replace her."

"All right, no need to hiss at me," I say.

"I wasn't hissing," the driver says. "But you do need to show me your pass."

I'm on the bus, but it's not moving and the doors are open behind me. An umbrella dangles from my wrist, and the weight of it, the movement as it swings about, is distracting. I can't find my bus pass — I know it's in my bag, I never take it out, but I can't see it. I have a thing for hair, for dragging out the tangles, a packet of Polo mints, a photo of a black and white cat and a thin plastic wallet. I push them all aside and put a hand in my pocket. There are lots of bits here. Lots of little bits. I can't think what they are, but they make me think of flowers and gardens and something else. Something to do with the bible, perhaps. A phrase from the bible?

"'Were it earth in an earthy bed,' " I say. That's it. I remember it from school. I wish I could think where it's from.

"What?" the driver asks, peering through his glass partition. "Come on, love, you're keeping us all waiting."

I turn to face the other passengers. They are sitting looking at me and I can hear their Helen-like sighs. My face feels suddenly hot. For some reason, they're impatient to go, but I don't know what I'm to do about it.

"Why don't you let her on?" someone calls out. "You can see she's old."

The driver puffs out a breath and tells me to go and sit down. There's a moment before the bus can pull into the traffic and through the window I see a man on the pavement, standing ripping the plastic from a pack of those things, little sticks, not whistles. The things you light up. He breaks the plastic and then goes on biting. First the cardboard and then the contents of the packet, bits of tobacco sticking to his teeth. His face is like a grin and he looks at me as he bites, and his quick, sharp movements are frightening. I think of the man running down the hill after his hat and my father telling me not to stare and I wish suddenly that someone was with me. Anyone. I'm grateful when the bus moves on.

We drive past the park and Elizabeth's house. Past the acacia tree. With its long milk-bloom. There. That's the same bit of something from school. I'm not sure it *is* the bible. I can't remember any more, though. The bus vibrates whenever it stops and I feel as if my bones are turning to jelly. There's a newspaper on the seat next to me and I hold the edge of it, fluttering the pages in my fingers. You can put adverts in this newspaper and all you have to do is go to the office and ask. I smile and read the shop signs and road signs aloud. It's starting to spit out there. Tiny drops of rain appear on the windows, like flecks of toothpaste on a mirror. An old couple get off by the supermarket and I find I have a sudden longing for Patrick. He would always hold my hand when we took the bus together. Just for a few minutes getting on, and the same getting off. Then we would break apart naturally and sit or walk side by side. He would do the same in a crowd, putting a hand out behind him, reaching for me. I miss that.

I see the building I want too late. By the time I've got up and pressed the bell we're two stops past, and I have to walk back. The *Echo*'s office looks nearly the same as when I was a girl. It makes me think of the pictures. Very glamorous, it is. Very modern. But in a nice way. Not like the modern buildings they put up now.

Inside, there's a woman behind the counter; she has fat cheeks like a baby and they bunch when she smiles.

"How can I help you?" she says, and I think it sounds like there is a word missing at the end of her sentence, like she wanted to say "love" or "dear" and stopped herself.

We look at each other and I try to think of something to say, but the word "baby" just goes round and round in my head. I rummage in my bag and find a photo of a cat lying in a bed of nasturtiums. I can't think where it's from.

"Was it a competition entry?" The woman bends slightly and her arms disappear from view; I can hear her leafing through papers under the desk. "I think all the winners for this month have been notified. I'm sorry. But you haven't lost. Just give it another try next month."

"Lost," I say, dropping the photo on to the counter. "I've lost Elizabeth."

She pauses a moment and straightens to look at the photo. "Oh, was it an advert you wanted?"

Breath floods into my lungs. "Yes. Yes, that's it. I wanted to place an advert."

"I'll get you a form. Awful, cats, aren't they?"

I nod, feeling as though I've missed some part of the conversation. I nod, but I quite like cats and I wonder what this woman has against them.

"I remember when my auntie lost her Oscar. She was frantic. Missing for weeks, he was. Found him in a beach hut in the end. Have you asked your neighbours to look in their sheds?"

I stare at the woman. I can't imagine finding Elizabeth in a shed. But perhaps it is a good suggestion. Perhaps it's just me it doesn't make sense to. I borrow a pen and write *beach hut* on a scrap of paper. The woman slides me a form with lots of boxes and spaces for writing. I look at it, and I must look at it for some time because she leans over and puts her head close to mine.

"Write what you can. I'll help if you're struggling."

"Right," I say, lifting my pen and pointing it at the form as if it were a wand and could think up the sentences for me.

"People do love their animals in this country, don't they? Makes me proud, actually. Not like that in

264

Turkey. My brother's got a place there and you wouldn't believe the number of skinny cats wandering around with no one to look after them."

I look at her and then back at the page. I've written "Turkey", for some reason. I cross it out.

"Here," she says. "Let me." She spins the paper towards her and rests against the counter.

She asks when I last saw Elizabeth and where. I'm not sure about that. I look through my notes and find my name and address and telephone number. I give her those in case they're important. She asks what colour I'd say Elizabeth is, and I'm surprised for a moment, but I suppose she could have been black, or Indian. She asks if Elizabeth has a collar, and it seems like an odd question. I look at my notes, but I can't find an answer. I do have my name and address and telephone number, though, so I give her those.

"And these are your details," she says, taking the note. "Thank you. I'll keep them there. See, I've written them in already. Okay, and is Elizabeth microchipped?"

I don't recognize the word. I shrug.

"We'll leave that out, then. Never mind. Hmmmn. It's not very detailed so far, and it seems funny to put her name in when there's no collar. I mean, she's hardly going to identify herself, is she?"

"No," I say, laughing, but I don't quite understand the joke.

"Well, have a read over what we've got."

I look at the sheet. It's a strange jumble of words and lines and I'm not even sure which bit I'm supposed to read. But there is a title: "Missing Cat".

"I don't want this," I say. "I don't want this word." I put my finger over it, trying to lift it off the page.

She waits for me to move my finger before she reads it. "'Cat'? But I really would advise . . . You see, we don't mention it anywhere else."

"Don't we? All the same, I don't think 'cat' is right."

She crosses the word through. "Up to you," she says.

"I'd like her last name too. Markham. Elizabeth Markham."

The woman makes a face, one fat cheek bunching, but she writes the name down anyway. "Part of the family, is she? Wait." She stops suddenly and covers the paper with both hands. "We are looking for a cat, aren't we?"

"Cat." I can't think what it means. "I don't think that's the right word. Cat. No, I don't think so."

"Oh, sorry, love. Elizabeth Markham. It's a person, isn't it? You must have thought I was off my rocker. Right. Let's begin again."

She pulls out a new sheet of paper and writes something down. I show her my phone number.

"I've kept it simple," she says. "I'm assuming it's an old friend? Yes? At the moment it would cost seven pounds twenty-two, but if we put it in a box with the phone number up large, it'll only be four pounds fourteen, don't ask me why. Something about price brackets. I just do what the computer tells me. That suit?"

I feel a bit stunned. The numbers roll around in my head. I get my purse ready, but I can't work out what she's asking for, or what I have.

266

"All right if I have a look?" She takes the purse and counts some coins on to the desk. "There. Four fourteen, okay? It'll be in this weekend."

And somehow I'm out on the pavement. Rain is coming down, slanting over the road, and drops hit my face like pinpricks. A lorry roars by and the noise of it makes me shudder. I look along the street after it, not sure where I am. All the buildings seem to be made of glass, reflecting the traffic back at me. Drizzly, wavering traffic. There's something hanging from my wrist, heavy and swinging. I can't think with it swinging there. I try to shake it loose, but it won't come off.

A car swerves round me, beeping, screeching, as I start to cross the street and I stumble on to the kerb, clutching at my cardigan. It's soaking, and so are my trousers. I feel up and down my body, squeezing the fabric of my clothes. I'm wet through; there are drips running from my hair and my toes squelch when I move. The rain seems to send the smell of petrol up into the air and I stand, shivering, looking out at the wet road, where rainbows of oil shimmer. I was on a kerb like this when the mad woman chased me. Hitting and shouting at me. The thought makes me hunch in anticipation. I start to take off my wet things, pulling my sleeves over my hands, and an umbrella slips off my wrist. It rolls on to the road and a car whizzes past, sending it hurtling into the middle. I'm too frightened to go after it but look at the umbrella where it lies and think about the shock of the bang! on my shoulder and the way the mad woman shouted.

I thought at the time I couldn't hear her words, but now I find I can remember them clearly. "Saw you," she said. "In the car with Frank. Playing at being her. Wearing her lipstick." I rub at my mouth now: the sleeve is wet, but so is my face. "You can't replace her. You can't ever replace her." And then I ran into the kitchen and Ma went out to tell her off, to tell her I was too young to be knocked down by a bus. And Sukey said, "Thank you, Mopps," and kissed me on the head.

No, that's a jumble, but I can't work out where I've gone wrong. There's a ribbon by my feet. A green, checked ribbon. It could be Sukey's. The ends are frayed and the silk is stained and grubby, but I wind it carefully round my finger as I walk along. My pocket's full of something. Seeds of some kind. I must have brought them for a snack. I pop one in my mouth, but it doesn't taste quite right and I spit it out.

At the end of the road I find a mass of people huddled beneath a glass ceiling which stretches over part of the street. They are holding shopping bags and looking up at the sky. The rain patters above them, the sound mixing with their chatter. I think I hear someone call "Grandma". I walk under the edge of the shelter and hear it again.

"Grandma! Grandma!"

Katy is tugging at my cardigan, her eyes big. "What big eyes you have," I say. But it's the wrong way round: she should be telling me.

"You're soaked," she says. "What are you doing here?"

"Oh, Katy," I say, clutching at her hand, limp with relief. "I don't know where I am. I'm so glad you're here, because I'm lost, and Katy, I don't know where I live. I can't remember. It's really terrible."

A couple of other teenagers are sitting on the back of a bench, their feet on the seat. One has a bright streak in her hair.

"I've got to take her home," Katy calls to them. "Come on, Grandma."

She takes her jacket off and puts it round my shoulders, rubbing my arms. I start to feel wobbly. I'm tired and want a sit-down.

"Shall we get something to drink?" she says, pointing out a café.

It's one of those dimly lit coffee shops where sleek-haired women sit at tables in the window and a man with suede shoes lounges on a leather settee. Katy opens the door for me and waits, her head on one side.

"Aren't you coming?" she says when I pause.

I peer in through the window again and scrabble in my bag for something, anything. There's a bit of seed in my pocket and I arrange it carefully on one of the tables outside. No one is sitting there, with it being so wet. Inside, it's very noisy and smells of damp clothes and hot milk. The people behind the counter seem to be doing a sort of dance and the customers shout instructions for it. I would be too shy to come to a place like this usually. But Katy seems to belong here with her piercings and bright clothes. She is even wearing suede shoes.

"What would you like?" Katy says, already in a queue.

"Tea."

"Oh, Grandma, the tea won't be very good here," she says. "How about a latte or something?"

I say, "All right, I'll have that," and go to sit in a big armchair, watching her order and pay and come towards me. If I look away will I forget who she is?

"Here we are then." She puts the cups down.

My drink has a sort of foam on top. I've seen her drinking something similar. "Milkshake or something, is it?" I say.

"No, latte. Milky coffee."

So that's what she meant. It's quite a relief. I never did like milkshakes. There was a place that did them on the pier when I was young. It was like an American diner, only it served tea and fish and chips as well. We used to go there after the pictures.

Katy pats a wodge of paper napkins over my head. For a moment I'm taken aback, outraged.

"Dry you off a bit," she says.

Am I wet then? I look out of the window. It's raining. And now I can see that this is the street where the ABC Cinema was. "Tub Street," I say, nodding at it.

Katy stops her patting. "No, Grandma. Bath Road."

I smile to myself. Tub Street, that's what Douglas called it. He went to see some film about gangsters not long after he moved in as our lodger, and he started making up nicknames for the local roads after that. So Blackthorn Road became Tree Street and Heron Court became Bird Street and Portland Avenue became Stone

270

Street. Dad asked him one day why he couldn't leave the bloody names as they were. He rarely got cross with Douglas, but I suppose as a postman he felt that the names of streets were sacred in some way.

Tub Street's changed an awful lot. They must have pulled down the cinema to make room for these ugly great buildings. No wonder I didn't recognize it. The place I knew has been buried. Soil upon soil.

"It's such a shame, Katy," I say.

"I know, Grandma, I know."

She's humouring me. A wet lump of tissues folds into itself on the table. It looks like that Plasticine stuff the children used to play with.

"I can't get hold of Mum," Katy says, holding something to the side of her face. "She's probably on the phone to the police or something."

"What's that you've got against your ear? A shell? Who is it you're listening to?" I say. Douglas had a shell, I remember. I watched him discover it in Sukey's case: he felt all around the edges and found it in the lining. And then he held it to his ear and her voice came out and she told him how she'd met the man she was going to marry.

"Handy," Katy says. "But this is just a phone, I'm afraid. And at the moment I'm listening to a woman telling me the number I have dialled is busy. Never mind. We'll go home in a minute. After you've drunk your coffee."

"Coffee is good for the memory," I say.

She smiles and sits back. I think of telling her that I've forgotten why we're here. But she looks so happy and I'm worried about how she might react. She curves her hands round her cup and sips. Her nail varnish is chipped. The nails are very short and I wonder if she bites them or if she's just broken them all. Broken them and left them in a box. Every little nail in a separate little box.

"Your coffee's going cold," Katy says.

I have curled my fingers tightly into the palm of my hands, protecting the nails, forcing them against the skin. It's an effort to uncurl them, but I hook one finger into the tiny handle, which, as it turns out, is not much use. The cup is huge and heavy and I spill quite a lot of coffee on the shiny wooden table.

"Whoa!" Katy says, springing forward to hold the cup steady. Helen would make an irritated noise now, but Katy laughs.

"Bit too big for your hands, isn't it?" she says, and makes me feel delicate rather than clumsy. "Let me get you something."

She pushes the lump of Plasticine into the spill and goes off. Brown seeps into the white like a sugar cube held on the surface of a cup of tea. Katy comes back with a tiny cup.

"It's for espresso, really," she says. "But we can just decant a bit at a time."

She pours some coffee into the little cup and hands it to me, grinning. I sip the warm liquid, feeling like a giant in a fairy tale. I can't help smiling at her. When I've finished my cup she refills it. I wish I could remember why we're here.

"We'll go in a bit," she says. "You'd better go to the loo, hadn't you?"

I get up to do as she says. The Ladies' door has a wooden cutout of a girl on it. Inside, there's an old woman, hunched into a cardigan. I step aside to let her pass, but she steps aside too. I step back; so does she. I walk closer. It's me in a mirror. I put a hand up to rub against the glass where my mouth is reflected, leaving a mark which makes it look as though I'm wearing smudged lipstick. I go hot at the sight, feeling embarrassed and uneasy, and I scrub at my mouth with the back of my hand. It's awkward getting the cubicle door closed: I seem to have too many layers on, too much padding. Once I'm inside, though, I have the urge to stay. It's cosy and safe in here, like my mother's larder. And I remember a moment when the children were small, when I'd had enough, I remember I went and stood in the larder and shut the door.

Tom and Helen clattered about, calling for me, whining at each other, but I stayed very still and made no noise. I don't know how long I would have stood there, perhaps not for very long, but Patrick came home unexpectedly and found me. "Hiding from our own children?" he said. He was shocked, but I don't remember him being angry. And years later when he'd been away working for months he remembered my hiding place and pulled me into the larder for a kiss while the children were occupied with the gifts he'd brought home. But the two of us together were too noisy, laughing and knocking against the rows of jars, so the kids knew we were there and made yuck noises and told us we were too old to kiss each other.

"Grandma?" A familiar voice comes through the gap between the door and floor. "Are you all right?"

I pull my layers straight and struggle out. It's a girl. She looks like Helen, but younger, with blondish curls and a "piercing" in her lip. She smiles and I feel as though it's a question.

"Shall we go?" she says. "Are you feeling up to it? Bus stop's only across the road."

A jacket is held up for me. It's not mine, but I let her tuck it round my shoulders anyway, not liking to say anything. I hope the owner doesn't mind me wearing it. Through the door is a coffee shop. I don't recognize it, but this young Helen leads the way. She walks ahead, and puts a hand out behind her all the time to make sure I can keep up. I follow her to a bus shelter.

"Do you know," I ask, when I've caught my breath, "where is the best place to plant marrows?"

There's a grin and a shrug. "I don't know, you'd have to ask Mum. Though probably you shouldn't. That question winds her up like crazy. It's almost better than asking where Elizabeth is." She gives a squeal of delight at the thought and helps me to sit down for a moment. We don't have to wait long for the bus, and Helen, or whoever she is, finds my pass quite easily in my bag.

"Where are you taking me?" I say. I say it several times, but I can't catch the answers. I hope we're going somewhere with a kettle. This trip has really taken it out of me. I can't wait for a cup of tea. We get off the

274

bus and walk a few streets. There is rubbish all down the middle of the road. Mostly newspapers. I suppose the bin men have been this morning. Helen leads me up the side of a house. It's a new house, newly built. I don't like it. I never liked new houses. You don't know what's buried beneath them. Elizabeth has a new house; I never liked that either.

"Helen, this isn't right," I say. "This isn't my house."

"I'm Katy, Grandma," she says. "And you live with us now. Remember? You moved in with us."

I look back along the road. The rubbish on the street swells round the lamp post. And suddenly I remember what I was going to do.

"Oh, Helen, I have to go to town," I say, turning. "I have to go to that office."

"What office, Grandma? You can't. We're home now."

"I have to go to the *Echo*'s offices," I say.

"Why? You going to be a papergirl?"

I can't smile, it's too important that I don't forget. "No," I say. "I have to put one of those things in the paper. A thing. For Elizabeth." I can't think of the word. "To say I'm looking for her."

"What?" Helen says, walking beside me. "Like an advert?"

I'm not sure if that's what I mean, but I nod anyway.

"I don't think that's a good idea," she says. "I don't think Mum would like it."

"Aren't I your mum?" I say.

"No, you're my grandma. I'm Katy. Katy, your granddaughter."

I stop and look at her face. Yes, I know her. Of course I do. But apart from that piercing in her lip she really could be Helen, years ago, with her blondish curls. Except she looks happier somehow. My daughter must be a good mother, I think. Better, anyway, than I was. We walk back to the new new house. There are seeds scattered over the pavement; the head of a sunflower has been pulled off and is lying on a wall. Katy gets out a key.

"This isn't right," I say to her, pointing. "This isn't my house."

Katy squeezes my hand in hers. "Come in for a bit anyway, Grandma," she says. "Mum said she'd get some coffee cake."

"I don't like that."

"Well, what about a banana sandwich then? You liked that yesterday."

"Oh, yes," I say. Banana sandwiches were a real treat when I was a girl and I even used to ask for them instead of dinner. I remember I was hoping to have a banana sandwich for dinner the day I met Nancy from the Station Hotel again.

I was in the queue for the greengrocer's. It was a long queue and there was a line of prams parked outside, each with a little head rising up from time to time to squawk for its mother. The pile of bananas just inside the window was what everyone was queuing for; it was huge and looked like it would last to my turn, but I tried not to think too hard about them in case that caused them to disappear. I leant against the brick wall of the shop and made faces at the babies in their prams, the smell of sun-warmed fruit washing about me like bath water.

Ma had sent me out with the ration books as she and Dad were spending the day talking to the police and following up any leads for Sukey. Sergeant Needham had suggested they retrace her steps from home to the hotel, from the hotel to our house and from our house to hers, looking out for anywhere she might have been "lost". I had a fairly good idea that the sergeant was just suggesting things to keep them occupied, but I hadn't said anything to Ma. She'd seemed more hopeful than she'd been for months and I hadn't the heart to tell her I'd already followed those routes myself, again and again, looking for answers.

Instead I'd set myself the task of getting the ingredients for a really good dinner, but I hadn't had much success with the shopping so far. Someone had told me there was haddock at the fishmonger's and I'd rushed off to see if I could get hold of some, but by the time I reached the front of the queue there was only cod left. So all I had so far was a tin of Heinz tomato soup. If I could get us a banana each, though, that would be a bit of a triumph.

I was still six or seven places from the front when Nancy tapped me on the shoulder.

"Hello. It's you," she said. "I thought I recognized you. Feeling better now?"

I said I was.

"And any news about your sister?"

"None."

She nodded. "Sorry about that." She shifted her shopping bag from hand to hand, puffing her flat cheeks out. "What are you after? I'm for the bananas if they hold out. My husband loves them."

"Was it you who signed Sukey's name on the register?" I asked.

"Oh. At the hotel, you mean? Yes, that's right."

"Why?"

"Frank asked me."

"But couldn't Sukey have signed it?"

"She was outside in the van. He wanted to pay and get the key and everything first so he could take her straight up to a room. She was in a bit of a state, he said. Poor love, so was he. Worried for her, I expect. That wretched mad woman had got into their house again. Not that I'm one to talk — my husband's got his own problems."

"So you did see her? Sukey, I mean. I thought you told the police you hadn't?"

"Er . . ."

"You saw Frank take her to her room?" I stared up at the pout of the woman's lips, hoping for even the meagrest description of Sukey. The idea of her living, still in our town, our world, dressed in her own clothes and fresh from dinner at our house, made me feel weightless for a moment.

"No. That's right," the woman said, causing a crashing sensation inside me. "I had to cover one of the telephonists, so I missed them going up. He was going to sneak your sister in as soon as he had the key, to make sure that mad woman didn't see where she'd

278

gone. Seemed a bit over the top to me, but I s'pose once you've had a fright like that you want to make sure you don't have another."

"So you never saw them go up?"

"Well, I saw Frank come back down — I was back on reception again by that time. Poor Frank, he really was in a state, so worried for his wife. I said, 'Why don't you stay with her?' But he couldn't, something he had to do that night in London. I didn't ask too much about it, because, well, he's a charmer that one, and wouldn't hurt a fly, but you don't get to sell razors that cheap without knowing a few of the wrong sort of people. My husband has to be clean-shaven, you see, he can't bear even a day's growth on his chin. I think it must remind him of the camp. He was a prisoner of war, near Singapore. You knew that, did you? Anyway, I offered to look in on her, but Frank said she'd gone straight to bed. And the bed certainly looked as though it had been slept in next day, covers rumpled about and that."

CHAPTER
SIXTEEN

The inside of this drawer smells of old putty rubbers and is stained and marked, but the things it contains are clean and new: unopened rolls of Polo mints, boxes of tissues, sheets of paracetamol. A few pictures of a family, smiling, in various places in Germany, have been clipped together; they must be cuttings from a magazine, though I can't think why I'd want them. And there is a packet of lamp posts, tiny lamp posts with lead through the middle. The right word for them is gone and I pick one up, trying to remember it, pressing the end into the wood of the drawer until the tip breaks off. It's satisfying and I pick up another just to break it.

The doorbell rings. I drop the pencil and bang into a bookcase in my hurry to leave the room. There are two dirty cups on a shelf. I collect them, and in the hall realize one has some tea in it. I drink it up, though it's cold, and then put both cups on the bottom stair. I stumble back. The staircase is at the wrong angle. It doesn't point at the door any more. I try a couple of steps. They're solid enough. The doorbell rings. Twice. Three times. It's a harsh ring, not at all tuneful. I open the door and a man bursts through.

"You really have gone too far," he says.

He's waving something, shaking it at me, but it moves too fast and I can't see what it is. I back away, finding myself against the banisters. I can't work out how they can be here. They're in the wrong place.

"I mean. A bloody advert. It's the fucking limit."

"The limit," I say, looking at the stairs. They've shifted and I can't understand it.

"Yes, exactly. Hey, are you listening?"

"Do you know how the stairs moved like this?" I say.

The man is in the middle of taking a deep breath. He stops. "What?"

He's familiar, but I don't know him, and anyway I can't think about him at the moment. "The stairs," I say. "They've moved. They face the wrong way. How could that happen, d'you think? Has there been an earthquake or something?"

"What are you going on about?" He is very tall, this boy. But stooped, like Douglas.

"The steps," I say. "Douglas. Douglas must have moved them." I can't think what I was going to say. My thoughts have got tangled somehow.

"Who's Douglas?"

"Our lodger."

The man seems to crouch, very slightly. "Upstairs, is he?" He puts a hand on the newel post and the banisters shake a little under his weight as he leans to peer up at the landing.

"Upstairs?" I say, following his gaze. "Who's upstairs?" I look to the man, feeling a sudden shiver. I wonder who could be up there. Not only that, but the banisters are in the wrong place. They're in the wrong place and I'm frightened. I study the man's throat above his shirt collar; it is raw from shaving. This is Peter. This is Elizabeth's son. I feel my stomach fill with anger.

"Was it you?" I say. "Was it you who moved the stairs?" That must be the explanation. "It's exactly the kind of spiteful thing you would do."

"Eh?" He rubs the back of his neck, frowns.

There is silence for a second. I hear a rook cawing, cawing in the distance. I am making fists of my hands. "Must have been money in it for you."

Peter glances up at the landing again. "I haven't moved your fucking stairs," he hisses.

"How do you explain it then?"

"I don't know, that's how they were built."

"Oh, ridiculous. What a thing to say. That sort of lie might work on your mother, but it doesn't wash with me."

"Shut up about my mother!" Peter shouts, raising both hands.

The front door opens behind him. It's Helen. Helen with the heavy, honeyish smell of wisteria, and the rumble of traffic and the rustle of the orange plastic bags in her hands. These are the ones that make her grimace and feel guilty, the ones she screws up into egg-shaped balls and hides in drawers.

"What's going on?" she says.

"This man has moved my staircase, Helen," I say. "I think I know why he's done it, but I don't know how. Make him tell me how he did it."

Peter turns to Helen. "Your mother has put an advert in the paper asking people to contact her if they've seen my mum."

He thrusts a folded newspaper at her and Helen lifts the bags to show her hands are full. Katy slips through the door behind her, picking up some cups from a step. She goes into the kitchen and I wonder if she will make me some toast, but a moment later she's back for the bags, untangling them from her mother's fingers.

"Better hide these, huh, Mum? Don't want anyone to know you use *plastic bags*." The last two words are said in a whisper, and I wonder if Helen hasn't heard. She doesn't react anyway, only looks at Peter.

"An advert?" she says.

"It's one thing calling me or leaving notes at the house. But this."

Helen finally takes the newspaper; she glances at the folded page and then waves it at me. I try to catch it, but she isn't looking and it misses my hand.

"I'm sorry," she says. "I don't know when — how — she could have put it in."

Peter shakes his head. I start to do the same. He shakes his head as he walks out of the house, and Helen darts after him, footsteps crunching across the gravel. Her voice is raised, but I can't make out the words. A car starts up and drives off.

"Well, that was a nice welcome home," Helen says, coming back in. She opens the newspaper she's carrying. "Here it is. 'Looking for Elizabeth Markham. If you have any information please call —'. Oh God.

It's the old house number. I didn't know you'd placed this."

"No. Wasn't me," I say.

"What made you think of doing that?" she says. "Putting an ad in the paper, I mean."

I peer up at the landing. "'Women. Contact your husbands,'" I say.

Helen hands me the newspaper and goes to put the kettle on.

"Contact your husbands." I kept that article. And I gathered any stories I could find about people leaving home. Adverts, too, men asking their wives to come back or write to them, parents hoping for news from missing sons. There weren't really that many — the reporter had obviously overestimated for effect — but each one I found seemed to catch at me like a parachute line, my hopes winging their way into the air. I knew, of course, that even if a hundred men and women had left without a word it didn't mean Sukey had. But it was better than the other possibility, that the murderer who had hurt those other two women had hurt Sukey too. It meant there was a chance, that one day we might find her again. I tried asking Ma which fishmonger's Sukey went to, but it only made her cry, and Dad was cross.

I wanted to find out what Douglas thought — after all, he always read every bit of the paper — but I was beginning to be frightened of him. I couldn't rid myself of the image of his face, looming and angry, as he'd smeared the lipstick across my cheeks and chin, and

284

though I'd spent days putting cold cream on just to wipe it off again I still felt as if a waxy stain lingered. I started to watch him in the house, thinking about how he hadn't seemed to grieve for his mother and how he had stared at Sukey and how that neighbour had said he was at Sukey's house all the time. And I remembered the policeman saying he recognized him, and the food going missing, and the umbrella in his room that was just like the mad woman's. And his saying he was going to the pictures and then never seeming to have seen any films. If he caught me watching he'd scowl and I would think about the film villains he looked like, but sometimes he would duck his head in that old shy way and I would think: It's only Doug, and feel sorry for suspecting him of anything at all.

With no one to talk to I was left to follow the meagre advice I found in the newspaper cuttings. I looked to see if there were any clues to where Sukey might have gone amongst the clothes that Frank had given me, or in the suitcase the police had returned. One man in an article had left a brochure for Torquay in a drawer and they'd found him that way. I remembered Douglas running his hands round the lining of the suitcase, and did the same, but I didn't find anything.

Eventually I showed the collection of cuttings to Frank when he took me back to the Fiveways. I was drinking my ginger ale, not very happy about being in a pub with him again. It was quieter, though, what with the shortage of beer, and smelled of damp rather than tobacco smoke, and Frank seemed to know fewer people now. When I showed him the papers I had a vague idea he might cry, but he didn't.

"So," he said. "You think she's left me, is that it?"

"Well, wouldn't that be better than the alternative? What happened to that woman at the Grosvenor Hotel?"

"P'raps."

He was staring into his beer glass, where there was only an inch of liquid left. I looked at the deep lines on his forehead, shadowed under the pub lights, and at the way his hands turned the glass, and I waited for him to finish the drink.

"You'd prefer her to be dead?" I asked, but I couldn't believe he'd really want that, and I didn't like saying "dead".

His hands didn't stop moving, the glass smoothing the skin of his fingers to whiteness, and when he looked at me it was with tired eyes.

He sighed. "No," he said. "No, of course I wouldn't prefer that. He's a maniac, that man: did you read the stories through? There's killing, that's one thing, and there's what he did, and that's another." Frank raised his hands, the last of the beer slopping about in the glass. "I mean, accidents happen, they happen and there's nothing you can do, no way of undoing them. But what he did was no accident."

I agreed the man was a maniac, and that his killings hadn't been accidental, and I asked Frank again if he thought Sukey might just have gone off somewhere, but he refused to discuss it any more. He just wanted me to remember Sukey's story, to tell him again how they first met.

"And then she said: 'That's the man I'm going to marry,' " I repeated, hardly having to remember at all, and watching the beer glass turning and feeling the newspaper twisted up in my hand. "'I just know it. He's the man for me.' "

When Frank walked me home that night, handing me a parcel of ham for Ma and standing again at the corner to watch me go in, I saw Mrs Winners hovering at her window. She was talking on the telephone as I went past her hedge, and she ran out after me.

"That mad woman's been prowling about again," she said, looking along the street. "I've called the constabulary, but I'd get inside quick-like, Maud."

She noticed Frank, but you couldn't see his face where he stood, in front of the street lamp, his hat pulled forward.

"You courting already?" she said. "Why doesn't he walk you home properly? Dad don't like him?" She chuckled and pushed me on towards home. "Go on. Get inside. God knows what that woman is capable of."

Frank was still at the corner when I looked back. I could see the lit end of his cigarette. So could Douglas.

"Been with him again," he said, giving me a fright. He was standing in our dark front garden, looking out on the road.

"What are you doing there?" I said, annoyed.

"Your mum asked me to look out for you. The — er — that woman has been here."

"Mrs Winners said. I suppose you're waiting to hand over our food."

He nodded, not seeming to have heard me, and stayed standing in the front garden, staring down the street to the park. "Have you seen those new houses?" he asked, though he didn't turn to me, and I wondered if it wasn't a question for himself. "The ground was churned up for months, soil upon soil upon soil. And now it's flat and smooth as anything. You'd never know what was under there."

I moved closer to Douglas, expecting the smell of liquorice to breathe up from the earth, suddenly too frightened to cross the wet, shadowed garden alone, and I stared hard into the dark, trying to see what he saw. But I knew he meant the houses across the park and there was no hope of seeing them from here, even during the day. I tried to remember what the new houses looked like, but all I could think of was the shell of Douglas's old house with its pictures and ornaments arranged in the exposed room, as if someone might walk back in at any minute.

"People could live somewhere for a hundred years and never know what was beneath their feet," he said. There was a rustle in the hedge and although it was probably just a hedgehog or something we both started. "You'd better go in," he said.

I went round into the kitchen. Ma and Dad were clearing things away.

"Your dinner's on the stove," Ma said, not looking at me. I'd told her it was Frank I was seeing that evening, and she'd kept it from Dad. She'd also asked if Frank could get any soap or matches, because there were none in the shops. I held the package of ham up when Dad's back was turned and her face brightened for a moment before the tired lines fell back into place.

I ate my mutton soup, expecting Douglas to come in any minute, but when I went upstairs he must still have been in the garden. I waited at my window to see him go in the kitchen door, listening to the occasional thuds of ripe apples falling from the tree, and it was nearly midnight when I finally caught sight of him, a black figure against the dark night. By then I'd finished writing to the murderer, Kenneth Lloyd Holmes.

"You smell funny," I tell Helen as she bends to put down my tea.

"Smell funny how?" She is indignant, though I've hardly insulted her.

"It's a sweet smell," I say. "I'll know it in a minute." It's sweet but it's not pleasant. It gives me a headache and it makes me think of the mad woman; it makes me rub at my shoulder as if I've had a whack from an umbrella.

"Is it the tea?" Helen says, holding her own cup under my nose. "It's fennel."

"Ugh, yes, that's it. How horrid. You haven't given that to me, have you?"

"No, Mum." She takes a sip from her mug and then grins. "I'd forgotten how much you hate the smell. You never used to let Tom and me buy Liquorice Allsorts when we were kids." She pauses a moment as if this is a fond memory, though I remember her whining about it

289

for hours when she was a child. "What are you writing?" she asks.

I look down at the paper under my hands. There are just scribbles. Lots of black scribbles on white. I can't read them. Helen says something about Peter.

"Talk about overreacting. What does he think you're going to do?" She pulls out a chair, scraping it along the floor, obscuring her last sentence.

I'm staring at a paper full of scribbles, meaningless scribbles. Except I have a feeling that some of them might be words and I just can't read them. I want to ask Helen, but I'm embarrassed, frightened. When I look she is biting the inside of her cheek, staring at me. I wonder if she has guessed about the scribble-words.

"Don't worry," I say. "I'll ask Elizabeth." This seems the right thing to say. I smile at Helen for a minute, but there is something not right. I try to remember what it is. An idea keeps slipping away from me. "I can ask her, can't I?" I look through my notes, but I don't even have to read them. I know already. Elizabeth is missing.

I drop my pen and fold the scribble sheet up, putting it in my pocket. Helen takes my hand. She's being nice, "making an effort". I should too. I wonder what I can say. "You look nice, dear."

She makes a face.

"I am glad to have a daughter like you."

She pats my hand and starts to get up.

"Can we go to see Patrick's grave?" I ask. "I'd like to put some flowers on it."

That's done it. She smiles, widely, sitting again. She has dimples, my daughter. Still there, buried in her cheeks at fifty. I'd forgotten. It's as if they were hiding and have finally broken out.

"We can go now," she says.

And we get our coats on and get in the car. It's all done in a whirl. We stop at some point, and Helen gets out. I hear the doors lock around me, see her mouth something through the glass and run off. The street isn't busy, but the odd person walks past. I don't recognize them, though. I don't think I recognize them. A woman with long, dark hair turns the corner and comes towards me. She peers into the car as she goes by and stops, tapping on the window, pointing at me and then at the car door. She smiles and nods and says something I can't quite hear through the glass. I pull at the handle, but the door won't open, and I shake my head. The woman shrugs, waves, blows a kiss and walks away. I wonder who she was. What she wanted.

Helen gets in suddenly, bringing a warm petrol smell with her.

"Was that Carla?" she says. "Just now?"

"No," I say. "I don't . . . Who did you say it was?"

"Carla."

It's not a name I know. Helen passes me a bunch of flowers and starts the car. "Are these for . . . that woman?" I ask. "Who did you say?"

"No, they're for Dad."

We pull out on to the road and I settle back, the flowers dusting me with water. I like being in the car. It's comfortable and you don't have to do anything. You can just sit. "Is he in hospital?"

"Who?"

"Your dad."

We stop at a light and Helen looks at me. "Mum, we're going to see Dad's grave."

"Oh, yes," I say, and laugh. Helen frowns. "Oh, yes," I say again.

The cemetery is huge, but it doesn't take her long to find the grave. She must come more often than I'd realized. We stand in front of the stone. Reading it. Silently, because Helen doesn't want me to read it aloud. We stand for a long time. I start to get tired. And it's boring, waiting here. Helen has her head down, her hands clasped as if she's praying. She doesn't even believe in God. There's a mound of earth not far from where we stand: someone's going to be put into the soil — what do you call that? Planted, someone's going to be planted. I stare at the earth for a long time. "Helen," I say, "how do you grow marrows?"

She doesn't move, but murmurs her response. "You never stop asking that question," she says.

I can't remember if that's true, though I don't know why she'd lie about it, and I move away to think, drifting towards a great yew tree. There's something frightening about its size and the way the dark branches block all the light from the ground. The grave here has a flat stone and the name has weathered badly. Only the date of death and R.I.P. are still readable. "That was the mad woman," I say, as Helen catches up with me. "Her name was Violet, but everyone called her the mad woman."

"How sad," Helen says, standing with her head bowed again.

292

I think she's overdoing the respectful pose. I screw my heel into the turf. "She chased me once," I say. "She chased me and stole my sister's comb. She ripped it from my hair." As I speak I can feel the strands break, the pain as they tear from my scalp, but it doesn't seem real, I've got the memory wrong somehow. "She watches me," I say. "She knows all about me."

"Who does?"

"Her." My hands are in my pockets, so I point at the gravestone with my elbow. I want to kick the stone. I want to stamp on the earth beneath it. "She's always there, always bloody watching."

Helen's head is no longer bowed. "She's dead, Mum," she says. "How can she be watching you?"

I don't know. I can't think. I pull my hands out of my pockets, looking for a note. There's a folded piece of paper with black writing on it and I scrunch it into a ball. I want to shove it into the earth, push it in where the mad woman's mouth is. But Helen takes my hand and lifts it, crushing the paper between her hand and mine. And in the little gap between our thumbs, I can just read the name Kenneth Lloyd Holmes.

He was the man arrested for the Grosvenor Hotel murder, the man I sent a letter to, asking if he'd killed my sister. I still hoped that Sukey had run away, but news of the murders was everywhere — even on the wireless. I said in the letter that I wouldn't tell anyone, but that I had to know if he'd killed her. I described Sukey, her hair, the way she dressed, and told him which town we lived in. I thought if he didn't write back it might mean she really was still alive. And if he said he'd done it, well, at least we'd know what had happened. I couldn't think what to sign after "Yours sincerely"; I had a horror of putting my own name. In the end I put Miss Lockwood and asked the grocer at the top of the road to accept a letter for me addressed to that name. It was Reg's mother ran the shop then. I remember her raising her eyebrows and laughing.

"Waiting for a biyay-doo, eh?" she said. "Miss Lockwood. Vanity of vanities." She smiled and tutted and I blushed and sweated under my coat. I was horribly embarrassed, knowing she would tell Mrs Winners, at least. But she agreed to accept the letter and keep it for me, and that was all that mattered. I tucked the newspaper cuttings away in a drawer and waited. I never got a reply, but I told Frank I'd written the letter when I met him in the Pleasure Gardens one afternoon.

"Have you gone mad?" he said, hardly waiting to let out his lungful of cigarette smoke. "Writing to a nutcase like that? What made you think he's got anything to do with Sukey?"

He stalked about in front of the bench I was sitting on, drawing violently on his cigarette so that the paper burnt down quick and bright. He'd arrived with packages of soap for Ma and chocolate for me — Cadbury's Dairy Milk, which wasn't anywhere in the shops. I bit a piece off, though I'd promised myself I wouldn't eat it till I got home. It was so overwhelmingly creamy and sweet that I forgot for a moment we were arguing, and grinned up at him.

294

"And if he says he hasn't done it, what does that prove?" he said, thankfully ignoring my grin.

I wrapped the rest of the chocolate up and put it in my pocket. "If he didn't do it, then it proves she might still be alive."

"No, Maud, it proves nothing."

He flicked his cigarette into the river and shook another from its packet, all the time staring down at me. I had to stop my hand from straying to the pocket with the Dairy Milk in it.

"What exactly did you write?" he asked, once the new cigarette was lit.

I told him, trying to remember word for word, but he kept interrupting, repeating my phrases and coughing out smoke.

"'She has the same look as the other girls you killed'? Bloody hell."

I sucked my lips in at my own words. "It's true, she does."

"Why?" he shouted, and an old couple looked over from another bench. "Why are you doing this? You bloody little idiot. He wasn't even here long enough to have met her. You'll probably just end up as his next victim."

I shrugged and turned away. The man had been caught and would be hanged, so that seemed unlikely. Frank swore under his breath and made off down the path. For a moment I thought he'd left me for good, but he wheeled round before he got to the old couple and swung his hand up to tear the cigarette from his lips. It was a strangely airless day, like being indoors,

295

and the smoke hung between us almost still, though I could hear the wind in the pines far above our heads.

"Where did you use to take Sukey dancing?" I asked, wishing I hadn't told him about the letter, wanting to make up, wanting to get back on to old ground.

"The Pavilion. Why? You going to tell that lunatic you've got a thing for?"

I flinched at his tone and he let out a long breath, flicking his second cigarette away and coming to stand in front of me. I'd given in and unwrapped the chocolate bar again and when he leant down to take my hands in his, it began to melt between us.

"We always went to the Pavilion," he said. "And she even used to make me dance before the interval. I'd never done that before. One thing I remember that you don't, eh?" He shook my hands lightly, and one side of his mouth curled up in a smile.

I smiled back, like always. "I remember now," I said. "Perhaps I'll go there to look, then."

He let go of me, and the chocolate bar landed on my lap, a little lick of it blotting my skirt.

"Why can't you leave it alone?" he said.

And I thought he meant the chocolate, and answered: "You brought it for me," before I realized he was talking about my search for Sukey.

But I couldn't leave it alone, and I wore Sukey's green scalloped dress to the Saturday-night dance at the Pavilion Ballrooms. There was a chance, I thought, if Sukey was still in the town — even if she didn't want to contact us, didn't want to know us — there was a chance that she wouldn't be able to resist going out dancing. It was as good a bet as anything. And I thought I would just go there to watch and see who turned up, making sure she wouldn't spot me by curling my hair into a new style and bringing a copy of Ma's *Britannia and Eve* magazine to hold in front of my face.

The Pavilion Ballrooms had a large foyer with red velvet benches and palms in big china pots. There were wicker chairs dotted around the pillars, but they seemed more conspicuous than the benches. Anyway, when I arrived, all the free ones faced away from the door, so I wouldn't have been able to watch who was coming in. I sat on a bench in the corner and held the magazine up. The dance was due to start in the main ballroom and occasionally people came into the foyer to sit and wait, chatting to each other, laughing, or jiggling their legs in anticipation. The air began to fill with a mix of perfume, shoe polish and mothballs from all the dresses left in wardrobes during the week. I'd got there early so I could watch for Sukey and had a quarter of an hour until the orchestra started. I half read an advert for Dr Williams' Pink Pills and half watched the door. My heart was beating hard and each beat seemed to send the blood straight to my arms so that it was difficult to keep the magazine steady.

At one point a man came in and paused on the threshold, scanning the room. He was tall and had a blond moustache, and his clothes looked as though they belonged to a fatter man. I sat up a little, watching him as a neat woman in a violet dress came out of the ballroom and called his name. Her voice seemed

297

familiar and her hair was a soft, dark colour. I hardly dared look at her, breath pooling in the top of my lungs. The man waited till she was near and then put an arm round her shoulders, and the woman helped him across the foyer to a wicker chair. He limped badly and I thought he must have damaged his leg in the war. As they came closer I could see the woman was plump, and more motherly than Sukey, and though she was light on her feet she wasn't as elegant. I was numb to the disappointment for nearly a minute, before it began to pinch, like a stitch in my side.

I pretended to myself that it was hunger and searched for the last of the chocolate Frank had given me, but I must have left it next to my bed or in the pocket of my school coat, because I couldn't find it. It was nearly six and the light from outside was very yellow. The colour was reflected on to everyone's clothes and hair by great mirrors fixed to the walls. The corners still had bits of brown paper stuck to them where they had been covered to protect them from air raids. I was sitting near the bottom-left corner of one mirror and, feeling desolate, I turned and raised a hand to pick at the brown paper. It was satisfying, tearing it from the smoothness of the glass, and I'd removed about an inch of it when someone came up behind me.

"Sukey?" a voice said, and I turned.

It was Douglas. He closed his eyes when he saw it was me. His mouth opened and his chin jutted out.

"Maud," he said. "I should've known."

He dropped on to the bench next to me, stretching his legs out, and the limping man in the wicker chair glanced across at him. I waited for Douglas to say something, but he just stared at his feet.

"Why are you here?" I asked finally. "Did the mad woman tell you to come?"

"I come every night there's dancing," he said. "In the hope —"

"Yes," I said, not wanting him to finish the sentence. "You come here instead of going to the pictures. In the hope."

"That's why you're here too."

I nodded.

"Wearing her clothes. Sure you're not meeting Frank?"

"Oh, for God's sake, Doug," I said. "It's not for Frank. And even if it were, what business is it of yours?"

He gave me a brief, bitter glare and I huffed and tutted, repeating my sentence, muttering it to myself, trying to be angry with him. "How long will you go on coming here?" I asked.

"As long as I can bear it."

We faced away from each other towards the sudden bustle of the foyer. The dance was starting and people were heading in.

"I don't know where else to look," he said. "I don't know what else to look for."

I nodded, studying the side of his face. I really loved him then. Loved him for carrying on, for caring enough to carry on when Frank had given up.

"Doug," I said, needing to know one more thing. "You and Sukey."

"She was kind to me, that was all," he said, gazing intently at the departing dancers. "Gave me somewhere to go, someone to talk to."

I wanted to ask what it was they talked about, but I didn't know how to without it sounding like a challenge. I always seemed to worry at Douglas, taunting and nit-picking, though it was never what I meant to do, and I didn't want to risk saying the wrong thing now. I also couldn't help feeling left out and resentful, despite it being far too late for that. Douglas looked blankly at the backs of jackets and cocktail dresses and I watched the way the colour came and went in his cheek and the way his soft hair ruffled in the draught from the door. And I smiled at him, though he didn't see it.

I meant to go back with him the next Saturday, but when I suggested it he didn't seem keen and I missed him leaving, or I was out, or busy. I tried the next week, after I'd been to my friend Audrey's for tea — Ma and Dad had gone up to London again to try to talk to someone about Sukey's case — but Audrey had pinched a bottle of gin from her father and insisted we drink it, despite us both hating the taste. By the time I arrived at the ballrooms the dancing was finished and Douglas was long gone.

The sky darkened as I walked home. It had been raining and the pavements by the new houses were shiny, and snails were making suicide dashes from every neat front garden. The smell of creosote was in the air, curling off the freshly constructed fences. Soon I couldn't see the ground in front of me and I was stiff

300

with the fright of crushing a shell. I could already feel the way it would collapse under my shoe, hear the crunch.

When I was younger I would have edged forward slowly, picking up each snail and carrying it to the safety of a garden, or at least to an opposing shrub, but I'd grown out of that, I suppose, and so I just watched for the glint of syrupy flesh as I walked, and followed the silver stream of their tracks, trying not to commit my feet to any area of ground. I'd made it halfway down the road when I heard the first hollow grind against the pavement. But I hardly had time to curse, barely a moment for that sick feeling — a mixture of sorrow and disgust — to envelop me, because in the same instant I saw the mad woman.

She was the other side of a car, the only one parked on the street, standing in the wet road and peering through two windows' worth of glass. Her fingers curled uselessly against it, her scratching unable to find purchase. It was the light from a house, switched on suddenly, that had exposed her, sending her shadow slipping towards me. A man had come out into his front garden and was shouting, and people had started to collect around him. He stood by his garden wall, running his hands over the top of it, where he, or someone, had cemented on a lot of coloured pebbles. Neighbours had come to hear him, and he shouted all the louder, but I could hardly concentrate on his words because of the mad woman, who was tapping on the car's window.

She seemed to shiver in the light, her white hair fluttering like a moth. We stared at each other through the glass and I wondered how long she'd been there, whether she had followed me along the road or had been waiting here, hiding. I wondered what her plan was, whether she had a plan. I felt paralysed, my foot still suckered to the pavement by the snail carcass, and I thought for a moment the man was shouting at her, but I was wrong.

Someone had been trying to dig up his vegetable marrows, he said, and they'd nearly got away with it. He was a prize marrow grower and his crop was just swelling to perfect size. He was certain it was sabotage. He'd even seen the back of the digger as they'd run away, and he could swear it was old Mr Murphy, who was his chief rival.

"It was the white hair gave him away. It gleamed in the moonlight," he said, making the gleaming itself sound like a crime. "I could tell his hair anywhere, I could. Bastard."

Some ladies muttered, and he apologized for swearing. A man suggested they go and knock up Mr Murphy and get him to show his hair. There were chuckles and the murmuring of people fast losing interest. In a moment it would be pitch black and quiet again, and yet I still couldn't move. The mad woman's eyes were fixed on me, her fingers tapping out some kind of demented Morse code, but it was the sight of her hair shining that made me shudder. It was she who had been digging in that man's garden, I thought, it was her white hair he'd mistaken for this Mr Murphy's, and I imagined her out there in the dark, fingernails full of dirt, pressing the flesh of the vegetable marrows against her teeth.

There was a call of "Goodnight! Goodnight!" as most of the women went back inside to tend to children and wirelesses and hair curlers, their men following. But a straggler with a kind of winking voice suggested that the culprit was one of these vegetable-marrow addicts and a shout of disproportionate laughter made the mad woman turn, just for an instant. And I ran. Along the street and past the marrow grower, maiming more snails as I went and not even lamenting their injuries, knowing I would find splinters of shell and gluey flesh on the bottom of my shoes the next morning.

CHAPTER
SEVENTEEN

My house is dark when I get there. Ma and Dad are out looking for Sukey. I stand in the front porch trying to find my keys, checking my bag and each of my pockets twice. The keys aren't there. My stomach seems to float into my chest, and my heart beats against it. I breathe carefully in, and turn out my pockets, shaking everything on to the ground. The rattle of the contents hitting concrete is mixed with that old familiar sound of my front door opening. The click of the latch, the heavy creak of the hinge. Someone, who isn't Ma and isn't Dad, is opening the door. It's a man, youngish, small and fair, who stops just inside and stares at me. He seems startled, as if he didn't expect me home. He doesn't look like a burglar. I stare back, disbelieving. I don't think I recognize him, but I don't trust myself. "Douglas?" I say.

"No, I'm Sean," he says, backing into the house. My house. "Stay there," he calls.

But I've no intention of waiting outside while he does God-knows-what inside, and so I follow him into the dark hallway. There's something funny going on: everything's different. The shelf above the radiator's gone and there's a bike propped against the wall. I can't think where I am. There's a smell of vinegar, and the man is on the phone. He smiles at me, showing off, just like Mrs Winners.

"Do you need to sit down?" he says, covering the mouthpiece with his hand.

"They won't be able to hear you like that," I say.

He nods and takes his hand away, says something into the phone and puts it down. "Would you like to come into the kitchen? We've just had fish and chips. Lots of chips left."

A small child slinks up the steps, keeping close to the wall, and studies me from behind her father.

"Poppy," the man says, "this is the lady who used to live here."

"Don't you live here any more, then?" I ask.

The girl squirms into laughter.

"Well, shall we go through?" He walks down the steps, and the girl twists away and runs down before him.

I'm not sure what to do. I can see a light on in the kitchen, but I can't think how to get there. It all seems so familiar, as if it should call up memories, but I can't reach them. There's a layer of other people's lives on top. I look at the front door, still open. It's just like mine — the same glass in the windowpanes — and it makes me think I should be getting home, only I'm stranded on this bit of carpet and there's no way out. I feel in my pockets for notes, but there's nothing there, just a few threads and emptiness. I've no notes at all. The lack makes me feel sick; I'm cut loose and whirling about in the wind. I wring the fabric of my coat, scrunching up and down in panic. And then, inside the ripped lining, I find one small blue square with my writing on it: *Where is Elizabeth?*

"Elizabeth is missing!" I shout. I shout so the part of my brain that forgets will stop forgetting. "Elizabeth is missing!" I shout it again and again. When I look over my shoulder there is a small girl holding on to the banister, half hidden under a mass of those things for winding round your neck. Wool and silk, long and deadly, they hang limply over the newel post, like clever snakes, pretending to be asleep. The girl widens her eyes at me and then shoots up the stairs. I shout in her direction.

And then I feel a hand on my shoulder. The weight of it makes me hunch into the front door.

"Mum?" someone says.

It's Helen. She rushes to put her arms around me, pressing my face against her collarbone. She smells like wet soil. When she stands back she gives me a little shake with one hand. Her phone is in the other.

"Who were you shouting at?" she says. Her eyes run over my face, and the hand on my shoulder squeezes. "Mum, you don't live here any more. You know that, don't you?"

"Elizabeth is missing," I whisper, looking up at the house. It's familiar, but I don't know whose it is. I put a hand to my throat.

"No, Mum, she's not. You know where she is. And you have to accept it. Or you have to let it go, and either way, you have to stop telling people that." She speaks very low and starts to lead me away towards the road.

"Telling people what?" I ask.

"Elizabeth is missing."

"You think so too?"

Her face freezes into a closed-eyed smile. "No, Mum. Never mind. Let's get home, shall we?" She opens a car door and helps me in and then goes back to the house to gather some things that have been strewn over the path. A man bends to help her.

"Thank you so much," I hear her say. "I was only out ten minutes. I thought it would be okay."

He says something I can't catch.

"I know. I know it isn't the first time. She's still adjusting."

I try to make sense of it, but it's impossible. There's such a jumble in my head. My house and strange people and Katy on the stairs and fish and chips for dinner and Sukey gone and Elizabeth gone and Helen. Gone? But, no, Helen's here, getting into the car and driving me off somewhere. I look back the way we've come. "Helen," I say. "I moved house, didn't I? I moved in with you."

"Yes, Mum," she says. "That's right." She reaches a hand out for me, but has to take it back to change gear.

"Well," I say, "at least I've got one thing right today." I watch the road swerve about in front of me with satisfaction, and Helen doesn't stop me reading the signs aloud. I concentrate very hard on them: they are solid and unjumbled and I don't have to understand what they mean, because I'm not driving.

A man wavers ahead of us, thin and fragile-looking. I think at first he's hovering on a single slender leg, but soon I see it is one of those things to move about on: two wheels, handlebars. Not a wheelbarrow. We catch him up and pass very close, and for a moment I think he will be pushed off centre, we'll make him topple, one touch on a spinning top. My insides go tight.

"Helen!" I say. "You nearly knocked him down."

"No, I didn't, Mum."

"You did. You nearly got him. You ought to be careful. People can die from that."

"Yes, I'm aware, but I was nowhere near him."

"That poor woman got knocked down in front of our house. When was that?"

"I don't know. I don't know who you're talking about."

"Yes, you do. She was standing over my bed and then she ran away and you knocked her down so she wouldn't come back."

"I have never knocked anyone down."

"Well, I don't know," I say. "I wasn't in the car at the time." I was in Douglas's room, playing the "Champagne Aria".

I heard the sudden screech of car brakes over the deep laughter of Ezio Pinza, and then my mother's voice, calling. I couldn't make out her words as I banged through Douglas's door and followed the shouts out on to the street, but I soon saw the huddled shape in the middle of the road. It was the mad woman. She lay on the ground, her head bleeding, her arms and legs at

308

funny angles. Ma was kneeling over her, a hand on her cheek. Mrs Winners must have heard the noise, too, as we arrived at the same time. She hurried back inside to use her telephone to call an ambulance and Ma sent me for blankets to cover up the misshapen limbs.

After that I didn't know what to do, so I just knelt by Ma and held the mad woman's hand. Her eyes rolled about and she whispered things I couldn't catch, but she didn't seem so frightening now, crumpled up and tiny on the tarmac. She didn't even have her umbrella. There were bits of plants lying by her sides, things she'd had in her hands when she fell: stripped hawthorn twigs, red nasturtium flowers, brooklime and dandelion leaves, honeysuckle, watercress and lemon balm. They lay scattered about her so she looked like an old Ophelia who'd mistaken the road for a river.

"It's all stuff for eating, look," Mrs Winners said. "Dandelion leaves, nasturtiums. Making herself a salad. Not so daft, after all."

When I began to gather up the leaves and flowers the mad woman made a harsh noise in the back of her throat. Ma bent to hear her words and the woman, with her eyes on my face, found my hand and pushed something against my palm. I took it, unresisting, feeling the thing, small, delicate and crisp, but not looking down at it.

"*Birds?*" Ma said, trying to catch the low words. "What birds? Whose head?"

But she couldn't seem to get any sense from the woman and so we just made soothing noises while Mrs Winners paced about wondering loudly where the ambulance had got to and asking whether we thought she ought to make use of her telephone again.

"How old d'you think she is?" Ma said to me, adjusting the blanket so it lay as lightly as possible over the mad woman's jagged form.

I told her I didn't know. "Does it matter?"

"I don't suppose it does. Only, she's younger than I thought. Might even be my age."

By the time the ambulance arrived the mad woman had stopped whispering, her mouth had stretched open and her cheeks had turned concave. There was a moment when she seemed to come round; her eyes met each of ours in turn and she closed her jaw once as if trying to say one last thing. But then a dark trickle of blood ran from the corner of her mouth and she faded back.

"She died in my arms," Ma said, as the men took away the small figure, still wrapped in one of our blankets.

We, all of us, stared down the road for several minutes, long after there was anything to see, and Mrs Winners was the first to shake herself and rub her hands and glance up at the sky to decide if it looked like rain. Eventually she ushered us into her house for tea.

"Was bound to happen," she said, settling us into her front room. "Always in the road, that one. Jumping in front of buses."

"It wasn't a bus that got her," Ma said. "It was a Morris."

Mrs Winners said she didn't see how that made a difference. She switched on her little electric fire and put a shawl round my mother's shoulders before pouring the tea and I realized Ma was shivering. I asked her what the matter was, but Mrs Winners made a face and waggled her head, and I knew to shut up.

"What you got there?" she said, nodding at my closed fist.

I put down my cup and finally opened the hand that held the mad woman's gift. It was a flower from a marrow plant, dry and faded and falling apart, like an old gramophone horn.

"From the woman, was it? Vegetable-marrow flower by the looks. A real treasure, I don't think. What did she give you that for?"

"You can eat marrow flowers, can't you? Same as nasturtiums. But I think it might be because she dug up some marrows in a man's garden," I said. "He nearly caught her digging them up. I was passing, and she knew I'd seen her." I thought of the man shouting to his neighbours in the dark and running his hands over the pebbles on the wall.

"And that's her confession? Blimey, she *was* barmy. Oh, I don't wish to speak ill of the dead, and she was honest, I suppose, in her own way. I'm fairly partial to a vegetable marrow myself."

"It was Frank who helped plant them," I said to Ma, thinking she might react if that was significant, but she only nodded, cradling the warmth of her cup, but not drinking.

"She said all the little birds were flying round her head," Ma said. "Like one of those cartoon films at the pictures. And then she talked about her daughter. Told me we'd both lost our girls. I s'pose she meant Sukey. I didn't think she knew anything about me; you wouldn't expect her to be aware, somehow. But she kept talking about our girls."

"Sounds like ravings to me," Mrs Winners said.

"No," Ma said. "She knew me."

"It's just for the weekend, Mum. I'm sorry, but I'll be back on Monday morning to take you home. Mum?"

I don't say anything. We're in a small room with plain blinds and pretend flowers in a vase, there's a strong smell of cheap gravy coming from somewhere, and disinfectant. Helen is crouching by the bed I'm sitting on; she says she'll be back, but I know she's lying. I know she's going to leave me here for ever. I've been here weeks and weeks already.

"It's only two nights. And they'll let you do some gardening."

"I don't like gardening," I say, and then am annoyed at myself for answering.

"Yes, you do. You're always asking about planting vegetables, and you certainly seem to enjoy digging things up when we're at home."

I remember not to answer this time. She's lying about this, too, I never liked gardening. I'm not like her, out in all weathers, telling people where they should gouge the earth to put in great ponds, or explaining what kind of soil is best for growing vegetables. Not that she ever thinks to tell *me*. She never thinks *I* might need to know how deep you have to dig to sow marrow seeds, or how far into the ground the roots grow. I resist asking now. Anyway, the room is empty except for me. At some point, Helen must have gone, and now I'm just sitting here. There's a notice up on the wall. WELCOME TO KEEBLE HOUSE. It's an old folks' home, and I can't think why I'm here. I look at my notes and find the home's name is written on a bit of pink paper, along with the address. Keeble Road. I used to have a friend here. She's dead now, and I can't remember her name. It wasn't Elizabeth, though, I know that; it was a different friend.

"Tea in five minutes."

A big, solid young woman ushers me into a corridor with bedrooms all the way along it. I think for a moment of the Station Hotel, but these doors stand open and I can hear television sets droning on as I walk past, and people calling out in low voices. I catch a glimpse of legs stretched out on beds, of slippers and surgical stockings. There is a constant beeping coming from somewhere. We reach a lounge and the smell of gravy recedes. I'm folded into a chair, facing a lot of other similar chairs, which slowly fill up with old people, their clothes and faces creased as if they've just got out of bed. Another TV is on in the corner and the noise of it confuses everything.

"I've been waiting hours and hours," I say to the solid girl.

"What have you been waiting for?" she asks.

"Ages and ages I've been waiting. Over two hours."

"What for?"

But I can't think what for, and the girl sighs, pushing her fringe back with her forearm. She passes me a cup of tea and I watch an old woman on the other side of the room. There is a bright scarf over the old woman's hair and she is very bent over. She can't seem to help dipping her nose into her tea as she drinks. Droplets drip off when she lifts her head, soaking her jumper. When she's finished she puts her head in her hands, taking the weight off her bent back. Someone comes to get her crockery, a man, elegant and smiling with light-brown skin. Spanish, perhaps. I watch him stack cups into a gleaming spine. The sun starts to angle in through the window and he rolls a blind down with a quick movement like a bullfighter shaking out his cloak.

It's getting late and I've been here a long time; all the dancers are heading home, but I can't go home yet. I must wait to see if Sukey turns up. There's a bit of tape on the seat of my chair and I begin to pick at it. "'When will the dancers leave her alone?'" I say, the poem's words clearer than the ones from the television. "'She is weary of dance and play.'"

"What?" a woman with long white hair barks as she comes in, leaning on a Zimmer frame. "Is someone in my seat? Where the hell is it?"

I have a sudden panic that I'm sitting in it, but the Spanish man points to the chair next to me.

"Here it is," he says, dancing to the left and waving at it.

She puts her head down as if she'll charge the chair, but twists at the last moment and lands gracefully.

314

"You're not doing that very nicely," she says, pointing to my fingers picking at the bit of tape.

I can't think of the next line of the poem, so I don't know how to answer. I smile instead, trying to sing the beginning, so at least she'll know I remember the tune.

"She thinks it's funny," the woman says to a man on the next chair. "*I* don't." She rounds on me again. "If you went home and told your mother and father that you were doing that, they wouldn't be very pleased."

"She can't go home to her mother, can she?" the man says, brushing some crumbs off his pullover.

"No, not yet," I say. "I have to wait here until someone comes. A matador with a great cloak. He's got my sister. He's got her under his cloak and he won't let her go until I dance with him." No one seems to be listening and the image of the matador is too vague to hold on to. A dark woman sitting by a vase of cloth flowers waves at me.

"These are fake, you know," she says. "But quite nice anyway."

I look at the flowers and nod.

"Fake," the dark woman says again, rubbing the petals between her fingers. She pulls one of the flowers from the vase and hands it to me. "Quite nice, though."

I take the flower and close my fist around it as she pulls the whole bunch of plastic stems from the vase and thrusts them at me. They hang their heads sadly without the vase's support, and the petals look worn from handling. There are several stems without any heads at all, and they make me think of Douglas, in our

315

kitchen, and the way his stooped back echoed the shape of his shabby bouquet.

The electric light was flickering, and ghostly insects had begun to flatten themselves to the outside of the kitchen window by the time Douglas got back. The range had nearly gone cold and we were drinking the last of the tea. Ma often couldn't sleep and I sometimes stayed with her, doing the crossword in the *Echo* and listening to Dad snoring at the top of the house.

"Your dinner's in the top oven," Ma said as Douglas came through the door. "It might be a bit cold. I'd have done something about it if I'd known you'd be late, but I didn't know."

"Yes, I'm sorry," he said, not sitting down but looking as though he might drop. "I'm sorry, I didn't think. I . . ." He had the flowers in his hand. A bedraggled bunch, wilting in the heat of the kitchen, petals falling with every twitch of his body. "I didn't know what to do," he said, holding them up to us. He swayed on his feet, and Ma waved a hand at me to do something.

"What's happened?" I asked, getting up and pushing my chair into his legs, to make him sit.

"My mother," he said. "She died this afternoon."

I flinched. Ma looked worried, spooked even. We must both have thought he'd gone off his head, lost his memory, something.

"Your mother's already dead, dear," Ma said. "There was a bomb, d'you remember?" She waved her hand again, towards the kettle this time, and I filled it with water and put it on the range, adding fuel.

"No," Douglas said. "No, she survived that. I hadn't known at the time, but she survived. And then, remember you saw her, Maud? She chased you."

"What, you mean the mad —" I stopped myself and rattled the kettle to cover the words I'd nearly said. "But how could she be . . .?"

He ducked his head and set the flowers down. I supposed he had collected them for his mother and I wondered whether to fetch a vase, but it hardly seemed worth it for such a sorry-looking gathering of roadside weeds.

"I thought perhaps you'd have known about Mother already," Douglas said. "Sukey knew. I told her. She was so kind, tried to help, made up parcels of food. I had begun to think everything would turn out all right. I don't know how I could be so dense, but I thought it just might be all right."

"But Douglas, your mother," Ma said. "I don't quite understand."

"She'd always been delicate," he said, his eyes shut against the maddening light. "Ever since my sister died. Dora was run over by a bus, before the war."

We nodded and urged him on because, of course, everybody knew that.

"And then my dad went to France in 1940 and never came home again. That's when she got a lot worse. Used to be out all hours, didn't sleep, didn't eat, not properly anyway. She got into trouble with our neighbours — when we lived on the other side of town.

317

The police were fetched. Several times I had to go and ask for her at the police station."

"That's how Sergeant Needham knew you."

"Did he? Yes, I suppose that's how. Anyway, in the end we had to move. Did a moonlight flit and used my milk cart to shift everything. I'm not proud of that. But at least it meant no one knew us, I thought that was a blessing. I avoided our new neighbours, and kept hold of our ration books so the shopkeepers wouldn't know Mother's name, wouldn't connect her to me. I don't think anyone even knew she lived with me, she kept such odd hours, and she used to sneak about the back gardens rather than use the road. In any case, we'd only moved in a few weeks before those bombs were dropped. I thought she'd gone in the raid. I'm ashamed to say I almost found it a relief, but then it turned out she was living in the wreck of the house. I tried to help her, but she was so difficult. You couldn't make her see sense. She only wanted to stay in the house, bombed as it was, because Dora's dolls and her Woolworth's handbag and her *Rupert* annuals were still inside somewhere."

"Poor woman," Ma said, looking about the kitchen and somehow not letting her eyes rest on anything.

The kettle had started to boil and I poured hot water over some beef-tea granules, sliding the cup towards Douglas. The smell of it clouded the kitchen and made my mouth water.

"We were with her," Ma said. "In the road. Did they tell you?"

318

Douglas sipped his tea in answer, and I took his plate from the oven and set it in front of him. He sat stiffly in his chair, the flickering light giving him a false animation.

Ma turned a knife and fork his way and pushed them across the table. "She didn't seem in pain. Just slipped away."

He nodded and then began to eat, neatly and quickly, not looking at us when he spoke. "When they started to clear the rubble from our house she went and slept in that boarded-up shack on the beach. Then I lost her again, for a while, until I found she'd been hanging about at Frank's, living in the old stables. I think she wanted to be near Sukey. You see, she looked a bit like my sister." He took another sip of the tea. "So do you, Maud."

I wondered whether that was what had made her chase me. "You had her umbrella," I said. "I saw it in your room."

He paused over a curl of onion, perhaps wondering what I'd been doing in there, and I suddenly realized I'd left the "Champagne Aria" on the gramophone and I wondered if he'd notice later.

"I took the umbrella off her," he said. "She . . . She got into your room when you were ill, and I was nervous of what she might do."

"I thought I'd seen her," I said. "But then I thought I'd seen a lot of people."

"She got in here, and she took food too," he said. "I should have told you, but I was ashamed. And she didn't take anything else, anything valuable."

"But the records," I said. "Smashed in the garden. That must have been your mother."

"No, that was me, I'm afraid. I'd put them aside for Sukey and, well, anyway, one night she got into Frank's house — my mother, I mean. I don't know how, or why, but she did, and Frank was out and Sukey got a fright and came running here. It was about ten o'clock and I was coming home from the pictures and I met her in the street. We had a row. She was angry, having been so frightened, and I was angry because she said things about my mother. They weren't meant to be cruel, but I was hurt all the same. And then Sukey went off home, back to Frank, and I went up to my room and smashed the records and, not knowing what to do, put them at the end of the garden, and you discovered the bits before I could move them."

"'Please let us be friends again,' " I said, quoting Sukey's letter aloud without thinking.

"What?"

I shook my head. "Did she tell Frank? About your mother?"

"She wanted to tell him, but I asked her not to," he said. "I didn't want that brute to know. He'd have used it against me."

Douglas carefully finished his last mouthful and I took his plate to the sink, staring at the pale underside of a moth, its body lit up and exposed against the glass.

"What did Sukey say," Ma asked, "that made you so angry?"

"She told me I should send my mother away somewhere, to an institution. But I couldn't do that. It was bad enough the old house being gone, and then my sister's things were buried beneath the rubble of the new house. I couldn't lock Mother away too. All she ever wanted was to go home, to touch the things my sister had touched."

CHAPTER
EIGHTEEN

"I want to go home," I say. But there's no one around and the words dissolve in the empty air, muffled by high, thick shrubs and deep turf and precisely clipped trees. I've got a tiny sort of shovel in my hand and I'd use it to make some noise if I could find anything else hard to bash it against. I don't know where I am. I don't know how I got here. There's a smell of cut grass, but there are no flowers. "Please," I say again. "I want to go home."

Beyond the hedge someone is walking, bobbing along. I try the tiny shovel on the trunk of a tree, but it only makes a faint thud, so it's no surprise whoever it is doesn't hear me. I wonder if I'm supposed to dig my way out, I seem to have been given the tool for it; but how do you start a tunnel? I never paid much attention to all those old films, never thought I'd have to escape from Colditz myself. I walk across the lawn towards the street and stop by the hedge, plucking off leaves and holding them in my hands. I fold them up and rip them into bits and scatter them on the grass. But I'm not going to eat them, no matter what anyone says. A woman crosses the road; she waves and I duck down behind the hedge, landing sorely on my knees.

"Hello, Mum," she says, leaning over, making the hard strands of glossy leaves bow and bristle. "What are you doing down there?"

She has short blonde curls, this woman, and freckles in her wrinkles. I get up slowly from the grass, pushing my arms into the hedge for support. My trousers are covered in little bits of leaf and my hands are stained with green.

"I've come to take you home," she says. "Was it okay?"

I ignore her and peer at the houses opposite. I don't recognize any of them. They are too new, too clean, for my street. There are a lot of builders in shiny jackets on one side and a great mound of that stuff, sharp gritty stuff. It makes me think of the beach and Sukey and bleeding fingernails. It makes me think of before the war when I was seven or eight and Sukey buried me up to my neck. I tried to dig myself out, but I couldn't and the grains got pushed into my fingernails and my wrists were sore and I was so panicked that I worked my way further down into the stuff and it covered my mouth and I was choking.

"I know you're very angry with me," the woman says, "but I'll make it up to you."

"Very angry," I say. "I was so angry I went home and smashed all her records and buried them in the garden." I can feel the anger now and see the records, but somehow the two things don't fit together.

"I thought we could visit Elizabeth."

"Elizabeth," I say. "She's missing." The words are correct, familiar, but I can't think what they mean.

"No, she's not, though, is she?"

The hedge makes another bow at the words and the shimmer of it frightens me. I don't trust this woman and I can't see her below chest height because this plant has grown too tall. I study her face but I can't remember what people look like when they're lying. "You've been feeding her," I say, and I pull a leaf off the plant.

"No, I haven't. She was in hospital, Mum, a stroke unit, remember? Remember we talked about it? Again and again and again." She says the last bit through her teeth. "And we went to visit her, didn't we? When you sprained your thumb. Anyway, she's still at the rehabilitation unit, because she's not swallowing properly, but we can visit her again now, if you like. Do you want to visit her?"

I don't know what this woman's talking about and I can't see her arms or legs. I begin to wonder if she has any. "What do you call this?" I say, holding up the tiny shovel.

"It's a trowel."

"Ah ha! I thought you'd know that," I say. "I've caught you out there, haven't I?"

"Mum? Do you understand? Peter said you can go and see Elizabeth. But remember last time — it might be a shock. Elizabeth doesn't look the way you remember her, does she? She's still the same person, though, and she does want to see you."

The woman smooths a hand over her hair, and I can see one arm now. I keep saying the word "trowel" in my head; I have a feeling it will be important later.

324

"We can go today if you want. I can call Peter. Would you like that? I'm so sorry I had to leave you here, Mum," she says, starting to walk along the hedge. "I want to make it up to you."

I can see all of her once she is standing behind the garden gate; it's made of thin iron bars, and she can't hide behind it. I can see her navy-blue wellingtons and grubby jeans. I can't think why she's here; I can't think of her name. She's like one of those people you mistake for someone else, one of those people you think is the person you want it to be. I always want it to be my daughter now, but it never seems to be her. I used to want it to be Sukey and I saw her everywhere: in the precise movement of a shop girl as she pressed powder to her nose, or the dancing step of an impatient housewife in a grocer's queue. I carried on seeing her in other people long after I was married and settled, and a mother. She was still in the smudge of a face seen from a car.

There is a car now and driving, and a bird flying up from the road, and someone sits on a bench by a shop and a dog is tied to a lamp post. "Helen . . ." I can't think what else I want to say. I pull the seatbelt away from my body and let it snap back. There's something important. "Trowel." That wasn't the thing. Not even close. Images blur together, words, too. The bandstand in the park, the ugly green and yellow house.

"Oh, Mum. Cheer up. I'm taking you to see Elizabeth." She looks at me quickly and then back through the windscreen. "I thought you'd be pleased."

325

Light bounces off a mass of cars and I feel dizzy. And then somehow we're in a long, white corridor and a man is squeaking by. His shoes seem to make a tune from long ago. A song about lilacs. And, as if they are part of the same production, two people carry bunches of flowers past us. "Those for me?" I say, and they laugh as if I've made a joke. We walk along corridors, corridors, each one the same, and I think we must be going round in circles. "Are we lost?" I say. But it seems we aren't. We've arrived. It's a room full of people in bed. "All these people should be made to get up," I say. "Can't be good for them, just lying there."

"Don't be silly," Helen says. "And keep your voice down. They're poorly."

The room is very bright, with white sheets and big lights and railings everywhere like a sort of indoor park. My mind won't focus.

"Mum?" Helen says.

I can only think of one word, and it isn't right, I know it isn't right. "Bandstand," I say. "Bandstand."

Helen walks towards a bed. And there, that tiny little thing with the crumpled face, that's Elizabeth. Her eyes are closed and she looks scrunched up and withered. Has she always looked like that? I stand by the curtain for a few minutes, staring. And then I move closer and pull the curtain round us, closing us in, hiding us. A man is standing over the bed. He has a very raw-looking throat.

"She had a rough night," he says. "But she'll wake up in a bit. Just be quiet."

I sit down quietly. Very quietly. I don't want to disturb her. Elizabeth is here. I smile at her, but she doesn't smile back. She is tucked tight into a huge bed. "Yes, have a rest," I whisper. In a minute we'll have a cup of tea. I might even have some chocolate in my bag. Or perhaps I could make some cheese on toast. You'll need something, Elizabeth. That son of yours keeps you on starvation rations.

"Starvation?" the man says. "Rations?"

And then you can tell me which bird is which, just by looking at their shadows, and I can dig up the broken records from the garden and we can listen to the "Champagne Aria".

"It was digging in the garden that got her in this state," the man says. "Do you hear me?"

He leans over, his raw throat stretched taut. Elizabeth is asleep half sitting up; she lists to one side and her mouth does, too, and it makes me feel as though we're rocking, as if we're on a ship. I hold on to the side of the bed to keep myself steady.

"You were digging, in the garden. Do you remember?"

I imagine my eye as a tiny point on the side of my head, and I turn as far from him as I can. "I don't know," I say. "Where was I?"

"In my mother's garden."

"No, I don't know where that is."

"In Elizabeth's garden," Helen says. "Peter, can I have a word outside?"

"No," I say. "I wouldn't dig there. You never know what's buried under the ground by those new houses. Douglas said there could be anything."

327

"Is that another accusation?"

"No," Helen says. "It's not."

She asks Peter again if they can talk outside and he whips the curtain open and shut, making a sound like a saw. I swish it about myself, trying to create the same effect, until I find the material tugged from my grasp. The room seems small now that it's just me, and the walls don't look quite right; they move with the breeze and I have a feeling of being on a boat. A tissue sticks up from its box like a sail and I pull it out before slowly tearing it to bits, listening to the voices outside. A woman sometimes, a man mostly.

"It was the shock of the fall that caused the stroke," he says. "And I've been asking myself what the bloody hell she thought she was looking for. I know for a fact she found something and didn't tell my mother what it was. If it's anything valuable we want it back. It's ours by right."

A carton of juice sits next to the tissues and a little white plastic comb next to that. I drop the bits of tissue on the floor and start to brush Elizabeth's hair with the comb. Gently, gently. Her hair is all white now, no streaks of grey left, and the comb looks dirty in comparison. It makes me angry: this isn't good enough for Elizabeth, she should have something better. I go through my handbag again and find I have a tortoiseshell comb, but it's curved and curved and for keeping your hair in place, not brushing it.

There's a laugh from beyond the curtain, nasty and sharp. The man again: "But then gardening's in the family, isn't it?" he says. "I suppose ruining people's lawns is some sort of big joke for you lot. And don't think I've been kept in the dark about your sneaking in to see my mother before."

I wonder what it's all about, but I only wonder for a second, because, finally, Elizabeth is opening her eyes. She makes a croaky sound, and I know she's speaking, but I can't understand her. The words are too soft, too wet and runny. Her hands push a little way inside the opposite sleeves, but I can still see the flesh of her wrists. They look unnaturally soft, boneless and puffy and the skin is smooth, as if she has been filled with air. Her lips are cracked, but she pulls them into a smile, she pulls one half into a smile, and tries again to speak. I feel as though I'm failing to catch something precious. The words tumble out and hit the floor and are lost.

None of us went to bed the night the mad woman died; instead we kept a kind of vigil, Ma and Douglas and I, and the insects that plastered themselves against the windows. What we were watching for, waiting for, I don't know. For some sense to come of it all, I suppose.

When the light of dawn worked its way into the air outside I went to stand in the garden and breathe it in. But my limbs were heavy and my eyes stung as I left the house. I walked blindly into the thick bramble hedge as I made my way up the path, and the hiss and sway of it made me jump in fright before I remembered that the mad woman would never again appear between the leaves of any hedge, would never shout or point or raise her dress to a bus, would never again chase me with her umbrella. And I regretted the relief I felt at the thought.

Dad went off to work while I was in the garden, stopping to pick a couple of blackberries from the mass that hung along the wall. He did it furtively, as he didn't want anyone to know he could still see the fruit, or enjoy the taste of it. But I copied him as I watched him go, popping the berries into my mouth. It seemed the right thing to do, fitting somehow, and anyway, it masked the stale morning taste on my tongue. I ate a few more, the sour ones making me search harder for the truly ripe and sweet, and then began to collect them in earnest, filling an old watering can which had been left in the grass.

The berries broke from their buds with satisfying ease and I wove my arms further into the brambles to reach the ripest. Douglas said nothing when he came to find me, but he, too, began to eat and collect and carefully pull away the branches so that he could get deeper into the fruit's nest. I watched him for a moment and there was a resemblance between him and the mad woman that was obvious when you knew about it, but I thought perhaps that was partly the situation: his arms buried in the foliage. And soon my own mother was out with baskets and bowls and her own share of the harvest.

We stripped the branches, greedy and quick, the berries collapsing between our fingers. As we picked we filled our mouths, silently, intense and certain. I kept going until I could hardly lift my arms and the skin of my fingers was flecked with tiny cuts from the blackberry thorns. It was then that Frank appeared. We heard his step on the path and turned together.

"Christ!" he said. "You all turned cannibal?"

I looked at Ma and Douglas and saw how their faces and hands were bloodied with the fruit as if they'd been devouring some animal alive. I could feel the juice clinging to my own mouth. We none of us laughed, but gazed at each other as if we'd just woken from a dream, our clothes stained, our skin pale, our eyes watering.

Frank had brought sugar and Ma wiped her hands and face on her apron to marvel at it, feeling the packages as if they were Christmas presents. "We could make jam," she said. "We've got the fruit for it."

"So I see," Frank said, and he laughed, but still he eyed us, side on, uneasy, and he lit a cigarette with nervous hands, one cuff flapping at his wrist like a greedy seagull.

Ma went inside, carrying our crop, and Douglas went on eating berries, but I'd lost my appetite for them. My skin itched where the juice had dried and I felt irritated. I wished Frank wasn't there; I wished we could have gone on picking blackberries all day, not talking, just gathering, doing something that I didn't have to make sense of.

I'd put off seeing Frank for days, walking the long way home when I saw him waiting at the end of our street, crossing the road when I was too near the Fiveways, or any other pub I thought he might frequent. I didn't know what to say to him. I couldn't tell him that Douglas was waiting at the Pavilion Ballrooms every night, in the hope that Sukey would arrive.

"Looks like you've got smudged lipstick," Frank said. "Like you've been kissing someone." His hands had stopped shaking and he put a thumb up to my mouth, letting it hover a fraction of an inch from my lips.

"I don't wear lipstick," I said, the effort of not moving towards his touch making my words stiff. There was a scuffing sound as Douglas kicked at the wall behind me. Frank didn't look at him, but stroked his thumb lightly over the last of the wet blackberry juice on my top lip and then smeared it on to his own.

"What d'you think?" he said. "P'raps *I* should start wearing it."

The absurdity of the action, the remark, made me giddy. "Now *you* look like you've been kissing someone," I said, as Ma called us in.

"I was going to tell Frank," she said, when we got through the door. "About the accident."

I saw Frank start at the word. "What accident?"

"Douglas's mother. She was killed by a car."

Ma was washing the fruit and turning it out into a pan to soften over the stove, and there was a moment of quiet before Frank spoke. When he did his voice was watery.

"What a terrible thing," he said. And, unbelievably, he seemed close to tears. "When was it? Were you there? God, it's terrible." He let out a sob which made the rest of us jump, as if he'd smashed a plate.

"You might not think it's so terrible when you hear who she was," Douglas said. His voice was angry, but his face, violently stained, was serene.

"Never mind about that," Ma said, wiping at the blackberry juice on his chin and silencing him.

"I remember the first time I saw her," Frank said, and there was a pause, during which I think we must all have been wondering what he would say next.

But he didn't finish; he shook himself and went and stood close to Ma and helped her to force the heated, softened berries through muslin bags, dark pulp clinging to his fingers and slipping over his wrists. I boiled the fruit with the black-market sugar and Ma cooled it and poured it into jars and sealed them with wax. The jam came out clear and rosy and delicious. And all the time there was Frank, again and again on the verge of tears because Douglas's mother had died in an accident.

"God, that bloody man," Helen says, hitting her hand on the steering wheel. "Blaming you for everything. Blaming me! As if how I make my living has anything to do with it. Well, it's Elizabeth I feel sorry for, with a son like that."

"Elizabeth is missing."

"Mum, we've just been to see her."

"She's missing and it's my fault."

"No, don't listen to that idiot. He shouldn't have left her alone in the garden when she was so unsteady on her feet. It's not your fault."

"It is my fault because I looked in the wrong places, I collected rubbish from everywhere else, and all the time the real things were lying out there, waiting for me."

"What are you on about?"

"She was buried in the garden."

"Who was?"

I can't think of the name. "The one you were talking about."

"Elizabeth's in hospital, Mum. We've just been to see her."

"No, in the garden. Buried for years."

Helen shifts in her seat, slows the car. "Whose garden? Ours?"

"At the new houses. She disappeared and they built those houses. And Frank brought tons of soil to lay over the gardens and he planted things there. And the vegetable marrows were nearly ruined after someone was in the garden. Digging."

"New houses. You mean at Elizabeth's?"

"Elizabeth is missing."

"No, Mum, we've just been to see her."

"She's buried —"

"You've been through that. But it's not Elizabeth, is it?"

"Elizabeth is missing." It's the wrong name, I know it's the wrong name, but I can't think of the right one.

Helen stops the car. "Who do you think is buried in Elizabeth's garden? Is it Sukey?"

Sukey. That's the name. Sukey. Sukey. My chest muscles relax slightly.

"Mum?" Helen wrenches the hand brake up with an awful stuttering.

"It's my fault. I was there, I knew the place because of the pebble wall, and if I'd just gone to dig, too, I'd

334

have found it all out and Ma wouldn't have died without knowing. I thought it was nothing, just the mad woman doing something to frighten me. But Sukey's things were in the garden, waiting for me, marking the place. Her compact was there, I found it too late, far too late. Now I'll never find her, will I? She'll always be missing and I'll always be looking for her. I can't bear it."

"Neither can I," Helen says under her breath. "Right, that's it. Get out of the car. Wait! I'll help you out."

She comes and opens my door, and I see we're the other side of the park, beyond the green and yellow house and the hotel and the acacia tree, and while I am stroking my fingers over the pattern of black and white pebbles on the wall, Helen is getting something from the boot of the car. The side gate is closed, but she wedges in the point of a shovel and the wood frame explodes into splinters.

"Come into the garden, Mum," she says, standing by the tapestry of moss and toadflax and holding the gate open for me. "Come on. I'll dig the whole fucking thing up if that's what it takes."

The lawn is brown and scarred, and there is a lot of bare earth where there should be grass or flowers. Helen marches up and down, carrying her tools. She bends to run her hand over the turf as if she's feeling for something under a rug and then she stamps at various points, her left ear towards the ground. Finally she throws down the shovel and lifts the fork high in the air, letting it fall, sheer, into the earth. The prongs

335

sink deep and silent and she lifts them with a rolling tide of dirt and grass.

"I've bloody had it with missing people and with sick people and with dead people. I've had it with missing people's bloody sons, too," she says as she stabs at the ground. "So we'll dig to fucking Australia if we have to."

I don't understand what she's doing. "Is it for runner beans?" I say, pointing at the wound she's making in the scabby lawn. It seems a funny place to plant them. She doesn't answer me, but talks to herself, swears. I peer into a greenhouse, empty and forlorn-looking. It's familiar somehow, and I move to stand inside for a minute, trying to place the smell of mildew, of rotten plastic plant pots and woodstain. A robin lands by the pile of earth next to Helen's trench.

"Fuck off!" she shouts at it, waving her shovel.

The bird flits away to perch on a branch of the apple tree. "Helen?" I say. "Where would be the best place to plant marrows?"

"For fuck's sake." She whips her head round as if she could make the words hit me. "What's that got to do with . . .?" But whatever she says next is lost beneath the scrape of metal and stone as she starts digging in another place. "Get a lot of sunlight here," she says. "Good wall for wind protection . . ."

She's making an awful mess and I wonder what it's all for. Perhaps this is how you landscape a garden, but that seems unlikely. So far there are just great ugly holes in the ground. Unless they're for ponds, I don't see the point. A white plastic chair rests on a mound of sandy soil and one of its legs sinks as I sit down. I find I am bent forward, studying the infinite amount of life on this little patch, peeping through holes in dock leaves and blowing on the bits of feather fallen from above.

I brush my fingers over the bud of a dandelion, the thin petals pressed together like a nub of velvet. I can't help pulling them out, it's too satisfying to feel the moment of resistance before they break away, each one a millisecond after the last. A snail moves through the undergrowth. "I'll make you into jam," I tell it. "I'll squidge you up and push you through muslin and boil you with sugar." It pulls its horns in a moment, but doesn't stop.

And then there is a cry. "Nearly got a piece of metal in my eye. Fuck," Helen says, climbing out of the hole she's dug. Her language is really terrible today. "Bit of shoe buckle," she says. "Wait a sec." She kneels down and leans into the hole. "There's something here. Mum!"

I get up creakily and go towards her, and she hands me a scrap of wood, pale except where the soil has made it filthy. The edges are crumbling with damp. Helen pulls more fragments from the earth, and the removal of the wood makes a cavity. Dusty soil begins to trickle downwards into it. There is something yellowish underneath, something smoothly, frighteningly, round, with rows of teeth which bite into the soil as if they could carve a path to the surface. But what do you call it, this thing with no flesh and no hair, this face that stares without any eyes? Helen won't tell me when

I ask, and as more dirt is displaced I see it has a missing piece, a crack, a mark of violence, hollow and dark against the pallor.

"Mum," Helen says. "Go towards the house, will you?" She reaches down again as I back away and I see she's got more wood when she stands. More wood and something circular, a little shallow pot. I know even from this distance that it's navy-blue and silver. And I know it once held peach-coloured powder rather than blackish soil. Helen scatters the contents as she walks.

"Let's get in the car," she says, very low, her hands on my arms. "Let's just sit in the car."

The passenger door is opened and I'm pressed into the seat sideways. Helen kneels on the pavement at my feet and talks into her hand. There's something nestled in her palm and she pushes it hard against her cheek as she speaks, glancing at the side gate every few seconds, as if she thinks something will escape. Side gate, I think. The side gate is open. It seems important but I don't know why. Slowly Helen lays out the bits of wood and the half-a-compact on the paving stones. I feel in my bag for the other half, lean down to reunite the two silver and blue circles and squeeze my eyes shut against the image of Sukey at our kitchen table sweeping powder over her nose. My middle is pinched by the waistband of my trousers as I bend and the blood seems to rush to my head.

The bits of crumbling wood are like the pieces of a jigsaw, like the shards of a gramophone record. I try to put them together but they are too wet and rotten, like long-stewed meat. It doesn't matter: I already know

338

they are part of a tea chest, the kind that Frank always had lying around his house, the kind that he stored Sukey's clothes in after she disappeared.

"Frank," I say, and my stomach churns. I feel as though I'm back with Audrey, drinking her father's gin.

When she's finished speaking Helen eases a flat oblong away from the skin of her face and lays out more things on the pavement. A handful of broken glass, the edges smoothed like pebbles, a rusted shoe buckle and the tiny skeletons of two birds, the bones twisted together with wire. Glass eyes are glued still to their skulls and their beaks show traces of some kind of coloured enamel. And I know the last time I came face to face with these beaks was in Frank's house. They flew about her head, the mad woman said. The glass smashed and the birds flew about her head.

A bright, chequered car stops by the house and a man and woman get out. They have white shirts with bulky black vests on top and they've been labelled like my KETTLE plug and my TEA jar. Their label is POLICE. Helen jerks as if she's about to jump to greet them, but her legs shake and she kicks the compact halves apart again. I push them together so that the hinges match up and I brush more dirt away to make the silver stripes shine. I've been bent forward so long that my hands are a purplish red and I can feel my pulse in them. I am top-heavy with blood, which throbs against my ears and seems to whisper "Sukey Sukey Sukey".

The policewoman goes through the open side gate and comes back out again. "Right," she says. "I can confirm that you have found human remains."

"Yes," Helen says.

"And you've taken these things here out of the scene of burial?" the policewoman asks.

"Yes," Helen says.

She is told off by the policewoman, who says we mustn't touch anything else. She lists all the things we aren't allowed to touch, all the things that are in a row at my feet: bits of glass, a make-up container, some wood, bird skeletons. I push myself upright, away from the collection of things, but I have to touch them. I have to.

"And this is not your garden?" the policeman asks.

"No," Helen says, "it belongs to a friend of my mother."

The policeman looks at me. His eyebrows go up; he takes a few steps back. "It's you!" he says. "I can't believe it. It is you, isn't it?"

"Yes, it's me," I say.

"Don't you recognize me?" He hunches down so I can see his face better. There's a boyish grin on it that reminds me of someone. "I'm the one you always report your friend Elizabeth missing to."

I don't react quickly enough and a twitch of disappointment crosses his mouth. "Oh, yes," I say. "Hello."

"It's always me," he says, turning to the policewoman. "I should have followed her lead: she's been sitting on a centuries-old murder here."

340

"It's not centuries old and we don't know it's a murder," the policewoman says. She pulls at her black vest and faces Helen. "Why were you digging in this garden?"

"I was looking for the body," Helen says.

"You knew it was here?"

"No, not really."

The policeman is told to get something from the car and he and the woman begin tying blue and white ribbon around a tree; it flaps in the breeze like bunting, but there are no flags, only the words DO NOT CROSS. While he is occupied I move my foot so the edge of my shoe is against the tiny skeleton of a bird. The contact makes it possible to breathe again. Blood drains away from my heavy head, and still it seems to speak. Is this what they mean by the blood singing in your veins? And is there a way to stop it?

"You brought the tools with you?" the policewoman says. She doesn't notice my foot.

"I'm a gardener," Helen tells her. "I have a gardening business. I usually have shovels, forks, trowels, in the boot of my car."

The policewoman tells her she'll have to take the tools for investigation and Helen says she understands. Her hand lifts once from the pavement and there are red ridges on her palm. I offer my hand, wanting to sooth the marks away, but she doesn't notice. Instead she tries again to get up and the policeman comes closer to help her. The blood has stopped singing in my head and now the voice is gone I want it back. I lean

341

from the car to feel it throb again, to hear it whisper to me, and I press my fingers to the crumbling wood.

"Please don't tamper with evidence," the police-woman says, rolling up the leftover tape. She looks at Helen. "Why didn't you call the police if you suspected there was a body here?"

Helen lets her arm hang limp in the policeman's hold. "I didn't really suspect it."

"I'm afraid you'll have to come with us to the station," the policeman says.

He guides Helen away and I let my hand swoop down. In an instant I have a tiny piece of glass in my hand. I hold it hard, the edges smoothed by soil, and I can see the glass dome shining in the light of the fire, the eyes of the birds gleaming. I can see Sukey sewing on the settee, her hair curling up the fabric behind. It's so close and so far away and I wish for a moment the glass were sharper so that I could feel it properly.

"Are you sure you don't want someone to sit in with you?" This man has reddish hair and freckles, so many freckles that it's hard to make out his features, hard to tell when he smiles. "How are you doing? Would you like any water if you don't want tea? Are you comfortable?"

No, I can't get comfortable on this seat, my waist feels as if it's being pummelled by the top of my trousers. I look to undo the button, but there isn't one, only elastic. "I wish I could take these off," I say. "And have one of those things, like a cooking pot for humans. You know. For boiling humans."

342

He says he isn't sure what I mean, and I can't read his expression because of the freckles. His face is so marked it's blank. Like the walls of this room. They are so blank that I don't have to see them at all and if I look past the man sitting opposite me I have space to picture every detail of Sukey's sitting room.

"Where's my sister?" I say.

"Do you mean 'daughter'? Another officer is interviewing her in another room. As I explained before, your daughter is also a witness, so we have to interview you separately. We've decided not to caution you, but we are going to have to take a witness statement. Do you understand?"

He's very neat this man, despite the mess of freckles on his skin. He sits carefully, facing me, smiling, I think. I press a pebbly piece of glass into my palm. "I'm not a witness," I say. If only I could take my things off and slide into a pool of water.

"Bath."

"I'm sorry?"

"That's the word I was looking for."

"Right. Good. Can you tell us anything about the body found in the garden of the property of Elizabeth Markham?"

"Elizabeth is missing," I say, but the words are like dust.

"Yes, a colleague of mine said you've been in several times to report her missing. Was it Mrs Markham you were looking for?"

I stare at the bare walls, looking through them to Sukey's sitting room. "The house is full of things," I say. There's a shoe scraper by the settee, and a chipped Chinese vase under the window. It's full of carved walking sticks, frilly umbrellas and an old dress sword and it tips over whenever there's a breeze. A little writing box has been balanced on a music stool and two marble lions sit at the foot of a washstand. There's hardly room to move and I have to be careful.

"Mrs Horsham? You understand what was found in the garden?"

I try to picture it, but I can't, I don't have the energy to think of two places. I study every bubble in the grey paint of the wall, trying to be back in that room, with Sukey. If only I could get back there, if only I could be with her again. The smell of coffee interferes, she never drank coffee, and I glance in anger at the white plastic cup on the table.

"Have you any idea how long the body might have been there? We have information — in fact, your daughter suggested — that it could have been there since 1946. Have you got anything to add to that?"

"1946 is when my sister went missing."

"Susan Gerrard, formerly Susan Palmer. Is that right?"

"Sukey," I say, and I think of blood singing, but what has blood got to do with anything?

"Sukey? That's what you called her? And she went missing in the autumn of 1946, correct?"

"Yes. How long ago is that?"

"It's nearly seventy years."

I think for a moment of the cold earth around the pale bones and I feel the same cold creep inside me, and if I had known I would willingly have curled into that wooden chest and kept her company for seventy years. I would never have let her be alone all that time. I would have done anything to be near her the way this bit of glass was. I press it between my fingers, feeling how it has warmed from my touch as if some life has been forced into it.

"You've seen the body," the man says. "Or perhaps I should say the skeleton. There is evidently damage to the skull. Can you tell me anything about that?"

"The glass smashed and the birds flew around her head."

"Birds? It looks as though there's glass and the remains of birds in with the body. Is that what you're referring to?"

"It's what the mad woman said."

"The mad woman? Who do you mean by that?"

"She hated those birds, Sukey did, all dyed wings and glass eyes. One day they'd fly out and peck her. That's what she thought. I was more afraid of the other things; the house was full of things to trip over. I thought she'd fall and break her head. I thought it was a death trap."

"Which house is this you're talking about?"

"Frank's house."

"Frank? Is that Frank Gerrard? We have him down as a possible suspect. Can you tell us anything more about him?"

"He was a jealous man, was Frank."

"Was he?"

"I don't know. Someone said he was."

"Who said?"

"I can't remember."

"Okay, we'll come back to that." He takes a sip of the coffee and then one of water. "Do you have any knowledge of the whereabouts of Frank Gerrard?"

"No."

"Did you know he had a record? For disturbing the peace, accepting stolen goods, aggravated assault."

"I didn't know." The tiny bit of glass magnifies the lines on my hand and I think of Sukey sewing and not wanting to disturb her neat row of stitches, and of the fire warming me right through. If I could just get back to that room everything would be right again. I won't look at the birds on the mantelpiece, I'll cover them with her shawl and I'll help her to make a blind for the kitchen, and when Frank comes home . . .

"When Frank comes home? What? What would happen?"

"Nothing," I say.

"Okay, I'll ask you about that again later. Something else we have to do is to establish how the body came to be in the garden of Mrs Markham's property. Did your sister have any connection to it?"

"No."

"But you do believe the body we found to be that of your sister? What made you think she would be there? Did Frank Gerrard have a connection to it, perhaps?"

"He helped someone to plant marrows."

"So he had access to the garden?"

"I don't know."

346

"We know he ran a removals business from 1938 to 1946. Did he perhaps deliver furniture there?"

"I don't know."

Teeth show up white against the freckles. "You liked Frank, didn't you?"

"He loved Sukey."

The man takes another sip of coffee. I stare again at the wall and think of Sukey joking with the soft-faced removal man, and of the mad woman eating the hawthorn by the lane, and then I think of Frank. In a moment he will come into the room.

"And then?" the man asks. "What will happen then?"

Then Sukey will run out screaming because of the mad woman and Frank will tell her to go to the Station Hotel, only she never goes because Frank does something. Pushes her into the mantelpiece? Hits her so she falls? Brains her with the glass dome full of birds? Something that cracks her skull and makes the stuffed birds tumble about her head. I'm careful to think and not to speak, and the freckled man carries on asking me questions, but I can't answer because if I speak I'll say too much. I'll say the mad woman saw it all, I'll say Frank put Sukey into a tea chest and buried her in the garden of a house where he knew no one yet lived. I'll say he offered to help plant the marrows so he could control where the ground would be dug and how deep. I'll say these things if I speak, but they can't be true, they can't possibly be true.

"What will happen now? Do you know?" Helen asks, taking her keys and unlocking the car.

"They'll verify your stories," the policeman says. "Ascertain the age of the remains found, try to trace any other witnesses, as well as possible suspects."

"They'll try to find Frank?"

"If that seems to be a reasonable line of inquiry." The words sound like the correct ones, but he ruins the effect with a grin.

I rest a hand on the car, curling my fingers against the window, and try to imagine a young girl running in zigzags to avoid snails. But it's difficult to picture yourself in a memory and all I can think of is Frank telling me how the new houses were nice, how he'd been here to move people in and had helped with their gardens. I stare at the glass, expecting shadows to flit across the surface, like on a film screen, but the sky's reflection obscures whatever story might be shown, and everything is still until the policeman opens the door and helps me in. He puts a hand over my head in case I bang it and leans across me to put my seatbelt on. When he moves back again he winks.

"I s'pose you've found what you were looking for," he says, "but I hope you still pop in from time to time, eh? Don't be a stranger."

He shuts the door and I'm left wondering what he was on about. The car is stifling, though it's late in the day and the sun's not strong. I can't get the windows to wind down and I'm grateful when Helen opens her door and lets in a breeze.

"And. The — er — body, I mean, if it is Sukey?" she asks the policeman. "When might she be released?"

"They'll have to establish that the body is who you say it is, there'll be a lot of tests to do to work out an accurate date of death, any injuries, and cause of death, if possible. It might be six months, it might be longer. They'll let you know if and when."

She thanks him, gets in beside me and turns the cold air on full blast. We drive a little way, the policeman waving us off as if he were an old friend, but stop once we're round a corner. Helen is breathing as though she has been pushing the car, not driving it.

"You haven't taken up smoking, have you?" I was always afraid of that when they were kids.

"Mum, I'm fifty-six, of course I haven't started smoking. You do know what's happened, don't you?"

I pat her hand again. I pat it very carefully, but I have a falling sensation inside, as if some important organ is coming loose, as if it's coming loose and I have to be ready to catch it before it hits the floor. "Frank stopped me falling over the banisters in the Station Hotel," I say. "Did I ever tell you?" I remember thinking that, if I'd been killed, he'd have got the blame, even though he'd never have meant me to come to any harm.

"Yes, Mum, you did tell me. But I always had the impression he'd been the reason you were so close to falling in the first place."

She starts the car again and drives very slowly, staying close to the side of the road, and she doesn't seem to notice when I read out the RAMP AHEAD and NO FOOTWAY signs. Her hand shakes when she changes gear and she isn't irritated when I ask where we're going.

349

"What happened to Douglas?" she asks.

"He went to America," I tell her, watching the dark gorse and darker sea trundle by outside the window. "It's where he always wanted to go, and that's why he liked to test out the phrases, the accent. I thought he might write, but he never did, wanted to start afresh, I suppose. He sold everything he had for the ticket. Except the 'Champagne Aria'."

"Ha-ha-ha," Helen says, stopping the car by the beach.

She helps me over the sand to the water. We both have soil under our fingernails and we wash it off in the waves. A tiny piece of glass, like a pebble, is nestled in the crease of my palm and I drop it through the surf to lie with the real pebbles amongst the sand. The sun is setting behind the pier and we watch it sinking for a moment. I wonder what time it is and what we've been doing all day. I wonder how we got soil on our hands and why Helen is shaking. She kisses me on the head and my stomach growls. I check my cardigan pockets and my bag for chocolate, but there's nothing. My stomach growls at me again.

"And Frank?" Helen stares out at the sea.

It looks rough today, the waves misshapen boxes of colour, and I wouldn't like to swim in it.

"What happened to him?" She twists her feet about so they sink a little way into a damp dune.

"He asked me to marry him."

"What?" She turns quickly and one foot plunges further into the sand.

350

"Oh, a long time after. I was twenty-two by then. He'd been away. In prison, Dad said, but Ma and I could never be sure. Anyway, he turned up one day and asked me to marry him. Just like that. I said no, of course. I was already engaged to Patrick."

"How did he take it?"

I think about that for a moment, though it's painful to remember. "I suspect he was relieved." But the sick, greyish look on his face when I said no looms up, and I wonder again whether I would have said yes if I hadn't already been engaged, and whether I resented Patrick for being in the way. And I wonder whether I would have minded a marriage where I had to remember my sister every day.

"And of course, it's likely he did kill her," Helen says, a bite in her voice. "So that might have complicated things." She stares at the blur between sky and sea. "But do you think he meant to?"

I look back up the beach. "I buried Sukey there," I say.

"No, Mum, it was —"

"And then she buried me. And I got cross." I always felt guilty afterwards, for getting cross, and embarrassed for being so childish. She'd only been trying to entertain me. But the sand, closing around my body, heavy on my limbs, had made me frightened, and it was too easy to imagine the dunes rising over my head. After that she was always careful to be the one who was buried, and I would heap handfuls of powdery grit on top of her, compacting it until she couldn't move and smoothing it into shapes, giving her the tentacles of an octopus or the tail of a mermaid. And once I made her a dress. Of fingernails, which I'd gathered from the shore. I'm sure that's right. I can picture them now, spread around her. Hundreds of pink fingernails pushed into the sand.

Epilogue

"I think he was hoping that one of them would turn out to be worth a fortune, but no such luck." The voice is low, followed by stifled laughter, the direction of the speaker obscured by the mass of black-clothed bodies. "I can't help thinking she gathered all that junk just to make him wade through it. She might have known he wouldn't be able to resist taking the china for valuation."

"Majolica ware, eh? One last joke from Aunt Elizabeth. Poor Peter."

Thick dust swirls about in the heat and settles on shoulders and hips and thighs; the air is full of the smell of cheap new clothes. I'm trapped, suffocating. There seems to be no way out and nowhere to rest. I lean a shoulder on a sturdy-looking cloth-covered partition, but a fat woman makes a thin cry and moves away, turning to frown at me. I sag forwards, my face grazing the lapel of a blazer, and for a moment I see a gap in the crowd. There is a creamy wall and a patch of light, and a board, a board with legs, piled with things to eat. I push towards it, while the people in their stifling black make down turned smiles and gulp at their drinks. God knows what they're doing packed together like this, like peaches in a tin.

When I reach the creamy wall I find that dust swirls here, too, but it rises in the light and the air is cooler. I pull up a sitting thing, for sitting on. In a minute I'll have to go back. There's something I must do. I can't remember what it is just now, but I know it's important; someone will tell me if I ask. The filled breads, the stuffed-and-buttered breads, are cut into squares, and my stomach growls, but I can't work out what I'm to do with them. I watch a man take one and bite into it, his fingers crushing, his lips sloppy. I feel queasy, but copy him all the same, cramming the thing into my own mouth. It slips against my tongue, cold and sharp and foetid at once. Someone comes at me, smiling, and I move hastily out of the way, into the kitchen, where the oven's on, humming its own low, laughing comments, wearing its own hot black clothes.

"Pass me that knife, dear, would you?" a red-faced housewifely person says.

I look around the room, but I can't think what it is she wants, and so I wander through a glass door on to a patio. Most of the space is taken up with those things, not boats, they are full of flowers, large pink flowers bobbing about in the breeze. But there is a bench at one end and I can sit down. A tall woman brings me out a slice of fruit cake. She tells me it's fruit cake as she hands it to me and I can see amber currants huddling under the crumbly surface.

"How are you feeling?" she asks, sitting down.

Have I been ill?

"At least you got to say goodbye," she says.

354

"Oh. Have they gone already? I wasn't there to catch the bouquet."

"Mum, it's a funeral. They don't throw bouquets at funerals."

She smiles and then covers her mouth with her hand, looking back into the house. I stare past her at the bobbing flowers. The garden is very pretty, but it's not mine.

"Where am I?" I ask.

"Peter's house."

I nod as if I recognize the name and pick the currants out of my cake, pinching them together. When a girl with blondish curls steps on to the patio I throw the currants at her feet. She stops and blinks, doesn't skitter away, doesn't peck at the fruit. Perhaps because she has no beak. I think I know her. "Is that my daughter?" I say to the woman next to me, pointing at the girl.

"Granddaughter," the woman says.

The girl laughs. "You're too old to be my mother, Grandma."

"Am I?"

"You're eighty-two."

I wonder why she's lying. Does she think it's funny? "This girl's mad," I say. "She'll be telling me I'm a hundred next."

A man steps out and bends, swoops, to gather the currants, scattering them over the lawn. Two blackbirds flutter down to pierce them with their beaks, and the sight pierces me too. "Elizabeth is missing," I say, feeling a twist of something inside me, the memory of a smile. "Did I tell you?" I catch at the woman's sleeve before she's out of reach. "I keep trying her house, but there's no answer."

"I'm sorry," the woman says, standing to put a hand on the man's shoulder. "I have told her."

"Poor Elizabeth," I say. I haven't seen her since she came to our kitchen to collect currants from my mother's cake. Anything might have happened since. She needed the currants to feed the mad woman. The mad woman, who was really a bird and flew about my sister's head. My sister was frightened, and she and Douglas dug a tunnel to America. I tried to follow, but I couldn't dig that far. Perhaps they took Elizabeth with them?

The woman doesn't think that's the answer and the man begins to explain something to me. But I can't concentrate. I can see they won't listen, won't take me seriously. So I must do something. I must, because Elizabeth is missing.

Acknowledgements

I would like to thank my parents, Kathryn Healey and Jack McDavid, and my partner, Andrew McKechnie, for all their encouragement and support.

Also Karolina Sutton and the lovely people at Curtis Brown, Venetia Butterfield and everyone at Viking, and Andrew Cowan and my tutors, classmates and colleagues at UEA.

Thanks to those who read and gave feedback on the manuscript, including Anne Aylor, Oonagh Barronwell, Paula Brooke, Nick Caistor, Claudia Devlin, Hannah Harper, Tom Hill, Narelle Hill, Debra Isaac, Campaspe Lloyd-Jacob, Gerard Macdonald, Fra von Massow, Tray Morgan, Andy Morwood, Teresa Mulligan, Hekate Papadaki, Sara Sha'ath, Alice Slater, Charlotte Stretch, Beatrice Sudsbury, Catriona Ward and Anna Wood.

And also to Annabel Elton, Billy Gray, Vicky Grut, Christopher Healey, Eoin Lafferty, Anna McKechnie and Mabel Morris.

And I am indebted to a great many more people for their help and enthusiasm.

Also available in ISIS Large Print:

The Legacy of Elizabeth Pringle

Kirsty Wark

Debut novel from the respected Newsnight presenter

Born just before the First World War, Elizabeth Pringle has lived all her very long life on the Scottish island of Arran. A familiar yet solitary figure: a dutiful daughter, an inspirational teacher, a gardener. But did anyone really know her?

When Elizabeth dies, her will contains a surprise. She has left her home and her belongings to someone who is all but a stranger, a young mother she watched pushing a pram down the road more than 30 years ago.

Now it falls to Martha, the baby in that pram, to find out how her mother inherited the house in such strange circumstances, and in doing so, perhaps leave her own past behind. But first she has to find the answer to the question: who was Elizabeth Pringle?

ISBN 978-1-4450-9916-3 (hb)
ISBN 978-1-4450-9917-0 (pb)

The Guts

Roddy Doyle

Jimmy Rabbitte is back

The man who invented The Commitments back in the eighties is now 47, with a loving wife, four kids . . . and bowel cancer. He isn't dying, he thinks, but he might be.

Jimmy still loves his music, and he still loves to hustle — his new thing is finding old bands and then finding the people who loved them enough to pay money for their resurrected singles and albums. On his path through Dublin he meets two of The Commitments — Outspan, whose illness is probably terminal, and Imelda Quirk, still as gorgeous as ever. He is reunited with his long-lost brother and learns to play the trumpet . . .

This warm, funny novel is about friendship and family, about facing death and opting for life.

ISBN 978-0-7531-9292-4 (hb)
ISBN 978-0-7531-9293-1 (pb)

The Unknown Bridesmaid

Margaret Forster

When Julia was eight, she was asked to be a bridesmaid at her cousin's wedding. Her mother saw this as a chore, but Julia was thrilled, and nothing could ruin the day. But after this, things began to go wrong for Julia, starting with an episode involving her cousin's baby, a pram and a secret trip round the block. A lifetime later, Julia is a child psychologist who deals with young girls said to be behaving badly. Julia has a special knack with these girls. She understands which of them really are troubled, and which are just seen that way by the adults around them.

But one day, Julia's own troubled past starts to creep into her present. And as she struggles to understand her childhood self, she must confront the possibility that the truth may not be as devastating as she feared.

ISBN 978-0-7531-9212-2 (hb)
ISBN 978-0-7531-9213-9 (pb)

The House We Grew Up In

Lisa Jewell

Meet the Bird Family — all four children have an idyllic childhood: a picture-book cottage in a country village, a warm, cosy kitchen filled with love and laughter, sun-drenched afternoons in a rambling garden. But one Easter weekend a tragedy strikes the family that is so devastating it begins, almost imperceptibly, to tear them apart.

The years pass, the children become adults and begin to develop their own quite separate lives. Soon it's almost as though they've never been a family at all. Almost. But not quite. Because something has happened that will call them home, back to the house they grew up in — and to what really happened that Easter weekend all those years ago.

ISBN 978-0-7531-9296-2 (hb)
ISBN 978-0-7531-9297-9 (pb)